AROUSE

AND

BEWARE

Books by MacKinlay Kantor

God and My Country
Arouse and Beware
The Romance of Rosy Ridge
Here Lies Holly Springs
Valedictory
Happy Land
The Noise of Their Wings
Glory for Me
Midnight Lace
One Wild Oat
Signal Thirty-Two
Wicked Water
Gentle Annie
Don't Touch Me
The Goss Boys
Turkey in the Straw
Lobo
Frontier
The Unseen Witness
Spirit Lake
Story Teller
Beauty Beast
Angleworms on Toast
Hamilton County
Children Sing
I love You, Irene
The Valley Forge
Gettysburg
But Look the Morn

AROUSE

AND

BEWARE

A Novel by

MACKINLAY KANTOR

SPEAKING VOLUMES, LLC
NAPLES, FLORIDA
2017

Arouse and Beware

ISBN 978-1-62815-591-4

To

ELEANOR OLIVER

"I'll weave the chord and twine in,
  Man's desire and babe's desire, I'll
      twine them in, I'll put in life...
  (As one carrying a symbol and menace far
          into the future,
  Crying with trumpet voice, *Arouse and
      beware! Beware and arouse!*)"

WALT WHITMAN.

NOTE

In that nightmare realm of reality which novelists visit in search of persons and circumstances wholly unreal, the author discovered this tale written in two large discarded daybooks. It bore every evidence of having been set down painfully and carefully, but at white heat of enthusiasm, through a period of years. The caption was, "Oliver Clark's Journal of Events Occurring during the Month of March, 1864, and during his Escape from Richmond to the Federal army lines in North Central Virginia." However, scribbled in lead pencil on a neighboring page, the author found a quotation from Whitman's *Song of the Banner at Daybreak,* certain words of which lent themselves more readily to a purpose of title than did the somewhat awkward designation Oliver Clark had inscribed.

M. K.

CONTENTS

BOOK I

Babe's Desire

THE pine needles that shone in those woods have long been dust. But whenever my thought hurries back to that bright March morning, I see a woman with pale hair and gray eyes walking toward me down the years.

I hear again the far-away, convalescent murmur of crows, the spasmodic chirping of vagrant bluebirds as they worked their way along the quieter roads and hedges toward the north. No matter how many lines of forbiddance and fortification bristled ahead of them, they were creatures which could pass unchallenged—observed only with longing and freshened memory when they were noticed at all, even though they wore the blue.

I hear, when my mind hastens to awaken itself once more on that steel-cut day, the distant scream of ungreased wagon wheels, where men worked at their endless replenishing of the entrenchments around each nest of clean-swabbed cannon. There were dogs barking, too, and though in most memory their barking has the taste of rural domesticity or the hunt, the barking of those dogs near the Three Chopt Road still menaces my mind.

They had bayed in my dreams for weeks before the moment when I went out to meet them, and I am sure that they had bayed in the sleep of Prentiss Barstow as well, whether he would have admitted it or not. Never again, when I walk a dark lane in the middle of the night (a lane which seems to have no geography easily identified, but is only a dun-colored sluice-way stretching among shapeless and unexplored wildernesses) shall I be able to rest secure in confidence con-

cerning any dog that challenges me. For a fugitive distrusts
the friends of man even more than he distrusts man himself:
all are allies in a desperate league seeking to thwart and
punish him.

No matter if the fugitive once dwelt in another ordinary
age where he loved a dog, or a cat, or a snail, or a donkey.
All these now have given their allegiance to the forces of
dark evil. The very lambs that bleat in stony wood-lots for
their mothers and their suppers, are warning him—not in
charity but in mockery.

And the cattle which have not been slaughtered for food,
have turned beyond the explanation of zoölogists into those
bovine herds which, men say, roved this earth in a time when
tigers were as tall at the shoulder as people are today. They
bellow and fume when the fleeing vagabond goes by. The
fugitive imagines that their horns are sharp and their hoofs
ready for him, and he knows they are no relatives of the kind-
hearted oxen who go down on their knees, in song and
legend, to thank God for the Christ Child, amid the frost of
Christmas morning.

But I will not rest forever on the dangers which beset us,
though there were plenty of them, nor speak too confusingly
of the sounds to which we opened our ears in that pine forest,
east of the Three Chopt Road and close by the outer line
of fortifications. Before I tell who we were and how we came
there and how badly it had gone with us, I shall speak again
of the woman named Naomi Kincaid.

A long time has passed, and I can penetrate certain of
the mysteries surrounding her—as many as man can hope to
penetrate where such a woman is concerned. And I say
solemnly that no consideration of Honor or of Cause, was
the greatest encouragement and food for Prentiss Barstow
and myself in those days and nights. No thought of families
(who did not even wait for us in Iowa and New Jersey,

because they knew we were dead); no memory of a mother's steps in the pantry or a little sister playing in sunlight on the sunken doorstep; no echo of the martial music which had driven us lustily forth to war; no recollection of the vows we had made, those vows which are deadly serious to young soldiers and new ones; no conception of flag and country, and revenge against those who would separate part of our country from the rest; no distillation of every dream and ambition and impulse to which a passionate young man can subscribe . . . no one or all of these invoked us to go a league beyond our strength, and do what mortals had seldom done before.

We believed they did at the time. But now I know that she, Naomi Kincaid, riding into our lives behind the bay mare, was the watch-woman on our far horizon, the light that shone for us, even in hours when we resented it: She wrested our souls from the dogs' baying, to which we might have yielded them.

2

I was awakened by the sound of wagon wheels. The day was Thursday, the third of March; the sun shone clear and bright, but at first with no degree of warmth—as if it shafted through a pane of clean-scrubbed glass blown around the world, a glass which kept the heat outside.

There was no wind worthy of mention, though no pine forest ever grew in which some wind did not live among the more limber tips of its trees. I was a skeleton, and I lay close against a brown log, with Prentiss Barstow lying half beside me and half on top of me. We had scraped a sifting of pine needles to cover us, when we fell and died there in the darker hours; by this time most of the needles, with their scattered leaves, had trickled down and compressed beneath our bodies.

When a starved man awakens he does not come from a realm in which his dreams are definite and acute, into an existence untenanted by them; but rather they follow him vaguely for five or ten minutes. Hence, surrounded as I was by the coughing and the plaintive insistence of a race who crouched in the very tents of death, I had to work desperately to banish the false figments and leave the bird-chirping where it belonged. At last I lifted my head above the level of the log, though as yet I was unable to release my legs from their stiffness.

The wagon wheels came nearer, jolting slowly in a clay road, and I feared that Barstow and I were closer to that road than we had believed. I turned my head, forgetting in this growing alarm how much it pained me to do so, and whispered several times down into his ear, "Bar. Bar...."

"In due time," he said.

I whispered again and again.

"Nor rot here forever," he swore, seriously.

Then he was awake, for his black eyes darted out at me and he shook his dirty mane. "I know," he said. "I know where we are. What's ado?"

"There's a wagon coming."

He ordered me, "Lie still, whatever you do. We're in the pines; nobody can see us."

And he proved the skill of his hiding, exhausted as we had been when he led me to the place. We were a good thirty yards from the high-road, and close beside a trail that led into the heart of the forest, over which possibly a thousand wagons had brought their lumber to be used in building entrenchments and abatis. But Barstow could not have realized that; we had never crossed the wood road in our skulkings before dawn.

The wheels rattled nearer and nearer. We learned from the sounds accompanying them that one horse was pulling the load, whatever the load might be. I expected soldiers; Barstow told me later that he thought it would be only a negro's cart. By this time both of us had our heads above the log, and we remained there, motionless and screened by vines, when the rig turned in at the wood road and moved through the pines not twenty-five feet from us.

It was a light, single-seated wagon without springs, drawn by a bay mare whose hair was worn thin by saddle leather and girth, and never by the harness that dressed her now. As a cavalryman I studied her automatically, and felt her to be not above a five-year-old, and unaccustomed to working between shafts. The wagon itself was in bad condition, with the wheels mended by wire. In the single seat sat, driving, a square-shouldered man with a full, flushed face and yellow mustache. His uniform was Confederate gray, but

I could not make out his rank. He wore a red sash and had some sort of enameled badge or decoration on his breast. Beside him was a woman, a very slender one, wearing a blue gown and rust-colored shawl and a bonnet sprouting with pansies. This much I could see and this much only, for she held her face bent low, and the officer was talking to her rapidly in an angry monotone. I imagined that she did not care what he was saying.

Mended wheels and all, the wagon bumped over broken limbs along the track that took it deeper and deeper into the green woods until no sound of its passage remained.

"We must go," I said to Barstow. "There are folks here."

He shook his head stubbornly. "We'd be daft to leave this forest in the daylight."

A strange and awful ambition possessed me suddenly, though no cunning mixed with it.

"They might have food," I whispered to him.

"And side-arms," Prentiss Barstow grunted.

"They might leave it in the wagon, if they walk abroad, somehow."

He said, "No, Clark. I wouldn't trust that mare. She'd whicker her head off if we come within reach, no matter how far they've gone. That officer is some kind of provost or I'll never guess again. He'd have this timber full of dogs and men in two shakes if he spotted us."

I said, "We've got to eat, Bar."

He laughed quietly. "Pshaw, you had more last night, and counting what we ate on the Island, than you've had in any four days."

"I can't help it; it makes it worse."

"How is your stomach?" he asked, more seriously.

I rolled over on my back and felt of myself with both hands, but I was so lame that every part of me felt the same.

I drew up my ragged shirt and parted the opening in the grimy drawers I had worn instead of trousers. My abdomen was not so swollen as it had been the previous day, and that was odd, because it weighted on me with a hotter lead than before.

Barstow said, "I reckon it's only scurvy gas that's bothering you now. It'll leave you when we get moving. But we daren't move."

I began to cry. "Barstow," I said, "if it weren't for you I'd never have made it."

"Well, I reckon you wouldn't," he told me.

For a while I lay rolled over, with my face buried against the pine needles. They were wet and chilly, but I thought then that I had never smelled anything so sweet. There was moss, too: fuzzy bits of gray, and bearing tiny green blossoms, crawling up between the jackstraw tangle. I lay there more relaxed, and forgetting everything except the childish comfort which came to me in looking at the delicate spires of moss. Finally I began to eat it, but it took a great deal to make even a chewable cud, and when I had filled my mouth the taste was so bitter that I spat it all out.

The sun fought its way through the trees, and yielded us a little more warmth, and Barstow moved, bit by bit, away from me, for the need of animal heat grew less. I reckoned that it must be past ten o'clock in the morning, perhaps near eleven.

"Point is," said Barstow, "I can't conclude what became of Fatridge."

"They broke Voss's head with a musket butt, Barstow."

He said, wisely, "I know. And Sauers went flat at the water's edge when they shot."

"I heard him yell. Maybe he wasn't killed."

"That don't matter, one way or the other. Point is,

Fatridge got into the water with us, and he had the map and he had the route of travel, and he even claimed he knew who the principal Tories were."

I asked, "What's Tories? They used to have them in the Revolution, up in Jersey."

"Tory niggers," explained Barstow. "I don't know anything about the Revolution. But he claimed they'd give us cornbread and the like. Two prisoners named Lewis Seeley and Adam Alden made it north by the same route, and Alden was Fatridge's cousin, I guess, and told him a deal about it. But I reckon he's gone deep in the river by now."

I said, as harshly as I could: "I always hated Fatridge from the first moment he came!"

"I didn't bear the man no love, but he did have that map, and he was stronger than us, too, because he hadn't been on the Island so long. Now," he said, lowering his voice, "it would pay us to do like the Bible says, setting a watch upon our lips. There may be folks listening or coming near."

We lay there quietly, watching the spot of sunlight growing broader and paler and more misshapen, until it came across Barstow's head, and he had to turn his eyes away from it. The edge of sunlight rested on my shoulder, and I felt the slow comfort warming through the rags and dirt that crusted me, releasing some tingling life which I had never dreamed could move within my flesh again.

I imagined that my body was a city, like the cities in the North which I had seen, and that in part of it there must be this surprised and tantalizing degree of life, creeping about and puffing and growing apace. And I was aware cruelly that the most grotesque death was swollen in another area, and might never be driven out.

That division of me in which it persisted, was my brain. My shoulders were the fortunate region of the city, in which a brave little child cried at birth; my brain was the dark street, the charnel-house, the slum wherein all hope had been abandoned. Lulled by the whistling of bluebirds along the road and by the nervous, hopeful piping of tinier birds, yellow and brown, that broke restlessly through the under-brush like excited hounds following a trail, I abandoned myself to sleep and to the awful dream which lay in wait for me.

Once more I was crowded on the cold island that lay between the cities of Richmond and Manchester, and I lived the life that had been laid out for me ever since the Mine Run campaign.

Now my body weighed one hundred and seventeen pounds, though it had weighed one hundred and sixty-six pounds in November. The spirit which lived in this body weighed nothing at all; it was lighter than the pollen blown from dry March weeds on the hill behind the batteries; it danced along roads where I had walked in earlier years, and it ran in headlong scamperings up the ridges of the future. Successfully, it had eluded the snare of my body and did not need to obey me.

Cold as always, the wind slid down the river, paring the crests of brown waves that sang among a thousand bowlders gorging the rapids. When an ear was turned sidewise, it caught the barest whisper of the wind: *cold,* was the song. But when you fronted into the breath of it, or stood with shoulders humped and face turned away, the breeze rose up and howled for joy...ahhh, there is still snow in the Massanuttons and the Blue Ridge: the wind will put ice back into the James river and keep it there.

My spirit took a poem from my lips and scuttled away with it, dancing as it fled. A man named Pratt. Half of me watched the runaway spirit, and the other half concerned itself with a remembered steel engraving—brooding eyes, damp hair, and a face which suffered forever.

"And travellers, now, within that valley,
Through the red-litten windows see . . .
. . . ghastly rapid river,
Through the pale door
A hideous throng rush out forever. . ."

Poe, not Pratt. I had read about him.

I went back under the flapping bower of rags which once had been a Sibley tent. The name was Poe. "Used to be in the army, the Regular army," I told a big, brown face. The brown face was named Fatridge. I could remember that kind of name. It made me think of a big dinner, a greasy one.

"Who?" asked Fatridge.

"It wasn't Pratt," my voice said, knowingly. "I thought it was, but I was mistaken."

Sauers and Voss and Barstow were all spooned beneath the new U. S. blanket, and though the day was rawer than Labrador, you could not see steam rising through the blanket any more. So there would be spring, and coming soon.

"What do you mean?" demanded Fatridge.

A voice shrieked, *"Poe, Poe, Poe!* We had the book, up in Jersey."

That roused Voss and Barstow, though Sauers slept still. Voss began to creep from under the blanket. He wore the cavalry jacket in which he had been captured five months before; the yellow piping along its seams was crusted white with the lice he had killed.

He nudged Barstow. "He's going, Bar."

Barstow muttered, still half asleep.

And I thought of my spirit: it must be far beyond the river by now, running north and running hard. It was a naked spirit, but the wind could never cut it down.

"Look at them eyes, gentlemen," they remarked of me.

"Just like Poppy Whitten's before he run across the deadline."

"He talked about a book in New Jersey," said Fatridge,
uncomprehendingly, for he had been on the Island only
three weeks.

Barstow stood up. He was a skeleton, too, but a mighty
one. His digestive system was that of a mule; he was the
only prisoner in the mess who had not been flat and retching
when we bought the five pounds of cow-udder from a guard
and had our feast. His beard had grown out intensely black,
blacker than his hair.

"Say it again, Clark," he suggested.

I felt that I must back toward the door, and masquerade
as a crafty man. I said, "No, you can't suck in this Dutchman . . . but never caught by any one. I saw it run through
the air. 'And so I shall catch the fly, your cousin, in the latter
end, and she must be blind too.' "

"Look at his eyes," shrilled Voss again, and I despised
his seventeen-year-old face—round and dirty-white and perfectly smooth.

Barstow said, his deep voice honest and soothing, "Now,
Clark. That was Henry, wasn't it? Like the Shakespeare
book."

"Witches," said Oliver Clark, and I felt shocked to learn
that Oliver Clark was I.

"Get him before he gets loose," called Sauers from under
the blanket. "They'll shoot him if he sets foot in the ditch."

The other three started toward me, and I tumbled back-
ward through the door. "You can't do anything to me for
that!" I wailed, and then Barstow had me. All along the
row of tents other bearded heads popped from under cover—
cannibal heads, hairy and savage.

"Let's get him inside," said Barstow, and I was crying as
they dragged me in.

Entirely forgetful of my truant spirit, I had become several men: I struggled mightily to awaken from my nightmare into those free woods once more. And I was the watcher who stood grimly pronouncing judgment on a lunatic, and I was the one who tried to save myself from lunacy, and whispered kindly encouragement; and worst of all, I was the lunatic who screamed in his pit. Although I swear that in each case I recognized the identity, and saw my other selves, and knew how they looked.

Barstow ordered, "Lay him on the oilcloth. Lay him flat," and they did. Barstow got on top of me with a huge knee on either side of my chest.

"Hush up. Hush, now; hush. Hush!" they all said. Barstow added, "Can you understand me?"

I screamed.

Barstow slapped me, and then I lay silent, but I could feel my eyes narrow and wet with hatred, and knew that the mark of his hand was on my face.

He said, "Clark, you be quiet or we'll feed you to the hogs!"

I told them to make Voss stay away from me, and complained about his smell. Prentiss Barstow asked Voss to move, and he obeyed readily. "Now, Clark," said Barstow, "how are you?"

"All right. What's the matter?" I made myself whisper it, and made myself pretend that I never knew what had been happening, though I did know.

Sauers said, "His face is showing red marks. It's the smallpox again!"

The others crowded back, but Prentiss Barstow still sat astride me. "Smallpox, and hell besides—that's where I slapped him! And he hasn't got no fever. He's cold and chilly."

"Yes, I'm cold and chilly, but I'm not sick. I'll be all right now."

"Do you know me, Clark?"

"Well enough," I said, "well enough."

"What's my name?"

I told him, "Prentiss Barstow, Sixth Wisconsin V. I."

"Your name. What is it?"

I tried to wriggle out from under him, but he held me fast. "I'm all right," I said again.

"What's your name?"

"Oliver Clark, First New Jersey Cavalry."

"Where you from?"

"Westfield, New Jersey. Now I'm Mess Five, Squad Three. We all are. Anything else—" I heard my voice rising to a scream—"anything else you'd like to know?"

"No," said Barstow. I saw him climbing to his feet. He extended a hand, as if to help me rise. I felt his knuckles, and was aware that the wiry cords controlling his fingers were scantily covered by the loose skin. And then he had drawn me up through a spinning chaos wherein Fatridge and Sauers and Voss and the whole population of the camp, were jumbled and overlapping, entire circles of faces spinning around me. He drew me surely and stanchly as a rope draws a workman who soars aloft on a scaffolding; and I wanted to vomit, but the breath of pine needles came back to me like liquor.

Now the dream had left me, the whole variety of unforeseen remembrances and imaginings, and I stood beside that log in the timberland of freedom, and, sure enough, Barstow held me by the hand.

"What?" I asked stupidly.

His face was drawn tight with alarm. "Don't speak," he whispered. "Wait a minute; don't grunt and groan like you been doing. Maybe we'll hear it again."

I whispered, "What will we hear?"

"A yell. A kind of a yell. It came from over yonder, there." He pointed toward the shady green where that timber road wound its course.

I thought of the rig which had traveled there a long time before, and of the man and the woman riding in it, and remembered that the woman had kept her face low while the man talked angrily. I twisted my ringing head, and tried to see the sun. The sun had not moved far through gaps in the pine branches, and I had slept through but a fraction of the eternities which seemed to have gone before.

"Did that woman scream, Barstow?"

His shaggy head moved slowly. "You mean those folks in the wagon? I don't think it sounded like a woman screaming. It was a sort of wail. Maybe it was just the horse, but—"

Then we heard a rise and stirring of sound in the woodland's heart, a crackling soon identified as the mended wheels moving toward us once more, crushing dry branches, and muffled time and again by a mat of pine needles.

"God," whispered Barstow, "they're coming back. Lay low." And then we had both flung ourselves behind the log again.

The road made a turn opposite us as it angled out of the woods, and I lifted my head warily above the ginger-colored log just as the wagon emerged from its tunnel of pine. The crashing of branches broken beneath the wheels increased; already the horse was moving at the stubborn trot of a creature trained for riding but never for drawing a vehicle.

Alone, the Confederate officer sat in the seat, and we did not know what had become of his companion. He was driving with one hand, and held one leg braced up against the short dashboard; his head was lolling back and his eyes seemed half-closed. His left hand, as I remember it now, was squeezed against his chest or side, and he coughed repeatedly as if he had been visited by consumption in the half-hour just past.

In another moment he was gone. His second advent, pressing also upon the memory of the strange cry which had issued from the woods, was enough to set Barstow scrambling out of the vines that concealed us, even while the protesting wheels still smashed their way toward the high-road.

I crawled over the log after Barstow, and was well torn by the vines in doing it. There lived a green vine in those woods and in most of the forests we encountered for days to come: its seed was spawn of the devil. Its varnished stem was like green whipcord, and the thorns were half as long as steel needles, and worse than any needle for paining you.

I remember drawing my ragged arm away from the vine's embrace and thinking that it resembled very closely a growth which we boys in New Jersey called "bread-and-butter." I wished that I had some bread and butter.

"Clark," cried Barstow again, "the woman was nowhere to be seen!"

"Maybe he took her to a house back there," I said. "Maybe he didn't want to take her, and that's why he was so cross about it."

Barstow moved lamely but deliberately into the path, and stood between the fresh wheel-tracks; he gazed suspiciously toward the Three Chopt Road, but neither of us could tell whether the wagon had turned right toward the last fortifications rimming the city, or left toward Richmond itself.

"Somebody howled," whispered Barstow. "Did he look to you like a man who would take a woman into the woods and strike her dead?"

I said, "Remember—we've got our own skins to save,"

but still I was affected and appalled by the thought that this might be one of those tragedies mentioned by men when they talk in whispers.

"True enough!" Barstow exclaimed, after some study. "You have a knack of saying things, now and then. No matter what he done to her, we've gone through hell to save this much of our hides."

"There might be food, still," I said. "Maybe she took it out of the wagon with her."

I spoke with greater prophecy than I dreamed; but long lack of food gives a second sight to people seeking it, and a second smell as well.

Barstow struck his bony flank with a wide-open hand. He forgot just where he was striking himself and what the state of his skin might be, and I saw his bearded lips draw back like rubber around his teeth. "Maybe you said a good say that time, too, Clark! I reckon we better look. We'll go back quiet-like through the brush, and you keep behind the trees when you can. These woods are real open."

"I won't go into those vines again," I told him flatly. "Not for all the rations at Manassas Junction."

He said, "Then go slow. We got to move quiet," and he slid away from me cautiously, staring through the trees as if he expected to see a dozen banquets spread for him, and a dozen murdered women dangling beside them.

We did not see her until we were all too close. Her shawl was rust-colored, as I have said, and there are hoards of rust in a Virginia forest of yellow pine. The spines of a tender, newer growth lifted around her at twice the height of rhubarb; but when she turned toward our crackling approach, her gown flashed like painted blue. She let something fall from her hand, some object that gleamed.

Her life had been cruel to her much of the time ... as we grew to know her, we found that she carried brands most women could well do without. And yet, God being not too brutal, she had until this moment been spared the experience of doing what she had just done, and then seeing two heathen rise out of the forest to haunt her for it.

I spoke before Barstow did, and did not speak with as much sense. "Did you scream, Ma'am?" I asked.

She made a whisper in her throat.

Barstow brayed forth, "We won't hurt you, Missis," which indeed I should have told her.

For, as surely as we trod those woods, we were spawned by that same evil nourishing the thorny vines—that wickedness which sent the buzzards stepping around their breakfasts in fields thereabouts (black buzzards, turkey buzzards, and all of them horrid little ladies in stained black silk who wore black shawls on their humped shoulders). I will not believe that a Divinity created those buzzards, and it is hard to reckon that the Lord had a hand in making what He had made out of us.

Our heads were straw-stacks, soaked by river and rain. Our nostrils were pinched, our hollow eyes red and angry, and our beards the very hallmark of savagery. And the puny, scrofulous shells we called our bodies, broken and wet at every joint, studded with corns and felons and bed-sores—these carcasses were draped in mouldy rags a cat would not have curled upon.

But in spite of the fear and bewilderment which stood in her resentful eyes, I knew, then, that at least she was seeing some core of humanity in both of us. She had gray eyes; they were as hard as rifle-balls, and contrasted with the soft luxury of her face, the preciseness of the thin upper lip, and the startling, delicate contour of her lower lip and chin.

"Where did you come from?" Some grimness about her robbed the question of its rightful inflection.

"We were over there a ways in the woods, Missis," replied Barstow.

I asked again, "Did you scream?"

"I don't know."

Still we waited in the scrub growth, letting our wolfish gaze go out to her. It was not that we desired her as young men are bound to desire women; we had lived through all that and forgotten it, as the draw-strings of the Island sack tightened around us. When she went by, with the officer in the wagon, we had said, "There's a woman," just as we had said in the midnight, "There's a dog barking," or "I hear footsteps."

But now, caught face to face with her in the moment of her hysteria, we saw the ordinary mask of womanhood peeled from her like a useless skin. We wondered who she was and why her eyes should look like that.

"How did you come to be in these woods?" she wanted to know.

"We came—" I said, but no more than that, for Barstow's elbow was against mine and then he stood in front of me.

He declared accusingly, "We heard a yell."

She shook her head. "I don't know what you heard."

"Was that rebel officer your husband?"

"No."

No matter what had happened there in the glade, and no matter what she admitted or denied, I could bear no longer the maddening smell which came to me. "I smell something to eat," I cried.

She had not moved from the mat of needles where she stood when first we saw her. "You're starving, aren't you?" she whispered, without wonder. "Both of you."

I cried again, "I smell it!"

"It's in the basket," she said, and nodded toward a heap of things which we had not noticed before, lying on the ground not ten feet away: two large cushions or pillows, home-made and covered with pieces of old carpet, a pair of field glasses, and a willow basket with a splintered handle. The basket was covered with a yellow damask cloth, and the cloth itself was stained by the food against which it had been pressed.

I tried to go toward it, but Barstow held me. "Ma'am," he said, his voice hard and ugly, "I don't like that knife you had in your hand."

"Knife?" She looked at the ground beside her, and then she said, "Oh," and we bent forward, though the smell of food was choking us. A pair of embroidery scissors lay there, spread wide; I thought there was blood on one blade, but could not be sure.

Then I bawled, "Oh, to hell with this, Bar!" and plunged toward the basket. I wrenched off the napkin and flung it far. There were slices of cornbread with bits of fried salt-pork or bacon between; there was a small stone crock of preserved peaches, another of sliced chicken, and a bottle which appeared to hold wine.

"Go on," I heard the woman say from an unbelievable height above me. Immediately I had a mass of bread and meat in my mouth, and was pawing at the peaches.

Barstow squatted beside me. He began to eat, also, but he was watching the woman as much as he watched the basket. "Go slow, Clark," he cautioned. "Go slow; it's death to gorge yourself."

I laughed, "Yes. Gorge," with the tears running down my cheeks, and then I was after the food once more.

Barstow snatched the basket away from me; the bottle of wine fell out. "Damn you, Clark!" he said. "If you fall in your tracks you'll have to stay there! I can't agree to lug you out of these woods. And we've got to go mighty quick, too, for there'll be a big fuss.... Take some wine, now—a little bit—and then I'll take some. But I beg you to take it cautious-like."

"Nobody knows we're here," I made him understand through all my munching and swallowing. "No one but her."

Barstow nodded, and looked up at the woman again as if she were accountable for more crimes than one. "That's just it. That officer set so funny in the wagon seat, and I knew something had happened. You stabbed him, didn't you, Ma'am?"

I looked up, then, for this was the first I realized what had really happened. But I did not find the woman with her face buried in her hands. Instead she was looking at Barstow with a curious blankness, and seemed not dangerous, but only afraid.

"I don't know," she told us. "I never thought to stab any one. I struck at him with those little shears. I had them in my hand—I was sewing, and he—"

Her eyes went wide, and she opened her mouth to scream, but only part of the cry had escaped before Barstow sprang at her and seized her mouth.

"Oh, no!" she sobbed, as he struggled with her. "No! Don't put your hands on me."

He released her; his eyes were black and vengeful. "We'll have no screaming here! I don't want these woods full of soldiers, and you can wager they'll come if they hear any yelling. They'll come soon enough, if that officer wasn't struck too bad to tell them about it. Will you swear not to scream again?"

She nodded without speaking.

"Do you think you know who we are?"

"Yankee prisoners," she whispered. "Are you from Libby?"

We spoke together, "Belle Island." Barstow added

quickly: "But don't think you're going to turn us over to your rebel friends, lady!"

I said, "Bar, you'd better come eat," not because I wished to be generous, but because our lives had been measured in shares ever since November, and the habit was strong in me.

"We can take it with us," said Barstow.

"Take it where?" I asked.

He came closer, pounding his fists together and looking angrily over his shoulder toward the woman and the empty wood road beyond. "I'm not crazy enough to stay here, and you'd better not be! I can calculate just what will happen. This lady jabbed a rebel officer with those little scissors of hers, and she admits he wasn't her husband. It's a scandalous business, and maybe it's murder. I don't see why they couldn't have driven into some other timber, somewhere!"

By this time I was at the basket again; I had my hands full of bread. I told him, "If you hadn't heard that yell the officer made, we wouldn't have come down here."

"You ought to thank me," he said. "We're fair warned, now, and we wouldn't have been. We wouldn't have known anything, until they came through with dogs and guards and yanked us out by the heels. It's risky to travel by daylight, but travel we must." He took two slices of the bread, and some of the chicken. "How about those glasses, Ma'am? Are those his?"

All the while we talked, she had been watching us. I felt that her mind became less and less concerned with her own terror, as it occupied itself with measuring us and trying to decide how deep she must go within our ragged, filthy shells, to find what sort of creatures we were before we went to Belle Island.

She nodded slightly at Prentiss Barstow. "They belong to the Colonel."

"Is he a colonel?" I asked.

"What's his name?" demanded Barstow.

She drew the rust-colored shawl tighter around her shoulders; its folds covered more and more of her dress, and it was long since I had seen a silk gown with a lovely woman inside. . . .

"He's Colonel Stanislas Mokranowski."

"No colonel ever had such a name!" Barstow scorned her.

"He comes from Poland."

I gobbled over the food: "Bar, they even have them down here. The rebels have them—hirelings! They're not all working for the Union."

"What's he doing here?" asked Barstow. "Why isn't he with the rebel army?"

The woman regarded him just as scornfully as he had ever looked at her. "He was with the army, until he was wounded. He's been twice wounded. He's not fully recovered yet, but he's helping with the fortifications, and helping organize the guards in Richmond. He wanted to drive out here and around to the north, as well, and see what the Yankee raiders had done. That's why we had a lunch."

"That wasn't why you jabbed him," said Barstow.

Again her eyes held the grayness of granite.

Barstow declared, "We're going to get out of here, lady— out of these woods. And don't you try to follow us. They may send dogs, too, but if we can get to some water we'll be able to lose the dogs. I wish you had some pepper in that basket of yours."

She whispered, "Where are you going?"

"Well," I told her, trying to laugh through my beard, "we're not going back to the Island unless they carry us. I take it our lines are around Culpeper or Stevensburg, somewhere."

"Do you think you'll survive to get that far?"

"God willing," said Barstow, and ate some of the chicken.

He straightened. "Come on, Clark. Stow away those field-glasses in the basket; we'll thank the colonel for them. I hate to leave those pillows."

I cried, "Barstow, you're not going to leave those?" and the woman looked at me in astonishment, for she had never dreamed of an existence wherein each broken button, each fragment of wood or dirty scrap of cloth, had its price.

Barstow shook his head. "They'll do us no profit, and the carpet goods around them ain't wide enough to make any covering out of."

"It'll make one kind of covering," I said. "Hold fast while I cut it off."

He watched me as I crossed to the woman's side, and again I heard her cry in her throat when I retrieved the scissors from the ground where they lay. There was blood on one blade, just as I had thought. I wiped it off, though I would never have done that had not the woman been watching me.

I went to the cushions and began to slit them loose at the seams. "This carpeting is for our feet," I told Barstow. "Mine, anyway."

He nodded wisely. "There's enough for two. Sometimes you do have sound ideas, Clark. But you got to be careful about gorging yourself. . . . Get them loose and we'll be moving. Crossing the main road will be the worst; we've been here too long, now. Listen."

We all stood stock-still and tried to hear the ugly promise of pursuit: the voices of animals, and the people who would bring them. But only bird sounds came to us, and a thin wind in the higher trees. Far away in the northwest, I imagined I heard negroes singing drearily as they worked, and was certain that the wagon wheels we heard so distantly were not coming on our trail.

Then I bent to my work, and quickly finished lifting

the carpet covering from the cushions. Barstow put the pieces into the basket along with the wine bottle and the officer's field-glasses, and pressed the damask cloth tight around them. "I wouldn't be robbing you of this lunch, Ma'am, but you don't seem to be needing it like we do."

"I need so much," she said.

We waited, staring at her. "You need nothing that we've got," said Barstow.

"Courage," she said. "I guess you have that. I used to have it, until I gave up."

"Now God be with us!" burst from my companion. "What's she driving at, Clark?"

I couldn't answer him, for her distress had embarrassed me (so distressed as I was, myself). I thought that, layer by layer, she was showing herself to us, and I could not bear the sight.

She said, dully, "Do you realize what I've done? If he dies, they'll no doubt hang me, and perhaps they should. I've scarce a friend in Richmond, and none elsewhere that I know of. If he lives, I cannot go back to him. . . . I felt this coming for a long time—I knew that he would force me to do it. I still thank Heaven I had those scissors."

She choked, and then her voice was shriller and thinner than before. "I'm from the North, too! My father was born there, and so was I. If you won't turn me over to the hang-man or starvation, you can let me go with you. I'll be happier, starving that way."

I do not know what expression was in my face. All I could see was the desperate pleading of her eyes, and I wondered what had become of the flint that shone in them before. But Barstow laughed aloud, and swung the basket high with a trembling hand.

"Come on, Clark," he hooted. "We'll go, before she gets more crazy and starts to screech again!"

He started away into the pines, already bending his shoulders and carrying his head forward with the slyness of an animal. I took a few steps after him, then stopped. I could feel the woman's eyes on my back, and hear her breathing, although she had not stirred.

"Wait a minute, Bar," I called.

He turned as I came up to him. "Clark," he began, in a savage whisper, "I saved your life last night—you cried and told me so. Don't ask me to do a thing like this. We can't go parading towards Culpeper with a Richmond whore!"

I still had the scissors in my hand. "How would you like to have me gash you with this?" I heard a voice murmuring, and knew that it was mine, and knew that I was uttering blasphemy. But before he could answer, there was the swift sound of her skirts through the scrub growth; she stood beside me.

"I heard what you said," she sobbed. "I've fought that thing for two years!" She struck Barstow across the mouth. He growled and swayed toward her, and I caught at his arm.

"You spoke of madness," the woman said. "You've taunted both of us because of it. And now you're madder than any friend you left on that Island. Don't you realize what I'm offering? I may be a woman, but I'm stronger than either of you, now. Yes, even stronger than you, you big black beard, with your big bones! I haven't been starving, the way you have. I can go farther, and sleep less and eat less than you need to. But you know I can never travel alone. Something would happen."

He watched her for a while, breathing heavily; gradually his face lost its stubborn ferocity. "By God," he said, "you've got spunk and you've got a good clear mind. I don't care what kind of a woman you are."

"I'm not a good woman," she said, "but I'm not what you think. There was no choice for me."

Barstow turned and looked down at me, and then back at the woman and down again. He was half a head taller than I, and she did not come near his shoulder. He muttered, "I never thought to see the hour when a little woman like you would claim she was stronger than me, and be right about it." His skeleton hand caressed the crossed axes of the Pioneer Corps, which still clung, stained and barely recognizable, to the sleeve of his jacket. "Nevertheless, Clark— What do you say?"

My mind was made up long before, but I stammered, for this was one of the strangest things which had ever come to me. "I say we should try it, Bar. It's the only chance for her. What if it were your sister?"

"I ain't got any sister," said Barstow, "but if I had one, she would do better than a rebel hireling."

The woman moved past us and stood looking into the woods. She glanced at the sky, then, and, seeming to remember something, opened a tiny gold watch that was pinned against her bosom under the shawl. "High noon," she said. "He must have gone back to town, and not to the outer lines. But you were right when you thought he would send for me.... If we cross the Three Chopt Road, we'll have to cross hereabouts, for there are wood details up yonder, and cavalry on the road behind."

"Share and share alike," I heard myself saying. "It's an equal risk, and I think you've brought us some strength, Ma'am."

"Miss," she said. "I repeat, for your mutual concern, that I was never married. Tell me your names."

We told her.

"My name is Naomi—Naomi Kincaid.... I've nearly lost track of Providence, but let it be with us."

"Amen," said Barstow, a bit sullenly. But I thought there was a light in his eyes; I could feel one burning in mine.

3

WHEN we reached the high-road, we squatted low in a thicket near the forest's edge, and spoke in whispers.

"One of us has got to crawl out a ways in front, and see what's what," said Barstow.

Already the presence of Naomi Kincaid was working in my mind, and inspiring me to do things I would not have done had Barstow and I been alone. For a man will not suffer his pain alone in the dark, half as well as he will bear it when he lies in the white light of day, and has people listening to him; and so a schoolboy will be haughty and bold before a gingham dress, when he might cringe in terror at another time.

I crept ahead speedily, only hearing them say, "Wait," and "Where are you going?" and marveling, too, that I should thus exhibit a bravery I did not possess, at the unspoken behest of an utter stranger, and one admittedly not a good woman at that.

The timberland at this point had been cut off some years before. Thatches of yellow pine stood at a height of three or four feet, bending back to earth under the weight of their needled masses. I worked my way under them and parted the boughs until I could see the road directly in front. There was nothing except a wagon-pole with a sharpened point, which had fallen there, and not far away a scattered mound of tawny apples where a horse had passed. I listened, and hearing no sound close at hand, moved to the edge of the road where I could look both right and left. There was a curve not a hundred yards away, shielding the view toward Richmond and the inner fortifications, but on my right the road was unobstructed into the northwest. Sure enough, wagons were moving there. As I looked, a horseman seemed to detach himself from the mass.

I crashed back through the growth, and Barstow hissed in my face, begging for quiet. "It's clear," I said. "There's a bend on the left, but let's take the risk and move out."

The three of us hurried through bushes and across the road; it was as if a thousand people were watching us. But the thousand people did not lift their voices...across the highway we scrambled through a rail fence, which was easily done, the fence being neglected and rails lying every which way. There was an old cornfield here; along its north boundary grew a tangled hedge of wild fruit trees, vines, and here and there a solitary pine.

"Get rid of that bonnet," Barstow said to the woman, sharply. "It's bright and shiny, and folks could spot it a mile away."

"They could see my dress, too," she said.

"Your shawl helps to cover that, for the time being," he warned her. "Here, I'll put it out of sight." He seized the bonnet, which she removed reluctantly even as we were hurrying, and thrust it inside the band of his pantaloons. "We'll stick it down a hole somewhere, because it's dangerous. Make haste through this hedge, folks; there's more cover to the north."

We got through the vines somehow, though I heard them tear at the woman's clothes, and there was not as much cover in the north pasture as Barstow had thought. From the direction of the Three Chopt Road we began to hear a horse's hoofs.

"It's the mounted man I saw," I cried. "He was up there toward those wagons, and he may be looking for us."

"Or for me," said the woman.

The sound came nearer; we knew that the man was galloping. Barstow ordered, "Lie down!" and we all lay flat without more ado. I reached over and drew the woman's shawl more widely to cover the blazing blue of her dress, and she turned quickly when she felt my hand. The horseman went past, south and east. The road was somewhat muddy, and the beat of hoofs had been muffled. He was closer than we thought.

Barstow lifted his head from the weeds, and he reported that the rider looked like a young boy; Barstow could not tell whether' he was a soldier or not, for their uniforms were mainly make-shift. But the rider did not pause, and the hurrying feet went beyond our hearing, and now there were wagon wheels again—heavy ones, grinding closer.

At the foot of the pasture was another fence, a very old one and partly made of stone. The ground sloped toward the west; ahead we could see the fuzzy gray and green of woodland covering the lower valley. A small, unpainted house stood close on our left. No one moved in the dooryard, but wood-smoke came from the chimney. "A nigger house, likely," the woman suggested, as we sighted it.

"Whatever it is, we can't stay here," said Barstow. "It'll be death to stop here in the open."

After passing the wall, we had entered a grain field; sunshine held us up to the gaze of the whole Confederacy. Our shadows moved too languidly under our feet and on our right, and it seemed that they must be leaving a trail all their own which any one could follow.

A dog barked near the unpainted shack. The woman trembled, and Barstow began to curse.

"Now," I said, eagerly, "you both know better than that. I've had dogs, many of them. It's a squirrel or woodchuck he's barking at—not people."

"You're right," muttered Barstow. After that we went less fearfully.

For we had behind us a rail fence, a dotting of trees along the Three Chopt Road, and the gentle slope which would help to shield us; also the stone fence, however low. We plucked up courage, for each matting of half-chewed rye stalks we scrambled through, added to the screen. I began to guess at something I knew for a truth later on: the doomed fugitive, beginning his tortuous flight, does not fear what is ahead as he fears what has been left behind.

The grain field ended without any fence; we entered a patch of jack-oaks, fresh logged-off for the fortifications. The bright yellow stumps were everywhere, and pale chips, and the marks of men and wheels. I saw a burnt-out cob pipe beneath my feet, and kicked it aside, and wondered who had smoked it last and why I did not feel the hankering to smoke again. The oak tract ended in squashy ground where the snow had melted a day or two before, to flow down and build little lakes among the hummocks. But there was dense forest just beyond.

Barstow gloated when he saw the water. "There may be a stream, too, and it'll all help if they send the dogs."

I felt the insane impulse to pick up Naomi Kincaid and carry her through this wetness—insane for every reason in the world, but chiefly because I could not have carried a twenty-pound sack of salt. She went ahead silently, close behind Barstow; I followed in the rear, looking now and again over my shoulder, and seeing no one but crows.

There were more crows in the drowned woods ahead of us. They rose up, screaming.

"Those birds," cried Naomi Kincaid. "I think they were sent here for a purpose."

"Crows do give warning," said Barstow, "but they'd do the same if a lone negro came into the woods. Come along with you."

It was a crows' rookery; the ground showed that, and the

bushes, and there was one dead crow. His brothers swept above the trees, scores of them, flapping and talking about us, and I was thankful that they were not buzzards. The water grew deeper, more overspreading. The moss, the gnarled roots and rotten burls of bark showed that water lay here forever.

But it all made Barstow very happy, for he was still entertaining bloodhounds in his thoughts.

"The idea is," he said, "to work in one direction or the other, and not come out square on the opposite side when we do come out." He stopped for a moment, the water splashing halfway to his ragged knees as he felt for firmer footing. We waited beside him, breathing heavily, and Heaven knows we men were breathing harder than the woman.

Her face was set, but mainly expressionless. I had thought that her hair was ash-blonde; now it held an unearthly greenish-silver, the quality of phosphorus, in the sudden gloom of this swamp. Her skirts were drenched, and the water made them heavier, impeding her limbs. But she wore a good pair of leather boots, small and dainty, but not too high of the heel. And so she could travel faster than we, still.

"Have you a map?" she asked.

Barstow explained, "Five of us tried to get away from the Island, but we lost two men, and I don't know what became of the third. He had the map—Fatridge did. He had some knowledge, too, about forts and such. And there is, sure, a fort on our right."

She nodded. "It's part of the circle of outer works; cavalry are supposed to patrol back and forth between all those batteries. But there's a road running west, near here. It would be on our left, of course—the road to Goochland Court House."

"Goochland's a mighty long ways," said Barstow, and I

agreed. "It was marked on the map. If you got any sense, you ought to know we can't travel that road!"

"Not in the day," she replied, "but at night."

I said, "There's the colonel to think of, and those he'll order out."

Her eyes were hard again. "You won't understand . . . but I'm not hag-ridden by thought of the Colonel. I keep wondering only if he's able to send soldiers after me."

She went on rapidly; she might have been talking to herself: "After I struck him he didn't say anything. He went over to the wagon and sort of fell against the wheel. There was no blood that I could see, but he kept holding himself. He climbed up, somehow or other, and turned the wagon around. He drove off. He didn't look back."

"Did he have a revolver?" asked Barstow.

"He had his side-arms. Yes, he could have shot me. Perhaps he never thought of it."

I felt Barstow watching my face, and for the first time I turned away from him. We had shared and sacrificed together, and had been vigilantes together when the great riot occurred in the prison, and the New York hoodlums were hunted down and killed. He held some of my secrets, I held some of his. He had saved my life, or had aided me back into it, on the night before. But now something was happening to us with the first smell of freedom, and with this peculiar circumstance whereby our party had grown in numbers from two to three.

Barstow announced, "That's all well enough, Miss. Maybe that rebel officer was too much hurt to send a squad after you. But we can't take root in this swamp; they'd hunt us down. We want more land and water between them and us than we got now! I say, keep moving, and stick to the brush as well as we can. We'll work south until we get nigh the road you talked about."

"Get nigh?" I echoed. "We'll cross the road! Then we'll have the river and canal on one side, and that Goochland road on the other. As long as we're between them, and working northwest, we're in the right direction."

Naomi Kincaid said simply, "I'm ready when you are."

And now began a peculiar, nightmare journeying of a sort we had never imagined in captivity. For then we had thought that, once we eluded the guards and passed the outer fortifications, no one would know we were abroad, and we would be safe so long as we preserved our silence and kept from sight. In this present course, we were followed by the memories of this woman—the things which she had done—and they were sufficient to snap at our heels each time we lingered to draw breath.

We drove ourselves on, while the sun tired of its perch and began to lean toward the southwest. The groves, the increasing areas of pasture-land where there were no herds and fields where there were no farmers, began to blur together until we had no record of how many we had passed.

Cross the Goochland road we did, running across its ruts with our hearts in our mouths, but seeing no enemies of any sort except a weasel who squeaked at us. Now we were prevented from straying too far afield, with the road on our right, and the river on our left; and we changed our course full toward the far-away Court House.

On a high ridge somewhere in that mighty wilderness where we penetrated, we staggered and fell and slept—Prentiss Barstow and I—with uneaten food still clutched in our fingers, and the woman sitting beside us, her feet drawn up under her soaked skirts, her face turned stonily toward the horizon over which we had crept. In our exhausted dreams, we counted a hundred miles traveled that midday; whereas I reckon now that perhaps we had traveled five.

4

I WOULD not have any one believe that each time I closed my eyes and abandoned myself to the mercies of unconsciousness (which often enough are no mercies at all) I saw the Island before me, or stood upon it. That would be evidence of a certain orderliness of thought, which no one in the plight of Prentiss Barstow or myself could possess; and when I did dream, part of what went on before me was true and had happened, and much of it, praise be, never came about.

Thus I dreamed of the fields we had just crossed—as I rested on that lonely ridge. I was aware that I had come from Westfield, and what my people were like, and again I rode in strange fairy uplands astride a wooden horse which my uncle had whittled out for me. . . . Childhood and army life, the torture of coughing in the winter rain, the first peppery urge for procreation that comes upon a youth—all those thoughts visited me, netted themselves together, and through them strained unhappy dreams which had obsessed me years before, now magnified or enlarged in a hundred directions.

And over all like a veil, or a shroud as thin as a veil, was spread Belle Island. Only Naomi Kincaid knows to this day whether I tossed and wailed in my sleep during those hours, and whether Prentiss Barstow did the same.

But I think some words must have come from us, buried in exhaustion as we were, to make her know that the Island was not merely an elongated mass of sycamores and stones and clay hills, stranded in the James river opposite the state penitentiary, but a place of horror which no one individual could be answerable for. If blame must go out to some one, let it lie upon the head of him who first planned for war and said, "Perhaps this may not be wise, but it will be best."

In succeeding days when from time to time we spoke of this and that which had occurred, there was the purity of understanding in Naomi Kincaid's face. And though I may be dead when this record is observed by others, I hope the same pitying gleam may start to life in the faces of those who read it.

To begin with, there was little enough wood in the city of Richmond itself. When women and children are taken into account, one can well understand why a few thousand Yankees were allowed to spend their winter without wood and the comfort that its burning can bring. Yet somehow I lived there from November until March, and Barstow did as well; though his bearing it was more understandable, since he was sturdier to begin with.

And our strength still supported us, in small measure, in those first days of March. It was the strength which is obedient to leadership and authority, but cannot give birth to them. Much as I disliked the man Fatridge, I was grateful for the fact that he was not captured until February, and thus had a good share of his enterprise left to him in preparing for the great night.

For one thing, he called us all Comrades, and we hated him for it, though we were quick to recognize the wisdom of letting him be the leader in our project. He had been captured near the Rapidan while on picket duty; he had a good blanket and a well-filled knapsack when he arrived and by some ministration of fate, approached our tent and asked to come and live with us. He was sanctimonious, but he possessed physical courage and initiative, and a kind of primitive, woodchuck canniness.

In tiny rag-lined graves, in little houses hollowed beneath the floor of the tent, we stored the profit of his planning:

crusts of corn loaves, a few onions, scraps of rancid salt-pork. This hoard was to be consumed only at the proper time. Within five days after his arrival at Belle Island, Fatridge began plans for escape. Those plans took into consideration the manufacture of energy.

Our leader was not generous by nature, but he knew a good truth: there would be shooting and hunting when the break came. Certainly one man would be chased down and caught or killed; so would two. But if the escape were made in a black night, the guards would be unable to see how many prisoners were in the party, and the average possibility of success would rise with the number essaying it. If five attempted the James river, one or even more might reach the north bank.

It was this understanding which caused Simon Fatridge to share the fruit of his petty marketings. Needles, envelopes, postage stamps, a comb, a lump of soap, a tin cup—all the treasures of his knapsack had been hawked along the narrow cesspool which we called Market street. Jo Sauers' playing cards had been sold, and so had the sticks of hickory which Barstow had buried away, and so had my card of bone buttons and my Bible and my tattered copy of Shakespeare. Some had gone to the prisoners, some to the guards, but all were converted into food. The onions proved a specific for scurvy. Only Voss looked to be beyond redemption; his teeth were loose in their sockets, his gums raw and spongy.

We acquired oilcloth—a rag of it—and kept my four matches carefully wrapped. Sauers had a map of Henrico and Goochland counties torn from a bartered book. These treasures lay in a special chamber of their own, and were tended daily.

I remember every detail of the afternoon preceding our escape. I remember when Fatridge looked seriously into our faces and up at the gray sky, and said, "What do you make it?" He meant, of course, the time of day.

We guessed. Most of us agreed on four o'clock. "And we haven't heard a piece of artillery all day. That means the Yanks didn't manage."

"If it was Kilpatrick, he likely cut the railroads in two," said Sauers. "No rations yet. Hear them howling?"

The camp moaned and shook around us. It was a plaint which had risen toward sharp crescendo since noon; and yet in all these hours we men had taken no direct notice.

"The cavalry meant business, but the Johns were ready for them," Barstow nodded. "I hope our cavalry burns in hell."

"Why?" Fatridge asked in astonishment.

I told him, "It's always that way. If they cut a railroad, we starve just as the rebs starve. We starve harder than ever."

Voss wiped his bleeding mouth. "If it was cavalry, it wasn't Pennsylvania. It was your God damn Jersey cavalry, I'll wager!"

I flew at him, but Barstow and Sauers pulled me off.

"Anyway," said Simon Fatridge, "it's past time for our exercise. All get ready for a run."

Voss howled, "My knees and ankles are broke clean open! They fair kill me if I try to—"

"We've all got sores," cried Sauers. "I got corns on every bone—more than you have, you little feist!"

Fatridge was at the door. "Everybody out!" he commanded. "Outside for exercise." And then, in a lower tone, "How do you expect to get across that river without plenty of elbow grease?"

He led us at a trot, up the muddy waste between the ranks of flapping tents. People came out and hooted; people waved us on encouragingly, or mocked us with frantically obscene gestures. Still we struggled on, and turned from Broadway into Market street, and on toward the parapet at its foot.

Here we were compelled to break our rank and pick a path amongst the huddled bundles of rags sprawling in the track. Here was the center of commerce, the axis of community nightmare; here demented beings came to bawl their psalms or sing their lullabies, and here men came to die. The dead-cart had arrived soon after dawn, and would not come again until another day.

At the ditch-side, under the gaze of a starving North Carolinian with a rifle in his hands, we halted our dogged race. All were gasping for breath.

"We cracked a few scabs that trip," said our mentor, "but it'll help make men of us, Comrades."

"Oh, God!" sobbed Bubby Voss.

The North Carolinian called down from behind the wire fence, "The manner you-all rare around, you Yanks act like double rations."

Sauers crowed, "You never gave us our breakfast, Johnny. You keep treating us like that and we'll get mad and go home."

"What's become of the fried chicken?" I was inspired to ask.

Sauers taunted, "The gingerbread—what became of the gingerbread for our tea?"

The guard told us reprovingly, "If your cavalry once stayed to home, you'd be better off."

He looked up and down for an officer, and seeing none, he bent over the wire and lowered his voice to a whisper. "They tore up the railroad again, Yanks, and mighty near galloped into Richmond before they got beat off. But I heard tell there'd still be an issue made today."

Voss shrieked, "The Union forever!"

"Hush up!" growled Barstow.

At the front gate, drums began to roll. We five skeletons (or four skeletons and Simon Fatridge, who would soon be one unless he made his escape) went scampering away toward the sound. I looked back over my shoulder as I ran. The guard was gazing through the wind toward those gray hills where Richmond poured its smoke against the sky, and I wondered whether he was pitying us.

In the camp, four thousand men had come suddenly to life. It seemed as if the very corpses had risen from their cold reclining, and once more were brandishing eager claws in the air.

"Drums for rations!" The yell rose from every side. "Fall in. Turn out for rations! Fall in for rations! Drums for rations. . . ." The brass drums roared mechanically in a warning of phantom battles. The familiar column of blanket-carriers advanced slowly from the bakehouse.

They paraded through the gate, serious scarecrows, each holding his corner of a squad blanket with the brown loaves weighting deep in the center. Ahead of the burdened details came squad commanders . . . the guards watched with pathetic eyes, for the guards also dreamed of food.

One century had gone by, in whirring retrospect; Napoleon had fallen, and had risen, and had been born. The rolling frigates plunged through oceans a hundred years old. Time spread itself in a painful band around the universe— the minutes stretched exhaustingly, paling into taut decades. . . . The prisoners piled the loaves on flat-spread blankets, added a loaf to this pile, broke off a corner of that. There were Union army crackers eking out the first seven portions, but there was an extra corn-loaf on each of the other thirty-five. All must be divided fairly, fairly.

"Who gets this?"

The pack of human wolves swayed around, at the distance prescribed by authorities; they danced, and waved their fists, they clapped their hands, they jounced foolishly up and down like children kept too long from the toilet.

"Who gets this?"

A gangling prisoner with a Sixth Corps badge stood and looked at the sky. "Twenty-eight." His back was turned firmly upon the little mounds of food, but his thin nostrils twitched and his hands were quivering.

Squad Twenty-eight roared.

"Squad Twenty-eight. Detail, attention!" The detail picked up the blanket, sagging none too low with a meal for a hundred men. "Forward—ho!" They marched, and Squad Twenty-eight pranced eagerly behind.

"Who gets this?"

"Four."

The centuries hummed, unrolling and stretching . . . no ordinary time had ever been so elastic. There were the Crusades, there was Charlemagne; Jesus Christ walked again on the Mount of Olives . . . *Who gets this? Thirty-one. Who gets this? Eleven. . . .* The prisoner with the Sixth Corps badge pitched forward without a sound; he was dead before he struck the ground. I thought that perhaps his had once been a brave heart, but now it had failed him.

They lifted him aside. Some one else was delegated to his place. A foreign voice: the man was a Swede or a Jew, or something queer and uncouth. And I watched Lieutenant Boisseau, the camp commander, strolling along outside the gate. He walked toward the narrow brick home of the Belle Island Manufacturing Company, which stood against the hill. His dog was with him; it was too fat, and one day I had planned to eat that dog.

Lieutenant Boisseau looked trim and stern, in his shabby gray. He was from the Point, said old Regulars among the prisoners. *Who gets this?* I counted the guards at the head of the Manchester bridge. There were seven of them, and two small negro boys and a woman with a pink cloth wrapped around her head. Maybe she was a negress, maybe not.

Then Squad Three had drawn its corn loaves; we went screaming down Broadway behind the burden in a black blanket. Again the inescapable queries sounded five times over; again a soldier looked at the sky with his back to the rations. He called in no order at all, the five messes. Third Mess, First Mess, Second Mess, Fifth Mess, and the Fifth Mess did not wait to hear the Fourth Mess called. We made our babbling departure, sixteen men and boys in Federal uniforms, or butternut clothes traded from the Confederates, or parti-colored rags and scraps of blanket. Two men were down sick since morning; one had died, and one was so insane that he could not eat and would soon starve. We divided rations for twenty men amongst eighteen, and did little talking until the eating was done. It did not take long.

In the seventh hovel from the end of the row, Simon Fatridge cautioned us, "We'd better dig up what's left and eat it now, Comrades. It'll be dark soon enough, and we've got to get over so much food before we tackle the water."

There was no dissenting vote, so the remaining two onions and bits of potato peeling, the scraps of mouldy pork, were exhumed and eaten.

We looked to the packet of matches, and Fatridge and Barstow and I studied the map until dusk covered us. At about ten o'clock we made our bid for freedom.

5

WHEN I awoke, Barstow was talking with Naomi Kincaid; he had been awake for fifteen minutes or more. I did not move for a time, but exercised that stubbornness held dear by the awakening sleeper: I refused to open my eyes, except for a brief glimpse of the ground on which I lay.

Barstow was telling the woman about his capture, when the rebels had taken his watch from him. He was still very bitter about it. "If I got hit and lay out on the fields somewheres," he kept repeating, "I wouldn't mind getting peeled. There's battlefield peelers in every regiment, and most of us have done something like that a time or two. But to have to stand there and let that fellow take it, went sore against the grain!"

I heard her say, "Would you have taken a Confederate soldier's watch if he were your prisoner?"

"Not if it was his grandfather's and he set great store by it."

"That's as may be," she said.

"Well, I wouldn't."

I turned my face toward them, and Barstow nodded at me sullenly. "I've been stirring for some time, Clark. We'd all better shake our legs. We're none too far on the way."

Naomi Kincaid had taken the carpet goods from the basket and was working at it diligently. "I've turned bootmaker," she told me, without smiling at all. "I've made shoes for you men."

She held the embroidery scissors; she had clipped off

long strands of the goods to serve as lacings. It must have been necessary for her to use Prentiss Barstow's foot as a model or gauge, and somehow I resented that. Thin as they might be, his feet were much larger than mine. The method by which she worked was peculiar, but doubtless the only one to adopt. The slippers she had shaped were merely loose sacks, to be closed round the ankles by means of the improvised cords.

"How did you get the scissors?" I asked.

"I took them from you while you were asleep."

Still resentful at her having measured Barstow's foot— for I was confident that she had—I wished to accuse her of being a pickpocket, among other things. But even in the annoying disorder of my mind, I must needs realize that she was attempting to do us a kindness.

"Try them." She offered two of the sacks to me.

I said, "They'll do no great good, Miss Kincaid."

"That's heavy material. I should rather have it on than not, if I stepped on a sharp stick."

"Well," I continued, "I don't see how you could cut it out with those little scissors—"

"It was difficult," she admitted, and now I felt ashamed.

My feet were in worse condition than were Barstow's, for his shoes had been stolen six weeks earlier, and in spite of his weakened condition, sturdy callouses had developed. But I had worn shoes until four days earlier, when I traded the tattered uppers for pork, knowing that they would do me no good in swimming. In our flight of the previous night, I had pounded heels and toes and the balls of both feet into puffed and aching bludgeons; by this time they were numb; they gave me no great pain unless I tried to spread the toes. As long as I considered each foot a plummet of bruised flesh, without the quality of flexing and bending, I could get on tolerably well.

I looked at them, I say, and began to scrape off the dried clay as if I were shucking corn. There were raw slits between the toes; the heels were black-and-blue, and half again as large as heels should be.

"Don't do that," ordered Barstow, when he saw what I was about, "you'll take the hide with it! Let it work loose easy-like, inside the carpet. They'll be wet through, soon enough."

I managed to bind the vari-colored scraps tightly around my ankles, and felt that they should hold for a while. Barstow was working at his; he made a much better job of it than I.

I tried to get up, and couldn't. But Barstow leapt up like a goat, and my shame was lost in resentment once more when he gave me his hand and helped me to stand.

The sun was low; the air had grown much colder. We believed that the warmth of midday was waning forever ... hereafter we should feel nothing but sleet or the wind going through us. We could look from the barren oak ridge where we had established ourselves, and see the country falling away toward the west, ridge after ridge and cold valley after valley, where unidentified streams lost themselves in swamps and wandered loose again to follow dark paths toward the southwest and the James river.

"Would we be in Goochland county yet?" I asked, and the woman shook her head.

"Mighty nigh," said Barstow. "We'll be across the line before we sleep again."

"Didn't you sleep?" I inquired of Naomi Kincaid.

"Why should I sleep? I don't think I'll ever sleep again."

I picked up the basket.

"It's high time you carried that," Barstow told me.

"There's not much left." I took stock. Half the wine was still in the bottle, a bit of chicken, too; but all the peaches and cornbread were gone. Barstow and I bent seriously to the task of picking up the stray crumbs which had escaped our fingers before, and the woman watched us as if there were things in life of which she had never dreamed.

"Let's divide the chicken now," I suggested, "and let's each of us have a couple swallows of wine to wet our whistles."

Barstow laughed. "To make less for you to carry, you mean!"

"I'll carry it all inside me, if you'll give me leave," I retorted.

He said, in alarm, "No, you don't!" and motioned for me to put the basket down. He divided the chicken into three little heaps of shredded flesh and oily, yellow skin.

"I want none, thank you," the woman said.

Barstow instructed her: "It's share and share alike. That was how we agreed."

"But I'm not hungry."

I told her, "You had none of the cornbread, and we've gobbled it all. This may help your strength a bit."

She said no more, but took her share of chicken with some distaste, and did not again permit herself to look at Barstow's crusted hands, or mine.

Prentiss Barstow said, "Now the wine. Two swallows apiece."

"You divide everything else so carefully, down to the last smidgin," cried Naomi Kincaid. "I don't see how you can allow people to drink out of the same bottle and still believe each is getting his fair share."

"Simple enough," I explained. "You watch the man's throat. Everybody does. If he swallows more than the right number of times, somebody's apt to lay a club across his head. If he makes error, and coughs, or swallows without getting anything, it's his misfortune."

Barstow added, "Naturally, Miss, you make the swallows as big as you can. Come, now—two apiece."

"Watch me," said the woman. She took the bottle in her hand, looked at its mouth helplessly for a moment, then wiped it quickly with her shawl. She drank; she would have fared badly on the Island where things were divided in this fashion, for she had no notion of how to swallow largely.

I signaled Barstow; he took his share, and I followed suit. The wine was doubtless only a modest sherry, but it tasted like all the richness of a monastery's vats. It set my whole body awake and valiant; it made me forget my feet.

Now there were only the cloth, the bottle (mainly empty of wine) and the field-glasses to be carried in the basket, for worthless shreds were all that remained of the carpet goods.

"What of these little crocks?" I asked Barstow.

"Clark," he objected, "you wouldn't throw away good dishes like that, just because they weighed a mite?"

Naomi Kincaid cried, "Lord Almighty, you're both mad! What reason can you have for carrying those crocks?"

"He just wants a light-weight basket," sneered Barstow.

"No, I don't, Bar. But we're no longer on the Island; crocks have no value in these woods."

He watched me soberly for a moment. "That's mainly correct. Maybe the basket itself ain't much account."

"Not for us—honestly. I'll carry the next thing we get, double portion. I'll be no skulker about carrying things," I reassured him.

Accordingly, Barstow took the willow basket and the crocks and hid them under a windfall where a tree, torn out by wind long before, was rotting into the ground. I knotted the field-glasses and wine bottle in the damask cloth, and slung it over my shoulder.

"One thing more," said Barstow, remembering. He brought out the pansy-covered bonnet, which he had thrust inside his clothing and was now mashed badly by his body when he slept.

The woman burst forth, indignantly, "There was no reason why I shouldn't have kept that. If we're going to be seen, we'll be seen! And land knows when I'll get another bonnet."

"Land knows when you'll need one," I declared, the wine making me say it, and Barstow laughed heartily.

He offered the bonnet to her. She stroked the broken pansies, and felt of the ribbons. "It's only a rag, to you," she whispered, "but it was run through the Blockade. You Yankees have no notion of the store we set by ordinary things in Richmond."

"Haven't we?" I jeered, and this time she joined in the laughter.

There was a hole in the largest tree near us, one of those narrow, tapering apertures between the main roots where the acorn powder of countless squirrel dinners has sifted down. Naomi Kincaid crushed her bonnet into a ball and knelt beside the tree to stuff the bonnet through the concave opening, until no ribbon could be seen.

"Mice can have it for a nest," she said. "I declare, I'd never be seen wearing it when it's in such a state. Not even by cows. And—" she flung over her shoulder at us—"dirty people like you stuffing it inside your clothing!"

We started away down the west face of the ridge, in better humor than before and holding rather close together. Behind us, as an imagined safeguard, lay the hours of sleep. For slumber makes a certain bulwark in the passage of time, and each awakening is a new day. No hounds had bayed after us; according to the woman, no man or animal had shown himself to her while we lay there.

The late sunshine, chilling minute by minute, stared us in the face. In another hour we knew the light would fail.

Already a deep swamp toward which we headed was dusky, and it was easy to imagine that ice would form on the edges of every pool this night. But still the sky remained clear, and we gave some kind of thanks for that. We could do more, now, than set our bruised feet forward time and again, a thousand times and a thousand again, and count the yards that went so slowly under them. We could talk and ask many questions, and Naomi Kincaid answered us as best she could.

Our dream of Union cavalry was dispelled before ever we left the Island, but still we had hoped against hope that we might chance across some band of scouts who would feed us, perhaps give us horses, and take us with them as they fell back toward the north. When Naomi Kincaid told us of the attempt which had been made against the city, we saw our last thin hold on such a hope, vanish.

There had been two assaults. Her information came from Colonel Mokranowski, although she didn't mention his name. A heavy force of cavalry had made an unsuccessful attempt from the north, before and during the time when a smaller body came from the west; this smaller force was turned off by pickets and Home Guards not far from the spot where Barstow and I had been hiding. All the Yankees were said to have headed northeast toward the Pamunkey river, pursued savagely by cavalry who were endeavoring to cut off the stragglers.

In turn, we told her of hearing the guns, and how the population of Belle Island howled with glee at each distant thundering, and imagined how a stream of blue would look pouring down the hills of Richmond.

Naomi Kincaid shook her head. "There's a rumor afoot, or was this morning," she said. "Those Yankees were to burn the whole city, and liberate the felons from the penitentiary as well as the military prisoners."

"Sad pity they didn't succeed," I told her.

She looked at me coldly. "That's not civilized warfare. You should be ashamed of yourself."

I retorted, with heat, "I challenge any one to look at Bar and me, and say that we represent civilized warfare!" But after that she was annoyed with me, and walked close beside Barstow. I followed behind, the wine bottle and field-glasses bruising my back and chest, and my swollen feet afire inside their bulky moccasins.

Nevertheless, in spite of my feet and the empty weakness in me once the wine had worn off, and in spite of whatever such anguish besieged my companions, we made good mileage for the next hour. We crossed one swamp, an open ridge, and a valley where there was no swamp. From the higher ground, always we could see the dark timber of the James river bending steadily northwest, as if trying to block our way.

And during all the painful march, which was to be our last on that day, we saw only two human beings; we had seen no others since we were near the Three Chopt Road.

We came unexpectedly upon two negro children. They had two limp grain sacks, perhaps for gathering something in the woods, though to this day I cannot imagine what crops they harvested. They were playing near a stream which twisted through the second valley. The little girl sat on a lower branch of a tree which had been undermined and had fallen across the creek, and her brother crept on the horizontal trunk above.

There was ample warning, had we known to take it; we had heard their voices for some time, but imagined that they were crows. A wall of scraggly willows ended suddenly, and there we were face to face with them—staring into the frightened white eyes of the little girl and the open mouth of her brother. The children spoke no word; nor did we, but

after we splashed hastily through the stream we heard them
bounding away in the opposite direction like black rabbits
who feared the dogs even as we did.

Our fear, no doubt, was greater than theirs; Naomi Kincaid reasoned with Prentiss Barstow and me when we
would have despaired.

"They're wild creatures," she said. "I know their kind.
They have no idea who we might be or where we are going.
There are hundreds of lonely families like that scattered
in the woods hereabouts—refugees who have run away from
their plantations or were driven off by the Yankees when
they tried to take Richmond, two summers ago."

Barstow grunted, "We're not safe, having been seen."

The woman smiled quietly. "Were we safe before?" she
asked, and to that there was one answer.

Her face was haggard, but the cool resolve of her was
something to wonder at, and to take inside ourselves where
it might comfort us. I felt that I should not pry too willingly
into my imagination to seek the reason for her being with
us, and to discover just why she might have become a mur-
deress. It was no especial pity which prompted me to re-
frain, nor any such passion as climbs a man from his heels to
his head and makes him forget that the woman he desires is
a thing (of silk and beauty) in which the demons dwell.
For desire, as such, could not exalt itself in my veins until a
braver day.

But in spite of my high words with Naomi Kincaid and
my feeling that perhaps she was Secessionist at heart, I was
eager to count her as an intrepid companion who might well
carry me through any nightmare ambuscade that awaited.

And after our momentary fright at meeting those negroes,
the woman let my shrill retorts fall forgotten, and she helped
both Barstow and me to tie the sacks on our feet when they
loosened. Sometimes her elbow brushed me under its shawl,

and twice I felt hardy enough to hold the grape-vines out of her path.

The sun slid low behind thin lines of metal cloud; over the city of Richmond far behind us, the growing wind brought up softer clouds to be painted with pink. Winds rose out of the valleys on either side. They hurried to meet us and remind us that we were walking, near naked, on a star that held no burrow we might call our own.

On the next ridge we found a worm fence, and the trees ended there. Beyond, a long upland had been plowed many months before, and lay forlorn with the sodden, beaten aspect forever worn by tilled land when no thing grows upon it.

Barstow exclaimed, "There's a house, sure as I'm a foot high!"

The three of us pointed it out together: a turreted cube squatting among its barns and sheds in a meager grove of locust trees, beyond the field.

"We'd best bear to the right," I said. "That will bring us nearer the Goochland road when we've passed this farm."

"We're safer near the James," objected Barstow, and the woman agreed.

I looked again. "There's no smoke from those chimneys, Bar."

He observed the house for a time. "Maybe they're not cooking anything."

Naomi Kincaid said, rapidly, "But for heat, they'd need wood burning on a night like this! It's growing far colder every minute. Likely there'll be frost or even snow before morning." She moved forward and put her hands on the top rail of the fence.

Barstow looked at us both, and was puzzled. "What does it count, one way or the other, about smoke from them chimneys? We mustn't go near any house."

I wanted to say, "Maybe no one lives there. Maybe there are only mice and owls and creatures like that, who will let us share it with them," but I could not muster the courage to put such a hope into words. I wondered how long it had been since I heard flames seething in a chimney... Mine Run—that was November. I thought of the shebangs which the men had built at Stevensburg, and which Fatridge had told us about: how people lay before the fires on winter nights, and sometimes had apples to toast upon their ramrods.

And while I considered, shivering and dreaming by turns, Naomi Kincaid was speaking to Barstow in that assured, reasoning tone which we were to know so well.

"I do believe we should wait and see, Mr. Barstow. The plantation people have wood—have had it all the while, even when we went without in Richmond. There's no reason why any of them should sit around a cold fireplace. I think we ought to lie here until it's fully dark, and see whether any candles are lighted, or whether there's firelight in the windows."

The dusk came about us, thicker and chillier in the scrub oaks where we stood. "You've got that knack of saying things sometimes, Clark," said Barstow, to me. He seemed stubbornly unwilling to place his future in the hands of a woman. "What do you say to the idea?"

I could not get those ramrods out of my mind, nor the flames which scorched them, and I swear I heard the sizzle of fat in a pan.... "Our cavalry came through here, a few days since."

"By God!" Barstow joined the woman at the fence and stood tall against the sunset. "That's an idea. After all, quite a few of these rebel farmers might have been scared away."

"Driven away," said the woman, but he payed no attention, addressing the two of us when he spoke again:

"The half light's best, at that. And we've run other

risks today . . . at least one of us could get nigh enough to see whether folks were working around the sheds."

"I'll go," I said, but weakly.

"No, Clark, we'll draw lots." Moving deliberately, he broke off two twigs from a branch near him and began to work them around in his hand.

Naomi Kincaid ordered him, "Three lots. Make three twigs."

Barstow said, "You couldn't do it."

"Share and share alike," she quoted. "I'll take my risks with the two of you! And if I'm discovered, it would be safer for me, never forget that. I could say that I was a farm woman who had lost my way, but they'd know you men were Yankees."

Barstow broke off another twig. "She has a better knack than you, Clark. I reckon she's even wiser." He shuffled the twigs in his hand and said, "The short lot goes," and somehow I knew that the woman would draw it. And draw it she did.

She climbed over the fence promptly enough, though we had to help her because of her skirts.

"I'll go now," she said. "There's no need of my waiting until it's darker, for they'll have no notion who I am."

"Don't go from this direction!" cried Barstow.

She snapped, "I'm not the fool I seem to be, Mister," and went quickly toward the right just outside the rail fence, but keeping close to the edge of the forest. There was a rising slope on this ridge which soon shut her off from us, and we concluded that she would hold close to the woods until she reached the north border of the plowed field, and then go west along it.

We waited; we heard a few chilly movements of birds in the thickets behind us, and far off toward the river, the blatting of a calf. The sun was well down in the west; pink streaks in the icy sky deepened to plum and brown. Barstow and I put our backs together one against the other, for warmth, but did little talking. My mind was well enough occupied with all the eccentricity which had come about this day; and doubtless every fear and puzzlement I owned, every puny impulse toward rivalry, was reflected in Barstow during the same moment.

"Do you think she'll come back?" he asked at one time.

"Certainly I do. She could never travel alone."

"If she couldn't," retorted Barstow, "nobody could. Not any woman." And then he fell silent, listening eagerly and thinking, no doubt, and with his bony back shuddering against mine.

We were buried in the trees' gloom, though there was still bold light in the open spaces or wherever the paler earth or grass could reflect it. Naomi Kincaid came back, after a time of twenty minutes perhaps; she seemed to rise out of the earth in the plowed field, with her gown and shawl fluttering.

We climbed over the fence. "Why in time did you walk back here direct?" demanded Barstow.

"I marked the place when I left," she said. "I marked it by that big sycamore tree. There's no need for fearing capture, yet. I went all the way to that nearest building—it's a wagon shed, and no one's about." She shivered. "There's no one in the yard, nor any light in the house, nor any smoke," and she trembled again. "There's a dead dog. It's lying in the wheel-track. I could see it plainly, and it frightened me."

I asked, "Do you still want to go?" But Barstow was already moving directly across the field, and in that moment the black house against the blue-gray of the western sky seemed to me a place where no one but an ogre had ever lived.

"Oh, yes," cried Naomi Kincaid. "It was just being alone that I didn't like: that made me afraid. And the dead dog...I don't know why I should be so afraid of a dead dog."

"It's a sure truth that he'll do nothing to prevent our coming," I told her. "Better a dead dog than a live one." I gathered up the damask cloth with its bottle and field-glasses. We made our way across the plowed field, with Barstow well ahead by now. When we came up cautiously to the wagon shed at the end of the field, we found Barstow standing before the building, bending over the dead dog.

I looked about, for prudence' sake, then went to his side. The animal had been a medium-sized cur of the mastiff persuasion, and he looked as if an ax had severed his head nearly from the body.

"Two days," whispered Barstow to me. "Wouldn't you say?"

"A good two days. Maybe three."

"This dog was shot," he went on, still whispering. "Don't say anything about it to her, but I got my ideas. See—there's a hole in his shoulder. He was shot in the first place, before he got cut with the ax or whatever it was."

I swore in some terror, and added, "I don't like this."

"Well," said the big man, "you ought to know more about it than I do. I've never been with cavalry on a raid, and you have."

We heard the woman crying urgently from behind us, "For mercy's sake, gentlemen, let's look about. And don't stand there all day with that dog!"

The fall of dusk had reached that peculiar stage where it seemed to hang motionless, with no further darkening for whole minutes at a time. We went quickly among the sheds and out-buildings. There was a smoke-house, a slave cottage long untenanted, and a barn in which at least one cow and several horses had been quartered. But now no animals were about. I saw a few chickens roosting on a broken stall at the farther end of the barn, but did not go near enough to rouse them.

"Now the house," Barstow whispered. "I reckon nobody lives there."

We went toward the little front gallery together. Naomi Kincaid came out from behind a tree and caught at our arms. I could see that she was trying to keep from crying.

"Oh, it's a fearful place!" she cried. "The dark buildings and that thing in the road. I'm—I'm fully terror-stricken. Shan't we go on?"

Barstow lifted his shoulders. "If you think we can go on, lady, without stopping to see whether there's any meal or bacon in the larder, you've much to learn. Come along with you, Clark." And then we approached the front door more closely, with the woman following us for fear of being left alone.

"Clark," cried Barstow, "the door's been broken in!" We ran up on the gallery together.

There were no ornate panels of leaded glass beside this door; the modest house was that of well-to-do farmers, surely what the Southerners call "quality." The door stood half open on a dark hallway, and was battered badly—one hinge being pounded loose at the top, the doorknob knocked clean off, and splintered gashes deep in the painted oak.

It was not difficult to find the instrument which had been used. Barstow stumbled over it as he leapt on the low porch, and at first I thought the cry he gave was one of alarm, though soon I knew better.

He rose up, gripping in his hands a woodsman's ax, single bladed and obviously dulled by the way it had been misused.

"God alive," I heard him mumble between his teeth, "now I've got an ax again...."

Naomi Kincaid sobbed, "Oh, what has happened here?" Then we were in the dimness of the hallway, peering this way and that, and poising on our tip-toes, the woman and I for ready flight, and Prentiss Barstow for combat.

"Let me go first," he whispered. "I got this thing," and he waggled the ax above his head.

My foot touched something soft. I stooped to pick up the object and drop it again: a woman's shoe. There was furniture in this hallway—a huge dresser or sideboard with some of the drawers pulled out, and a chair. Rag carpets on the floor had been kicked this way and that, tumbled and wadded until they looked like fallen corpses. Overhead, the steep stairway shot aloft into a realm that seemed even more silent and forbidding than the one below.

I turned to find Barstow vanished. The woman leaned by the shattered door, her hands clenched together. "He went in there," she whispered. I followed Barstow into a square, low-ceiled room at the left, where there were more chairs and tables, an old sofa, and all the wealth of tiny, homely, worthless objects which count for nothing in our lives until we do without them. A winter kitchen lay beyond, and there, when I had made my nervous way through the dusk, I found Barstow bending over a long table before the black fireplace.

"Things to eat, Clark. They're on this table." One of his hands went out to caress some monstrous object on a plate. "This dinner's been here for some time, though."

"What do you think?" I asked.

"I don't know. I don't know what to think. Let's look in yonder."

We hurried back to the hallway, and Naomi Kincaid caught at our rags and begged us not to leave her again. Still I marvel how one could be as brave as she, serene in the chill of night, uncomplaining through leagues of rain—and yet collapsing like a child when faced with the situation we had found. Perhaps the reason lay in her conscience, but Heaven knows that for many of us, a stealthy approach among the leaves is not as fearsome as the same stealth heard upon a stair. Wiser men than I will explain, sometime, that the savage tribes from which we all sprang were brave enough in ancient, outdoor dusks made thunderous by the lions. Houses have wedded us to fear and trembling.

So we went on, all three, into the room on the right. Here were more dressers and chairs, and a wide bed neatly made up with a coverlet of patch-work, though drawers were disordered and open, as in the hallway and room across the hall. One drawer lay upset in the middle of the floor.

"Raiders," whispered Barstow. "Union cavalry, I'll be bound!"

"No," I told him. "I'd take my oath, it's not that." And after we had looked under the bed and into cupboards and crannies, we went out and climbed the stairs, three quaking explorers, with Barstow and his ax leading on.

The house was small, and possessed no attic. There were four doors along the upstairs hall, two on either side, but we were to find that there were only two rooms: as if partitions had been planned but never made, or else knocked out after the house was built. It was so dark that we could scarcely see, but I knew there must be candles.

A door on the left, or southernmost side, was open. We crept to it, still hearing no sound within or without. When at last we stood inside the room, I did find a candle—a very tall home-made one in a pottery stick.

"Let's light it," I begged Barstow. "You've got the oil-cloth with the matches."

He muttered, "We'll take a risk once more." While I held the ax and stood guard—guarding against I knew not what—he produced the scrap of oilcloth and found that the match-heads were dry enough to be ignited on the bit of scratching paper wrapped with them. The first sizzled and went out, its sulphur burned to waste, but with the second match we lighted the candle.

This room had two beds in it. One was made up with some neatness, the other disarranged. The marks of thievery and a minor vandalism were here, too, and when we looked into the closet we saw the clothing of both women and men —or perhaps a woman and a man. Wholly unable to fathom the awfulness of this desertion, we slipped back into the hallway and approached the opposite door, which was closed.

Barstow went ahead as before, ax held ready; I followed with the candle. The candle-light cleared the door-frame. I heard Barstow suck in his breath, and some instinct of protection made me stumble ahead of Naomi Kincaid and block her path.

The moment went on forever—Barstow inside, myself holding the candle across the threshold, but seeing nothing yet.

"Miss," cried Barstow, "don't you come in here!"

I was sure that he had found a dead person, though God knows I had seen plenty of those. I put my hands on the woman's shoulder and turned her away as assertively as I could, and left her in darkness while I stepped inside the room and closed the door.

"A body?" I asked Barstow, looking about in the yellow light, and seeing none.

He whispered, "No. But look at that."

Together we looked, then bent forward for closer examination. I felt sick. Barstow was already down on his knees to see whether anybody might be hiding under the bed. Whatever weakness and nausea now possessed me, I felt called upon to do my part as well as I could, and so I opened the wardrobe and felt about in it with my hands. But there was nothing but clothing: calico dresses, nightgowns, petticoats, and steel hoops that clattered like manacles when I upset them.

"What do you think?" I asked Barstow again.

"I never had anything like this to figure," he said slowly. "Not in my whole life. There's been trouble...."

I repeated, "Trouble. Christ, yes! And crime."

"Of a sort," he agreed.

"There are few worse sorts."

He opened the outer door. Naomi Kincaid's face was white. She stared at us sternly, her chin still quivering but her eyeballs catching the candle-light with a directness that showed she was becoming brave once more. We came outside, and I closed the door.

"What's in there?" the woman asked, huskily.

Barstow told her, "It don't matter. Not to you."

"Has some one been killed in there?"

I replied, "I don't think so. But you'd best not go inside. Come, now, let's get to the lower door and decide what's what."

My mind kept leaping like a colt, all the way down those steep stairs; I did not experience the childish relief I thought I would feel when again we stood in the lesser darkness of the front porch. There was horridness in this house, but not enough to overwhelm men who had been a part of iniquity for months on end.

"Well, Clark," began Prentiss Barstow, "how long do we wait before we go in the larder?"

"No time at all. But after that comes the question."

Close beside us, the woman shuddered in a wind that blew more raw with each successive thickening of night. "Tell me one thing. You saw no one, dead or alive?"

"No one." And then Barstow came forth with his opinion: "I think I got it figured. Folks lived here, of course.

Maybe a farmer and his family, without any niggers, because the nigger house hasn't been lived in. The Federal cavalry come this way and plundered the house, and drove the folks off and the animals, too. They killed the dog. Unless anybody should sneak up here soon, we're safe enough, as long as we creep around cautious-like."

I said, "You're wrong. That isn't it."

He turned, challenging me.

"Because you ought to know as well as I that Federal cavalry, or any other cavalry, wouldn't drive off horses and cattle when they were on their way to fight at Richmond—only a few miles distant, at that. This house is off the main road—"

Naomi Kincaid interrupted, calmly, "Far off. I saw the Goochland road from the hilltop when I went along that plowed field. I could barely see a covered wagon moving there in the dusk."

"That's not all," I went on. "I've seen houses plundered twice, and the people who did it went about it with their sleeves rolled up. There are hams hanging next to that chimney in the kitchen. Do you think the hams would have been left? There are a hundred things we've seen, that a body of cavalry would have carried off! Some thief has been here, beyond a doubt. But not a whole squadron. Though it's too dark to look for tracks."

Still Barstow waited, pondering and shifting about uneasily. He sighed: "I tell you, these folks have *puckacheed*. I saw wagon tracks, light wagon tracks, coming out of that shed; and there wasn't a wagon anywhere about, nor a horse."

So I turned to the woman, though I could scarce see her face; the night hung like rain about that house. "It's unlikely they'll come back before morning, and we know what all of us could do with a fire and things to eat. We might—" it

made me dizzy to think of it, but I got the words out feebly
—"we might even wash."

Prentiss Barstow laughed, and I swear that his laughter
sent any number of hyenas scampering in retreat. "That's
common sense, Clark—as good as I ever see! And don't forget
that we're no longer unarmed."

"Unarmed?" repeated Naomi Kincaid.

He lifted one of his bony hands away from the ax helve,
and spat upon it, and put it back around the club tighter
than ever. "I was born with one of these in my hand, lady.
If anybody comes within range, I'll carve a butt kerf in him
quicker than you can wink."

She sobbed once, quickly ... "If it weren't for that room
upstairs—the room you wouldn't let me enter..."

"Oh, that," I said, and I felt the brutality of an unidentified crime less sharply than before. "Don't stand worry-
ing over that. Whatever has happened here is over and done
with. Perhaps the Lord Himself led us in just the right
direction."

"Perhaps," she murmured, but not as if she believed it.
Then we turned back into the house, and I took up the
candlestick with its lighted candle, from where I had set it
down on the lowest step of the stair.

6

WE put the vile secret of the upstairs room far out of our minds, and set ourselves to the eager task of accomplishing a regeneration which we had dreamed might be accomplished only in weeks. For we felt, perhaps rightly, that the recent crimes visited on people unknown to us were in few ways more monstrous than the wickedness which had been done to ourselves, and which we had totaled already.

Three minutes after we entered the kitchen for the second time, I had a fire burning on the cold hearth. I fed it as a nurse tends a precious child, while Naomi Kincaid sat slicing meat from one of the great hams.

Barstow went outside, carrying his ax, for a last reconnoitering. He closed every shutter on the downstairs windows, to hold the light safely, and within the one window where there were no shutters he draped a cotton comforter. Then, when the ham was already driving me mad by its curling and sputtering, he was gone for a longer period than ever; which was surely unwise of him, for he visited the barn where the few chickens sat roosting, and dared to risk their cackling and outcry. When he reappeared he was grinning, his beard split wide apart and showing his great white teeth; he had a small wooden bucket which shook in his hands.

"Eggs," he said. "I'm already one ahead of you, because I ate it raw. But you each can have an extra one cooked."

I blubbered by the fireplace, my face spotted with hot grease, "You realize what this means? It means that we can eat until we fill ourselves. Nobody can take it from us!"

Barstow stopped his glee and warned me again about gorging. "You spoke of soap and water, too, Clark, and you want to remember it's dangerous to wash yourself after a hearty meal." But I scoffed him down, for I felt that the Fates were standing guard around that house, and no ill could come to us.

I try now to remember how the food tasted, to feel the crisp pinkness of the ham spreading and softening itself between my jaws—to reconstruct the matter of eggs, hot and soft and running down my raw throat, and to remember the smell of the cornmeal cakes which Naomi Kincaid dropped into the skillet after the first food was taken from it. But the most tender and valuable memories of man are those which elude him time and again, playing tag down the glades of the past, and permitting him only the briefest glimpse of their beauty as they vanish before him.

The room comes back, though: the long table of that desolate household shoved against the wall, its cargo of dry or decaying food forgotten and ignored by us who would have counted it choicest treasure a day before. I see the firelight red on our faces, and hear the shutters tapping in the wind, and I remember, too, a little bird which we disturbed—one which had taken refuge through the open door it found in that house, and which Barstow felt should be driven outside, though the woman kept him from it.

We ate less wisely than we had hoped, nor was I the only sinner. But at least we were still able to walk and think, and there was a fresh pan full browning for us when we had rested a bit.

The woman did not talk a great deal, though she relished her supper better than I could have hoped, after the terror that possessed her when we came there. She asked our pardon and removed her shoes, setting them to dry in the open heat; she rested on the floor with her back against an old oak dresser, and her small feet in gray-striped stockings held out to the friendly fire. She sat half doubled up, knees arched and head forward. With arms holding her gown carefully around her ankles, she looked like a child, and quite unlike the paramour of a Polish officer.

Still, I had never seen many paramours, to my knowledge; and Barstow and I were nowhere near the point where we might have considered the beauty of any limb and ankle in the world to outweigh that of food filling the air with its perfection.

I could feel little surprise at our sudden ignoring of the recent past, the uneasy present, and above all, the dark channel of the future. For I had ridden two years under Colonel Sir Percy Wyndham, and I had seen whole troops of boys, their throats caked with dust, and bodies racked by the sharp sob of fighting—I had seen them torn and bloodied, covering their brothers and friends with fresh dirt, and going off within the hour to quarrel heartily over scraps of paper currency in a Bluff game, or to pool their resources for brandy-and-peaches at the sutler's.

It is this fearful resiliency of the human soul, this rebounding ability to climb out of the grave and play marbles among the headstones, that gives to war its ghastly permanence, and the certainty that we shall see more people willing for war in the years to come.

Barstow said, poking at the corn-cakes with a long-handled spoon, "Clark, do you think these farmers would have a map anywheres about?"

"They might," I said. "We'll search."

I had no more than said the words when Naomi Kincaid rose quickly, smoothing down her skirts and bending to lift her shoes from in front of the fire to see if they had dried.

"I'll search for a map," she said. "That's something which I can do as well as you."

"Hold your horses, lady," said Barstow. "How do you know what kind of a map we'll want?"

"A map showing this part of Virginia, and all the way up to the Yankee lines. Around Culpeper, you said, though I've heard that our pickets—I mean the rebel pickets—are holding a line on the Rapidan at Orange Court. And we'll need a map, sadly, before we've gone much farther."

Her shoes were not yet dry enough to put on. So she lighted a candle from the blaze, and went away through the front room in her stocking feet.

Barstow still sat looking after her in some amazement, but I hurried at her heels and found her setting down the candle in that room north of the hall, where there were some books much disarranged and scattered, and an old secretary which held a miscellaneous litter of letters and pamphlets.

"You're not afraid?" I asked.

She glanced briefly at the ceiling and shook her head. "Not of what's above me. I have your word that no one is up there."

"Well," I said, helplessly, and returned to the kitchen, where I found Barstow scratching his matted head with one hand and selecting a corn-cake out of the pan, with the other.

He said, "She's an odd critter. Why did she get up and run away like that so sudden?"

"I think I'm well aware of the reason," and, unbarring the rear door, I went out upon the shed porch to get a wooden tub I had seen there before.

When I came dragging it back into the kitchen, Barstow was ready to sneer at me. "Jehoshaphat, Clark!" he cried, in an angry whisper. "Maybe there ain't any reason why she should relish our smell, but it didn't appear to give her much of a turn all day long."

"For reason," I told him. "We were out in the open air, and it was middling cold, anyway. It's so long since we've been near a good fire that we must have forgotten how heat brings out the worst in us."

He glared at me for a time.

"Maybe that's a true fact," he agreed, finally. "Sometimes I used to believe I couldn't abide myself much longer... I got over that, by the turn of the year. You needn't think we folks out west are inclined to go around dirty, either! Pa always made us boys get into the horse pond once a week, even when we had to break the ice."

It seemed wholly logical that we should finish the peculiar moment of our lives which had begun that morning, by learning what sort of bodies lay inside our filthy husks. The Lord knows that we made a great clatter and stirring about it, and only those who have been at some time long-uncleaned, will understand our reluctance and fear as we drew the water.

A cistern lay beneath a trap-door in the old planks; we drew our bath from that deep stone well. It smelled of brown leaves and lizards, as if it reached into the lowest belly of the earth to tap some reservoir collected from rains that fell before our time. We drew it up, I say, in a great, dripping, wooden bucket attached to a rusty chain that lay coiled beneath the trap-door; and Barstow for one feared the water might be poison.

"Take note, too, Clark," he warned me. "We're lousy. It'll take more than one washing to clean these things out of us."

"We'll be rid of them before we're an hour older," I prophesied, for I had found a pair of big steel shears, and I remembered the woman's little embroidery scissors. "Likely there are razors in that washstand upstairs."

We brought a fat iron kettle and filled it with more

water, and banked wood around it on the hearth. And while
Barstow went outside to make a patrol in the dark, for
safety's sake, I had a mind that there would be clothing in
this house sufficient to make us human again, though I did
not like stealing it. I had stolen food before this, but never
clothing.

When I went into the hallway, there were two candles
burning in the north room instead of one, and Naomi Kincaid was reading in a chair between them, quite as calmly
as if she had been appointed mistress of the house.

"Have you found that map?" I asked her, accusingly,
from the doorway.

"Not yet," she answered, and scarcely raised her eyes from
the book. "I'm reading poetry."

"Well," I said, "poetry or not, you'd best not venture
into the kitchen until we're done scrubbing."

She replied tartly, "I've no wish to," and I went up to
the south bedroom with one of her candles, turning my back
on that blank, closed door across the hall, and remembering
that there were no man's clothes in that room, anyway.

The pantaloons I found were to be of a wrong size for
me, and all too short for Barstow, but I brought down two
pairs of them: one of checkered woolen, the other of faded
blue jeans. There were home-knit socks in plenty, and by
searching the big dressers I found four shirts, though one of
them was of superior linen, with tucks well-ironed, and I felt
that we must not take it. There was only one pair of under-
drawers; and I wondered what Barstow would do with his
feet, for I knew that he could never wear either of the two
pairs of boots I found in the closet.

However, I discovered a razor in a shabby leather case—a
good one, Spanish steel, with a stone to whet it by—and a
mug for mixing lather. I carried my treasures back to the

first floor, and found Barstow struggling to drag one of the hall dressers against the front door.

"We can't fasten this," he warned me. "There's no sense in laying down tonight if we can be caught and killed in our sleep before we know it."

The woman came to help us, and when we had the mighty sideboard firmly in place, she went back to the front room. She said that she was reading a book of poems by Lord Byron, and it had been a birthday gift to a girl named Elvira on her fifteenth birthday, for the name and a birthday greeting from Cousin Earl were written on the fly-leaf.

"There's no sense in poetry," Barstow whispered to me in the kitchen, "though she's a queer kind of woman, and I don't doubt she's read a deal of poetry before this."

I retorted, "You liked my Shakespeare, and men agree that he was a poet, too."

"That's honest reading," Barstow declared. "I never had much schooling, but I can get the gist of that. I don't want to spell out poems about sunbeams and things."

So we argued about it while we were stripping off our rags, and eating bits of cornbread now and then—the kind of hoecake which Naomi Kincaid had made by mixing meal and salt and water, with an egg or two also, and dropping spoonfuls of the mixture into the bubbling grease of the great skillet.

We thought it wisest to trim our beards and hair before we washed, but when I was in a chair and Barstow clipping away at me with the shears, he soon declared that no ordinary trimming would suffice. "They're all over you, Clark," he said, and swearing about it. "I reckon they're all over me, too. I don't know what we're to do, unless we want to go lousy from now on."

"We'll do this," I said, and showed him the razor, and he found pleasure in whetting its blade on the little stone.

He cut me in a dozen places, but there was a clean feeling about the steel. Later, when I stood to my knees in the steaming tub, and rubbed with strong soft soap to the top of my shaven head, Barstow told me that I looked like something the Sioux left behind after they came down on the settlements. But I did not care how I looked, and thought I could never get enough of the soap and water; though Barstow cried that I had more than my share.

When I planned that an hour should work the ultimate change, I had not estimated how degraded we were, nor what an amount of flaying must be done to us. Two hours elapsed before we were both trimmed and garbed once more; Barstow had no shoes, and walked about in his stocking feet.

He wore the blue pantaloons, which were too tight for him and flapped short at his ankles. Nevertheless he was prouder than Lucifer that the color of this cloth was blue, and I had seen him remove the insignia of the Pioneer Corps from the smelly blouse which he abandoned, hoping perhaps to have the woman stitch it upon his sleeve when he should find another coat.

There was a watery looking-glass hanging over a wash bench in the kitchen; I held it in my hands before the firelight, wondering at myself. Prentiss Barstow said there was every reason for me to wonder. He hoped that he did not look as queer as I. At that I challenged him, for Heaven never shrank before a stranger specimen than he, and the mirror made so many distortions of my face that I calculated I was not the worse of the two.

I had shaved Barstow over the whole of his head. The bones of his big skull stuck through the fuzz in strange blue swellings. The mark of his shaven beard laid a purple mask over his cheeks and jaws, for his face was brown as an autumn leaf wherever the hair had not grown.

Cleaned and freshened as we were, we seemed lighter of

weight than when the thatch was still upon us. I knew that my body itched and stung in a hundred places, though Barstow did not once complain of his. We had found one bottle on a kitchen shelf and used it copiously: the label said that it was Father Emerson's Liquid Ointment and Brown Precipitate, fit to bring relief in any cases of cuts, burns, scalds, or abrasions. I hoped that it was doing us both good, for it burned like the very broth of hell.

Redolent of this mixture, feeling more thin and frail than we had felt for hours, we presented ourselves to Naomi Kincaid in the north room, and she swore that she had never set eyes on us before.

"Don't think, though," she warned us, "that I'll look the same when I'm done with myself."

"You don't need to wash," said Barstow, "just because we did. You could wade in that mud for a month, and not be half as dirty."

She told us, "I shall never try wading in it the way I did today," and then she wanted to know what had become of the scissors. I found them for her, and brought her shoes from the kitchen; she went aloft to the second story with two candles, while Barstow warned her repeatedly not to enter the closed bedroom.

We ate again while she was gone. Barstow set on more ham to cook, though now I was the one who warned against gorging.

"I could even do with a drink," he said.

Such was the nature of the treasure house in which we sat, that I was not surprised when he found a stone jug in a dark cupboard. He declared that it held applejack.

"It'll burn us, Clark. Don't take more than a smell of it, or it'll lay you low."

I replied that already I was laid very low indeed. He brought out two cracked cups and was lifting the jug for pouring, when we heard the woman on the stairs. Barstow set down the jug to wait for her.

"It's strong as spirits," he whispered. "Do you reckon she'd like a swallow along with us?"

I was ready to reply that for all her confession, she must be a lady of sorts, and I had never yet known a lady to drink liquor of such strength—when she appeared before us.

She wore a pair of black broadcloth pantaloons which I had seen in the wardrobe upstairs and had left, knowing the ones I brought were more suitable for our purpose; and she had, too, a shirt of checkered factory, thrown open at the neck. But of all the changes wrought in her, the chief concerned that region above the shoulders, for she had snipped off her hair close below her ears in a manner I never saw before or since, except in drawings of the children who live in Holland. Her own shoes were suitable enough for her still. And only she would know how much of her more intimate wardrobe she had retained.

We stood and stared as we would have stared on Belle Island had a regiment of Massachusetts Fire Zouaves come in to issue us our rations.

"Woman alive!" said Barstow.

I could say nothing at all.

She laughed shortly and lifted her hands, tossing the short-banged hair back from her forehead. "You don't need to stare as if you were looking at a witch, either of you. I couldn't go wandering through the thickets dressed in my own clothes! And these will be far better, though I hate to part with the others."

"That dress—" it was hard for me to get the words out—"you're not leaving that blue silk dress? Why, it must have been run through the Blockade, just like your bonnet!"

She said, quietly, "Almost everything I had was run

through the Blockade. That's one way in which Colonel Mokranowski was kind to me. He wanted me to have things that were very dear. There are few things dearer than those that have been won by the death of brave men."

This was no time for philosophizing, for already Barstow had set another cup on the table and was slopping out a small portion of the applejack for each of us. But I said to her, "How about those things won by the living of brave men?" and her eyes leapt up at me when I said it.

"Are you brave?" she asked.

"God knows," I answered.

"I reckon we're all brave," said Barstow, who must have been thinking of Fatridge, for he added, "comrades."

She took up the cup he had placed for her and motioned for us to take ours.

"We're on the very threshold of doom," she said. "Between two dooms, if such a thing can be. But let's all be brave."

We stood through a sudden silence in which there existed nothing but wind and the eternal swaying of shutters—the silent speed of ghosts moving beside us through that house. Then as sound grows which has been heard, unheeded, for some time and is at last identified, we heard the crying of a house cat, plaintive and sad beyond words. Barstow unbarred the back door; the cat rushed in—it was a large one, gray and white—and stood for a moment frightened at such grotesque strangers in its own home, but not so fearful of us as of the lonely, supperless night outside. Naomi Kincaid called "Pussy, Pussy!" but the cat dashed into the next room and fell silent, as if it had taken refuge beneath the sofa.

Barstow barred the door again.

"We didn't have our toast," said the woman.

Again we all took up our cups. "Let us be brave," she

said in a clear voice. Her hand trembled, but she downed her drink with the rest of us. And that night, the first we had known with her, she called Barstow, Bar, and called me Ollie, and said that we might call her Naomi; although in the past her friends had called her Na*om*, when she had them.

7

Even though we were sore from our recent washings, and from gigantic exertion of the day and night which had gone before, this evening was to hold to itself that rare beauty forever surrounding the origin of bold or important events which in themselves, perhaps, are never wholly beautiful. For we two starved scalawags, Prentiss Barstow and Oliver Clark, were not yet hardened or fed to the state where rivalry could chain us apart; nor was the woman more to us than a stray comet riving across our sky. She had not yet planted herself hurtfully in our hearts.

She was our sister at times, and perhaps at other times our child to care for; and persistently she served as our captain, too.

In one capacity or another, she was ready to hear of the astonishing feat we had performed before we met her in the pine woods, and I told her much of it because I have always been ready to talk to new friends with greatest enthusiasm. The differences between Barstow and me were more than those of geographical situation and rearing, and measurement of literacy or the world's goods. For Barstow, bred no matter where, would have found pain in opening his memories to another person save when driven by panic, or remorse, or perhaps by the passion of love.

But I could talk as always, and my father had told me chidingly that I talked too much. I had not got over it at the age of twenty-two.

We drew lots for standing at guard; the woman offered her watch to defend against the infringement of time. To my surprise, Prentiss Barstow agreed that she might stand her share of guard duty just as we did. Later I decided that he had intended to sleep with one eye open while she was thus serving; and exhaustion got the better of him, in spite of his plans.

I drew the first watch of two hours. Barstow flung himself down on the couch in that room adjoining the kitchen, and tossed in soft, squeaking agony until he had sense enough to climb off and lie upon the floor, where he soon became as one dead. It had been agreed that Naomi Kincaid could sleep in the north room if she wanted to, but she came out to join me at the fire, saying calmly that there was no sense in any woman lying down with a conscience like hers.

The applejack had exalted me to eager nervousness, even as it drugged Barstow. I was all for questioning Naomi Kincaid until I learned just what had happened in the woods at the Three Chopt Road, and why. But I soon found that her spirit was fully as reclusive as was Barstow's. Although not wanting in trust, she was never one to confide at the drop of a hat. She gave me question after question, there by the glowing logs: I found myself telling each thing which I had thought and felt throughout that desperate plunge we made, a scant twenty-four hours earlier.

She said that often enough prisoners had tried to swim the river, and I knew it, too. We saw them, knotted and shrunk from the cold, carried along the shore to lie in a burial ground populated mainly by those who had accepted starvation more calmly. Not one in twenty, perhaps, had ever been successful in his attempt; and the more I told her the more I realized that Prentiss Barstow had carried my life in his pocket, all along. Escape would never have come for me, without him. I gave him every credit when I talked to Naomi Kincaid, although I might not have done so a week later.

A thousand times I had imagined escape, and each time I was bold and forever successful. Though I had never considered a flight such as occurred in my delirious dream (that single hour of lunacy wherein my spirit extracted itself from the flesh and raced the north wind, bare and unwounded) nevertheless, I was plagued by the thought that once I had been less checked by corporeal limitations than I was on this night of actual escape.

I told Naomi how, one at a time, we crept from our tent and traveled by separate paths to the agreed place of meeting. No lights of any kind burned within the camp, and the March darkness contributed willingly toward concealment. In other months, before the New York Bowery hoodlums were killed or subjugated by vigilantes, the darkness had been an accessory to murder and even baser crimes. No night could forget what the other nights knew. Accordingly, the blackness was lewd and portentous.

Sometimes the red of the Tredegar Iron Works rose thick and high, and any one who stood would show like a tree against it. All about us the guards held their dogged beats behind the deadline. No stockade surrounded this camp. Only a ditch eight feet wide, and a low parapet made of earth which had been scooped from the ditch, and beyond that, a fence which few men had ever touched and lived to return. Outside the fence waited the rifles or muskets. Past the guns was a quarter mile of icy water, currents as tensile as wire, rocks, jagged bars. The bridge at the opposite end of camp crossed the south channel to Manchester, but a dozen minié balls would snap themselves into any prisoner who set foot upon it.

I told her that the matches in my pocket weighed me down; I might as well have been carrying a pick-ax. They were my own matches, but my stammering conscience had endowed them with the grossest tonnage.

Barstow would reach the opposite shore and I would not. I knew it.

Fatridge would swim the rough currents with quick and confident strokes. Even Sauers might blunder across. Voss would never get there, but that mattered little. Voss was puny in every way: it had been a mistake for him to try the army, or to try life in the beginning. Not Voss, but Fatridge or Barstow or Sauers would profit from the matches; and Barstow I had depended upon in more ways than one ... "Give up the matches," cried all chivalry.

I crept behind the last of the huts. Once a man came toward me; he was none of my squad, for this man wore an overcoat that brushed me as he passed. I murmured the first words that came into my mind: "I ought to let him have them. He's the one," and the man cursed me for a maniac and stumbled away.

Here was open mud, and the parapet loomed vaguely beyond. Flat in the mud I crawled forward, but soon I smelled another man.

"Fatridge," wailed Voss, and clasped me with trembling hands.

"It's Clark," I whispered. "Let me go."

Another shape roved closer, and spoke. It was Barstow.

"Barstow," I muttered. "Here..."

In his bewilderment, he came near speaking aloud. "What's this?"

"The matches. They—"

"They're yours!" Barstow gulped.

"I'll never make it. You can have the use—"

"No. I won't take them."

I hissed at him, "Yes, yes. They're something I'll never get to use." I did not remember New Jersey, nor any one up there who might be loving me and counting me as alive still. Only the waste of water: it would claim me, I knew well enough. I ground my teeth, thinking of treasured blankets and oilcloth in the tent yonder, and how others would salvage them and use them for their own.

"If I could use them," I said, "I would. But I don't calculate I'll get there."

Barstow accepted the little oilcloth packet. Voss tumbled against us again. "Will he shoot? The guard . . . Think he'll shoot?"

"He'll shoot," I whispered.

Fatridge crept up and ordered, "For God's sake, keep still, Comrades! We're at the edge. I got my foot in the ditch."

We heard the guard slapping past in the soggy path. One of his shoe-soles was loose, so we knew the pace of the upstream guard and how it differed from the downstream guard.

"Where's Sauers?"

"Here."

"We're all here, Comrades!"

Barstow asked, "Now, which one's the old guard?"

"Him on the right. You know where we are?"

"Just where the ditch bends. A shade west."

Voss groaned aloud, half because of fear, and because of a dozen pains besetting him, but the guards did not hear. With the river rustling on one side and the coughing on the other, they could not detect our faint stirring near the deadline.

Twenty-four hundred men had been removed from the Island during the two weeks just past, but still there were more than four thousand prisoners shivering in tattered huts, in rotten tents, or in solitary nests scooped from the mud and offal. It seemed, now, that every man who was awake must be coughing, and half the rest were coughing in their sleep. The unearthly chorus rose and fell over the four-acre tract: no two coughs sounding alike, no two throat-clearings identical in occurrence or tone.

"Remember the plan," came from Fatridge. "I'll give the word. Say Go or Forward."

Voss blubbered, "Charlie Becker got tangled in a fish trap and drowned," and somebody put a hand over his mouth. The guard stopped; he clicked his musket-hammer for a moment. We were conscious of his peering here and there in the darkness, but at last he went away.

"Keep scrooched down, Comrades! The next time the downstream guard comes and turns...he's an old coot—I don't think he can hit much with that Vincennes."

Barstow's whisper sounded, and seemed more comforting and assured than Fatridge's. "Never hit scat."

"When he Abouts, we're to cut and run. The young guard will be at the far end by then. I'll say Go or Forward."

"Well," grunted Sauers, "make it Go."

Voss sobbed, "Let's go back. In warmer weather we got a better chance. The fish traps—"

While we waited, chins sunk in the puddles where we lay, it seemed to me that the coughing rose in a sudden blare, concurring with us and aiding our scheme. The guard limped to his station; he turned and spat into the ditch fairly on me; we heard him breathing shrilly, and I remembered how he had looked in the moonlight a week before, when I lay watching him.

Fatridge forgot to say Go or Forward. What he said was *Now!* in an explosive blast. We stumbled across the ditch and over the parapet. The guard's musket-sling squeaked, his very knees and shoulders screamed aloud as he swung around. A strand of wire raked the lobe of my right ear, and another gashed my elbow. Then I was through. Our lame, bare feet made a tremendous thudding: you would have thought that at least fifty men were trying to get away. The guard yelled, "Halt." Then he exclaimed, in a lower tone and in surprise, "Hell-fire!" and the flame of his musket came close.

Somebody screamed. I thought, "That's Voss." But it wasn't—it was Sauers. He screamed again, *"Ow,"* as if a bee had stung him; then he made another sound and fell flat at the edge of the water.

"Fatridge," shrieked Voss, tangled in the wire. "Fatridge!" There were running feet: one guard and two and three, and the sound of a gun-butt breaking something, and not another word from Voss. I found the river and went headlong into it: I fell over a rock, but deeper water waited beyond. On either side there was terrific thrashing as Fatridge and Barstow flailed ahead into the stinging cold.

It strangled me for a moment, though I had swallowed very little. The cold froze every thread of muscle left to me, and tied me in a knot. "Why," I told myself, and all surprised at my own amazement, "I can never do this." The current turned me around and took me underneath into a void particularly chilly and encompassing, and a rifle bullet squealed when I came up again. I had not forgotten how to swim, but there seemed no reason for painful effort of any sort. Angry with myself, and angry at those heckling gun explosions, I made a few strokes...I had never learned to swim expertly. I lifted my right arm high and brought it down, I drew my left arm across my body and pulled up my feet and kicked them down, but it seemed senseless to do so.

The crashing strokes of the other men went away from me. They neglected me, they had forgotten, and I uttered a bubbling wail at the cruelty of it all.

The Confederate States of America were yelling, "Corporal of the guard, corporal of the guard!" Sometimes the bullets whined toward Richmond, sometimes they plumped like pebbles near at hand. I turned round and round; the tide yanked at my feet again, but I broke loose, and a rock drove against my shoulder to punish me for it.

All across the nearer face of the river lay intricate islands, lonely tufts of leafless willow, scattered granite ribs with the foam crushing among them. Here was gravel...the river bed rose under me, and I stood erect with the bullets hammering all around. The air stung the broken blisters on my thighs and elbows; it would be better under the water again. I stumbled into the next channel and was carried far.

I thought, "Alone. Sole alone." If enemies squinted through the windy darkness they could see that no one was aiding me. My own folly had made me a solitary target for persecution. When people had shot at me before this, they had shot at ten thousand other people as well, and at the same time, and there was always the notion that fellow soldiers would absorb the bullets long before my turn came. Forgetting all about Fatridge and Barstow, I saw myself twisted and turned, carried among a host of tiny continents, slammed here and there upon sharp-nosed limestone, but always exposed to the pitiless gunfire. I deplored to myself, "Why did I start? The tent was warm...spooned up between the blankets, warmed by the breath of others..." I was disgusted with myself for selecting this uncomfortable death. Abandoned fish-traps would mesh me forever.

Again my knees scraped the bottom; and as the current hurled me across some shelving rocks, I wrapped my arms around the highest cleft, and heard my voice say, "So cold." My arms began to slide. Below me something banged and slapped like a loose shutter. My wet finger-nails dug into it, and found comfort in their clawing: this was a plank, it was wood, and the rocks had wedged themselves around it until now. But my weight took it away.

In the distance, barely to be observed, some one had

placed thin arms around wet wood. Thin arms, wet wood, grotesque burden which pulled and resisted—the whole universe centered in them and rolled under and over, and grew steadily less important. I slept through it, watching, aware of crimson and purple sunbursts that spun at length into moon-bursts as I discovered that it was night. I remarked on it: the words popped inside my ears. My fingers held, they started from their joints, the thumbs squeezed out of the sockets and came back again. Such repetition was stupid, and why not put a stop to it?

Underneath, something was bending and breaking. After a breathless search, I knew the truth. Legs. Those were legs, bending and breaking. With evil eagerness I began to learn how viciously I could make them bend and straighten, crumbling into bits each time they flung themselves out. I assembled the bony blocks, the frozen portions, with all the delight of a torturer. I built them up again very quickly, destroyed them over and over, and felt an uncanny satisfaction that I had learned to do this.

Cruel? My father would think so. So would other men. But this was black magic which they did not understand, and only jealousy would cause them to censure me. I placed the advisers of my youth in column, made them wheel into regimental front: my father, the minister, the school-teachers, my uncle, good men who had written good books, nameless people with tender hearts. *Now,* I said, *the reason I did it was—this. Watch! Gather the pieces, so. Disregard the clutching fingers and human ribs growing into the drowned wood. Concern yourself with legs. Catch them when they're bent; fling them out as hard as you ever flung anything....*

But at this time, perhaps because I was trying to explain and had taken extra pains with the process, the pieces scattered through infinity. I tried to bring them back, I hunted here and there among the rocks in the water. At last I found my feet—one was thrust into the sand, one was braced against a shuddering bowlder. The river swept across my face, but I shook it off. All I had to show for my searching were two feet, bruised and sodden.

A voice called to me, begging an answer, and at last I was able to say, "I—lost—them."

"Who is it?" inquired the man who owned the voice. He got down and felt me over. "Who?" he asked, once more. "Who's it?"

I would admit nothing any longer. I heard the conversation of water around us, but my intimacy with the river was gone.

"Fatridge?"

"Nnaw," I said.

"Clark?"

Barstow was this voice, resolved to find out so much about me; solely by his voice could he be identified. "Clark," I admitted, reluctantly.

"I never thought you'd make it. I thought you were gone."

"Gone," I repeated.

"Get up. It ain't far now. I heard folks talking over there a minute ago—over there across that next water, by some buildings."

I discovered a body, and I was inside it. It moved, but the pain came back and frightened me. "I can't," and that seemed such an easy explanation that I wondered why I had never thought of it before.

Barstow gasped, "You'd better."

"Nnaw."

Barstow seemed debating something. "If you've gone daft, I'll just have to light out alone," he said.

I whispered, "Wait," and surprised myself. "Where?" I began to ask. "Where?"

"Where what?" demanded Barstow.

"Is this?"

"Looks to be an island, but it's the last. I heard men going alongside the canal over there, a minute before you landed here. There's buildings, too—I heard a door shut. We got to look out."

I crowed, "We're loose, Bar. The cavalry never took Richmond yesterday, but we're loose!"

Belle Island lay well above; an occasional gun-shot explored the water in between. The lights of Richmond were close—the red of furnaces, the unidentified, tiny lights which had been only a scattered yellow pepper when seen from the prison camp. Now they resolved themselves into high lights and low lights, nearer spangles, more distant ones. Wagon wheels traveled on cobble stones.

"I reckon," said Prentiss Barstow, "that there'll be guards all along the way, guarding that canal. We're not loose yet."

"No, we're not."

"We'll have to swim this last part real quiet-like."

"Where's—" I hunted for the name, and found it, and was proud—"where's Fatridge?"

"I don't know. We split apart, and I don't know."

I crawled up on my hands and knees. "That's the ticket," exclaimed Barstow. "I knew you'd do it. Rub your wrists and say a few prayers. We'll never go back to that stink-hole."

One of his words remained with me; I repeated it in some surprise. "Prayers." Men never considered prayers at Belle Island. Earlier in captivity, before the mildew of prison claimed me, I had written in my diary: "As a whole, the body of prisoners seems utterly abandoned to profanity, hatred, and all forms of depravity. No religious service has been held here since I arrived, and my companions tell me not for a long time previously."

I went hunting through forests of remembrance; the

forests were water-logged, freezing, and filled with bowlders. I told Barstow, "I was wondering what became of it."

"It's still there, friend! Up the river."

"I mean my diary."

The black shape cried in surprise, "Don't you remember? We burned it to get the sticks going, when we cooked that cow-udder."

"Yes," I agreed, and then said again, "Prayers."

"I've forgotten all I knew," said Barstow. "Maybe the Lord will forgive me."

We were tangled together, but now we had no blanket to cover us or to contain the warmth of our breath.

"Better start, than freeze here."

"I'm rubbing my wrists," I cried. "It makes my fingers have the blood in them. Let me rub a while first."

"Oh, my God, Clark! That water was cold. But we've got to try it again."

We heard the creaking of tackle as a barge hitched along the canal opposite us. A mule brayed: a hideous outcry, startling in its nearness, for the braying had sounded faint and elfin on Belle Island.

"I thought of a Psalm," I whispered.

Barstow was silent for a while, but he had heard and understood. "I'll go you," he said, at last.

"What?"

"Say it, Clark. Speak it." His huge, loose-strung body quivered, and not entirely from reason of cold.

I thought of a certain Presbyterian church, white and sturdy on its hill above the creek.... My father held my hand, I was a boy, we walked on a path among the red-brown tombstones, and there were anemones near the old stone fence. Deacon Howells drove home with us for dinner; I saw the dinner table once more, smelled the kitchen. Lights flew in front of my eyes.... "It's not the Twenty-third," I declared, trying to marshal my courage.

" 'The Lord is—is—' " began Barstow. " 'The Lord—' " He growled, "Forgot it."

"Not that," I cried, angrily. " 'Restoreth my soul...' No. I had it, and it's gone."

"We better start. *Forward!*" Barstow helped me to my feet; we stood with the wind going through us.

I said, "Pestilence is the first I can get. The first... 'Nor for the pestilence that walketh in darkness; nor for the destruction that wasteth at noonday.' He used to read it before breakfast. Afterward, sometimes. But usually he prays afterward."

"Listen," Barstow cried, "it was ten before we started. We've only got until daylight, and we've got to be hid by then!"

I stumbled with him across the narrow spit of gravel, and the willows knotted together, trying to restrain us. "By God, Bar. This is a kind of baptism. But I'm Presbyterian."

"Well, I'm a Baptist, Clark."

Cold and swift, the water rose toward our knees. Another mule began to answer the barge mule, from far down the river. We heard railroad engines breathing heavily at Manchester.

"I know what I wanted. This is it." And I restrained Barstow's hands, which had closed on the rags at my waist. I quoted: " 'For he shall give his angels charge over thee, to keep thee in all thy ways.' That was the one I wanted."

Barstow laughed, "Nobody gives any angels charge over us. That's a dirty lie."

I thought about it, with the river pushing me from my feet. "Blasphemy. I tell you that's—"

"Well, I don't care a God damn if it is," replied Barstow.

Then, dragging me with him, he struck out across the last stretch of river. I could have never crossed it without him. The current lessened as we came up against the shore, and we clambered sobbing over the sandy bank and fell amongst the willows.

This was the end of my tale as told to Naomi, for it was time to call Prentiss Barstow to his night picket duty. The story was not told all in one piece; I had tried to be a good soldier and make my rounds of doors and windows and lonely listenings, and there was also the barley coffee which Naomi stewed in a tall tin pot. Nor did I tell it in the words used here, for I could not handle words so well in those days; and I have employed quotation marks; but the story is the true one for all that.

8

THROUGHOUT the night I was wakeful, and so were the others. I do not believe that the woman feared us, for there was nothing to fear from such infirm species as we; and yet often enough I heard her stirring in the room where she lay, and sometimes she came to the kitchen fire. Our guard duty seemed but a well-ordered sham, for like as not both Barstow and I rested happier when we were on guard, and not when we took turns lying by the squeaky sofa with the cat coming out from beneath, now and then, to touch our fingers with a fearful nose.

It reminded me of the first night in camp after I became a soldier. Then I was sore and aching, as now, but for a different reason; and then the wild thrill of abiding as a picket in the dark kept each boy of us with his eyes and ears and nostrils open, trying to sense an ominous approach. On the Island we slept because we were dying of weakness, and because it was the sole manner in which we might take ourselves out of the place—though by no means might we escape each time we slept.

But here we had good food dissolving inside our bodies, trying to build them up for us. Water and soap and Brown Precipitate had made our festerings aware and feverish, busy with the first pain of healing. So we slept a hundred times instead of one, and on each occasion when we emerged from bedlam into the lonely house we wondered how long we might be allowed to live there. We reasoned and planned, and chased ourselves from ridge to ridge and planet to planet, and mapped the wildest journeyings on record, and abandoned each plan as soon as it was made....

The coldest hour came at dawn, when I felt a strong draft blowing across me. I saw that the dresser had been pulled away from the front door; our world was icy, a barren brown-and-blue in the opening. I took a kitchen knife with which I had provided myself, and crept to the porch.

Barstow stood in the yard, examining the landscape, while each shed and tree grew more noticeable in a pale light developing around us.

"I came out for a bite of air," he said. "I reckon I won't ever be able to live in a house again."

"Let's hope that all of us may live in houses, some time," I said.

He came toward the door, shivering, but seeming to enjoy the early wind in spite of its shrillness. "Maybe we ought to start, Clark. Maybe we ought to get marching."

"You were the one who advised against travel by day."

His shaven, felon's head stood like a knob against the sunrise. "We could be an hour's journey away from here before any folks were abroad! This is a good hour for travel; and then we could hide in the woods somewheres."

"There's food here," I objected, "and pans and blankets, and all kinds of things we could use. We'd be mad, to go away without taking them. Remember, too, that if any one approaches this house in the daylight we're really safer than if they approached at night."

Since I had come outside, the farm had grown many shades lighter. Now the sheds were separating one from the other, now we could see the dead dog in the barnyard.

Barstow agreed reluctantly, "I guess we'd be daft to leave without some kind of supplies. Lord knows I'd like to get a pair of shoes, but there won't none of these fit me." He came closer and lowered his voice. "Clark, what do you think of this business—I mean, taking her with us?"

"Thus far," I answered, "it's she who has been taking us. There aren't many like her."

He agreed quickly, "True enough. I never met none. But what if—?" and he mentioned an embarrassing circumstance which would doubtless arise many times when we went on again.

I was in some doubt, but I said, "Well, she'll just have to make out as best she can, and so will we. Didn't you ever go on a picnic with ladies?"

"I never went on a picnic at all," he said, slowly. "I never had much fun when I was a boy."

We returned into the house and found Naomi Kincaid feeding the cat in the kitchen. There was no milk for the creature, but Naomi had broken an egg into the warm skillet and let it congeal slightly, and then poured it into a saucer. She held the saucer at arm's length, kneeling as she did so, and the cat came closer and closer, stretching out its pink nose and lashing its tail fearfully, yet drawn on even as we had been by the compelling attraction of food.

"She's a mother cat," said Naomi. "She's afraid of us, but I think no one has ever been cruel to her."

"She kind of chewed my fingers when I was laying down," said Barstow. "She's still mighty fat, too, in spite of not getting anything to eat lately. She wouldn't have lasted five minutes on the Island."

The woman cried, "Mercy sakes, you wouldn't have eaten her?" We both laughed at such horrified astonishment; and the pussy went streaking away when we tried to pet her.

We had better fare than cat-meat for our breakfast: hoe-cake and more ham and eggs, and a whitish preserve made of melon rind, which we found in a jar. It was daylight by the time we finished. The wind had borne away every cloud that formed in the night, and the sun gleamed on endless coverts of bright-polished weeds.

We were of one mind by this time: we held it unwise to sally forth unless driven by necessity, and we would search the house at leisure, taking those things which we needed and were able to carry. Then, if undisturbed, we should rest until dusk before we set out.

Thus it came about that my conscience beset me seriously. As noted before, I had stolen food in my time—plenty of it, like any other soldier—and I did not think that Providence would begrudge us the few garments we had taken to wear. Yet wholesale burglary was not to my liking; nor, I believe, to the woman's. Though Barstow made light of it and said that the people who owned the house were lucky that an entire regiment had not come to visit them.

"Don't forget, Clark," he added, "that stragglers or cavalry, or whoever did the business in this place, have committed a sight more crime than we will by carrying off a few needfuls."

But each time I rummaged a dresser drawer, I was oppressed with that same nervous sense of ill-doing, and wondered what my father would think of it.

We found letters, too, and gift-books, and a few legal papers scattered by the hands of the unseen invader who walked those rooms before we did. Though we did not have time to humor our inquisitiveness by reading whatever notations we came across, we saw many names—Seddons, Halsey, Manikin, Duval, and Carpenter. The name of Carpenter was most evident, and appeared in many of the books and on two packets of letters, most of which came from Fredericksburg.

So, while Barstow jeered at me still, I sat down in the noon hour and inscribed the following letter, and fastened it carefully to the wall in the north room, close by the old secretary.

To Whom It May Concern (mainly the owners of this house, whose name we think is
Carpenter):

This is to state that on Thursday, the third of March, 1864, the undersigned, accompanied by Pvt. Barstow, 6th Wisconsin Vol. Inf., arrived at this place and found it deserted, with evidences of pillage and a very bad crime. Undersigned and Private Barstow, accompanied by a friend, remained here overnight, and fed and clothed themselves; we also washed, being in a bad state from incarceration by the rebel government on Belle Island.

Whatever vandalism and plundering has been committed here we did not do, except for taking the articles hereinafter mentioned: 1 ax, 2 blankets, 1 comforter; clothing and shoes, miscellaneous, to garb 3 people; 1 large tin cup and 2 small, 3 spoons, 3 forks, 4 knives, a packet of matches containing 18, flint and steel, 2 stew pans, 3 tin plates, 1 razor, also trunk straps and ropes and cords, with material for wrapping these articles. We have carried off miscellaneous foodstuffs and soap, with a flask of applejack—all to the amount, perhaps, of $1000 Confederate.

Also, appropriated for our needs whatever money we found, amounting to $145 Confederate, $2 in greenbacks, and 25¢ in silver.

We have mutilated one book, for which we should be charged.

Whatever other damage and wickedness has been committed hereabouts was done by a person or persons utterly unknown to us. Since we have no desire to make innocent people suffer, no matter what their affiliations may be, we are leaving this letter in the hope that recompense can be made at some future date. When, if ever, regular mail communication is established with the Northern states (probably only after the subjugation of rebellious states), please send a letter to the undersigned at his home in Westfield, New Jersey, of which town his father, Abraham, is a well-known citizen; and restitution will be made to any reasonable and just amount. Provided, of course, that the undersigned survives until that time.

We did not kill the dog, either, but found him lying dead on our arrival.

With regret for any further difficulty which we may have visited upon a household already stricken with misfortune, but with all thanks for material assistance acquired unexpectedly in a moment of great need, I remain,

Respectfully,
Pvt. Oliver Clark,
1st N. J. Cav.

The mutilation of the book was done by Naomi, who found a fine map of Virginia State in a school book, and who tore out the page very coolly. And she was the one who found the Confederate currency wadded in a jelly-jar in the kitchen cupboard, although I discovered the greenbacks and silver in a pocketbook which had fallen beneath an upstairs table, and probably had been overlooked by the plunderer who preceded us.

"Do you reckon you'll ever hear from these people?" asked Barstow, with amusement. And then when he saw that I was angry with him, he hastened to explain his stand: "I'm every bit as honest as you, Clark. Maybe more so! But war is war, and when Inkpahdutah come down on the settlements out home, we didn't complain because the Sioux ripped open the feather-beds and threw good wheat flour around, too. If we had been there and seen them do it, I reckon we would have shot at them. We're taking the Indians' chance."

"This is civilized warfare," I said with deep disgust. He laughed, and then I felt my cheeks growing warm, for I remembered my conversation with Naomi the day before.

We made three packs of the goods we had stolen (Barstow said that we had borrowed the things, and the woman contended that we had bought them, since I was going to pay charges at some time in the future). Barstow of course had his ax, nor would he let it out of his hand for a moment.

Yet again we prowled the house, peering from behind every shutter and watching down the lane toward the north for returning householders who never came. Barstow made bold, too, to go into the yard and scout for tracks. He reported that no troop of cavalry had been there, at least since the last heavy rain. There were the tracks of men and women on foot; a light-wheeled vehicle was the last thing which had gone away from that farm. He dragged the dead dog behind the slave cottage, and then came back, for he could be seen from afar if any one were watching.

We ate once more, of a stew which Naomi contrived from fat and ham-bone and meal and rice flour, with a few onions. It would not have looked like much to those who daily sit themselves down to discuss the decent fare of peace-times, yet I have never eaten anything before or since which afforded quite the satisfaction. So we toasted our companion again in applejack, and she wanted to read to us from the Lord Byron book, but Barstow would have none of it. He wrapped himself in a blanket beside the fireplace and cried out that he was ready to die happy, and would we take ourselves away from there and let him die in peace?

We were in the north room: the woman still reading, myself far from her, quilt-wrapped and half asleep on the floor, and the sky growing overcast outside—when some one trod heavily upon the little front porch.

I leapt up, the patchwork quilt impeding my movements, startled with the nerve-racking fright of one caught in a guilty act (that quick terror which is like a sword going through every nerve and sinew so speedily that one realizes what has happened only when, afterward, he stands aloof and looks at the quivering wounds).

Naomi spoke no word; her lips were a firm gray crease. We stood, turned to plaster, and in the hall we saw the dresser trembling as some person tried to open the front door.

Again the dresser shook. Outside, a man's voice spoke in a deep whisper. Then I was across the room, through the door, into the hall, putting my entire weight (whatever it amounted to) against the great slab of furniture which, inch by inch, had staggered away from the door.

There was no time for wonderment as to what person crouched with a shoulder against our barricade. In another second I saw the light blocked off from the north room and released again, as Naomi Kincaid sprang to take a position beside me.

"Barstow!" she cried. Though her voice had no scream about it, it lashed into the deepest dungeons of slumber to rouse him.

Before he came, however, the pressure at the door relaxed; feet retreated across the porch to be muffled by the empty ground. Barstow met us in the south room. Together we three crouched like trapped rabbits, peering through a window opposite a broken shutter-leaf.

I cried, "Union cavalry!" and for one rare moment we thought that we must be saved, but of course such a thing could not be.

For the lone man we saw there did indeed wear the deep-blue jacket and forage cap of the Federal cavalry. Though he had no saber, his belt and boots and soiled trousers showed that he was one with those buccaneering troops who had pushed against Richmond, while Barstow and I still lay in the mire of the Island.

But no command would have accepted him as he faced us now: a gigantic specimen of a man, quite as tall as Barstow, and heavier than the Iowan had been at the time of his capture.

He stood well out from the house across the wheel tracks, clenched fists planted on his hips and feet wide apart, his swift gaze running from window to window and, of course, seeing nothing but shutters. His face was pale and jaundiced under tan, but the lower half sprouted with an orange-red stubble that should have sent him to the guard-house at double time, if ever he reported for duty in that condition. One hand patted a revolver holster; the fingers twisted and played with the flap as if itching to draw and shoot; and now and then, to our amazed horror, he took a few steps forward and pointed a finger in mock accusation at the front door.

While we stared speechless and wondering, he cupped enormous hands around his mouth and roared toward the upper windows: "What did you do with the ax?"

He turned and ran to the wagon-shed, where he disappeared for a second, to emerge with a broken single-tree which he brandished threateningly and then threw from him. He ran to the barn, and then to the next shed, and then to the slave cottage; while we watched from successive windows as well as we could, knowing that for the moment flight was out of the question, since easily he could overtake any one or all three.

"He's drunk," whispered Barstow. "I tell you, he's a dangerous critter and we'd better not meet up with him!"

And all the time that enormous blue figure was lumbering from outbuilding to outbuilding, increasing his pace until he slipped and stumbled at every turn. His holster bounced, his forage cap was still jammed upon his shaggy head. Once he picked up a length of board, and once a grubbing hoe, but these he threw away as he had the single-tree; and it seemed that in his wild, threatening dance, he had bound himself to select a mightier weapon than any of those.

We saw the chickens go screaming away from the barn door, when he burst forth once more, carrying a short log which perhaps had been part of a manger or stanchion; and even his wide back bent beneath the weight. He was trying to come at a dead run, but the log was heavy, and he stumbled and fell. He got up promptly, his trousers smeared with cow manure; he came on toward the front door, log and all.

"He's not drunk," said Naomi Kincaid. "He's mad. He's madder than any bull," and I felt a chill down my back as I remembered the tales I had heard, of army stragglers—insane to begin with, or men whose intelligence had crackled to bits under the grinding of battle—who preyed worse than wolves off defenseless citizens in isolated parts.

But Barstow's eyes were filmed; he had his ax, he took a fresh grip, and yet another grip which he liked better. Already the man in blue was roaring before the front porch.

As for myself, I was taken in charge by terror such as I had never felt since the day of my enlistment. I cannot remember that my knees trembled or that my hands turned to putty, and yet I know that my body must have been hollow and useless, a thin shell housing my incompetent fear. Nevertheless, I leaned against the front door barricade, hoping to do what I might in holding it there.

Barstow dragged me away. "No, Clark," he cried. "He's liable to shoot!" The soldier outside did fire, twice. The balls went through the dresser and broke something in one of the drawers; we heard a tinkle of china or glass.

"Take her in there," Barstow ordered. "Naomi—take her in the other room or somewheres! I've got this," and he waved the ax, while the dresser jammed and resounded under impact from outside.

My terror would not have risen so shrill, had the creature besieging us been an acknowledged enemy wearing a uniform we hated, or the hairy coat of an ape. He was a sinew of the body to which we had been trained, whose purpose was never meant to be distorted in such fashion. The very rupture of this soldier's faith with us who had been his comrades (unknown to him in fact or fancy, but still his comrades) was cause enough for revulsion. He was Turk and Tartar alike, he was jungle savage and brown-faced Sioux: now we knew the trouble of families haunted on their prairie farms by a menace no more brutal or unreasoning than this.

With all my strength I was trying to draw Naomi Kincaid to a place of safety—what place I did not know. But I thought of the pantry and of the secluded corner next to the kitchen fireplace.

"He'll kill Bar," she cried to me.

"No, he won't. Bar has got the ax!"

And then we were in the kitchen; the blows no longer resounded against the braced front door. I lifted a fold of the comforter hanging over the north kitchen window, in time to see the cavalryman rounding the corner of the house, now without his log, and groping here and there for some new weapon.

I called out to Barstow. Our enemy found his thunderbolt. It was a half-a-brick, and he hurled it through the window with such force that the glass spattered all over the room, and the missile lay on the floor muffled in folds of the comforter. The man was singing, now—if one can call it that.

He was roaring *Saint Paul's Advice* which our regimental songsters (I was one of them) offered at a Saturday night glee when we were in winter quarters, more than two years before.

> *"He is the man,*
> *He is the man to suit us all...*
> *Hurrah! Hurrah! For doctors like*
> *Saint Paul..."*

He mouthed the words, and there was no melody binding them: only a voice like the deep-chested braying of a mule, chanting no humor whatsoever.

His hands, covered with orange hair, came through the window frame and brushed the broken glass aside. One hand disappeared and came back as a fist, to take the frame away. I swung Naomi behind the table in the far corner of the room and wrestled her to her knees, and then I crept to the north wall with the sharp kitchen knife ready.

The window-space darkened as the man squeezed his body against it. Through the doorway close beside, I could see Barstow coming. He held the ax high, and made no shuffling with his stocking feet, although I remember that the boards talked under him.

The giant pushed his head and one shoulder through the window, and he was still reciting the song. Our little bird, which had taken itself into hiding since the night before, shot in sudden agony from a secret perch atop the kitchen safe. The cavalryman's face lifted at the feathery rush; with a squeak, the bird went by Barstow in the doorway. But the man had not yet turned his shaggy head when Barstow's ax came down, blunt end first, on the base of his brain.

In all my recollection of the war and our numerous voyagings and alarms, I cannot separate one hour as grotesque as this. It held that quality of desperate unreality born only in derangement, or in the minds of those who write of ghouls and magic dragons and enchantment. In each battle, earlier and later, when I felt my horse sawing at his single rein and rocking me forward amid the mud flying from a thousand other hoofs, I grasped the knowledge that here was a moment uncertain and dangerous, though surely something which I had planned to experience, and a natural pattern in my life. . . .

But there had been no foreboding of this frenzy. There could be no excusing it, now that the happening was done. Prentiss Barstow had killed a man in his defense and ours; we had drawn blood in our striving for freedom, rather than let the blood be drawn from us; but it was nightmare for all that, and so remains to this hour, and those who read it may feel that I have recounted frenzy which never occurred in Virginia or any place else. I shall hold no blame against them if they do.

9

NAOMI cried to us, as if excuse were needed, "I tell you, he's crazy. He is!"

Barstow held the ax ready for another blow. But it was not needed; his first stroke had done destruction.

The body was still wedged in the window, one arm dangling inside. We debated as to whether we should drag him into the room or pull him down in the yard. Finally we did the former, with great labor, and Barstow was compelled to go out and lift the heavy-booted legs. Naomi stood beside the table watching us, biting the knuckles of her hand, though still unable to draw away.

"Second New York Cavalry," I reported to Barstow.

"Clark, I never thought to kill a Yankee when I went away to the war. But I reckon it had to be done."

"Oh yes, Barstow!"

"He was the one," Barstow said, and repeated it several times under his breath. "A straggler, I reckon—a straggler from the Union cavalry when they came through here on the way to Richmond. God help the people who lived in this house!"

I said, "I guess He is helping them well enough, for they got away, and weren't here when this man came back."

I took the belt and holster and cartouche. No one of us knew what he had done with his saber or his horse, or just how all this villainy came about. At least he had a revolver loaded with ball—in all, seventeen rounds of ammunition, besides many extra caps. There was no watch in his pocket, but a jackknife and several dollars in greenbacks and silver, which we took; we wanted nor needed anything else in his pockets, though we found some crude notations and a misspelled letter, obscene as to nature, which some one had written to a man named Ryan.

I buckled on the revolver—a Colt's, army pattern. I loaded the empty chambers, and saw that they were freshly capped. Barstow got down on his hands and knees and worked to remove the cavalry jacket, though the woman begged him not to do so.

"I'll make better use of it than he will," returned Barstow. "Clark, do you want his cap?"

"Not I."

"No more do I. What I want is a wide-brimmed hat like I used to have, to keep the rain off my neck, and I reckon maybe we'll find one somewhere. I got to have shoes, though, and maybe his boots will do me."

Now the woman was ill, and fled away. But Barstow and I went on with our robbing of the dead, and the boots were large enough to serve—though well worn at the toes, and one was split high on the side.

"What will we do with him, Bar?"

"Leave him lay. When these folks come back, if they ever do, they'll see that he settled his bill."

And then, when first he jammed his hand into the inside pocket (which we had missed before) Prentiss Barstow found evidence which showed that, beyond any doubt, this man was guilty as the very devil himself. For in the pocket was a torn yellow envelope filled with a great wad of Confederate money—five hundred and five dollars, as we soon ascertained —and the envelope was from a letter addressed to that same Henry Carpenter, Esq., whose name had appeared in books and letters we found there.

Barstow looked down at the dead face, which stared at the ceiling as if surprised out of all sullenness. He lifted his leg, and no one but such as myself, well acquainted with the worst brutalities, could understand and forgive when he implanted a sturdy kick against the defenseless clay. "May the fat fry out of you," said Barstow. "I reckon you'll never go around raping any more virgins."

He stopped speaking. He heard what I heard and what Naomi Kincaid heard as well: the cry of hounds coming over a ridge, and none too far away.

Now there was no more corpse-gazing for us. The hounds warned, in a second, that we should be fleeing or else establishing ourselves for defense, unless in our turn we wished to be flat and sightless—while people went through our pockets, and stripped us of boots still warm with the heat of our living.

Those dogs roamed from an easterly direction, and Naomi and I were first to reach the east windows. Barstow came trampling after us, the unfamiliar leather impeding him. I raised one of the windows in its stiff frame, with more strength than I had thought I owned, and Naomi held it there while I reached out to draw a shutter ajar.

Far across the field we could see them coming—two men and two dogs. But they cast about as if uncertain of the trail; one dog hung back, and half the time he was being dragged in a sitting position. The other hound, white and smaller, sprawled at the limit of his leash, and both of them gobbled with open mouths.

Barstow asked, "Are you any great shakes with a pistol, Clark?"

"Third money," I said, "in the squadron match, last year . . ."

"That's well. I could never learn to shoot one of them little things!" and the dogs chorused closer at every word. "You stay here, Clark. Lady, you come with me and get our packs!" He went leaping into the hall. There we had set our stolen goods, tied in the blankets and strapped for lugging them with us.

But Naomi never stirred from my side. "Do you mean to stand them off, Ollie? Look! That one has a gun—"

"They're boys," I said. They were near enough now for me to tell that much. "They'll never take us—"

She cried, "Don't shoot them!"

"And go back to the Island?" I jeered.

She held my left arm, hurting the bones with both her hands. "Look," she wailed, more frantically than before, "they're not coming after us! I tell you they're not! We never crossed the field there. They're coming after *him.*"

Barstow had dragged the bundles close; now he came down on his knees beside our window. We saw that the dogs were holding more sternly to their purpose, though one of them still sat whenever his master would let him. The boys managing them were undersized and thin; I remember that one of them wore a tattered straw hat even in that cold season, and a long gray overcoat which hung clear to his shanks. He had a belt around his waist, but we could not see whether or not he carried a holster.

"Don't shoot till they're this side the wheel tracks, Clark!"

I lowered the revolver. "She's dead right, Bar. They're not trailing us. We weren't up at that end of the field. They're trailing that fellow in there!"

He cried, hoarsely, "We're here, aren't we? They'll see us, won't they?" and made as if to get the revolver away from me. I jerked myself free and fell back from the window, to pick up the bundle which I had called mine.

Naomi wrung her hands. Though her voice was urgent and decisive, even so. "You're a fool, Bar! We'd gain nothing by shooting them. Let's run out the back way while they're still at the front—"

Prentiss Barstow's face was more colored than I had seen it for months. "Who's captain, anyway?" he demanded. "Me or you?"

"Nobody's captain," fairly screamed the woman. "Oh, for God's sake, men, come on!" Then, though we obeyed her at last with all the speed we could muster, she turned in her tracks and ran into the north room; and when she came flying back she was forcing some object into her pocket.

Her pack lay ready. From this moment our space of safety could be measured by fractions: surely, as the woman had said, those boys were scouting the trail of the dead cavalryman. For, passing the wagon shed, the foremost dog turned off on one of the invisible trails which the giant had followed in his dartings about the landscape only a few moments before. It went carolling into the empty shed with its master after it, and then out again and criss-crossing its own trail with screams and challenges.

We got the back door open. We tumbled out into light which hurt us in every sense, even though the sky was becoming overcast. There were chicken-coops here, smothered by weeds of a previous season, and each of us must have fallen at least twice before we got over and around the discarded fencings, to enter the sloping orchard itself. We labored down-hill, struggling with our unfamiliar burdens; the tines of a fork had worked through Barstow's blanket in sharp-pointed menace. We sprawled across a disordered rail fence and into a field better kept than most of the others—where some unidentified, tiny, green growth had fought its remarkable way through the sod.

From here we reckoned our progress by the sum of agonies: too much destruction and besieging had fretted us who were so little qualified to bear them. We tussled like fiends to hold our first terror-stricken galloping. But Barstow and I fell behind the woman, and God knows his ax was tons heavier than the weapon I carried at my belt.

Now the hounds went rallying against the walls of the house, and they circled the corner under urging of the boys directing them. From the yelps that seemed only a yard behind us, I imagined they were on our side of the building now—and quite able to see us, had they peered beyond the orchard.

Centuries later (so many thousand days of threat and lung-burning) we got ourselves over a second fence that marked the nether boundary of the grain field. Foremost in the woodland was a thicket of scrub oaks; we skirmished into it, never minding the vines.

I felt the ground writhing beneath me, trying to toss my weak body aloft as a wild horse tosses a novice. But I only dug my fingers into the leaves, clawing for a more desperate hold.

"Got to go on," said Barstow at last, gulping for breath between each word.

Naomi told him, "Not you, Bar. Not yet. Nor Clark. I could go on—"

His breath was a tonic dearly bought, but he expended it in profanity.

"Save your rage, mister! I shan't stir until you're able."

There on the earth I closed my eyes again. In the manner of the blind, I transferred the power of their sense until my hearing told me that a new and well-grounded fear would be realized.

"Your boots," I gasped.

"What say?"

"They're his, Bar. You took them off of him before he was cold!"

Naomi clenched her fists. "Oh, I see what you mean!

That man's scent is on his boots still. All the way down to these woods—"

"Coming on it," I cried. "Coming this way, now!"

Close together in the saplings, we reared up to observe the pursuit which my ears had brought to me.... There were only two of them, we saw as they broke from the apple trees and came on toward us: the small, white, eager dog and the boy in the straw hat, though now he was the one who carried a musket. I thought that I had never seen a hound or a human being move with such hideous deliberation, yet now I know that they were running as fast as their legs would let them. Those boys had found the man they chased, and we, or rather Barstow, had attended to him before their chance came. It crossed my imagination that doubtless the house on the hill was one of several, and the evidence of that upstairs room could be multiplied in other houses of the neighborhood. There were a day and a night, perhaps two days and two nights, when he had prowled mercilessly abroad.

He was prowling no more, but the animal most anxious to seek him would not be balked by the mere process of death. Boots were boots, and the smell they imprinted upon the cold ground possessed a certain immortality. So these persecutors were crossing the field where we had walked; I wondered, as I braced my pistol for firing, whether the boy was puzzled at three pairs of tracks crisscrossing under his gaze.

"God," said Naomi, "he looks so young..."

"You ought to have seen some of them on the Island," Barstow whispered.

I cried, "He'll never smell your boots! Just the dog—" I waited until they were ten yards from the fence, and I could see sputum dripping from the little animal's open mouth. I fired—a very bad shot—and tore the earth so close behind the hound that he spun around with a snarl. The second ball took him amidships, while his master turned and ran.

There is a picture I do not like to build again before my eyes: the dog which had gone forth wisely and furiously, to do the task for which he was trained by nature and by men— his blood, his rollings and bitings, and the rapid squeal he made in his undignified yielding to death. So I fired a third time, though we could not well spare the charge; we saw the stained, white body leap under impact of the lead; after that he moved nothing but his tail, and did not move it for long.

The boy kept running, a clumsy figure in his long over-coat, until he was half-way across the field. Then, possessed by defiant rage which had not come to him in the throes of surprise, he turned. He took aim intended to be careful, and sent a bullet spitting into the trees high over our heads and to one side. With empty gun he retreated less rapidly to the orchard, where we heard him yelling, "Paul! Paul!" and saw the other boy and dog hastening to meet him.

Then we rose up and ran away to the northwest, moving as silently as we could in the thick growth. We found a road at the foot of the woods—one side lined by a fence—a wide road curving southwest and then northwest again, and which could have been only the chief road to Goochland Court House. There was no traveler in sight. We scampered across, tortured ourselves through a steepening ravine, and crouched in a clump of wild cherry trees on the first hill beyond. There we lay for half an hour, watching the road throughout its nearby course: no enemies approached in all that time.

We moved twice more before night, speeding in con-fusion, lugging our blanket-bundles of food and clothing and sharp-pointed utensils. Each time when we reached a copse commanding a view of the country toward the south and east, we cowered in expectation of gun-shots and dogs and the muddled howl of pursuit. In each den we felt that we were at bay, without the endurance to surmount further hills; and each time a renewed ambition goaded us into fresh onslaughts against distance.

From three varying opinions we were able to construct a theory: that one dog was dead, that his survivor was never ardent for the trail. Of the two boys who had conducted the hounds, neither had seen us, though the one in the gray overcoat must have believed that our bullets were intended for him. No matter how earnest the boys' desire to ferret us out (unseen and unidentified avengers that we were, and surely no foe of theirs) they would go first to seek reënforcement and wiser counsel. We were sure that there must be Home Guards in the neighborhood, for every southern community was said to abound with them. But as yet we discerned no trace of an organized military.

Elude pursuit, we said, until night! And then we would have our chance at walking the road—a course far and away more profitable than the vagrant track we now deployed among worn-out pastures.

10

O N this fourth and fifth of March we explored our first highway, pushing ahead rigorously until dawn. Never before, when I imagined the kidney of our erring sister-states, had I been able to estimate just what subversion now befell them.

Whenever I had made an expedition with my regiment, the turnpikes filled with the unmistakable human and animal clatter of cavalry. We had no reason to believe that a stricken desolation lay in broad tracts on either side. When the army moved as a whole, it was a teeming migration of militant tribes who had their own biscuits and horse-shoes and overcoats and canister, with the wheels necessary for transporting them. We spread out on more roads than one; the woodland alleys had their mud churned or their dust disturbed by countless errand-boys and messengers. We occupied the country as surely as we passed over it, and substituted our own weariness, our enthusiasm or busy-body sins, for the civilization which had gone deep into hiding.

I had read Holmes, too ... in this first night of travel by the ordinary routes of men, I could agree that his prophecy became fact: the harvest was rotting black in the soil—whatever harvest might be left, after winter had frozen it there. The wolves and the catamounts were loose, their caves had been burned about their ears ... I fancied a dozen times that I heard them shrieking in the hedge-rows.

There was one village which we avoided, and another through which we slipped in the midnight emptiness. We came upon it unawares, seeing the roadside houses rise up without warning until they stood blankly and accusingly, a pole's length away. The windows were plain as the faces of school slates; the doors were closed against us. A warped sign, hung from a store-front, squeaked on its rusty flanges and became a talkative ally eager to disguise our progress. Two dogs assailed us, one in a dooryard and one which came out to trot threateningly until we had left his town. Behind the houses' unpainted walls, behind the shutters and sidings, there was certainly a life—an enemy life drugged and secret from the laceration of armies.

I knew also, when we saw a single light, that humanity suffered its wrongs: misfortunes beneath notice when one reckoned the existing myriads, tortures overwhelming when one was a part of them. We saw that light (a single tawny lamp-flare through an unshuttered window) where a woman with spectral hair bent over the lamp, heating a small tin which she held with a pair of pincers.

One flash as we hurried—the anxious face; the yellow hand rebelling from proximity to the lamp's hotness; the projection of anxiety which sits beside every cradle until the cradle has been emptied by death or time. I told my companions, when later we talked of it, that my own mother used often to mix turpentine and lard in that fashion. Vaguely I could remember how the stuff felt—thin and greasy and burning—when she rubbed it on my chest, and smothered the aroma in flannel. And Barstow said that in Iowa, the old grannies were forever heating skunk oil or the gall of bulls, but there they melted them above candles. ...Naomi Kincaid wondered only who was sick, and if it were a boy or a girl, and what the mother would do if it died.

The solitary picture, the single square of actuality in that lame village where the dogs resented us, and where doubtless a dozen men would have put us in irons could

they have known we were feeling our way along their road!
Then at last it became a keynote of the past, and the hills
shut it away from us. The road went on toward Goochland
Court House.

At times we thought we should never accomplish another
mile . . . we dropped into the weeds and felt the blood
pounding at our wrists and temples. We had essayed a campaign beyond our strength; at least Barstow and I were not
fit for it. But we kept on, not wanting to die on Belle Island,
not wanting to be fired upon, nor to be easy prey of the
wolves and the catamounts which Doctor Holmes had seen
in Dixie, all the way from New England.

No one passed us coming up from the rear; and only
twice did we meet people who were traveling in the direction
of Richmond. Both times we lay down and choked back our
breath; both times we arose to go forward more rapidly than
before, sliding in mud of the lower places and tripping over
loose stones that were left high and dry by the cold wind's
shrinking.

First we met a lone horseman, a mile or two beyond the
village, and I think he was asleep in his saddle: his horse
blew in alarm when it came abreast of us, and he—dark,
besotted shape—never stirred or spoke to the animal. Sometime before daybreak, too, we heard a vast complaining of
wooden wheels, and took refuge in a ditch to let a covered
wagon lurch past and vanish into the region through which
we had come. But no sound of laughter, or singing, or crying
of a child, crept through the towering frame of canvas. God
alone knows what the cargo was, and what remote destina-
tion the driver had in mind.

We crossed six brooks. I estimate that we traveled ten
or eleven miles, or perhaps even farther. For men in our
condition it was a march as stupendous as any managed by
the vaunted foot-cavalry of Stonewall Jackson, when they

were chasing our General Banks here and there through the northern portions of Virginia. And it was an enviable accomplishment for a woman unused to such doings. As our strength wore down, the road went higher and higher; at last the countryside showed a drab crust of horizon on our right, and it was wise for us to be hid before the day came close.

We wallowed beyond the fences and traversed a field sprouting with hop poles. The best we could manage, at long last, was an abandoned pig-pen from which the pigs had departed more recently than we could have wished. It lay in a valley, and that was unsatisfactory; in our prostration we must need be content, and trust to fortune that any one approaching could be seen on the higher ground before he came down. There was a roof over our heads—a roof of sorts—made from long, thick shingles which Barstow called "shakes" and which were curled like clover, chinked poorly by the leafy rubbish of winds.

But we were glad to have any structure, even as crazy a pile as this, doing its part to shelter us from the steady drizzle which set in soon after daylight. On one of our blankets we laid forth the last scraps of ham, the greasy corn-cakes mostly broken apart, a glass of jelly, and half-a-loaf of dark bread which I had taken from the abandoned supper (that most frightfully interrupted meal, mouldering on its plates) in the house of the Carpenters. Each of us had his swallow of brandy, too.

We were no longer two men and a woman, no longer did any distinction of sex or politics or morals beset us. We were half human, now. We had killed, we could kill again if it were required by our inclination toward freedom. And, in a lurid fashion, we were becoming hunters in the same hour when we lay ticketed as the hunted. Barstow and I were stronger and bolder than we had been, even taking into account how stiff our little wounds had grown and how life-less our arms and legs became under the night's abuse. One would keep watch, we pledged, while the others slept. But we boasted, and I say now that I was the first on watch, and likely slept as soon as the others.

The wind had changed from southeast to southwest, and back again to the south; it drifted steadily, angrily through the open face of the sty. Inch by inch, half sleeping and half waking, we drew together, dragging our wraps with us. In a strange time which may have been midday, I awakened to learn that we were nearly in a single pile—not men and woman drawing close, as such; but only organisms on whom ice and dampness had laid their compulsion, demanding inti-macy and proximity—a tangle of limbs and arms and blankets, a feeble amalgamation from which, no matter how inferior our state, our roots went deep and supplied us with the sap of existence.

11

Y manhood returned to me late in that afternoon. Its visitation was marked; it could be identified, and I was proud enough. When one is able to experience the delights of his sex, or even to entertain such design wholeheartedly in his mind, he rises far above those glutinous fish which persons of science declare to have fathered and mothered the race without intent or pleasure on their part.

I crept back from driving away three pigs which, in my sleep, I considered to be the catamounts or sharks designated by Doctor Holmes when he prophesied the terror of this civil war. I heard them growling and rooting about the door of their home, and was delighted that a few cobs and balls of mud could discourage them. I crept back, I say, and found Barstow still burying his head beneath the fold of dirty blue comforter in order to contain the warmth of his breath—a trick men learned on the Island. But Naomi was awake, and she wanted to know (inquiring without much alarm) what had happened.

"Pigs," I said.

"We've taken their house," and she tried to laugh about it.

"They shan't have it until we're ready to leave. God knows it's bad enough, that we have to lie in their bed!"

Her eyes looked out at me from above the edge of blanket which concealed her mouth; perhaps she was smiling, though her face was drawn and pale from physical weariness and the constant, savage impress of danger. "Belle Island was a sty, wasn't it, Ollie? Would you rather be back there?"

I mumbled something—no matter what—and took my own place which so closely adjoined hers and Barstow's. Here was the section of mud which I had tenanted since dawn, and which now held a comforting warmth that even the frailest chemistry of me had placed there. I lay down, but not to sleep. Although the lids closed over my eyes, although I may have wished to return to the disordered pioneerings of slumber, I could not contrive as wisdom would have commanded.

The woman was there; we were a family welded closer by ambition and primitive encounters than any family of civilization. *Will she be my sister,* I thought, *or my mother?* ... The vagabond voices within me went on to discuss all range of possibility . . . she cannot be your wife; you must never consider her as such; no woman can have two husbands; but this notion prevails whenever men and women lie down together. . . .

Once in my life I had done the thing—when I was in the Academy—and I had been frightened out of my wits by it, though willing enough to attempt it again if the young woman had not returned to New York City. I was smugly aware that she was wicked; I fancied her as degrading me, and conspiring to keep me out of Heaven.

For I had been well taught that such acts were conducted by only two: God or the devil. God controlled them when the participants were married, and wished to beget children according to the style of the Bible. The devil organized all other relations of the kind, though often enough women (their faces covered by noticeable layers of paint) acted as his hired hands, and were regularly in his pay.

And the devil had managed my single transgression when I was sixteen, and doubtless Miss Angelina Sifert had long since collected her wages (when she returned to Manhattan and the apartment which she occupied adjacent to her uncle's livery barn). Somehow, at sixteen, I had imagined

her being paid in gold—half-eagles—rung into her palm
piece by piece, by a solemn-faced devil who had his clothes
imported from Paris. Though to be sure, I had never seen
such a devil lurking in the vicinity of Westfield at those
houses which he was said to inhabit, or at least visit, every
now and then.

The tales of my father's cousin (whom we called Corporal
Jerry and who had been in Mexico, Texas, and even the
Crimea) were sufficient to send me scuttling away from ad-
vertised sin, the first month I went to war. The boys talked
of it often, and many of them bragged, and I lied twice in
order to save my reputation or even to enhance it.

However, I was honest enough with myself, if not with
others. When maturity was forced upon me during the next
two-and-a-half years, I began to doubt that the Creator super-
vised pleasures of the flesh thus inquisitively. Barstow swore
that he believed God did watch, eye-to-eye, inch-for-inch,
throughout the whole succession of individual vicissitudes.
He could reach out at will and pluck you, untouched, from
a contested fence-corner where every other man got a minié-
ball in his vitals. He watched over your other appetites, too,
said Barstow; and He recorded charitable acts in a ledger;
and He had a special place for recording carnal offenses. If
so, there was half a page of fine calligraphy under Prentiss
Barstow's name, for when he was first on the Island, he
bragged insufferably about some women in Juneau county,
Wisconsin.

Here at my right hand was she who might be the means
of fulfilling any pent-up anxiety of manhood, if she were
willing. She had done as much for a rebel colonel; she made
no secret of that; and I fancied myself infinitely more righteous than any rebel colonel who ever walked Virginia. Yet
there was about her, lying in the bog where we nestled, an

unconquerable worthiness and challenge to respect which I had never met before.

Thus, if conquerable or eager for persuasion, she could be overcome only by those means with which a man might undertake to contend against a frigid wife, or to march a timid woman into marriage.

I saw her body close at hand, under the woolen cloth. I felt her knee touching me at one place and her elbow at another, and I knew that I was basking or at least surviving, partly because she contributed to the warmth in which I had slept. I had breathed the breath from her lungs in that sequestered intimacy; the crumbs which came to us, we had shared.

"Three ways," I said, so loud in my mind that I believed the thought transmitted to my lips. "We've shared three ways," and one part of me rose up in wrath to stand with legs apart, hands on hips, and dark face accusing, to fling a brassy bugle note at me: *Reveille!* Stand on your feet, Clark, and admit to perfidy. She is as much his as yours, and make no doubt of that!

In the swift changes of sickly emotion (for I was far from being a strong man again, and thus marveled all the more at my recapturing any froth of desire) I lived again over the recent past, the midnight journeying, the long march in clay, the baying of dogs—back to and beyond the murder which we had done. I saw us unshaven, vermin-ridden, diseased in the sight of man, when first we attained to the lowest decency of life, and washed ourselves, and cut off the badness, and heard Naomi Kincaid urging us to a toast. "Let us be brave," she had said.

I raced farther and farther, and crossed the swamps; I frightened the negro children and was frightened by them; and again Naomi rode in the old wagon beside her Polish colonel. Beyond that hour, the past was rotten with chuckholes wherein the snakes coiled and the dead men grew fat. One hand—one only—had helped to draw me from that morass. Unredeemed (one with the snakes and the cadavers) I would be lying now, were it not for my tall companion.

I writhed for a long time, endeavoring to recount to the Judas within me what had happened—the debts that I must tally, or be forever condemned.

So I shall try now to set it all down. There were a million disasters ready for any lucky man who crossed the river. The shore of Richmond was no far shore beyond Jordan, where the blessed came out in white to meet you. There were miles of guards, forests, entrenchments, and patrols which walled off the Confederate capital to the north and west, guarding the river and the Kanawha Canal from exploring cavalry which might come against them, and had tried so recently. Through that area of fright we had to travel; and for all I did to save Barstow's life I might as well have been carried in his knapsack, if he had had one.

My debt, haunting me, importunes from the moment when first we were lying in the willows and sand, having attained the Richmond shore, only to see two lanterns moving closer and closer on the canal embankment high above.

One of the lanterns spoke to the other: "Hi, Pettey."

The lantern named Pettey seemed to turn and halt. "I'm not going up there too distant."

"We're ordered to patrol!"

"Well, I'm not going to patrol up there too distant."

Barstow cried in my ear, "Guards. Lay low . . ." and his whisper roused me to new shivering.

". . . Sneak around to see if we're obeying his orders!"

"I'm sure I don't care if he does. The Island guards don't keep their fire low, and we're liable to get hit, that's why."

The lantern named Pettey swung back and forth indecisively. It declared, "They ought to take good care how high they fire." Then the lanterns moved west slowly and cautiously; they kept talking, but their voices faded in the breeze.

Prentiss Barstow announced, "Just boys—size of Voss. I guess they mainly keep young soldiers and old ones, to guard the town." He began to slide off through the tangles ahead.

"No," I whispered. "Don't. They'll hear us."

"Come on, Clark! We got to move."

"Never go back to the Island," I murmured.

"You won't get a chance, if you're caught."

" 'Give his angels charge over thee, and keep—' "

He tugged at my suspender rope in one last signal; then he crawled stealthily into the waste of sand and broken bricks, which lay between the river's edge and a tall levee propping the canal against the hillside. Now I had to follow, or remain to meet a solitary fate.

I considered weirdly: a number of voices argued in my brain...legs are cold and you can't feel them...you'll be unable to walk....Yes, but if you lie down you'll freeze, and rot, and freeze again and again; the sand will blow between your ribs and construct a hummock, a landmark without any history...when they catch **you** they will shoot you, and it will hurt worse than anything in the world...if you follow Barstow, he may find something to eat, and he may share it with you....

It was the thought of food which drove me on, in final persuasion. My feet picked out a path running parallel with the river. Eventually I ran against Barstow, standing like a scarecrow in the gloom with his head bent forward.

"Where you been?" he asked. "Do you hear that noise?"

We listened: it was a groaning mechanism which labored with suffering breath. "I used to hear it on the Island," Barstow whispered, as if the Island were ten years behind him. "Charlie Becker used to say it was Jeff Davis talking in his sleep."

I sobbed, "He tried to swim, and got drowned in a fish trap. Charlie Becker, I mean."

"I tell you, Clark, it's some kind of a pump! A water pump. It's near to us."

Our prisoners' eyes (tomcat eyes which had learned to know the differences in mass and shadow and fell blackness, in a community which had no night lights whatever) poked here and there, penetrating the tarns around us. There was danger of our being seen here on the ragged edge of Richmond town lights; the reflection from mills and furnaces had a pronounced effect on even this extraordinary dark. I could see the bank sloping up to the canal, and the bulk of higher hills beyond it; I saw a whitewashed sycamore stump, and could sense the importance of miniature sand-dunes underfoot.

"You heard a door shut, before we swam that last channel," I reminded Barstow.

"That was downstream a ways. But no lights—it was a building without lights."

A cataract of gravel spilled from some higher point beyond. I thought of the guards; the warmth of my urine sprayed my leg. I heard Barstow catch his breath, and then say, "No lanterns," decisively.

And while hope bloomed in my mind again, there was the light squeak of rusty wire, the brushing of feet in the path, and the wind brought an odor smashing against us: a man, an oncoming man who smelled nothing like a prisoner.

He loomed up out of the night. I arched my body away from the path, but could not move my feet. There were more odors emanating from this newcomer; they pierced my brain with the force of fire. "Eat," I gasped, and the man stopped in his tracks.

Barstow towered beside him. There came a thud, the stranger fell at our feet, while something heavy rolled into the weeds beyond. His smell was a pungent oil. *Bloodhound that I am,* was my thought, *I said he wasn't a prisoner, all along.*

"Bar," I whispered, "that's a darkey."

He muttered, "I know. I had a rock. It was likely we'd meet somebody along here." He went down beside the dark bundle and then got up again. "Never killed him at all."

"Oh, Jesus Christ!" I wailed. "I smelled something baked, and now it's gone!"

The fallen man groaned aloud, and rolled back and forth. "Find it! ..."

My sodden foot came in contact with a rim of wood. I picked up the bucket, while the wonderful smell possessed me again. It was food, wrapped in cloth, perhaps in a handkerchief.

Barstow cried, "Forward!" Together we stumbled ahead, and he had me by the hand. The path bent toward the canal and crawled the steep ascent at a steady angle.

That unseen pump, or engine, was sobbing uncomfortably close. We toiled into a wider path bordering the canal, where a yellow lantern, unseen from below, stood glaring at us. ... Good God, we thought, this guard could not help but hear us, and his gun would resound in another second. But the soldier did not shoot; he did not move his lantern, and there was no signal from him. Slyly as a rat, Barstow began to fall back toward the declivity.

"Wait," I whispered, experiencing satisfaction that I should be in any way responsible for our deliverance. I scooped up a few pebbles and tossed them. They spattered around the lantern, and still the rays regarded us without motion.

"Canal lantern," I said. "They have them up in Jersey."

I was proud that I should be able to recollect New Jersey and invoke its memory when needed most.

The narrow length of water was black grease; it accepted feeble parts of the lantern light, and played with them.

Barstow took my arm again. "The guards went straight ahead. We should have remembered—they're far gone by now."

I sought out the bundle of food. My nervous fingers went over it, seeking lumps in the cloth, squeezing and fondling them. "Let's take some, Bar."

"Certain."

On the ground, we tore the wrappings. "Meat," said the westerner. "And this—it feels like a big root."

I felt, and said, "Sweet potato."

"I know, I know," stammered Barstow. "The rebels call them yams." He wrenched the potato apart, and his fingers must have quivered with ecstasy when they sank into the heart of it. He held one half aloft toward the gloomy sky. "Who gets this?"

I growled, "You," and when he gave me my share, the richness immediately surfeited my mouth; my tongue wallowed in it. At last I could speak again, and I said, "This pork's got a rind. I'm trying to tear it. There it comes. Who gets this?"

"I do," crowed Barstow, and I slapped the meat into his outstretched hand.

From the valley behind us sounded a wail. I dropped the remainder of my potato, but found it again.... The negro whom we had waylaid was yelling. His cries were incoherent, but they sounded as one thing: the complaint of a man who was hurt and frightened, and besought the world to help him.

A great distance ahead of us tiny stars which were lanterns had stopped, motionless. Now they began to bob as if the soldiers who carried them were running.

"They're on this side of the canal," cried Barstow. "We got to swim again!"

"Bar, I wager that's a bridge lantern." We stumbled forward, and again I was correct. The bridge was a narrow draw of planks with a windlass for lifting it above the channel. We trotted across, the planks squeaking under us, and the negro's outcry leaping high behind. Barstow ordered, "Lay down! They'll never see—" We fell flat in the tow-path, amongst heaps of mule manure.

On the opposite embankment the two guards soon sprinted past with a jingle of accouterments, their lanterns bouncing as they ran. Both wore the overcoats of United States infantrymen, doubtless impressed or traded from prisoners.

One of them halted, swung back, and picked up something. It was pink in the lantern glow. We had left the negro's handkerchief lying in plain sight. "This wasn't here when we came up, Pettey."

"It's just an old bandana," said Pettey. "Law, he makes a hullabaloo! I reckon that's Captain Turner's nigger man Bijah. Sounds like he fell and broke his leg." Then they dropped from sight, sliding down the sluice which we had climbed only a few minutes before.

Barstow crushed a last husk between his teeth. "Now we'd better skin along! Fast—even if it kills you. . . ." We were up and running again. The chalky sycamores limped wearily toward us, and stayed with us for a time, and finally drifted behind.

"My side!" I gasped.

Barstow said, "We'll catch wind in a minute," but it was a long minute before he would let me lie down and grip my side, and gulp at the cold air. And this surcease was not to be for long. The devilish little lights ascended in the background; they pushed together, then separated in a horrid team of pursuit. And we saw the suggestion of other lanterns advancing in their rear.

Barstow would not stay there to be shot. "They know what's up," he said. "The nigger told them."

"Won't know it's us ..."

"They found the rag. They know there was shooting on the river. You better get up and travel!"

I put my teeth together until they bent. "No more," I said. "If I can't—catch wind—I'm—"

Barstow swore at me, and started west at a run. I licked the wet clay of the tow-path and thought I could feel its vibration as the guards swept down, hunting me out, bayonets ready.... The ground did wriggle; it was not my imagination. Then Barstow was back, and dragging me to my feet. Through the agony I saw those dabs of light. Now there were more than two.

"Over the edge," Barstow ordered, and together we rolled down the north side of the canal wall, twigs and uprooted weeds snapping under us. Here was a soaked area—mud, sucking mires of it, with hummocks between. "Little valley," said Bar, "thanks be!"

He helped me across a low stone wall, and the gloom of many trees settled around us. We heard the Confederates crashing closer, calling to one another as they came, though the nearest hill blocked them from our sight as yet.

My ears were ringing louder and louder, my legs were indignant in their refusal to support me. Barstow seemed a giant; his arms were as long and strong and insistent as the arms of any creature in a fable.... A square-hewn stone came between my feet. I went down, with all existence lifting on a hasty level above me.

"Well," said Barstow, from a remote place in the clouds,

"here's bushes, anyway," and then the soldiers came up the path a hundred feet away.

The first were Pettey and his unnamed companion; we recognized the Union blue accompanying their lanterns. They scouted past; something bland and white reflected the splintered beams of light. But before they had gone out of sound, there appeared a third lantern. Unidentified shapes accompanied it.

"Deak!" rang a shrill voice—an old man's voice trying to give itself rigidity and importance, and failing at both.

"Yes, sir!"

"Any signs ahead, Deak?"

"No, sir. Pettey and I can't find no trace."

Another man spat, and said, "Just tramps, Turner. Let's go back."

"Tramps be damned, sir!" the old man cried. "The prison guards were firing for half an hour by the clock. Some one's made the crossing."

Another man laughed. "You can't kill a nigger by clouting him over the head."

"Oh, Deak!"

"Yes, sir."

"You go and root around in the woods alongside you— you and Private Pettey."

(Barstow whispered, "Almighty God—" I was conscious of murderous tension in the great rack of bones that lay beside me.)

"In the cemetery, Captain?"

The old officer inquired, in surprise, "Why, are we up as far as Holly Wood?" and there was a murmur of assent. "Cross the wall, boys, and search behind the tombstones," he ordered. "Don't be worried—those prisoners will not be armed, if prisoners they be."

"Tramps, I tell you, sir," said another of the group.

They huddled together, and one struck a match; they guarded the flame jealously, for matches had come to be rare things indeed. One after another, orange faces shoved forward into the cupped flame. They waited for the young guards, with the lantern set upon the ground.

I moved my leg. "No!" whispered Barstow.

"They'll come this way, Bar."

"Lay low," he insisted. "We're in some bushes."

Then the first lantern bobbed up over the incline, and I shut my eyes against it. As is said to be the habit of ostriches, I imagined that I should achieve security if I did not follow that yellow fate with my eyes. But the sound of footsteps, the jingle of gun-slings and the report of twigs beneath the boys' heels—all were sheerest torture. Again I looked at the lantern, at both lanterns.

They had halted indecisively, perhaps ten yards away. "And look behind the tombstones," one of them was mocking. The other youth giggled. Metal clinked against a shaft of rock.

" 'Our Julia,' " read the voice called Deak.

Pettey said, "Look here. Right next me. 'Sister Fannie. A tribute from Sycamore Sunday School.' This young lady is Miss Fannie Douglas; Aunt Cad used to know—"

The other boy read, " 'In the seventeenth year of her age.' Just as old as me—"

"Deak!"

"Yes, sir."

"Stop your palavering over the tombstones, sir! If you can't find any Yankees, go back over to the river side. They're somewhere about, and we've got to capture them."

The boys told him, "No Yanks hereabouts, Captain Turner," and they rejoined the men in the tow-path.

One of the others, whom I thought might be a citizen, insisted, "Tramps, stragglers, deserters! I tell you, Turner, no Yankee could swim that river and live to tell the tale."

But the old captain retorted, "They do it from time to time."

The little band moved away past the shoulder of the hill; they retreated into darkness and wind, and only when two lanterns swung close together could we see why the elderly Confederate captain directed the search without aiding in it. He had but one leg, and he moved on crutches.

Barstow stood up in the bare bushes and struck at an imaginary foe. "Trot out your Psalms, Clark! It looks like God was saving us for breakfast." He added, in a different tone, as he helped me to rise, "It's a big misfortune that Fatridge never made it. He knew the route—the prisoners' route—and he had the map with him."

At that moment I did not believe we should ever be able to pierce the outer defenses and acquire a haven, however temporary, in the unarmed country beyond. And we came near enough to failing. My first energy, exuberant through the hysteria of escape, was long since departed; this effort of wandering was no concern of mine. Still Barstow persuaded and impelled me, though my few muscles had long since ground themselves to shreds, and my joints were frozen like old hinges. The measure of Oliver Clark, and the cruel things which he did to his body, was not to be attained in a study of flesh and tissue and straining heart. No, measure what I did in terms of Prentiss Barstow! To him goes the credit, whatever it be worth, and in him is found the explanation.

If my Revolutionary ancestors whispered in my ears, I never heard them. I heard dogs and other animals at their lonely farms along the Westham Plank Road: that was the dangerous boundary which lay somewhere on our right. I heard guards marching beside the James River & Kanawha

Canal: that was the deadline to our left, and we dared not depart to any distance from it.

Only athletes in Greek stories had ever driven their bodies as Barstow drove his and mine. We traveled perhaps one mile in every hour...the ground we could see, the dun sky, and deeper blots of forest when we were well away from them. Otherwise, our eyes were unneeded things which irked and annoyed us, and should have been torn out and thrown away.

We had never traveled these ravines and briery fields before, and would never travel them again, but for this race we had been trained more wisely than Pheidippides. We had spent our days in a madhouse which spread without walls over whole acres, and if we had chosen to listen, the yells of maniacal comrades would have chased us against the wind. The chill of scurvy, the stink of diarrhea and vomit hung behind us, and would pollute our air all the way to the Union lines.

For such boldness as we undertook, it was necessary to be fitted by starvation and insanity. You who read this—you can never walk a hundred yards in the unplumbed darkness, you can never outrun the guards or lie slyly in windbreaks when they rattle past, unless you nourish yourselves with fever and toughen your determination by watching two half-grown boys claw to the death over a rind of cornbread. At night it shall be necessary for you to swallow the breath of dying men, to hear the moan of the consumptive adolescent, the chuckle of the masturbator, the yowl of the patriarch who has come a thousand miles to die in his own filth.

We had our tasks—Providence had set them for both of us, and Barstow set the tasks again for me. To elude pursuit; to crouch and back-track and gallop when a negro's shack rose up ahead; to judge the depth of gullies we had never scaled, and measure the contour of ridges we had never wandered; to keep warm in a world which had no heat, keep hearty in a wasteland where all the foxes must have died for want of food; to believe on a God who let this occur, and was letting it occur to others in other places—each of these was a single plan in the great program of labor laid forth for us. We were compelled to be the greatest workers of miracles since the Christ, in whom we still trusted so earnestly, so without excuse or reason.

Oh, the world was kind enough to some people, and it let them crumple with small holes in their foreheads! But without the gardening by which we were propagated, man was unfit for the process of escape, and would never survive to see again the striped flag of the nation which surely had betrayed him. He would never be able to hear the yodeling of fifers at guard-mount, or the laughing of the new recruits.

I remembered those recruits well enough, for once I had walked among them. Each had a picture of a girl, it seemed, and each wrote letters to her. They named their captain the Royal Monk; they played a game called baseball when they were off duty; they contrived to steal the sergeant's peaches; they became fumbling and drunk on two fingers of the sutler's whiskey; they drilled sternly and anxiously, and fainted sometimes of the heat. Most of them had promised their mothers that they would read a Chapter every night, and had promised their fathers that they would not stray among loose women if they could help it. Their eyes grew damp when they pushed out their honest chests at Retreat; they whispered what the rebels had done to a Loyalist in Kentucky; they read the plans for campaign in the newspapers and remapped them twenty times a day, gratis. And when they went out to march, one church-school tenor would soar from the ranks: *Or from foul treason's savage grasp to wrench the murd'rous blade, and in the face of foreign foes its fragments to parade* . . . and the whole column would roar back at him:

We're coming, Father Abraham, three hundred thousand more. And many of them would live to tell future generations, "I was a soldier. I served my country in the field. I was proud to do it."

Oh, we too had been recruits, but surely we were recruits no longer. We were men who accomplished much. And at the risk of wearying by repetition, I swear again that my accomplishment was dependent on Barstow. True, our feat was not done in a single night, but we were a highway's width from completing it when at last we lay down in the woods and awaited the coming of March third—its sun and comparative warmth, and the person it would bring to walk our lives. We had passed more than one fortress and dodged more than one band of Home Guards. The tricks we played—barefooted and short of breath, in the brambles—will do credit to us until we die, at least in my own estimation. But Barstow played sturdier tricks than I (though at the time it was seriously unwise of him to do so, since there was little I could contribute in turn to his encouragement and safety).

His arms dragged me, his fingers wrenched at my suspender, he propelled me all the way from the cemetery across the lonely area guarded by the Westham Plank Road. As I write this now, I realize that I have not heard the clatter of dry magnolia leaves, winter-worn but still clinging to the twigs overhead—I have not heard the ruffling paper of their sound for some years (or at least have not lingered to take notice of it, although there are a few magnolia trees in Westfield). But when I do hear them again, they will evoke the torturing memories of our escape from Holly Wood Cemetery to the pine-land far west of Richmond; again I will be beset by strange agonies that only such a night could devise, and again I will be aided out of them by my comrade—then comrade in an alliance of blood and desperation, but soon to be an enemy in person.

The roar of the river will leave us and sink lower behind its steep defile, as we swing away from it. A few dogs will complain—perhaps about us, perhaps about other dangers of darkness. But we will reach refuge in spite of them, and again we will lie down to sleep: strange, stinking skeletons wrapped in one another's arms for pure tenacity of life.

BOOK II

Man's Desire

1

Before dark the wind went into the northwest; the sky was blown clear. A day's drizzle had done damage for us: we had slow work climbing out of the valley, delving through the blackness of early evening, and finding ourselves stuck time and again in great clay sores on the hillside where other waters had taken away the top-soil. This was the dark of the moon, too, as it had been in that long-ago time when we left the Island.

Larger stars gave us some light, however, once we were up where we could see them, and Barstow wondered which might be Mars. He had colloquial, layman's names for all the stars—the hunter's star, the evening star, and so forth—and he spoke commonly of the Great Bear and the Little Bear, though I had been taught to call them Dippers. But Naomi could tell us the astronomers' identification of each, and she did it in so scholarly a fashion that we came near blundering upon a farmstead before we reached the road again. The dogs must have been begging around the table at that hour. They took no notice of us, and we marched away toward the northwest, wondering how far we must go until we reached Goochland Court House.

It was far enough, we discovered before that campaign was done; our bodies had been misused in hazard and panic of the previous night, and there were no heroics we could perform now. We dragged along stiff-limbed or loose-limbed by turn, and aching constantly. Each time we dropped exhausted, we rested longer than before. We remembered our experience at the Carpenters' farmhouse as a legend of luxury and bountifulness. . . .

It turned out that we had not acted wisely in the matter of provisioning. We should have cooked another of the hams, slice by slice, during Friday forenoon, and brought as much with us as we could carry. The ham itself, brown with wood-smoke and hanging like a rock beside the chimney, had frightened us out: it looked to weigh twenty pounds. We had brought beans and rice and meal, but a fire was needed for them unless we wished to assault our gums and stomachs by chewing up the flinty grains. So now we had only bread and jelly and a little pot of fat, and our energies suffered from such short rationing.

Barstow alone retained enough of his new-found sturdiness to be alive with suspicion; he skulked ahead looking for ambuscades. He said, lucidly enough, that he did not like the feel of this night. At times even I could sense a different spirit in the vacant miles around us: a stealthy wheel-creak, the opening or shutting of a door, and twice there were vague murmurs which might have been voices lingering on the borders of our hearing. The dogs barking in the farther reaches of midnight seemed to speak with more purposeful opinion, as if they welcomed or challenged the movement of men who went armed, and who never went about such fugitive piracy as ours.

True enough, they were hunting us, although we did not know it at the time. Only the half-wild sense which Barstow had borrowed from his western Indians reflected the dangers now portending.

We went by the court house at daybreak (seeing two or three lights of different size and color, and knowing that two or three lights meant a village of size in that hour). So we entered a field on our right and crossed a series of board fences and walls, and two thorn fences, striking along the eastern scarp of the highland where Goochland Court House sat.

The northwest wind bit angrily, coldly at our faces, trying to turn us off the higher ground. When we looked back, in clear blue light dotted by stars of surprising beam and yellowness, we saw the buildings orderly among their cedars, and we gulped in satisfaction at placing this landmark behind us.

"Clark," said Bar, "we've got to have food."

"We have it in our bundles."

"That's well enough if you want to chew up a mess of dry beans!"

Naomi pointed. "There's timberland ahead—a bank of it. Daren't we make a fire?"

Barstow adjusted the ropes of his pack and hooked them to the handle of his ax, close below the blade. That was the way he bore his burden, although I thought that it would have killed my shoulder to have done it. He frowned at the paling zenith; all of us saw the sky turning warm and ominous, and we knew that we must hide once more.

"It's a risk, folks, whichever we do! We can hunt for a nigger cabin and maybe see if they're Tories. Or we can get into the woods a good ways and hope nobody sees our smoke."

"I'm for doing that," I told Barstow, and Naomi Kincaid agreed. Then we were terrified by the sight of riders moving out from the village—a noisy blot of them, brown in the dawn—and one was laughing loudly as he rode. They headed north on the road which led from the heart of the hamlet, the road we had abandoned only a few moments before.

We ducked behind a fence and hurried north in a course parallel to that of the horsemen, but falling lower and lower as the ridge narrowed until we were out of their sight, fence or no fence. In this extremity we had nothing to say, but trooped along without further discussion, Barstow ahead and myself bringing up the rear.

We fell into a ravine and followed a creek that rose in the woods Naomi had pointed out. The vines were cruel; boundaries of the forest were alive with holly. Small trees, thickly-leaved, obstructed us severely. Minute by minute the gloom was lightening, even among the pines, and when we came upon an old cart-path we followed it without caution, so long as it twisted toward the north.

Studying the whole record of our journey, I cannot imagine just what our fate would have been had we chosen to lie down then and there, and wait (no matter how thorny our beds or how clamorous our stomachs) until another night. Perhaps we should have got off scot free; perhaps we should have been rooted out sooner or later. But we did not stop. . . . A coon-hound pealed forth on our right flank and slightly in the rear. At his outcry we increased our speed—until we rounded a curve and ran smack into three men, one on horseback and two afoot, who were every bit as surprised as we, although not as fearful.

They yelled, I think; I cannot be sure that any of us fugitives said a word. It was so long since I had worn a weapon that I never thought of my revolver until the capture was complete. My arms were pinioned in a second. Barstow had his ax wrenched from him and a rifle muzzle under his chin before the coon-hound, baying up to its master on some imagined trail of sport, had smashed through the shrubberies.

At this point the road became an open glade, where timber had been taken out long before. With the bright cobalt of the late dawn overhead, the astonishment of the three men had changed to warlike antagonism, all on an instant. One of us wore blue—they could see that—and it was enough. So we were captured, by what hands we had yet to learn, and Naomi dropped her bundle to the ground and sat upon it.

The coon-hound, a white-and-liver bitch who carried pups, went clamoring to the head of the glade, and back again. Each moment the day (which might well be the awful day of reckoning) stalked nearer: while we stood gaping, I saw a pink light on the skin of the man who sat mounted and confronting us.

He was elderly, white-haired but still erect and well-fleshed, his face truly distinguished; and he had a silver beard combed out to luxuriance. He wore an old shooting-coat stained by years of service, and a fine silver-mounted shotgun rested across the pommel of his saddle. First he had leveled this fowling-piece at our whole party, but shortened his aim to cover Naomi only, when the other men fell upon Barstow and me.

He still kept a ready hand around the stock, with finger inside the trigger guard.

I could not see the fellow who held me, but his arms were too strong for comfort. They squeezed like a corset of wire, pushing my elbows into my sides. The third man was as tall as I, and middle-aged, with a sallow face and brass-bowed spectacles from which one lens had been broken. But still he wore them, clamped tight on his nose; and he had ragged moustaches hanging like twin mink-tails from either side of his jaw.

It was his weapon, an old-fashioned rifle with a six-foot barrel, which threatened Prentiss Barstow.

"Little Victor," he called, "get that pistol!" and while one arm squeezed me tight, my assailant fumbled at my belt-buckle and got it loose.

"Now," said the man with the broken spectacles, "leave him come over here, beside this one!" Thus I was prodded to Barstow's side, whereat our captors called upon Naomi to join us. They dropped back a few paces and examined us with hostility, while the sun made a bonfire through the trees.

Little Victor was huger in frame than the man who had ordered him about, though he was young and gangling, and not more than seventeen years of age in spite of his six-feet-one. The two Victors (we learned that this was so, and Big Victor, smaller in size, was the father of the other one) wore trousers of Confederate cloth, nondescript hats, and identical jackets cut from a yellow horse-blanket. As for Little Victor, he had been unarmed until he acquired my revolver; and from his face I knew that he had long wished to own one.

"Mr. Summers, sir," he said, without turning his head, "do you reckon these are the Yankees?"

And now to our astonishment, the fine-faced man on the horse bent forward: a series of strange sounds, sibilant and painful, came from his beard. He seemed to open his mouth twice for every word he made, and God knows none of us could understand what he said. I might best describe his speech as something between a squeak and a hiss; but the two men on foot nodded slowly and knew what he was telling them.

Sometime later we saw bandages wound close about the old man's throat, and knew that he suffered from some injury or ailment of the larynx. As yet the light was not clear enough for us to fathom his incapacity—and so we gawked, all three in a row, like culprits waiting to be shot.

"Pappy," said Little Victor, "that one's a lady!"

Big Victor nodded. He shifted his rifle, though still covering us with it. He brought a plug of tobacco out of his pocket, and both he and his son bit off their morsels.

"Lady—" began Big Victor. "You *are* a lady, ain't you?"

Naomi said nothing; she risked death with her fool-hardiness. Their guns jerked quickly, and turning, I saw that she had sat upon her bundle again.

The old man turned his horse closer behind the two. He leaned out to speak again in the same mystic, hard-won syllables.

"Well, Mr. Summers, sir," replied Big Victor, "that ought to match up! There was supposed to be three of them at the Carpenters', according to what Mr. Pope told yesterday."

Once more the old man gave a series of suggestions or orders, at which Little Victor tucked the revolver into its holster and, reaching up, took the shotgun from Mr. Summers' saddle. He motioned us out into the center of the cart-path, whereat Mr. Summers' horse, an old chestnut stallion turning gray, became excited and waltzed in circles. Firm in the saddle, the invalid gentleman dressed the horse down, and brought him behind us docilely enough.

Barstow whispered to me, "Money," and then commenced to the enemy, "Look here, you bushwhackers! We'd like to talk a little—"

"No matter what you want to talk, it can wait," Big Victor growled at him. "Pick up your bundles and carry them."

"Stolen, too, I'll be bound," added the youth. "And don't call us bushwhackers no more. We're from Captain Argyle's Home Guards!"

Thus they marshalled us through the sunrise. They spoke sharply, threatening death the next time Barstow made as if to whisper to me. Still Naomi had nothing to say; from her eyes, set and brooding, I was sure that she contemplated some desperate escape.

The hound marched coolly at our heels, but Mr. Summers' stallion grew restless again, and presently he circled past us through the low bushes and cantered on into the north, whither the cart-path was taking us.

It was shortly before we reached the road bounding this forest, that I really came to myself. From the moment of our capture I had been in that state of blank amazement akin to fever, in which one lies idly and watches his body march through events of droll insignificance, no matter how badly he may be circumvented or betrayed. Like the others, I had counted every detail of our capture: had obeyed, had been made silent, even humble, and was now marching without protest to whatever doom these make-shift soldiers had in mind. And yet, until the sun got above the stump-ground in the east and burned my eyes and truly awakened me into this reddest of all Sabbath mornings, I felt no inclination to count the cost.

Realizing at last that Belle Island, or worse, was in store for us again (and Heaven knew what harsh discipline for Naomi Kincaid), I did not fear these men—not as I had feared the Federal straggler or the intent boys and cross-bred hounds who came after him. Set apart from the scene of our capture, watching it as I might have watched some uncouth Punch-and-Judy show, I had been amused at Little Victor's eagerness to don the revolver and the ammunition pouch, and I felt sorry for Mr. Summers because of his throat condition, and for Big Victor on account of his not having two lenses in his spectacles. This was romance, I had imagined, as in the records of highwaymen and Prince Charlie's patriots, which I read avidly until I joined the army. I was stupid and hungry enough to fancy that these people would feed us on the best they had; I had even planned French leave, if thus and so should come about, with a sentry overwhelmed by the winning way Naomi might be able to exercise upon him.

But my imaginings and dawn-dreams fell from me in the coldness, like the leaves and tufts of dirty straw scraped from our clothes by the bushes. I began to count the bitter price of our capture, and the sum total was staggering. Barstow mumbled beside me; his very respiration was furious and painful. But with the somber countrymen close upon him, he had to be as meek as Moses.

Led by Mr. Summers, we soon wheeled left on a narrow road which certainly would take us by roundabout fashion to Goochland Court House. There was no house at hand; more woods to the north looked warm and hospitable in the sunrise, and Barstow swore because we had not attained them.

We had not yet intercepted the main highway north of Goochland when we heard a tremendous yelling ahead, and a party of riders—the same who had frightened us as they burst from the village not long before—advanced at the gallop, threatening to pile in a horse-leg tangle at every second. There were five in the party, four of them being not more than fifteen or sixteen years old, and one a red-faced fellow with the soapy, squinting eyes and stable-bred smell of him who takes a bottle to bed.

They pulled in respectfully to let Mr. Summers ride through, which he did with a slight nod and lifting of his hand, but after that they closed around us and the two Victors. The fat fellow trampled too close to Naomi on his sprung-backed white mare, blind in one eye, and he roared, "Hang them up to dry! Nail them up to dry!" until Barstow had the boldness to strike his horse on the nose. The mare reared back; the fat man was nearly hurled into the ditch, and he assaulted us with an outpouring of threats and bad names.

At this display of resentment, the younger Guards ranged in front of us, holding their pistols and carbines ready and desiring to shoot us in our tracks. Discovering that one of us was a woman, they began to stare and giggle, and overwhelm the Victors with queries.

"Don't balk us in our business," said Big Victor, with the

way of authority. "Mr. Summers said to take them to Mr. Quarles's house, and that's what we'll do!"

"I'm for hanging them," retorted one of the boys, at which their rheumy-eyed elder compatriot set up his howl of nailing us to dry.

But both Big Victor and Little Victor shook their heads. "Mighty unwise for anybody to go against Mr. Summers," they said. So we were allowed to march on, now desperately worn from carrying our bundles so far and running so hard before we were caught, and feeling more angry than uneasy because of the whoops and hurrahs with which the Irregulars herded us.

At the juncture with the main road, Mr. Summers sat waiting, stern and disapproving. I thought from his mien that he would have rebuked the whole party, had his voice permitted it. But he merely motioned with a long finger, back toward the southeast where there was a small white house on a knoll to the right, and chimneys and cedar hedges of Goochland Court House swelling up behind it, gold-rinsed in the morning.

We reached the house in less than five minutes, Mr. Summers having ridden ahead to give the news of our coming. When we filed in at the gate we found that he had dismounted and was holding his horse's bridle, and conversing with the master of the house, whom we took to be the Mr. Quarles mentioned by the Victors. Mr. Quarles was a man of fifty who had lost most of his teeth and had cheeks shrunken in around his angular jaw-bones. His eyes were gray-green; he had a very direct gaze, and his face and neck were rutted in intricate wrinkles, weathered brown. He wore a suit of homespun, shabby but neat and clean, and he seemed not one with those sky-larking rustic soldiers, but more the stamp of Mr. Summers himself, no matter how modest his deportment.

Two other armed boys had been sitting on the wide front porch, and now came down to give us their scrutiny.

"Take the prisoners to the leaf-house, Big Victor," ordered Mr. Quarles. And when they had marched us to this structure (a tall, narrow shed of dressed logs with a snug roof and small apertures for ventilation, as commonly used throughout that region for the curing of tobacco) Mr. Quarles produced a key and with some difficulty opened the door on a black interior.

We would have taken our bundles with us but they said, "No, you don't!" and relieved us of them. So we were penned in darkness, until our eyes became accustomed to the gloom and we could make out the corners and walls, and the small quantity of tobacco in storage there.

Naomi was crying.

"I never thought you'd do that," said I.

She wept on for a time, but could say at last, "I'm relieved, that's all! I was certain they'd shut me away from you because I'm a woman, and we can't escape unless we're all together."

Barstow went to examining our prison. The whole posse of Irregulars skirmished outside, with much horseplay; and they hurled brutal forecast at us, through the logs, as to how we would look dangling from a gum-tree.

"Folks," I whispered, "there's not a man of them knows how to conduct a search."

"What say, Clark?"

"They never went through our pockets. I've still got that little knife."

Naomi cried, "And the money. Mercy sakes, they never took our money!"

She had the wad from the kitchen jelly-jar concealed somewhere about her, and her watch also, and now she produced the embroidery scissors and let us touch them to be reassured. Barstow had appropriated the five-hundred-and-five dollars, Confederate, which we found in the cavalry-man's pocket; he wore it pinned, as he confessed with embarrassment, in the band of his under-drawers. I had silver and greenbacks in my pocket.

We were debating as to whether we should conceal our capital in the building and trust to fortune that there would be an opportunity for us to retrieve it, when we heard the Guards set a curb on their boisterousness; the door opened again and we blinked into the face of Mr. Quarles.

"We want to talk to you," he said, not at all harshly.

"Who?" we asked, but he said, "All of you."

The boys and the mouthy fat man surrounded us on the way to the house. An old colored woman and a half-grown slave girl stood at the rear door; the woman was muttering vulgar threats against Yankees. "Anna," ordered her master, "take yourself off." Her small eyes red and spiteful, the slave stepped to the ground, and jerked the girl with her.

We were taken through a long kitchen which had a wide chimney at each end, but a fire was lit on only one hearth, and pots of different sizes steamed and bubbled close to the flames. Perhaps they would feed us, I thought—but no, we were sent into the front room where another fire burned on a narrower hearth, and Mr. Summers sat coughing beside it.

The room was plain and much used, with old-fashioned country furniture nicked and marred and scarred on every face. There were rag rugs on the floors—not enough of them— and a wildcat skin close to the hearth. The walls held two religious prints, a fine steel engraving of children being frightened by a lamb, and a framed scroll ornamented with cannon and flags, and colored by hand, which I took to be a company roster. There were neat cotton curtains at two of the windows, though the others were bare. Spindling, half-blighted geraniums grew from pots on a shelf at the southern window.

"Remain standing," commanded Mr. Quarles. So we stood, with the Home Guards crowding the door behind us; looking back, I saw one of them steal johnnycake from a pan in the kitchen, and I wished he had the human decency to share it with me.

Mr. Quarles did not observe the theft, though he had his own ideas about what sort of court he wished to conduct, and he sent the youths packing. "You stay, Victor Parrish, and that boy of yours," he said. "I understand you made the capture. . . . The rest of you go out in the yard—"

Mr. Summers motioned to him, and spoke briefly in his ghostly whisper.

"—and less sky-larking, if you please!" added Mr. Quarles. "This is a serious affair." His words had little effect, for we heard the whole party yelping as soon as they were past the kitchen door.

Now the Victors sat guarding us, one at either door. Little Victor was so interested in examining the mechanism of the revolver that I thought seriously of attempting to snatch it from him.

Mr. Quarles pulled out a center-table less scarred than the others, and placed it so that Mr. Summers might rest his arms upon it. The latter had provided himself with a notebook in the shape of a yellow ledger. He had a lead pencil, and from time to time he made notations. Mr. Quarles seated himself on a hassock close beside the gray-bearded 'squire and together they eyed us for a season—so pontifical and all-seeing in their manner that I felt naked, and wished that we had more of such men on our side of the contention.

"Your names," Mr. Quarles spoke at last. When we had given them, he went into a whispered conversation with Mr.

Summers, during which I heard the word "Carpenter" mentioned again. He turned back and motioned at me with his thumb. "Are you the man named Clark?"

"I am."

"Did you leave a letter at the house of Henry Carpenter?"

"Yes, sir."

Barstow growled at me, "I wouldn't 'sir' him—not if they shot me for it!" But I continued the address for all that; there was a compelling austerity about the man.

"Who was that other Yankee at the Carpenter house?" and when I asked what other man he meant, he said, "The one who was murdered."

"I killed him," said Barstow. "Are you going to hang me for it?"

Mr. Summers held further squeaking discussion with the master of the house. About this time an inner door opened behind us, and when we turned nervously, we saw a little black-clad woman with smooth gray hair, slip quietly into the room from a bedchamber beyond. She sat on a corded chair, and throughout the rest of the interview remained there motionless, looking at the floor most of the time and holding her red, work-worn hands neatly folded in her lap.

"The man named Clark," said Quarles. "You will answer all questions for a time, sir!"

I said, "If you are acquainted with the letter I left at the house—the place you say was the Carpenter house—you are acquainted with the facts. You will admit there was no compulsion about my leaving that letter."

"This man whom your friend killed—tell us more about him." So accordingly I gave a brief account of how the cavalryman had come back and besieged the house, and us in it, and how he met his death. I told them, too, about the room upstairs; they sat without interrupting me. The face

of Mr. Quarles was expressionless, though Mr. Summers
looked ill and horrified once or twice.

I say they did not interrupt me while I was in the midst
of my recital, but once Mr. Quarles arose silently, brought
a chair forward so that Naomi could sit upon it, and went
back to his hassock without pausing to acknowledge her
thanks.

He began, when I had concluded: "You say that you
were incarcerated at Belle Isle. Tell us briefly about how you
managed your escape. I warn you, if you withhold any information about collusion with guards, it will be found out
sooner or later. You'll suffer accordingly."

I cried, "Nobody helped us! The guards tried to kill us,
and they did kill at least two."

"This woman. Did she meet you after you left the
Island, by previous arrangement?"

When I turned, not knowing what to say nor how much
of Naomi's own history I should give, she motioned me
aside and left her chair. She advanced to the table and stood
looking down at Mr. Summers, addressing her remarks to
both but always looking at him.

"I didn't know these Yankees," she said, quietly. "I
never set eyes on them until Thursday morning. I was outside Richmond, near the fortifications, when we met. I had
every reason to get away from Richmond. If you return us
there, you'll find out soon enough why I left. That is all,
gentlemen."

They palavered for a time. Mr. Summers had another
fit of coughing, whilst Naomi returned to her chair and sat
with her jaw hard, watching the steel engraving above the
mantelpiece and seeming to disapprove of it. At length the
man Quarles asked us if we were hungry, and we were so
distraught that Barstow and I laughed wildly and made jokes
about it.

The woman in black went into the kitchen, and in another moment Quarles had the two Victors take us there. We were seated, all on one side at a long deal table, with the guards watching us and chewing tobacco in unison. The negro woman gave us each a large bowl of mush and thin milk, with a small quantity of brown sugar, which tasted very good. She brought bread, too, and a sour preserve made from plums.

When the meal was concluded (and speedily enough) our jailer—or our host, since I hardly know which to call him— had us conducted back into the front room. Mr. Summers had been writing a letter. He was folding it when we came in, and Mr. Quarles held a stick of brown sealing-wax into the fireplace until it was soft enough to use. He gave this letter to the youth called Little Victor, whispering a few words we could not hear, and Little Victor rode away in a hurry on Mr. Summers' stallion.

"Now," said Quarles, singling out Naomi, "you are to stay in the house—"

The look she gave us told me, for the first time, that in three perilous days Barstow and I had become her people.

Mr. Quarles saw the look. Though he could not understand all of it, he attributed her dismay to the fear of what might happen to her. "Young woman, my wife will see that you meet with no harm, and so will I!" He added, as serious afterthought, "Not today, at least." Turning to the little wife in black who had followed us from the kitchen, he asked, "Carrie, is there a lock to Thomas's room?"

The wife nodded.

"Then see that she's locked in safely, and Victor Parrish can guard the stairway. As for you two," he said, turning to Barstow and me, "you'll have to go back to the leaf-house."

Accordingly, we were marched away, with Naomi looking anxiously after us. I think we felt sullen and personally

resentful, for the first time since our capture. We were
heartened by the sight of our three bundles ranged against
the wall in a kitchen pantry where we had not seen them
before, and apparently they were not yet tampered with.
But Barstow said that if the old slave got her claws in them,
there'd be little of value left, and we would shoulder addi-
tional blame, should authorities press a special charge of
plundering against us.

Once more in the tobacco shed, we settled ourselves on
the floor; we were so gloomy that we could scarcely speak.
It was cold, and we wished for our blankets. In his rummag-
ings Barstow had found a tatter of canvas much folded and
full of tobacco siftings, which seemed to be part of an old
wagon cover. We wrapped the relic around us and huddled
against the wall, listening to the Irregulars outside. They
pitched horseshoes for a time, but Mr. Quarles came out
and stopped them. When we heard him assert his authority
we learned that he held the rank of lieutenant in this band
of Home Guards.

He sent home our personal enemy, the fat man with
the bleary face; we wished that we could have seen him
doing it, even through the narrowest crack. "Claybaugh,"
he cried, "I thought you were drunk before, and now I
know it!"

The man wheedled and whined; the younger guards
tittered; but Mr. Quarles would have no excuses, and drove
him off the place. "None of your sass, Claybaugh," he said.
"I'll report you to Captain Argyle if you show your face outside, this day. What if the Reverend found you here on duty
in this condition?"

We tried to see what we could, through chinks and vent-
holes, but the day outside grew overcast; our spirits were
equally somber. The logs were thick; the door a strong one,
and the boys in the yard would surely have enjoyed shooting

us. So there was no dream of flight any longer, and I could only wonder how Naomi was faring in the upstairs bedroom, and whether the silent farm wife sat in her jail to keep her company.

It seemed half a day later, though perhaps but two or three hours, when the guards went away from our vicinity in a body, leaving only one of their number behind. We heard the solitary youth on the log step outside, humming lugubriously to himself, and presently we realized that he was carving at the wood with a jack-knife, perhaps cutting his initials in the jamb as boys are bound to do. But above and beyond the scraping sound he made, we heard other noises: the indefinite chatter and trampling of women as well as men, accompanied by the laughter of children and loud crying of one child. Since we had seen no children about the place (except for the Home Guards themselves, who were little more than that), we could not imagine what sort of convocation was in order—unless it was intended to hang us immediately, with the entire village looking on.

A mule brayed, wheels squeaked and rattled, and two men came behind the tobacco house to perform a private act. When they returned to the front, they questioned the guard:

"Are they in there, sure enough?"

"Two of them. The woman's up yonder."

"I reckon," said one, "that Leander Argyle will string them up pretty smart, soon as he gets back."

But the other man, whom I blessed, disparaged him. "He couldn't do it without orders from Richmond, Hazey. Not possibly." And then they went away, arguing about it.

Mr. Quarles appeared, with three of his soldiers. He unlocked the door and let us step outside, and this time the youths examined us for weapons. They took my little kitchen

knife, but none of the money from my pockets, and they did
not find Barstow's roll of bills.

The sky was heavy and dun-colored; it looked like a
summer sky presaging rain and humidity. But the March
wind still whipped out of the northwest, keen and shrill, and
Mr. Quarles let Barstow go back into the leaf-house for our
canvas covering.

At the side of the residence, crowding over into the front
yard where we could not see them, was an assemblage of
people—men and women accompanied by their children.
Several mules, saddle horses, and other teams with wagons
were tied along the fence.

"We are about to have divine service," said Quarles.
"Every human being has got such need. I would be the last
to say you Yankees didn't need the Word." He hesitated,
looking first at Barstow and then at me, and asked suddenly
if either of us was a Roman Catholic. When we said no, but
confessed to being a Baptist and a Presbyterian, he told us
that the people of his group were followers of Alexander
Campbell; although there was that in his explanation which
made me feel that they were not true Disciples of Christ,
but a group of mild dissenters. Their church, he said, had
recently been burned, and we could attend the service held
in his own front yard if we would conduct ourselves decently, and listen with open hearts to what was said.

So we went along after him, the two of us side by side,
with the canvas dangling across our shoulders to keep off the
wind, and the guards prodding us with their guns now and
then when they thought it safe to do so. The congregation
gave us all too much attention, and we could hear the nearer
people muttering that we were not fit to be among them in
this event. God knows we tried to be bold enough and to give
them stare for stare. Two little boys and a girl got behind
the fence and pelted us with stones, until admonished

shrilly by their mother and exiled to a cart far down the line.

There were stumps in the yard, and some flower-borders made of stone, high enough for people to sit upon. However, the women sat on the steps all together, and their daughters with them—a custom no longer practiced at my home. The rest of us stood there in the wind. Barstow and I looked for Naomi to appear, but she did not come. Perhaps it was because the Quarleses felt that her attire would disrupt the meeting.

They began by singing:

> "Won't you come over and help us?
> Sinners and wicked are we,"

and neither Barstow nor I knew it, and probably would not have sung if we had. Mr. Summers sat on the porch in a chair brought from the living room; the minister sat near him, with Mr. Quarles and two other men whom we had not seen before.

I can shut my eyes now, and recreate them all: the shabby women in their capes and shawls, and some of them wearing sun-bonnets even in March; the wan-faced little children staring at us steadily, moment after moment, as if hell and the devil were far-away mischiefs, but Yankees you dared not let out of your sight; and I remember the minister, who mentioned twice during his sermon that he had been a student at Bethany College, and seemed proud to mention it. He was young and owl-eyed, with a sparse beard. He was thin like many of the Island prisoners—undoubtedly a consumptive, for he had the hot, dull red in his cheeks that nature should never have wanted there.

He read the eleventh chapter of First Corinthians complete. I began to think of Naomi Kincaid and how she had cut off her hair, when he got to the sixth verse: "For if a woman be not covered, let her also be shorn: but if it be a shame for a woman to be shorn or shaven, let her be covered."

I strayed away with Naomi, and Barstow was not with us ... we wandered in a new little nightmare all our own, until the minister was well toward the end of his reading, and informed us that when we are judged, we are chastened of the Lord. He closed his Bible with a bang which made us jump, and launched eagerly into a discussion of the Apostle Paul and his relations with the men of Corinth—a sermon which must have been days in the preparing.

He came back to Virginia and the needs of his flock only at long last, and then it was to remind them that there were scarce two years in which to prepare themselves for Christ's inspection. Alexander Campbell had informed the world that Our Lord would be here in the year 1866.

Then he prayed. Much to Barstow's astonishment and mine, he prayed for us. It afforded a melancholy augury when he spoke of the two enemies who might meet their Maker sooner than the rest. Apparently he knew nothing of Naomi, locked in Thomas's bedroom upstairs; or if he did, he considered her not worth praying for, as she had traveled about brazenly in male attire. Then some one struck up another hymn, "Let the New Lights shine out," and I remembered hearing that the followers of Campbell had once been known as the New Lights.

Mr. Quarles ordered us back to the leaf-house. The church meeting was at an end, and little boys raced each other to see who could get to the door before we did. Sealed once more in the snuffy darkness, we waited for food, not daring to believe that these people would offer us the Bread of Life without other bread as well; and when the food finally came it was good, but there was not enough of it.

2

As I consider that afternoon we spent, Barstow and I, locked in the shed together, I wonder that we did not clutch each other by the throat, and settle our rivalry before it even came about. Yet I am conjecturing out of later knowledge and experience; there was then little reason for either of us to guess what discoveries the other had made within himself.

But Barstow prophesied what was to transpire, with a rareness of vision I would not have attributed to him. In this bitter exigency, I did not suppose that there would be a chance for his forecast to take shape as the monstrosity which we two would make of it.

"Clark," he said, when an hour had gone by, and we had talked lugubriously of our recapture, "in some ways I reckon it's just as well."

"No. Anything's better than the Island."

"Well, it would be a bad problem."

I knew well enough what he meant, but I kept after him with the savage persistence with which a morose person gratifies his cruelty, drawing forced explanation from one who is made inarticulate by nature or by emotional stress. "Problem?" I echoed. "What's a worse problem than trying to get away from the Island? We'll never manage it a second time."

"Well, I was thinking about her, Clark."

"Yes," I said, "if she killed the colonel, perhaps they'll hang her for it."

There he was, wrapped in the same cloth which wrapped

me and which had been a comfort bought by his own ingenuity; and yet I plagued him into unwilling confession, perhaps because I did not have to look at his face, though benefited by the warmth of his body as I had been benefited before.

"I didn't mean that! I meant if these bushwhackers hadn't gobbled us up the way they did—"

I cried, "You mean you're glad we were captured?"

He swallowed again and again, and shifted his legs into a position away from mine. "Two men and one woman. I reckon that's a problem, any time."

I lied, "Bar, that's something I hadn't thought about," and the walls slapped the falsehood back into my ears.

Barstow got up, leaving the canvas behind him, and went exploring into the gloom. He had his hands against the logs, sounding them to see if one might be looser than the rest; yet there was no purpose in his doing so, since we knew that our jail was all too secure.

"Clark," he cried, from the farthest corner, "I reckon that's a lie. You must have thought about it, or else you ain't the man I think you are!" And then, considering more and more the truth of his own challenge, he built a case against me: "I reckon you've thought about it over and over, just like I have."

"I've thought about freedom. I've thought about the Union lines."

Having assured himself just how I felt, he would only laugh at me. "Oh, I'm not educated, Clark! I didn't go to no academy, and I never read a novel in my life. I never read much of anything except the Bible, and Rollo, and newspapers once in a while. I never set eyes on Shakespeare until I met you on the Island. But don't keep treating me like a plain fool, because I'm not one."

Outside, the guard banged at the door and told us to quit

talking. Barstow only swore, and I reached over and beat on the drum-head of the door in derision. For the barest second we captives were comrades again, facing an opposition presented against us both, but when the boy outside fell silent (not knowing how to deal with the situation, and choosing to ignore it) we aimed our suspicion again.

"You talk about my being a man," I said to Barstow. "What kind of a man do you think you are? All you can care about is a full meal. Do you think any woman would look at you, or look at me either?"

"Well, she looked at us, and she was willing to come along. She'd rather be with us than with that rebel colonel, wouldn't she?"

"I don't know."

"She stabbed him. She stabbed him with those little shears—"

"Maybe she did, but there was something queer about it. She was frightened, but don't think she didn't like him well enough to live with him!"

He stood above me: the vaguest sort of shape, more felt than seen, and yet I was convinced that he towered with his fists clenched. "You won't admit the truth, Clark. Well, I'll admit it for you. You've looked upon her, the same as I have."

"What difference does it make, now?"

He was silent for a long time. At length he sat down beside me and wrapped the canvas around him; as a gesture of surrender and forgiveness and admission, I gave him more than his full share of cloth. "Oh, I can't say that it does make any difference," he muttered. "It would make a sight of difference if we went on traveling."

In that instant I dreamed of a thousand men coughing on Belle Isle, and the coughs of Barstow and myself were as racking and hopeless as any. So I fell silent, pretending that the two of us traveled to our liberty, sharing the woman between us (with her quite willing to be shared); and shrinking back in revulsion, at last knowing that it was not a true picture of what would have occurred, I found contentment in making a romance, high-sounding and decorated, out of the shabby encounter which had terminated our excursion.

I had read a romance not many weeks since, or at least part of it. Since our reading matter on the Island was limited, I had committed much of the romance to memory. It was from the pen of Mr. Wilkie Collins and came printed in a copy of *Harper's Weekly* for January 24, 1863; and it was past imagining how those sixteen pages of type had survived for a year to find their way southward, in the pocket of a newly captured Federal musician.

Yet I owned the paper which I had traded for some leaves from the Bible, our ordinary stock-in-trade, and all our tent devoured it eagerly. We got more than the prescribed six cents of benefit from the study.... The pages wore thin and separated into bits, along folds fuzzy from much handling. A few pages survived up to the week of our escape, and those were the ones I committed to memory.

I remembered a stirring picture in which the ironclad *Monitor* was in the process of shipwreck, carrying its doomed crew to the bottom; and there were parlor or floor skates for sale, warranted to work with the best, and having their wheels arranged by fours; and an advertisement of a manufacturer whom Barstow and I considered associating ourselves with professionally, if and when we could get a letter through to him. *AGENTS. SOLDIERS in camp or discharged, can make easily $15 per day selling our GREAT NEW and WONDERFUL UNION PRIZE and STATIONERY PACKAGES*, etc. We concluded that fifteen dollars per day would go a long way towards stocking our larder, and there were greenbacks circulating on the Island, though few of them came our direction. And passing from contemplation of riches to be gained by this method, I committed a good share of Wilkie Collins' tale. It was entitled "No Name," and the heroine was a woman of character and spirit.

Now I could quote with bigoted satisfaction, a bit which might be an appropriate epitaph for any one of us, and an ornate valedictory to our enterprise: *The end I dreamed of has come. Nothing is changed but the position I once thought we might hold to each other. Better as it is, my love—far, far better as it is!*

So I kept wondering about the romance in which we had found ourselves involved by this second capture (unlike my capture during the Mine Run campaign, when a rebel hit me on the nose while two other rebels held me and ravaged my pockets, all in the same instant). I recollected further remarks from *Harper's Weekly,* and tried to make myself believe them, although wondering whether Mr. Wilkie Collins had ever been captured by Home Guards in the woods when he was tired and hungry.

Our four-day record of jeopardy, inscribed across two Virginia counties, would never be broached for the readers of *Harper's Weekly.* And still it would be published to us, I thought, in our resounding memory, throughout all future privations.

Barstow snored, dragging more and more of the thin cover away from me—until I sat denuded of it, but feeling no worse chill than I had felt before. My imaginings were my cloak again, as they have been the blanket or bread or dungeon-light of prisoners since the world began; I wound myself closely in them. Thus laced in invisibility, I was able to stalk through the thickness of the logs and across the littered farmyard; I scaled the house walls to Naomi's window, went in and found her there on the high bed of some vanished denizen by the name of Thomas, and I lay down beside her and whispered, "It's Ollie, Naom. Didn't you think I'd come?" I whispered it again and again, and finally spoke aloud, and then I was shouting. But no one heard my words clearly enough to sense their import—not even the men downstairs—and Naomi would not listen to the most appealing whisper in my solicitation.

3

About ten or eleven o'clock, as nearly as we could estimate, we heard a great deal of whispering outside. From the sounds which followed, we judged that our guard had been changed. There were divers ways in which we could sense as much: the former sentry had bounced his gun-butt on the door-sill every minute or two, and there was no noise of this kind any longer. Too, the picket who came to relieve him did a great deal of throat-clearing, and it struck me that recently I had known some one with the same mannerism.

We had received no attention for some hours, except that a bucket of water was handed in to us. We grew restless in the grasp of absolute darkness, and again turned surly, though we did not talk much. Another fifteen minutes went by; then, simultaneously with the arrival of two other persons, the guard unlocked and opened the door.

"Little Victor!" said Barstow, recognizing him.

"We want you at the house," came Mr. Quarles' voice. Big Victor was with him, holding his rifle at the ready.

We came out, shivering, into lesser darkness of the farm-yard. There were lights in the kitchen which faced us. The windows of the second story were not lit up; we supposed that Naomi was prisoned in black solitude as we had been. We marched willingly, though stiff at the knees from much sitting and from ancient aches and pains which fell upon us more in that tobacco-house than they had in the unroofed woodlands. There might have been opportunity for us to break away and run for it, but there were three partners to our ill-fated enterprise, and one waited in the house.

They threw open the kitchen door, and we were welcomed by smells of frying meat and barley-coffee. The old slave woman looked up, at the edge of the fireplace flame; her eyes caught the gleam from candles and fire, and menaced us accordingly. Then I spoke out, not knowing what I said, for Naomi sat on a stool beside the table.

Her gaze was calm and steady, her lips twitched in a tight smile. Looking behind her, I saw Mrs. Quarles in the shadows, with a handkerchief against her nose. Now, close following the gratification which sprang up when I saw Naomi Kincaid, came an ominous fear that Mrs. Quarles mourned because one as beautiful as Naomi (no matter what laws or ethics she had violated) was well on the road to being hanged.

I could not see Barstow's face; he was ahead of me, but he stepped forward as if he would have grasped Naomi by the arm. Little Victor jerked out the revolver, and ordered him back. With him out of my way and the guards drawn aside as well, I observed that the Quarleses were not alone with their slaves and the two guards named Parrish.

On the farther side of the table sat a slender, middle-aged man who held a wide-brimmed black hat on the board in front of him, and turned it round and round like a toy. Although the firelight was ruddy over us—redder than any sunset, ominous and intent—the face of this stranger was the waxy face of a corpse in its casket. He looked at us, Barstow and me, with a blank indifference which was in no way casual, but the product of some secret compulsion. He had a shabby coat of woolen plaid, loose-hung around his shoulders and falling back against the chair on one side; his face was smooth-shaven except for whiskers in a square patch below the chin, and he was as bald as an egg.

"Sit down on this bench by the door," Quarles directed us, but the man across the table shook his head slowly. I thought that he was watching through the thickest haze that ever sat upon a human mind.

"No," he said, "bring them closer, Mr. Quarles," and so we were allowed to take stools along the table, a few feet distant from Naomi.

Behind us, the door had been shut and barred; Little Victor made a great to-do about jamming the bar into place. I wondered what had become of Mr. Summers, and concluded that he must have gone to his home before this, since he was in no way a healthy man, and Heaven knew what the night air would do to him. But much to our surprise, he was aroused from the front room by the thudding of the great wooden bar; he entered slowly, his throat still close-wrapped in its bandages. He stopped behind the bald-headed man opposite us. We endured their combined scrutiny until, with all those odors of cooking, and the horrid certainty of Belle Island in the future, I wanted to whoop aloud.

"These are the men, sir," said Mr. Quarles.

Big Victor went to the foot of the table and stood there, with his gun in his hands.

"You came to my house?" inquired the bald stranger.

We looked at him, not understanding, until Mr. Quarles bent forward and whispered, "This is Mr. Henry Carpenter, in whose house you spent the night," and thus we stared fearfully into the patient eyes of him whom we had robbed and avenged.

At length he lifted his head, and nodded. "Their tale must be true, Quarles. Neither would fit the description."

"Did you see the body?" asked Mr. Quarles.

Mr. Carpenter leapt suddenly to his feet, upsetting the stool, and he stood there for a moment, pounding his blunt fists together. Behind him, old Mr. Summers fumbled around, trying to reach the stool. At last, mastering his agitation, Carpenter himself recovered the stool. He pulled it upright, and sat down again. "I haven't been back to the house—not yet. Gilbert brought me the note."

From an inside pocket he produced the letter which I had written and left in our awful refuge. For a moment, indeed, I did not recognize the note, dirtied as it was by much handling, and creased and re-creased in a dozen different directions.

He patted the paper against the table top; and Mrs. Quarles left the room suddenly.

"Which one of you shot the hound?" he asked.

I nodded, but found it difficult to speak.

"Why didn't you shoot Gilbert?"

I thought of the boy in his grotesque overcoat, the boy who had trailed us through that orchard and across the field, two days before, but I could not yet frame an answer.

"The boy with the dog—that was my son Gilbert."

"There was one named Paul..."

He nodded, but again asked me, "Why?"

"Well," I said, "he was just a youngster."

"You shot the hound, easily enough."

"Yes, but—"

Barstow cried, "God damn it, what's all this business about?"

I thought they would drag him back to the leaf-house, or perhaps gag him at once, but nothing of the kind happened. Instead, Mr. Carpenter turned and looked at Barstow as vaguely as he had been looking at me. "I take it," he said, "that you're the one who had the ax."

His round chin began to tremble, and the little beard with it. We had that stark, comfortless embarrassment which comes upon men, when another man breaks into tears. Mr. Carpenter bent one arm on the table top and put his head down against it, and we shifted uneasily, and then remained very quiet. We could hear an old clock ticking somewhere.

Mr. Quarles tiptoed down the room and muttered to the two negroes, who began to dish up food from the pans at the fireplace.

In another minute or two, Henry Carpenter got control of his emotions, and sat up to face us. He took out a crumpled red handkerchief and wiped his eyes, though there were no tears in them. "Quarles," he said, unevenly, "they can have it all."

"I don't think that's wise, sir!" replied our jailer.

"Then you never had a daughter," said Mr. Carpenter.

Old Mr. Summers started around the table, beckoning to Mr. Quarles, and our jailer went forward. There was no sound for a time except that grave-voice, the anguished conversation of the man who talked without the physical implements which nature had provided and taken away from him again; and the spoon scraped at the pans, and Naomi bent down and rested her head in her arms, much as Mr. Carpenter had done.

"Well, sir," said Mr. Quarles, "Mr. Summers is for it, too. But there'd be trouble, if word of this got about. You mean, I suppose, that you want these people to be turned loose?"

Mr. Carpenter told him, "I don't care if they're Yankees, ten thousand times over."

"What about the woman?"

"What about her?" repeated Henry Carpenter. "I don't know what about her, sir, and I don't care. I have nothing but envy for any of them!" His voice went higher on the last phrase; he screamed, "Oh, God, why did I ever leave them? Why did I ever go to the mill?" Groping to his feet, he got up and disappeared into the front room.

The table, the staring faces, the fire itself, all melted and commingled before my eyes. I heard Barstow breathing heavily; I tried to look at Naomi, but could not single her out from the desperate, swimming illusions.

"Victor Parrish," I heard Mr. Quarles saying, "you and your son, both—we'll have to trust you," and I heard Big Victor answer in a monosyllable which must have been a satisfactory response. When my vision cleared, I saw Mr. Quarles down by the fireplace, standing with his muscular arms straight at his sides. He was looking into the faces of the two slave women. He said nothing that I could hear; but they muttered earnestly, punctuating their remarks with appeals to their Creator. A new, fearful sweat gleamed on the older woman's forehead.

Barstow whispered, "Clark, it's not reasonable. They won't do this!" But indeed he believed that they were going to, and presently he dug out the money from his drawers and offered it to Mr. Quarles.

"I won't hang on to this—not if you're going to let us loose!" and he was all for forcing it into the man's hand.

"Is that Confederate money?" asked the householder. When Barstow said that it was, and that we had even more, Mr. Quarles only shrugged. "I'm sorry to say that it's more worthless each day. Half the people won't accept it; we rely mainly on barter, in these parts. You may as well keep it, since he wants you to. I believe that Mr. Carpenter will be little the poorer."

They fed us; we ate corn-bread and fried spare-ribs, and drank quantities of barley-coffee. The two Victors had plates of their own at the other end of the table, where they ate every bit as heartily as we, though Little Victor regarded me sourly throughout the meal.

Mr. Quarles and the dignified Summers did some more private planning in a far corner of the room. The result of it was that they sent Big Victor Parrish away before he had finished his meal, and the rest of us settled into the most appalling siege of silence I have ever experienced. It seemed an hour later when Big Victor returned; without more ado, they motioned for us to follow him out of the kitchen door. Mr. Summers stayed behind. The last we saw of him was the sparkle of firelight on his silver beard—he seemed a figure carved out by the ancients, stern and prophetic, but with an air of forgiveness about him.

Mr. Quarles and Little Victor brought up the rear, as we slid and stumbled until we reached the front road. There a prodigious shape loomed before us. When a lantern was hoisted on high, and lowered again into the hands of Big Victor, we saw that this towering shape was a wagon covered with canvas, with a broad-shouldered negro on the driver's seat. He had a three-horse team harnessed up in a fashion unknown to me, and to Barstow as well, for I remember that Barstow commented upon it several times.

I turned, and asked Mr. Quarles in a voice as level as I could make it, "What are you doing with us? I thought we were to be set free."

He hesitated; the lantern-light did not extend as high as his face and I had no clue as to his emotions. "We can't turn you out, not in these parts," he said. "Our boys would pick you up in no time. You'll be taken north to the county line. That's what Mr. Carpenter asked, and Mr. Summers sent this wagon and the boy to take you."

Barstow put one foot on the wagon-wheel, and then stopped. "What about our packs?"

"That's right," said Mr. Quarles, quickly. He sent Little Victor back to the house for them, and they were handed into the wagon. The ax came as well, but Mr. Quarles whispered to the driver, and the slave put the ax under his feet in front.

"You have your instructions, Parrish," said Mr. Quarles. The two Victors climbed aloft, and disappeared into the equipage. Naomi put her hands on my shoulders. I grasped her around the waist, and Barstow reached over quickly to

share in assisting her. Between us we lifted her bodily, and
it was the most urgent summoning of strength in which our
arms had indulged; my shoulders ached for hours afterward.

Another light advanced from the house—a candle in a
home-made tin lantern, and Mrs. Quarles was carrying it.
She had something folded over her arm.

"Give this to her," she said to her husband. "Thomas used
to have it on his bed." Without a word, her husband passed
the thing to Naomi. It turned out to be a kind of shawl or
coverlet, home knit of rough wool, and dyed black. It was
kind of them to give the shawl—more kind than we then
realized, for that night Big Victor told us that Thomas
Quarles had been killed at Cedar Mountain.

Now Barstow and I joined the others, our ears ringing
with the drunkenness of a freedom so newly awarded (one to
which we did not hold the title we had established for that
earlier freedom, won solely by our own efforts and not
through the charity of others). Still the driver did not speak
to his horses. We waited in silence, the wagon cover flapping
on its bows.

We were waiting as the Quarleses waited, for a last inspection by the citizen whose disaster had, in its roundabout
way, been our gain. He must have known that we waited for
him; perhaps he was standing near the porch all the time.
For presently he came down from the house into the frail,
insignificant light. We saw its yellowness gleaming on his
bald head; he still held the hat in his hands. When he spoke,
his voice was more impressive than we had heard it, sea-
soned by some fervency within himself.

"Trouble may come of this," he said, "but we're acting
as we believe best. Isn't that so, Mr. Quarles?"

I do not believe that Quarles approved of granting us
our liberty, though God knows we had established the right-

eousness of our claim as decent men; and we were no common marauders, however desperate and unshaven we seemed. ... Henry Carpenter said something else, but we could not tell what it was. A signal was given; the horses settled into their collars, and we started north through the overcast, windy darkness of a new journey.

We rode as free men and free woman, in a more sublime state than we had traveled before. We had walked on sore feet and sprawled in the mud-holes, to be apprehended in the end for all our striving; and now the very people who had beset our path, were an accessory to salvation. Naturally we could not believe it, in our hearts. We expected to awaken from our dream, behind locked doors.

I touched Barstow's foot, I felt the elbow of Naomi Kincaid. They were an active part of creation, they were flesh and bone and cloth; and surely those were the two Victors, chewing tobacco up there beyond, and not exchanging a word for three miles at least. Reason could not persuade me. I sat up stiff and fearful, doubting that such generosity might develop without treachery attached to it.

But, swinging among the ruts and pitching down each precipitous slope, with the wooden brakes screaming against the wagon wheels—a few miles of this, and the very persistency of our journey was convincing in itself.

Barstow was the first to speak. He amazed us by the manner of his address, requesting, as he did, tobacco. Tobacco had once played its part in our scheme, but I had not yet experienced the reawakening of any desire to smoke, and chewing was beyond me. Beyond Barstow, too, as yet; for he crawled back to the tail-board after five minutes, and got rid of it. Nevertheless, he had broken the ice, and now he began to talk with the Victors. They were averse to answering even the most casual queries, at first, but seemed to take courage from each new question we put to them. Before another hour went by we had gained a good share of their confidence.

They told us about their home near the Quarles place, and how a pest killed their hop vines but still they had plenty of sweet potatoes and a fair crop of corn; and about the two mules they owned; and how the wife of Big Victor had died from bowel affliction two years previously. Big Victor had been a soldier in the army of the rebel General Johnson, and he had fought in the Peninsular campaign. He got a fever, and was sent home, and would just as soon not return to service in the line, although his son aspired to join the raider Mosby, if ever he got the chance.

And they cleared up some points which had plagued us in the last hour at the Quarles house. From what they had overheard between Messrs. Summers and Quarles and Henry Carpenter (at least as much as they were willing to tell), we reckoned more accurately the history of that farmhouse on the ridge; we pieced it together with what we already knew, and in later conversation we had the events well mapped, though bewildered by Mr. Carpenter's charity, and wondering how mere revenge could give rise to it.

A large force of Federal cavalry had gone through Goochland county the previous Tuesday, and among other property destroyed by them had been a mill belonging to Mr. Carpenter, near a place called Manikin's Bend. Word of this incursion being brought to him, Mr. Carpenter had ridden hastily to the scene; the wild straggler came, in his absence, to find the house occupied by Mrs. Carpenter and a young daughter, defenseless before him.

The boy Gilbert, lone survivor of three sons (the other two having died of disease in the army) was a member of the Home Guards, and had taken to the woods with his fellows in order to pester the Union advance. The New York cavalryman did not linger overnight at the Carpenter's, but went preying into the neighborhood; and the woman and her daughter fled to the nearest village as soon as they were able.

The story of their calamity was cried around, and Gilbert Carpenter and his friend Paul were but two of dozens who took up the search. They were no Pinkerton men, but they could reason that not sufficient time had elapsed, between the soldier's return flight to the farmstead and their finding of his body there, for a letter such as ours to have been written. Accordingly, they took the thing at face value, although regretting the loss of their hound, and they carried the letter to Manikin's Bend.

The country was in arms that next night, as we had guessed. The rumor went out that more Yankees were prowling close, and it is a wonder that the bare facts of the story ever got as far as Goochland Court House without more distortion. It is a wonder, too, that the Victors or Mr. Summers did not shoot us in our tracks, when first we came upon them. But in their zeal to save us for appropriate justice, if indeed we had been guilty of heinous crime, they unwittingly worked out our salvation.

A crime of gross nature is indeed a logical by-product of war itself, for no moral qualification contributes to the making up of armies; the orang-outangs are gathered in with the men. Now I marvel that I did not hear more of such things during my years of campaigning, and I feel a certain fright this day (possessing children of my own) which was not equalled in that overcast hour when the red-headed man scrambled through the window, and Barstow wielded his ax.

We had done, with dispatch, what half a county longed to do. Or Barstow had done it—he saved our skins with his ax-blunt, more surely than if he had dictated a commutation in the office of Jefferson Davis himself. There was some fas-

cinated envy, accounting for this illegal parole they gave us
... in the dead of night, I used to wonder what had happened to the carcass of the New Yorker, when I heard how
the body of a man like Colonel Dahlgren was thrown into
a hog-lot and stripped of its clothes. There is a relentless
understanding between political enemies of a decent stripe,
when such things occur; and on Belle Island, the Confederates stood willingly by, and let us mete out vengeance to
the hoodlums who had robbed and murdered among the
prisoners, and even urged us to the administering of such
justice.

Still, we fugitives had money and food and clothing taken
from a man who, I am sure, could little afford to furnish
them, especially to Yankees. I prayed that I might survive
to settle the account with the eagerness, if not the hysteria,
which had prompted Carpenter to his own program of settlement.

Long into the night, we were jolted to and fro in the
flat box. The road was bad; this wagon crept like a crippled
snail. The sky had lightened to lead-color, when we halted
and were told to get down. "That's Gum Springs over yonder," said Big Victor. "I reckon you'd better steer clear of
there, and hide in the brush." He told us that we were the
most fortunate Yanks he had ever seen, and that he hoped
no one would get into trouble because of us.

He and his son gave us back our bundles; the ax appeared
again, and was seized thankfully by Barstow. Then, to my
astonishment, Little Victor unbuckled the revolver belt
and gave it over to me, holster and all. I suppose he
must have had his orders or he should never have done it,
though surely he was bold enough to capture another revolver when opportunity came his way.

Meanwhile, the negro teamster climbed down to see after
his horses. He felt his way from the lead horse back, tight-

ening harness, and devoting meticulous care to certain buckles and traces. It was a sham on his part, as Naomi soon discovered. For she was the first to stand beside him, and when she did, she shivered at hearing a whisper from the man.

He repeated several times: "Mr. Vestry's place, missy! Find Mr. Vestry! You go there." She bent close to him, trying to hear the name again, but the two Victors were near. The slave only shook his head, and climbed up on the wagon-box.

There was not yet chance for her to tell us of the strange advice she received, so Barstow and I knew nothing of it. The westerner whispered to me, "Clark, they've been fair and square. Maybe we ought to give them some money?" And so I broached the subject, rather hesitantly.

The men looked down at us from the wagon. It was too dark for us to see their faces, but there must have been a kind of scorn there. "We don't want no money," said Big Victor. "Not none of yours."

"None of Carpenter's!" his son corrected, angrily.

"We don't turn Yanks loose, for money," went on Big Victor. "We come up here with you by order of Quarles; and he sent us sole on account of Mr. Carpenter. You'd better take to the brush." And then, with much jolting and clamor, the negro backed into a squashy side-road, and swung his team to the south.

We dared not huddle there for long, listening to our peculiar enemies (and even more peculiar friends, they were), as they rumbled homeward from their illicit mission. We did not know what Gum Springs might be, but supposed it to be a town; later on, when the morning was close, we looked back and saw a little country church blocked against the horizon. Still, we believed that in obedience to their instructions, the men would not have let us down in the midst of a populous community.

This was a main road: under our feet were ruts, and hard-patted ground between, where hoofs had churned the wet soil loose and pressed it down again each hour as it lay drying. Strange revelation which came to me, many years afterward! this was the Three Chopt Road, a distant continuation of it—that same highway leading out past the encircling forts of Richmond. Long after the war was over, I saw a map; I thrilled to learn, even so late, among what ruts we had stood. What were the Chops I may never know, nor why there were only three of them; and I have seen the name written down as Three Chop Road.

But there it was, under the metal sky, going west by northwest into farther reaches of the Confederacy. The stars in their dawn positions, when we could see them through dissolving clouds, were valuable sentinels for us. They declared that we must get away from these tracks and from the highway itself, which might have taken us to the Allegheny Mountains instead of among those friendly videttes we sought.

We hurried along, scrambling awkwardly, our eyes untrained to the journey. Each of us tasted the tiniest morsel of liberty in his mouth, but dared not sit down to discuss the entire, extraordinary banquet. Presently the open fields on either side led up against solid woodlands, and another road cut to the right (north to the north star, or a little west of it), more certainly in the direction we wished to follow.

The sky cleared under compulsion of dawn and of a braver wind rushing from the same quarter as ever, but now seeming to talk to us from Stevensburg, and not from the poverty-stricken tobacco fields across which we had toiled. We heard a bird, and then another of a different species, frightened in her matutinal flutter.

Trees guarding this narrower road began to separate, and offer apertures fit for hiding. "We can't be sure," muttered

Barstow, "but we'll have to chance it, and find some kind of a thicket."

I said, "There's no one near, and woods all around. Let's keep going as long as we can."

"Well," returned Barstow, "what do you say, lady?"

She was ahead, striding willingly through the gloom, and this was the first time she had walked in the lead. I saw her hair shine out amid the slightest reflection of dawn there, and I thought of how it looked in that first swamp we explored on Thursday forenoon: it was phosphorus, it was fox-fire and will-o'-the-wisp together, and I wondered if its shine might not be leading one of us men to a solitary doom. She did not turn; she went on, half running, slim arrow released from the bow of her captivity, and she cried, "Let's travel just as long as we dare."

Accordingly we went two miles farther; and this day oaks instead of pines sheltered us, and the sun spread on us agreeably when we slept.

4

THEY say that the bolder animals of the jungles roam at night and go to their beds by day, and this had become the fashion of our lives. But the sharp edge was gone from the woman's desperation; and something had happened to Prentiss Barstow and myself during the day we spent ankle-deep, at least, in a civilization where there were plum preserves and hymns and ordinary citizens. No more could we embrace in a single nest, covered in common by blankets. Each had his separate lair in the oak leaves, though we all burrowed against the same fallen tree, and trusted out-flung branches to shield us.

Naomi told us, before we slept, of what the negro teamster had muttered to her. We decided that Mr. Vestry, evidently a dweller in these parts, might be one of the Tories anticipated by Barstow. We agreed to find him if possible, since we considered Mr. Summers' slave to be above any treachery except that of aiding the Union cause (and that was no treachery whatever, in our minds).

Spiritedly, the birds objected to us; we turned and twitched a hundred times, before we were able to forget the oncoming day and the stress which we had borne at the Quarles house. In the first flush of thanksgiving, I could not work at keeping alive my irritation with Barstow, and I do not think he harbored a conscious grudge towards me; yet probably both of us were aware that the discussion begun in the tobacco-house would take even more poignant form in future days. We heard the birds, and felt the dawn about us with its meager warmth; and then, one by one, we tumbled down the channels of slumber.

I remember awakening when the sun was square above us, and shutting my eyes under its stare, until I drifted to unconsciousness in the tomato-red world its light had made through my eyelids. I stirred in mid-afternoon, and again sometime later; and this time I stood upright within a few seconds, for I realized that Barstow and the woman were not at hand.

Their coverings lay where they had left them, and the packs, too. But the bare thickets gave no sign of their presence. My first belief was that they had been captured and carried off bodily, while I lay drugged. It was a notion wild enough, but I dropped my comforter and sprang past the barrier of stumps and water-sprouts.

Even when I heard their voices, after five minutes of heedless rummaging in the woods, I was not relieved; thus soon was I ready to attach a peculiar motive to their absence, and likely Barstow would have done the same, had I been the man who was missing. The woods were thick, but small in area at this point. In the west they fell away steeply to the bank of a creek, beyond which, as I poked out of the underbrush, I could see a house on a hill. Low beside the water's edge, Barstow and Naomi did not see the house, and they thought that we enjoyed the security of the most isolated hiding-place we had yet found.

She had gone for a drink, they told me when I came down to them; and Barstow, awakening almost at the same moment, had followed her. When I reached them, crying warnings about the farmhouse beyond, their hands were orange with clay and their clothing spotted where they had lain down to drink.

I drank too, pretending that I had come for that purpose and had not even missed them. Then we went back through the bushes, though Naomi and Bar still talked aloud despite my remonstrance. There was a personal sort of interest here which I did not appreciate—possibly because I knew the story by heart, and more likely because I objected to any show of concern on the part of the woman.

She was wanting to know just why, if Barstow were an Iowan, he had served with a Wisconsin regiment. He was telling her the whole tale, even to a physical description of his cousin Frank, whom he had visited in Juneau County, Wisconsin, on an errand of family importance. He discussed with excitement, as always, the outbreak of the war, the organizing of the Lemonweir Minutemen, and their eventual incorporation as a company of the Sixth Wisconsin Volunteers. It was no more important, said I to myself, than the story of how the First New Jersey Cavalry was born, with a titled Englishman commanding it. But no one had ever seemed much interested in that tale, since I was native to New Jersey.

When we came back to our fallen tree, I lay down sulkily and covered my face with the soiled comforter, and hated Barstow.

In another half hour, he began to whisper, "Clark, Clark!" until at last I sat up to face him.

"Can't you let me sleep?"

"I didn't think you were sleeping. You kept swallowing, and making noises."

"What do you want?"

He whispered, "Not here! Let's go over in the brush, so's not to wake her."

However, before I had time to resent his solicitude, Naomi herself crawled out from the soft pod she had made of her blanket and black-knit coverlet; she stretched, enjoying it without disguise or prudery, and sat down on the tree trunk.

"I wasn't asleep, Bar," she said. "Maybe none of us needs any more sleep. We've had plenty of that, and you both look stronger than I've seen you. There ought to be some sort of strength in your beards—like Samson's hair. They're growing out fast enough!"

There had been a mirror in the Quarles' kitchen. I had thought that, with shaven head and three-day beard, I looked even more revolting than in the tousled mane of captivity. "That don't matter," I said, sharply. "At least we're not lousy any more," and I demanded to know what Barstow had in mind.

"It's this Vestry business," he said. "Do you have any notion of how we could find him?"

"I don't even know that he's worth finding," I replied, still disagreeably. Then Naomi reminded me that we had agreed to undertake the venture.

Barstow began to gather the small articles which had been in his pack; he shook out the blanket, and shaped it into a bundle for the march. "I've been thinking," he said, "our best hope is to get hold of a nigger. A darky talked about it to us, and plenty of other darkies must know. If this Vestry is a good Union man, they'll tell us."

"Maybe they will," I said, "and maybe not."

He roared, "Well, we've got to try, haven't we? What's got into you, Clark?" and I felt ashamed. But Naomi swung her battered heels from the log and reminded us that, after all, Mr. Vestry's house might be miles in the wrong direction, since we had traveled some distance after the wagon left us.

Barstow tried the edge of his ax and found it not to his liking. He searched for a decent whetstone, and discovered none. "Even if we have to go back," he said, over his shoulder, "it's well worth it, if this Vestry's a Union man. He may be part of the underground railroad, that Fatridge told about. Anyhow, he's liable to feed us."

There was plain common sense in this. The woman and I

prepared our bundles, and we slipped away among the trees when the sun was still shining on their tops.

We came to the edge of the road in time to hear the sound of wheels, and shrill voices; we knelt in gum-wood sprouts and watched a two-wheeled cart, drawn by a mule, approaching from the south. Here were Barstow's negroes, surely enough: a thin, raw-boned woman with skin the color of raisins, sat on one corner of the box, her bare legs hanging close to the wheel. The cart itself was filled with what we took to be her children—a weird bouquet of ginger faces and fuzzy wool, string-tied in every case to keep off the witches. These children (of whom there must have been four or five, and all of them very small) were piled in with stone jugs, a basket, canvas sacks, and a striped cat. And so serious was their disorder and so effusive their laughter, that I saw Naomi put her face between her knees in order to remain silent.

But before I could do more than gulp, Prentiss Barstow had run out from between the trees, and had clenched his hand on the crazy bridle by which the mule was driven.

The negro woman sat motionless, a long club held stiff in her hand like a scepter; all her children rose up to stare at the bandit in their path.

"Where's Mr. Vestry's place? Answer quick, now!" demanded Barstow.

Still the negress stared at him, her eyes wide and her full purple lips hanging open.

Barstow let the ax handle slide through his fingers, and closed them around it, a scant six inches below the blade. "I want to know, woman!" By this time Naomi and I were standing up in the bushes; I got my revolver out, in case some horseman should come quickly upon the scene and take Barstow unawares. I do not think that any of the negroes saw us, so stupefied were they by Barstow himself, and the sudden interruption of their jaunt.

When Barstow had mentioned the name of Vestry a second or third time, and with due menace, the negress cried out, "What you mean, white man? What you trying to do? That mule belong to Mr. Gideon Sylvester," and she put one big, bare foot on the cartwheel and jumped to the ground.

"Lay down in that cart. The whole passel of you!" she yelled at her children, and they obeyed as one body. Then, to our horror, she advanced upon Barstow with her club waving, and I could not but wonder whether he would have to defend himself with the ax. Afterward, Barstow told us that he had no time to think what he should do, astounded as he was when she came at him with her yelling ferocity.

But when she was close, she said in a low tone, "Don't take this road, Mister Yankee. Go round through the woods, over along Owen's Creek," and she pointed towards the east with her elbow. She whispered again, "Houses ahead, Mister Yankee! You go around to the creek, and then back, and you find Mr. Vestry. He's got a white-washed gate."

Then she jerked the mule's bridle out of his hand, and as he stepped back she led the beast ahead, cart and all, groaning terribly and brandishing the club until Barstow ducked out of reach.

Now her children were standing up again, and she let them watch with all their eyes as she led the mule some twenty yards down the road. Running back, she scrambled quickly into the cart. She stood up, tall and thin, showing all her teeth as she yelled, "Now! I reckon you stay out of my road. Now! Don't you lay hand on Mr. Sylvester's mule again!" Until the party went out of sight around the next bend of woodland, she roared back, threatening violence in one breath and admonishing her children in the next.

We two in the bushes were well amazed, but it was easily explained when Barstow came back and told us what the woman had whispered.... There was a canniness about these slaves which I had never imagined before. I had thought them barbaric or stupid or lazy, as the case might be, and doubtless many of them were. And many others, too, were loyal to their masters and the Confederacy; but somehow I cannot hear jubilee singers chanting of Moses, and bondage and their freedom from it, without thinking of this thin, brown-faced wench with her high shoulders and long strong arms, shouting vituperation at Barstow in that narrow sunset road.

Owen's Creek, she had said. And God knows we were aware that there would be no sign pointing the way. But she had gestured toward the east; so now we crossed the road and followed tortuous tunnels through a narrow, sloping woodland, turning to the northeast as the ground fell that way, and the trees took us there. My own petulance wholly forgotten, I let Barstow travel ahead as our captain, since he had won the necessary information through his own resourcefulness, and through good luck as well. And Naomi told with joy that the last time we traveled by daylight we had been close pursued, but now no enemy was at our heels.

It was during this day that we had been first conscious of a new life stirring in the bushes around us, and underneath the very soil where we lay. As yet we could neither taste nor smell it, nor hear its voice raised high. The only whispers we had heard, while the sun was warm, came from birds which had been our companions all the way from Richmond. They scouted along the vine-grown fences and into unfenced timber tracts—flicking now toward the east, now toward the west, but twitching their course north again each hour, nor caring how provokingly the wind tried to turn them back.

Even so, we were prepared for what we would hear, in

this hour when we took up our march. We heard it first beside Owen's Creek, a clay-filled stream that lay buried in ancient vines, and shone sulphur-colored when the last daylight hunted it out. We paused there, sinking deeper into the mire each instant, yet loath to lift our feet out of the morass which had given birth to spring (as forgotten swamps gave birth to the earliest germs that grew, through changing generations, into the men and women of today).

It was a frog, so small that we could not even see him. Somewhere among the trailing roots he put his mouth out of the water and talked to us, and the endless winter retreated at his singing. Now I wish that I could have seen him and touched him with my hand, to win childish reassurance which a wiser man would not have needed. He croaked valiantly beneath tangled rubbish of the watercourse; and we fancied him calling to his relatives in other sloughs, as if he urged them to take up the burden of his signal, and rush the tidings across Louisa county and north to Spotsylvania, and on to the opposing lines along the Rapidan.

We walked in silence for a long time, a silence which permitted us to know finally that this bold frog had indeed inspired the fellows who swam in pools not his own. For they echoed the solo and made a mysterious chorus of it; the valley grew darker and darker, but took unto itself a certain tropical charm, and ignored the wind.

Each of us was busy, I believe, with thoughts of the separate springs he had known, just as a sentimental person pauses at Christmas Eve, and glances tearfully over the file of hoary Christmases stalking down the past to the verge of his trundle-bed. Barstow would never talk of his springs, but he must have heard wild geese and swans going to Canada above the prairies; and Naomi told me once that the damp buzzing of the frogs made her see her father more clearly than at any time since his death, and that she could fairly smell the rain-wet leather of an old buggy in which she jolted through much of her childhood.

And I wandered the Watchung hills again, as I had done before ever there existed a New Jersey cavalry to spirit me away from them. I stood in an open place among the beeches, and saw how hazy the tree-tops were, all the way to the Highlands along the Atlantic Ocean. I found anemones, and raked them up heedlessly with my fingers, and got a kind of nourishment when my hands were moist with the juice of their frail stems. I strode on into kinder, warmer weeks when there were violets and May-apples; and once on a far ridge by my uncle's farm (it was an endless journey to get there, and I visited it only twice during my boyhood) I saw a bear ranging wearily through the underbrush, reluctant to desert the log which had sheltered her and her new-born cubs, but responding to a thousand concertos instigated by the frogs. I heard the deer which I chased with my dog, but never caught; again I tried to find the fabled, encircling thickets where young deer were said to lie in the liverwort, and to be deserted by their mothers if you so much as breathed upon them.

All these fancies trooped back, to tag me in this lone valley of Louisa county; and more trivial, roguish memories came skipping as well. I remembered how our potatoes sprouted in their bin, when spring came close; I could recall my mother coming out of the cellar with the last jar of peach preserve, and saying that we should have no more until the peaches were ripe again. The half-moons of March and April, with clouds dancing across them like women's veils blown in the wind ... the peculiar sound of men's footfalls in the early morning, when they went past our house on the wooden sidewalk, and found an echo in the trees—one never living there when the winter was hard upon us: this sound was drawn up out of secret wells, till I had to turn my head and stare back into the sloping dusk to be sure that no person followed us now.

We came out of the valley at last, and began to talk of finding Mr. Vestry's house, with its white-washed gate. The all-important discussion of food arose; and underneath this business of managing our immediate present lay the primitive antagonism, submerged and held in check, ready to boil forth whenever pricked by a word or a gesture. Yet we held our heads high and breathed more willingly, even with a cold breeze sucking into our nostrils. For the frogs labored forth in another pool somewhere ahead, and still they sang.

5

I<small>N</small> our willingness to take at face value the advice of the
negress, we were now perhaps a mile east of the road.
We had worked our way north, crossing a tributary brook
until I thought we must be beyond the latitude of the houses
concerning which we had been warned. But Barstow was for
keeping north beside this creek valley; he feared now that
the slave might have regretted being his accomplice, even
in remote fashion.

"I wouldn't trust one of them," he kept repeating, "man
or woman. Not one. No more than I'd trust Indians."

I objected, telling him that negroes were of the Ethiopian
race, and he had best not gauge his association with them by
experience in the west, since they were nothing like Indians
at all.

"How do you know?" he countered. "You never saw any
Indians." And to that I could not retort, although a legend
in the Clark family said that there had been an ancestor, in
Colonial times, who doctored all the Delawares in his neighborhood, and they would not burn his house on account of it.

At last, with Naomi teasing Barstow because of his trust
in the blacks one moment, and his suspicion of them the
next—at last we got him persuaded to try the road. When
we had crossed the creek again (trying to cross on stones
which we could not see, and thereby getting wet), we climbed
a steep embankment and found ourselves on the summit of a
barren hill, with the new moon ahead; a sharp bent blade
in the purple sky. The moon fell lower before we had reached
the road; Bar informed us that the next month would be

rainy, because a hunter could hang his powder-horn on the lowest prong of the moon, and thus should stay at home instead of faring forth.

But there was no rain menacing above—only the faithful stars, new-born and riding steadily abreast of us. Off in woods toward the south, where we had slept that day, we heard a cow mooing. A man called to her, musically, and we dove into bushes until we were sure that the herdsman was not chasing his stray cow in our direction. Then we went on, not having to feel our way now, as there was no timberland beside the road and we could see the track easily.

The white-washed gate of Mr. Vestry's house loomed on our right hand, long before we expected it. It could have been discerned in the blackest night that ever blew: a teetering rack of poles all white in the gloom, and with a kind of transverse sweep suspended from the tallest post, whereby a driver could reach up and, manipulating the contraption, open the gate without descending from his wagon. But we dared not step in without due vigilance. We crouched in a row outside the rail fence, and tried to see just what was happening at Mr. Vestry's, and whether he was offering any visible evidence of National sympathies.

All lights look alike at night, whether rebel or Yankee. The lights in the Vestry house told us nothing of their owner's faith. At last, hearing neither dogs nor negroes about, and only an occasional clatter of pans or pails somewhere at the rear, we knew that closer investigation was essential. We talked in whispers about it; and I went forward instead of Barstow, because I wore no Federal jacket, and might have been an ordinary but dishevelled farmer, were it not for my shaven poll. Barstow kept my revolver belt; I put the weapon inside my shirt, and held it in a tight grasp while I advanced.

The house had a wide front. Even in the early darkness,

one could see that the high porch was rickety and had no steps to it. As I approached, there sounded a violent grunting, and several bodies came scrambling from under the porch, in all directions. They were pigs, but I had my revolver out before I realized their harmlessness. The front door opened a moment later. Whilst I remained motionless, a man looked out, to see what had disturbed his hogs. He went back in; I skirted the end of the house and came into a backyard cluttered with a well-curb, chicken coops, cauldrons and the like. A hill—the steep prolongation of the last ridge we had crossed—rose up behind the house, leaving room for a big barn built against its flank, and a shack or two beyond. I went in this direction, rather than toward the house itself, and on passing the barn I could see a shower of sparks pouring from a chimney on one of the shacks—undoubtedly slave quarters.

Behind me, a figure walked from the barn door. I turned with my finger bent against the trigger.

"Who's there?" came a man's voice.

I whispered, "Hush up!" and went to him.

He was a squat negro with very long arms, so round-shouldered as to be deformed, and he carried a dripping pail. I looked down at him for a moment; he must have seen the revolver, but he did not budge from his place. "Is that you, Mr. Jack Mayo?" he asked respectfully.

I said, "No. Is this Mr. Vestry's place?" When he replied, "Yes, boss," I was not so delighted at the confirmation, as I was astonished to hear him speaking like a northern negro.

"Don't move," I said, "and don't yell, if you don't want me to kill you. Is Mr. Vestry a Union man?"

He set the pail down, and I came near shooting him for it. "Boss," he said, "I just work for him. I'm a free nigger, I am. Do you want I should take you to Mr. Vestry?"

I thought of Barstow, and especially of Naomi, waiting

out there beyond the fence, but decided that I could shoot
my way to safety so long as I stayed in the yard. "Lead on,"
I ordered. "You can call him out, but don't do more than
call him outside."

"Boss," asked the man, in a whisper so low I could scarce
hear it, "are you a traveler?"

"Yes. Of course I'm a traveler. Lead on, now!"

He abandoned his pail and went ahead of me, his hunched
back giving him a false air of humility; I am sure he was
not alarmed or over-awed, in any sense. Near the back door
I halted him and told him to speak, and promptly he let
out a hail.

The door opened a crack, a woman looked out; when
the negro repeated his request she went away, leaving the
door open, with the crack widening each second as the wind
moved it. I waited, the muzzle of my weapon against the
round shoulders of the servant. Presently the door swung
wide, closing behind the figure of a man—the same man
who had come to the front door.

"What's wanted, Ernest?"

"Mr. Vestry, there's a man out here who asked was this
your house; and he says he's a traveler."

"A traveler," repeated the man on the porch, and then
he said "Oh!" in a different tone. He came down into the
yard.

I drew the negro in front of me for a shield. "Don't
come armed," I said.

"I'm not armed, my friend." Mr. Vestry came close to
us, and stood looking at me through the gloom. "Are you the
kind of traveler I think you are?"

I told him, "Perhaps."

"Where did you hear of me?"

"There's a Mr. Summers living near Goochland Court
House. He has a negro teamster."

Mr. Vestry said, "Oh, yes. I often go to Goochland Court. I know the boy you mean; his name is Jove. Where are you from, my friend?"

"Richmond."

He bent nearer and whispered, "Libby?" and I told him that I was from Belle Island.

His next query was, "Are you alone?"

"No," I said, "there are two others."

"Where are they now?"

"Waiting."

"Are you hungry?"

I burst out, "God, yes!" for the smell of the kitchen, when that door was opened, had been a fair insult to me.

Mr. Vestry (still a dark shape without a face, and not so tall as I, but nearly as thin) told me, "Well, I'm one of the Right Sort of People. I'll do what I can for you, my friend. I daren't take you into the house, because there's relations stopping here tonight, who don't subscribe to our cause. Do you want to spend the night in my barn?"

"Not necessarily. It's easier for us to travel at night."

He went on to say that even though we could cover greater distance at night, it would be a wise thing for us to stop in his barn. He and a friend, whose name he did not mention, were sending a wagon north to the railroad the next day, and he said that we might ride in it. He said that the negro man, Ernest, would take us to a good hiding place, and that he himself would be out to talk with us soon. Then, before I could do more than caution him against telling any one that we were there, and warning that at the first act against any of us, some one might have his brains blown out— he had gone back into the house, provoking me with the smell of food when he went through the door.

I demanded of the freedman whether or not Mr. Vestry often sheltered fugitives of my kind, because he seemed not at all surprised at seeing me there. "Oh yes, boss," the negro responded. "We have them by here, mighty frequently! Some comes from Richmond, but not so many this year, and some comes down from the mountains. There's the Right Sort of People up there, too, and they send them to Mr. Vestry."

"Ernest," said I, "how would you like to earn a five dollar bill?" and when he said that he would like very much to, I made him wait beside his bucket. For the contents of the bucket shone white and steamy in the gloom, and it was long since I had tasted milk still warm from the cow. As a boy I had thought that I did not like milk warm from the cow, desiring it cooled in a crock in my mother's cellar, instead, and drunk when I was eating baking-powder biscuits and honey for a treat. But now I ran around and got Barstow and Naomi, with the packs, and when we came back, the man Ernest was waiting there in all faith.

We grouped around the bucket, unwilling to take the time for fishing out a cup from our bundles; each, in turn, got down and drank from the brim of the wooden pail until it was half empty. And then we stood up and grinned at one another; Barstow and I were hoary with milk foam because of our whiskers. I had no five-dollar greenback, but Naomi produced a Confederate bill and asked the man if that would do for him, and he seemed willing enough to get it. He kept laughing, and whispering to us as to how he would explain the lesser quantity of milk. He intended to declare that the cow had given the pail a kick; but he insisted on taking his bucket to the kitchen, before he showed us to our hiding place.

There was a long wait. We rested inside the open barn door; horses or mules were rustling their forage, and stamping on the dirt floor behind us. Barstow was sure, now, that the negro had fled away to tell the Home Guards where we might be found. But at length he came back with a lantern.

Round the corner of the barn he guided us, past manure piles and openings that gave on subterranean stables, and we climbed the slope until we stood opposite the second story.

There was a window to the mow, easily seen beyond. Instead of taking us there, Ernest reached out and began to wrestle with a corner of the eaves. Presently several of the boards lifted all together like a door, still bearing their uneven shingles: he had forced open a carefully prepared refuge, on which this false sloping roof lay like the lid of a box. Into this mysterious den we clambered, and the freedman lowered the lid, reassuring us through the cracks, and pointing out that, if the barn were fired from below, we could easily escape by climbing the hill an arm's length away. Then Ernest went back to his barn-yard duties. We crouched in this little box, not more than six feet square—locked in with the odor of musty straw and blankets, and the odious inheritance from previous transients who had been more filthy than we, though still befriended by the Right Sort of People.

Barstow was the first to grow restless. It was difficult for him to cramp his great length into this uncomfortable space; and after the first flush of foolhardiness in which he had challenged the negress, at sundown, he had grown more uneasy with every hour. Before we had been crowded into our hiding place for ten minutes, Barstow was cursing Mr. Vestry and Ernest, terming the latter a black scalawag not any more to be depended upon than a drunken Mesquakie.

"I'm warning you," he said, "we've seen the last of them. They'll never come near us again. What's Vestry got to gain by it, anyway? I reckon he's *pukacheed.*"

Naomi said, through the darkness which was somehow cold and stifling in the same breath, "What's *pukacheed,* Bar? You've said that before."

"Gone," he answered. "Run away. It's Dakotah talk, and I'll bet he's done it."

"Well," I told him, "you were the one who wanted to trust these Tories."

He swore, and reared up suddenly with his shoulders against the lid of our box. "Help me," he gasped, and I did help him, though counting it unwise and wondering whether Mr. Vestry would be angry.

We tipped the roof back on its hinges until it was folded completely over, resting on the slope of the barn. A thousand stars seemed chiding us for our action, but Barstow cared nothing for chiding from the stars or from his comrades, and he clambered promptly out onto the hill.

"One thing," he whispered. "I'm going to see that this ax is whetted up proper, before we go another mile. I'd rather have blisters than a dull ax! There must be a grindstone somewhere about."

I warned, "You start turning a grindstone, and you'll have the whole place about your ears." But he went past the corner of the barn and groped down toward the stables, without heeding me.

I muttered, cursing him as he had cursed those who promised to help us.

"Don't," said Naomi. "His nerves are all unsettled."

"We've got every right to be just as unsettled!"

She said, quickly, "Oh, every bit as much right. Probably more."

I take my oath that I had not planned it . . . nor had I, in the instant since Barstow left us, entertained any thought fit to stir up a hurricane. Yet, during the long moment which followed Naomi's last speech, I could think of nothing but that first day following our escape from the Carpenter house, when we lay in our nest at the hog-shelter, and the primary passion of the male made itself known to me.

And now it made itself known in powerful ways, so hastily that importunate words crowded my mouth, and still I could not speak . . . Almighty Father, I thought, what have I been carrying with me? . . . It seemed that my desire for Naomi had stowed itself inside my pack, at the first moment I made it up—then as small as any snail on a berry-leaf, but growing larger, more potent and dangerous throughout the hours of journeying—fed not only by the food which I ate, but by sunshine, the black nights, the sharp sickle-light of the first moon. Now it had grown to murderous size, and occupied me completely, folding its rough coat around my arms and legs, arming my extremities with its claws. Now I wore the skin of passion, as it had never fallen over me before.

"Naomi," I said, still looking at the stars.

"What?"

"Give me your hand."

She did give it to me, but only after hesitation, as if she chose to mistake the emotion which had prompted me. I felt her hand carefully: so small a hand, though not thin like mine, and with a feeling of purity about it, in spite of the clay that crusted around the fingernails. My own hand slid higher along her arm, now; it was pressing her wrist and the roundness of the forearm, squeezing the coarse shirt against her skin.

She spoke in a different tone—lower, sharper. "Ollie. What—?"

I whispered something, no matter what. Though admitting to any wrong I achieved or contemplated, I will say that I fought against it and had my jaws hard-pressed together, and the words were slow to come. . . . She snatched her hand away and rose up on her knees; I saw her profile beside me and above me, against the lights of the sky, as if she were searching there for an answer to the riddle I now challenged her with.

"Ollie," she said, "no good could come of this."

I heard myself whisper: "Good? Of course not. Maybe no good at all. I didn't ask you that! I—"

"Companions," she whispered, "companions in misery. That's all we can be."

So I tussled with her, and in another moment (though surely her strength matched mine, in ordinary occasion) I had her shoulders against the straw and the matted blankets, and was trying to reach her face.

"Ollie," she whispered, evenly, "he'll kill you for this."

"Oh, no, he won't! I'd have something to say about—"

I said no more, for she made a kind of sigh. Her lips came against me, not on my mouth but on my forehead. She left off struggling, and I left off my compulsion; and then, lightly, she had turned my head away and she sat up. I heard her brushing straw from her shoulders and arms. . . . "That's all I can give you, Ollie. All I can give to either of you."

I muttered, "You'd be willing to kiss him, too?"

Her whisper was nearer a cry. "Why, of course I would—like that."

"Then it meant nothing at all," I wailed, in a rage.

"Ollie, do you think I want to kill you? Or do you think I want to kill Barstow? I don't: you know it well enough, or will if you stop to think. . . . I'd be killing one or the other. We'll leave that for the rebels to do. Or starvation, or—"

We heard some one climbing toward us along the end of the barn, and I thought that it must be Barstow, until a shimmer of lantern light came past the cornice. A head and shoulders appeared; in one second I believed an enemy had discovered us; the next moment we realized that this was Mr. Vestry, whose face I had not seen close at hand before.

He was annoyed at finding us with the lid of the shelter raised, and wanted to know if Ernest had left it that way.

"They watch me like hawks," he explained. "I have to use all care."

"Well," I told him, "we'll put the roof down now, if you say so. But it stinks inside."

He swallowed. "You may as well leave it open, for the time being. You see, the brother of my wife is a doctor well known hereabouts, and a strong Secessionist." He lifted his lantern higher, sliding it quickly inside the trough of our prison so that it could not be seen from the house; and now, with light filling the closet where we crouched, Mr. Vestry saw that Barstow was missing, and became more fearful than annoyed. I explained that Bar had gone to hunt for a grindstone, at which Mr. Vestry showed the greatest excitement and went scrambling down the slope, leaving his lantern and the tin bucket in which he had brought our supper.

We looked into the pail. There was an iron spoon apiece, and the supper was a single substance which we should have recognized by odor long before. It consisted solely of mashed turnips, flavored with bacon-fat, and we saw that Mr. Vestry stood in no danger of bankrupting his larder by stray kindnesses of this sort. Nevertheless, we set to at once, pressing the turnips flat and dividing them by line into equal thirds before we began, and Barstow's third was an isolated promontory in the pail by the time Mr. Vestry herded him back.

Bar had found no grindstone, but somewhere or other he discovered a whet-slab such as hay-makers use for their scythes, and how he ever smelt it out in the darkness of that farmyard, is more than I knew then or know now. He dropped down beside us, his face sullen from the upbraiding which Mr. Vestry had given him.

"Man alive!" said the farmer. "If you use that stone in here, you'll fetch all my hands!"

"Well, I'll use it after we're gone."

Mr. Vestry hesitated; then he said, with all politeness,

that he could not afford to part with the stone unless he were paid. Barstow argued with him, but at last they settled on ten dollars Confederate; and turning away from the woman, Barstow got out his roll of bills.

Naomi said, "Just a moment. If you're doing any trading, I want to have a hand in it."

We both asked, "Why?" Leaning back, she held one of her legs forward until her shoe was close to the lantern, and we could see that the sole was worn through.

Mr. Vestry leaned his elbows on the eaves, and considered. "Yes," he said, at last, "I think I can find a pair of shoes small enough for you. They were a pair my daughter had. She grew too large for them before they were worn out."

"Are they better than these?" demanded the woman.

"Oh, yes. A trifle shabby, but with good heavy soles. But"—he coughed—"have you any United States currency?"

By this time Barstow and I wanted to join in the discussion, but Naomi made it known that she preferred to conduct her own bargaining. "If the shoes are what you say, I'll give you two dollars in greenbacks, Mr. Vestry!"

He argued for a time, saying that the shoes were worth at least five dollars, and that he had intended to offer them for sale when he went to town again. At last, since Naomi was so firm, he agreed to accept the two dollars. He went away to get the shoes.

Barstow looked at the woman and shook his head, with his mouth full of turnips. "I didn't offer him currency for the whetstone," he said, when he could speak. "I only offered shinplasters."

Naomi remarked, coolly, "It's a great wonder he didn't demand pay for the turnips! Get out your money, Bar; you too, Ollie," and she brought forth the Confederate paper she had. "We'll divide it, share and share alike. We should have done so before this."

I poured out my store of silver and greenbacks, and close beside the lantern we counted our hoard. We had left to us six hundred and thirty-five dollars in Secession scrip, and Naomi insisted that the five dollars spent for milk was a benefit to each of us, but that Barstow must pay for his own whetstone. "Two hundred and fifteen for Ollie and me, each," she said. "Two hundred and five for Bar," and Barstow admitted that it was fair enough. Then we divided the National currency, which came to two dollars and thirty cents apiece. Mr. Vestry came back as we were completing the transaction, and Naomi tried on the shoes. She said that she was willing to keep them and part with two dollars, if Mr. Vestry would throw in a pair of woolen socks, as even these girls' shoes were a bit too large for her.

"How about you two?" asked Mr. Vestry, when at last he had brought the socks and had folded the greenbacks which Naomi gave him.

Barstow wanted to know if, indeed, he was in the shoe business; but the man said humbly, "Not at all. I merely have things here—a few things—for people who might need them."

Barstow laughed—ungratefully, it seemed to me. After all, he might have realized the risks which Mr. Vestry bore in behalf of escaping Unionists. "These are good Federal army boots, mister; they'll do me for a while longer, and Clark hasn't got a hole in the ones he got down there below Goochland. Why, God damn it, you stand to make a pretty fair living, if enough prisoners come past here!"

Mr. Vestry caught up his lantern, and blew it out. The darkness rushed about us. Our new moon was long since gone, and I imagined that the chilly northwest wind had whirled it away like a scrap of paper. Mr. Vestry stood there on the hillside, seeming taller than he really was. He had a noticeable dignity when he replied,

"I told you, my friend, that I was one of the Right Sort of People. I belong to the Sons of America; you would recognize as much, if you knew the grip and password."

I demanded, "Who are the Sons of America?"

"Conservative people." He informed us in a manner not at all plaintive: "As you go toward the Rapidan, you will find fewer people of my notion. Then you will appreciate what food and shelter have meant to you. If you were in the mountains southwest of here, things might be easier: last week a man came past who told me that in Wilkes county, North Carolina, there were at least a thousand Unionists hiding out. I trust you will make due allowance for the fact that I must provide for my family. I cannot give away things, much as I might like to."

He started away. But Naomi whistled at him to come back, and asked if he would sell her some tea.

"Tea!" Bar cried, in the darkness. "What in tarnation do you want with tea?"

"I want to drink it," she said. "I'll even give some to you and Ollie. I can feel half civilized, if I have tea."

Mr. Vestry cleared his throat. "It's expensive, miss." And then I realized that not once had he addressed her as "Madam," and I wondered if he meant any insult by the omission. "I have a little green tea," he went on. "The prevailing price is around one hundred twenty dollars Confederate, per pound."

Barstow called on his Maker.

"I could let you have a pound, at only small profit to myself. One hundred and"—he hesitated again—"one hundred twenty-seven dollars Confederate." Naomi agreed to pay the price, and sent him to fetch the tea, though it seemed the wildest sort of extravagance to Barstow and me.

"You'll have less than a hundred dollars left, woman!"

"I know it, Bar. Maybe we ought to have a common fund

to buy other food, along the way. I'll contribute seventy-five dollars to that." So we followed her suggestion, and Barstow was made our treasurer.

Later we heard Mr. Vestry picking his way up the hill, bringing the tea for Naomi, carefully weighed out in a little sack and bound with cotton string. He was carrying an unlighted lantern; but he had to touch a match to it within the walls of our shelter, so that Naomi might count the money for him. Then he returned to the house, saying that we could leave the roof open if we chose; and he cautioned us against prowling abroad, as his relatives were still at the house.

It must have taxed him to measure out the tea, and secure the shoes, and do the other fetching and carrying which he had done—when enemies were settled at his hearthside. Still, I do not now think (as I did think then) that his motives were purely mercenary. His face, shining yellow in the lantern light, was serious and intent; but it was the face of a small-minded man. He believed firmly in certain causes and purposes, and I do not consider that he would have grown treacherous unless driven by the utmost terror. There was no ardent generosity about him, such as some people can boast, which impelled him to meet unfortunate persons on any level but the level where he met those more fortunate. The inclination to business for business' sake, was firm inside him.

Let it be as it may: we were not the first prisoners who had lain in the refuge of his barn, nor probably the last. And it is likely that more than one soldier crept up to the Rapidan—heartened and fortified by the sleazy fare of mashed turnips which he got at Mr. Vestry's, and for which Mr. Vestry charged nothing at all.

6

M Y CONSCIENCE stood forth like an evangelist incarnate, impressing me to the point where I could see its belligerent proportions; and it proceeded to accuse me by every authority at its command. It was egged on by the immediate presence of Barstow, who ate up the last of his turnips in the darkness beside us, and who was kept from righteous attack upon me only by the thinnest chain of all: ignorance, for the moment, as to what had come about. And again, I saw my conscience go to doom—a drowning disciple if ever there was one, submerged in the water of my own private desires—struggling up to wave a last feeble threat, and then going down with finality.

I thought (the acrid satisfaction of a man not yet guilty but eager to achieve guilt!) that my conscience lay in his water-logged cerements, in the deepest pool of our mutual existence; it would take more than the voices of spring-time frogs to arouse him now. For Naomi's lips had come against my skin in a gesture which any woman would consider as humane forbiddance, and which, as it has affected men time out of mind, nerved me only to a fresh assault when the hour should be ripe.

Whether a similar litter of passion had been quietly suckled inside Barstow's pack, I did not know. I was aware only of the full-grown monster to which my boldest cub had grown, and how she had mated herself to my former self, producing the impetuous hybrid I now became. "There will be more nights," I thought. "Perhaps tomorrow night or the next. . . . Barstow will sleep; no, he will wander away.

He will go on errands yet unimagined, and I wish I might dare him to go."

In another moment I was entertaining the hope that this same night would offer me a better opportunity; then, unable to support the palpitation of a power for which I was not yet fitted, I broke down. Bereft in the dark, with Naomi's elbow on one side of me and Barstow's knees on the other, I felt the strident tautness leaving me, vanishing from my very fingertips—not scourged out by any dire strokes of shame, but whipped by the intensity of the fire within itself.

It left me empty and stupid, but still aware of a future that once was too distant to be gained, and now seemed promised within hours which I could count.

Five days we were gone from the Island; this was the start of the sixth night. I admitted the futility of comparing time in which nothing happens but the trivialities of existence, with time wherein every hour is sharpened like a razor by distracted minutes grinding against its edge. Still, I was bound to recognize that the thrusts of those hours had not bled any of us to our downfall. Perhaps this was the ministration of leeches, who brought a man to his strength by taking it away from him.

A secret had been born between Naomi and myself, and every secret is a link manacling its possessors together. . . . I was ready to sleep where I lay. I drew up my knees, and moved my shoulder to a spot where the straw was not so rocky. My arm went back, my fingers touched some part of the woman; and sliding coolly in the darkness, her own fingers came forward and took mine away. I believed that she felt no offense, but only the sympathy and resolution she had shown before.

The straw rustled under my hand as I dragged it back, and Barstow asked about the sound.

"I just moved my leg," I said. "What did you think it was—a mouse?"

"No matter," he said, sharply, and then we all remained silent, and the stars walked above us.

We heard the faint murmur of the countryside, fancied mutterings of animals and men: the silence of rural regions, beside which an untenanted forest seems vocal. But our ears, close to being stopped by slumber, opened quickly at a new vibration that approached. One by one, we sat erect to hear it.

A vehicle came down from the south, each wheel complaining at stones in the roadway, and the horse slipping and scuffling as his driver urged him to a pace unwise for so narrow and uneven a road. The night was still clear, and sounds came readily from a distance, in spite of the constant swishing of the wind.

All of us grew tense and frightened when the driver cried, "Whoa!" and the vehicle stopped squarely in front of Mr. Vestry's house. But we were relieved by hearing a hail, and an answering response which mentioned the name of Charlie —as if they at the Vestrys' knew well enough who was in the buggy.

We spoke no more except for the vaguest whisper or two. I believe that Naomi had fallen asleep, before Barstow and I stiffened again at a stealthy approach alongside the barn. The steps came higher; we could sense the labored movement of one who tried to climb with the greatest caution. Presently a head rose up, close by the corner, and from the shape of the man I knew that he was Ernest.

"Travelers?" he whispered.

We answered him quietly, and then he bent down; we could smell onions on his hot breath. "Doctor Overton just come in his buggy," the man whispered. "They're talking out by the gate."

"Who's Doctor Overton?" Barstow wanted to know.

Ernest hovered us. "You better scoot," he said. "Doctor Overton, he's kin of Mr. Vestry. He's Secesh." And he repeated it several times: "All Secesh. Yes, sir. They don't wish no good to Yankees."

Now we were wide awake—more wide awake than we had been, and Naomi wondered aloud if Mr. Vestry dared reveal that we were hiding on his property.

"Yes, sir," cried Ernest, fearfully, "I reckon maybe the companies will come looking for you! No, sir, Mr. Vestry he won't tell, but maybe they'll burn this barn like they come near doing once before." Then he stood back against the hillside, saying that he would scoot if he were in our shoes.

"Folks," I said, "I'll go out there and listen."

"Find out what's what," Barstow counseled me. I could hear Naomi beginning to drag our packs from the rear wall of the cubbyhole where they had been piled. I went speedily down the incline at the barn's end, making easy work of it since my eyes were accustomed to the night.

Out in front, the buggy had not entered at the gate; it stood near the fence, and the horse was rubbing his neck against one of the posts. The hogs helped me, too, for they were grunting and complaining under the front porch again. I got within earshot of the vehicle.

Mr. Vestry was standing beside it. I heard the scrape of leather as he lifted his boot to a wheel hub.

A voice, undoubtedly that of Doctor Overton, said: "Andrews told me, when he came by for some ipecac."

"That's no reason for them to continue pestering me," cried Mr. Vestry.

Doctor Overton made a great to-do about spitting out some tobacco. "James," he said, "you've not only tried my patience before, but you're constantly endangering yourself.

I'm so almighty disgusted I wouldn't be here now, if it weren't for Susan and Bethel and Rose.... Andrews said they were all from Richmond. And they're desperate, for they escaped from the Home Guards at Goochland Court only last night. He fully believes that the woman is the one mentioned by Richmond. I warn you, James, if you value your hide—which I damn near don't—you'll not attempt to shelter them, should they come here."

Mr. Vestry took his foot off the hub again. "Charlie, nobody can say that every loose Yank in Virginia comes to my farm." And then his kinsman raised his voice, reproaching Vestry further, and calling him several species of a fool.

I got out of the yard as rapidly as possible, and fell against some kind of tripod, but apparently the men in the road thought the disturbance was caused by a pig. When I reached the barn eaves, Barstow and Naomi were out on the ground, and Ernest had vanished.

"What did you hear?"

"Enough," I said. "We'll travel again," and we all climbed down the hillside.

Ernest came out of the barn door and hissed at us. He herded us inside to heavier darkness. "Two nigger girls be down from the house in a minute," he whispered. "You don't want to run afoul of them, do you?"

So we crouched amid hanging harness and trampled straw, until the servants had ambled back to their quarters. Meanwhile, we heard Doctor Overton's buggy turning in the road; the rapid *clop-clop* of hoofs went away toward the south again. We were out of the barn door when Mr. Vestry came forth with his lantern. He wanted to know why we had left the hiding place. Fearing to expose Ernest to censure, we told him that we had become nervous and decided to wait no longer.

He was holding his lantern low, and we could not see

his face. "On the whole, perhaps you're just as wise. I have been warned that some Home Guards are coming to search the place. They may not come, but it's best not to run the risk."

Barstow asked, "Are they searching especially for us?" and when Mr. Vestry replied hurriedly, "Oh, no; not at all. Just searching my place, as they often do," I was the only one aware of his falsehood. Even I could not decide what had inspired it.

At any rate, he gave us meticulous instructions about the path we should follow: it was less than a mile and a half, he said, to a wider and better road known as the Old Mountain Road, which would take us directly toward the South Anna. We should avoid a village some four or five miles ahead—a place called Thompson's Crossroad, easily recognized by a store and a group of houses—but after that he described the journey as clear sailing.

"You will find a bridge across the South Anna," he explained. "There is a brick Baptist church just beyond, on the left, but it's far back from the road and hard to see in the darkness. It's immediately across the way from Lame Mercer's, and I want you to go to him."

He continued explicitly, informing us that Lame Mercer was a negro, a free blacksmith, and one of the Right Sort of People. "His cabin is east of the road in the woods, reached by a narrow path. There is a dead pine at the roadside. I reckon you can see it easily. Keep going past the bridge until you come to a dead pine, and that's the path to Lame Mercer's. He may be able to cook you some grits and gravy."

In another two minutes we were in the road, passing the last of Mr. Vestry's fence and fearing that we might hear Home Guards riding in from the south. I told Barstow and Naomi most of the conversation I had heard, and so they knew as well as I that Mr. Vestry was not telling the truth when he said that we ourselves were not the specific objects of search. I did not speak then of the reference to Naomi; and only when Barstow was striding well ahead, in the darkness of later miles, did I repeat to her the exact words.

"They spoke of you," I whispered.

She marched in silence for a time. "You mean, Ollie— the Colonel—" She halted suddenly and, turning, asked in a smothered voice, "Is he dead, Ollie? Did they say he was dead?"

"I don't know! They only said that they believed you must be the woman mentioned by Richmond. Dead or alive —I don't know, and probably they didn't. You were mentioned by Richmond," and then we were walking again, hastening to catch up with Barstow, and Naomi told him that she got a stone in one of her newly-bought shoes, but I think he doubted it.

Close-run by the thought of Irregulars prowling on our trail, we stepped along with more animation than we had mustered since leaving Goochland Court House. Our strength was greater, too; for the moment our purpose was more settled. The weak little lights of Thompson's Crossroad hitched toward us before we had advanced for more than an hour and a half, and we were able to avoid the place without rousing more than one dog. We found our road; it struck off into the northeast, and we believed that Lame Mercer's cabin was only a short distance ahead.

Oh, at best it was a peculiar pattern which we wove through those counties of Virginia! Somehow we were more intimately entangled with every other string to which we bound ourselves in the loom of adventure, than we were with Mr. Vestry. After these years, I find myself bothered by an impulse to apologize for him, to make him more complete, more heroic and self-sacrificing than he really was, for he was the only white Loyalist whom we met.

The colors of Mr. Quarles and Mr. Summers, the hue of the Carpenters and the two Victors were easily recognizable. One could say of each, "This is wool," or "This is hemp," or "This is linen," and name the exact dye. But Mr. Vestry was of another stripe, of a less definable origin. I have thought to term him the shoddy in the cloth, and yet God knows he deserves no such injustice from one who ate his food and drank his milk, even in a manner of theft and bribery. The lot of the spy and the traitor is not a fortunate one, and there was something of spy and traitor about every man who belonged to the Sons of America. Yet weakness and avarice are no synonyms for villainy. I prefer, now as then, to think of Vestry as a man who dared to risk the burning of his barn and the ostracism of his family.

But no such cogitation could retard my legs in their eagerness to escape; and my companions forced themselves into the north just as anxiously.

The road became a curving gully more precipitous than many of those we had passed. We knew from the deepening character of the valley that this stream we were approaching must be the South-Anna. The hill was of clay, and had that character (so disastrous to him who travels a clay road at night) of sweating out its gravel and bowlders in loose profusion, until they lay thickly in the ruts, and even formed them.

It is often said that the progress of a traveler journeying downward is happier than that of the man who sees an ever-steepening horizon ahead of him. The parable has been worn raw in oratory and religion, but teachers who prate of it never traveled long nor far over unfamiliar terrain at night. . . . Your midnight wanderer, knowing not where he goes, profits from every hill that rises ahead of him, and suffers discouragement in the downward trends. He tenses his knees and his thighs; he draws back in unconscious alarm from imagined, unmarked declivities which may slant to immeasurable depth. Whatever exhaustion he suffers from marching his body toward an eminence, and from tussling to break, with his footsteps, the dictates of gravity, is more than compensated by the assurance that earth waits not too far ahead of him, and when he falls, he will sunder the laws of nature, and fall upward.

It was uncertain business, but we found the bridge just as we had been told. I was for proceeding at once to scout out the path; but Barstow said that we must wait with caution, our breathing concealed by the water's sound, and see whether we were being followed. We stood for a time, and then we sat, our feet dangling over the edge of this log bridge; we felt somehow that spring had come very close to us.

Naomi lay back in a trough between two of the largest logs. She whispered soon that she had seen two whole worlds dissolved in fire before her eyes.

"They're not worlds," I said. "Only particles of worlds. Bits of planet dust. I thought you knew astronomy."

Barstow inquired, "What are you two talking of?"

"Stars," said the woman, "falling stars."

"I've got worries more important than that," said Barstow, "and you ought to have."

She whispered, "Just think: our own world may dissolve in fire, in the same manner."

I told them grimly, but not half believing it: "Likely this world would profit if it did!" and the rock-ripples lifted up their voices to approve what I said.

"Here's a thing, people." Barstow spoke in that excited tone he employed to recount a memory which had long escaped him, and had quite astonished him by coming back. "There was an old lady lived in our neighborhood, out home, and she said that whenever a star went shooting off somewheres, it was because somebody had died! She said that they weren't really falling stars, but just a kind of smear that people's souls made when the Lord sent for them."

Naomi said to us, in some disgust, "I've met souls who wouldn't make a bright spot in any sky! If anybody sends for them, it won't be the Lord."

Barstow rose up. His shape blotted out a great many of those worlds which were fixed in their places above us; perhaps loose flakes of infinity were even then scorching behind him. He listened, almost as if he had imagined the faint echo of hoofs, and feared to find that they were real.

"No pursuit," he announced at last. "I reckon we're safe, by this time.... Well, you can grin all you want to, but this lady was a pretty smart old woman! I saw her cure my uncle of proud-flesh in his shin, when nobody else could. She may have had funny ideas, but plenty times she was more right than wrong. Her name was Granny Frakes."

I clambered up and felt through the dimness for my pack. "If Granny Frakes told you to listen for sounds of pursuit on top of a bridge with a noisy river under it, that was one of the times she was wrong, Bar. It's just occurred to me—"

"Why?"

"Because the water makes this humming and rippling, and we could hear no one coming after us."

Barstow laughed. "First place, a horse don't sound like a river! Second place, if they come with hounds, we want to be around water when we leave the road . . . you remember what hounds sound like, don't you?"

But to this I had no answer, nor more scorn for his ideas.

"Hustle up, Captain Kincaid," he ordered Naomi.

She sighed at our feet, "I'd rather lie here and watch the heavens exploding."

"Maybe more than Heaven will explode, if we stay on this bridge too long!"

"True enough," said I. "Hell might explode as well." While Naomi was gathering up her burden, I went ahead and found what must be the path described to us—a deep indentation winding into dry shrubbery, a short distance past the end of the bridge.

Naomi cried, "Ah, this can't be the way! He said there was a dead pine."

"Come along with you," urged Barstow.

I explained, "There might be a hundred dead pines around here, and we couldn't see them. He only mentioned one path—to the right, immediately beyond the bridge."

"He didn't say that, Ollie," she dissented seriously. "He said, 'Keep going past the bridge till you come to a dead pine, and that's the path to Lame Mercer's.'"

Already Barstow had blundered beyond me, leading off into bleak fastnesses. I argued, "I'm hungry; so are we all. This must be the path to Lame Mercer's. Don't forget—Mr. Vestry said something about grits. And we've got a hundred and twenty-seven dollars worth of tea!"

Despite her doubts, we went pioneering over roots, through swampy patches, angling our painful way around fallen sycamores, and Naomi must needs come with us or be left alone. She came, but once I heard her growling to herself, and I smiled in the dark at woman's willfulness.

Women were not made, I thought, for such grotesque excursions; I went ahead, carrying the idea in my mind as a dog carries a bone—pausing now and then to drop it, turn it over, approve, and go to carrying it again. I thought that Fate might have been guilty of more wrongs than those noted already, if it had placed women in the saddles of the generals. For who would ever manage a campaign, when the leaders balked at bagatelles, and got together in frightened tumult, chirping shrilly that the plan of battle could not go forward because of this or that or so-and-so?

A dog startled me out of my musings. It leaped from some unknown kennel in the grimness ahead, blaring suspicion to the whole bottomland. But yet we saw no light.

Barstow's hand clamped my wrist. I felt the woman drawing close behind.

"That fellow didn't say anything about a dog, Clark."

"He did not," said Naomi Kincaid.

"He did!" I cried in my angry hoarseness. "At least—I can't be sure, but— All negroes have dogs. They feed dogs when they can't feed themselves!"

Still the creature came bellowing closer each second, and his voice sounded as if he were big enough to do us harm. Then, while he prowled furiously beyond the thicket, a crack of orange appeared in the landscape, widening slowly. We crept about, dodging this way and that, until the trees no longer prevented our seeing the dim bulk of a cabin which stood beyond—door half open, and householder thrusting his head and shoulders warily forth.

A deep voice demanded to know who was there.

"Lame Mercer," I cried, with no sense of caution, "is that you?"

The man called his dog back to the door, and when the animal passed before the firelight we could see that its roaring had belied its size.

"Who wants Lame Mercer?" asked that same deep voice.

Naomi prodded me with her fist, entreating caution. "It's code," she whispered. "Remember what we should say."

"We're the Right Sort of People," I called out, in answer.

The man seemed considering our reply, but with less suspicion, for he advanced into full relief against the light within, filling the doorway. In the wavering glow of fire which distorts and changes, he seemed in no way lame enough to have earned his nickname. "The Right Sort of People? Maybe you be. Come nigh till I see for myself. Who sent you here?"

"Vestry," Barstow and I replied, together.

"Come nigh, as I bid you. I want to see for myself."

We found the path again, though it was difficult when the glare of the big log fire had played such havoc with our gaze. We stumbled out of the clutch of trees and grapevines, and crossed a dooryard not thirty feet wide. That raw-boned figure still blocked the doorway; now we saw that he held a weapon, probably a shotgun, with its muzzle commanding the yard.

Behind him a middle-sized black dog slapped itself to the puncheons in a forbidding crouch, with nose pointing fairly between its master's feet.

"Come nigh, come nigh," repeated the man. "Step up, Right Sort of People. Lord condemn us all, I see right smart of the wrong sort! And this musket is loaded with buck-and-ball."

I retorted, "We're armed as well. So take care!"

"I can't witness you none too clearly, strangers. I see one of you grows as tall as I do. What's your name, friend?"

"Barstow."

"Who else?"

"My name's Clark."

"There's three of you. Who's that least one?"

I cried, before she could speak, "The name of the least one is Kincaid. I tell you, Mr. Vestry sent us here! Are you going to turn us out?"

He chuckled kindly, and his dog got up, retreating farther into the cabin. "Not no way, people! Step inside and squat; I do like to make talk with the Right Sort of People."

I have no way of knowing, now, what reason it was that made us abandon prudence, as indeed we did abandon it;

surely enough had happened to us, to build the veriest wild-
ness in our spirits. Perhaps it was the voice of this cabin man;
there was something of the Hebrew patriarch about him,
with his matted beard and the hair hanging to his shoulders.
Or perhaps it was the lure of giant flames that went sheeting
up the chimney in topsy-turvy cataract. And perhaps the lure
that dulled us, came from odors of biscuit and pork around
the hearthside.

Whatever the cause, we were as innocent and tractable
as puppies. No fear touched us until we were beyond the
threshold.

Our host set his musket upright against the wall. He shut
the door and dropped a bar into its slot. He swabbed the
hair back from his eyes with what we could now see was
only the stump of a hand. From the far corner of the room
there rose a stirring and twitching, in a mound of bedclothes
where some late sleeper sat up to gawk at us. The little dog
—black, with points of brown, and bulging buttons of tan
over the eyes—sat on his haunches, and laughed silently.

Well might he laugh. Our host, even with one hand, was
our enemy, or so announced by his attire. His pantaloons
and jacket, stained by grease and household tasks, were all
gray—Confederate gray—with brass buttons **dangling** and
glinting on loops where they had not dropped off.

He was not lame. He was merely a **man** minus one hand.
He was not Lame Mercer, for Lame Mercer was black and
had been a slave, before he became a smith and a freedman.
And this man was white; of our race, but surely not of our
persuasion.

I had my revolver against the man's flat belly, in no time
at all; and Barstow came all too near to splitting the dog's
head with his ax, when the animal sprang frantically forward.

But the man took up laughing where the dog had left off,

and he nodded wisely at Naomi. "Ain't you got ary pistol or ax, Least One?"

"He's a reb!" said Barstow, as if we didn't know that already. "Don't let him stir foot from that door." He advanced toward the bed, where the occupant sat higher, a bewildered peak in the mountain range of old quilts, and began to pray in a determined voice.

"Why, boy alive," cried the gray-bearded man, "I had no intent to make harm for you! I conclude that you be Yankees or bushwhackers, but there's nought for you to bushwhack here."

His eyes worked disaster on my eagerness to shoot him in his tracks. "Well enough," I said, lowering the muzzle a bit, "but where did you get that rebel jacket?"

"I come by it when soldiering."

Naomi addressed my back, "Oliver Clark, you were so certain that this path would take us to Lame Mercer's!"

"Get that musket," I ordered her, angrily, and she snatched the weapon from where the man had placed it. I stepped back a pace or two, and let myself glance again toward Barstow. Bar held his left hand on his hip; his right hand still grasped the ax, but as I watched he raised the butt of it and scratched his clipped head with the steel. For the person in the one-legged bedstead (a kind of crude bunk built in the corner of the room) was far gone into the Lord's Prayer, by now. She was a woman, doubtless the wife of our bearded Confederate; she prayed as if in a manner of ritual, but not stricken by terror to the point of quavering.

"Don't you harm Treaty," warned the old man, "or the Lord will come down on you."

"Who's Treaty?" I demanded.

"Wife to me these six year, since my second wife Evaline was buried. *En*treaty, if you want to go by the book. But mostly people have always called her Treaty, and she's touched deeply with religion."

"When did you do any soldiering?"

"Mighty nigh onto two years of it! I plucked me a ball out of the air on the way back from Pennsylvania, and hain't been fitten for soldiering since."

By this time Naomi was laughing. She retreated to a stool near the glutting fire, where she sat with the musket across her knees.

"Lord condemn us all," murmured the old soldier, "but ain't you a woman, Least One?"

"Yes."

I cried, "Now, hold on. No nonsense from you, Johnny!"

He grinned at me, with a humanity which I could not withstand. "Put that pistol by, friend; put it by!"

Naomi whispered urgently; so I slid the weapon into its holster, though Barstow cried out that we must be cautious. In bed, the wife came to "Amen" and ceased praying; but the shadows were such that we did not know whether she looked on us with hatred, or only with that homely interest beaming in the eyes of her husband.

"Barstow," I said, "I think he's safe, especially if we have the gun."

Our old Confederate was nodding violently. He came forward with outstretched hand; when we shook I gave him my left, and kept my right on the holster.

"I know just what you be," he said. "You've all fled from some prison pen, though I do see in amazement that they have women in them, too. Oh, don't look at me so sly! I've got ears, and I've heard talk. . . . We ain't native to this region. We come here from up behind Rockingham county five years since, when there was a plague. Treaty says the plague was a visitation of the Lord, but I don't conclude the Lord's got that much meanness in him."

"What's your name?" inquired Barstow.

"Tillingbee. Johnson Tillingbee."

"What was your regiment in the army?"

His fluffy brows drew down, and bright little eyes hid and laughed beneath them. "Yank, I beg you! Do you stand fast and believe that I lopped off this here hand when I was splitting shavings? Well, I soldiered in the Forty-first Virginia regiment, and I never needed to lose my hand if I had had a grain of sense . . . just waved some kind of tom-foolery at a man over acrost the road; next thing I knew, I couldn't do no waving!"

Then Naomi rose up and cried in highest indignation, "What ails you two? Perhaps you did take me on the wrong path, but now I believe it was the right one." She set the musket down decisively in the chimney corner, and came over to stand before the householder—standing like a boy, feet apart and hands behind her back, and in the firelight her hair had a sheen that the most skillful gypsy goldsmith might have envied.

"Johnson Tillingbee!" she repeated. "It's such an honest name that I know you could never make it up."

He touched his finger to his forehead. "No, ma'am, I never. There's Johnsons and Johnsons in these parts, but I reckon there ain't no other Tillingbee this side of Cutaway Mountain."

Barstow began, "Not so fast! I tell—"

"Johnson Tillingbee," asked Naomi, "will you feed us?"

The old man debated for a time, tweaking at various tussocks in his beard. "Well, I never admired to feed Yankees. But seeing how my soldiering is done until they start to fight one-handed, and seeing how you're fresh from a prison pen—for I conclude you are—I might not count that you was Yankees." He crooked a commanding finger toward the woman in bed. "Rise up, Treaty, and put on a gown."

The woman sat higher; she held the top quilt wide, as a shield of modesty. " 'These wait all upon Thee; that Thou mayest give them their meat in due season,' " she said hoarsely.

"Right enough, Treaty." The old man added, to us: "She has the knowingest ear for Scriptures. But oftentimes I've looked in the Book, and found where she was mistook."

His wife told him, "Johnson, I can't rise decently, until these men turn themselves at the far end of the cabin. And you, too! I ain't going to be wanton, no matter how many strangers we got to feed."

Naomi cried, "We have money—plenty of money!" And when the old veteran asked eagerly about greenbacks, Barstow spoke forth and said that if their stores were low, we would pay them in Confederate currency.

"But," he continued, "no funny actions from you, reb. I don't mistrust you more than I should, but I don't like the color of the clothes you're wearing. Naomi, you set tight on that stool and hold Clark's revolver, if we've got to turn our backs!"

The woman, Entreaty Tillingbee, quoted with indignation, " 'Whoso privily slandereth his neighbor, him will I cut off,' " and Barstow ducked his head at this reproach, and came down the room to join me.

So we endured, backs turned to the women, and our eyes regarding the logs before us, while Johnson Tillingbee stood at my right hand, telling us again that he needn't have suffered his wound if he had had a grain of sense. I was glad when the woman's task of garbing herself was done; I was glad that Barstow had thought about putting the revolver in Naomi's hand. Naomi herself scoffed, afterward, contending that any idiot would have known these people possessed a simple charity for whatever unfortunates passed their way. Still, considering the spectral trail by which we had traveled to a Confederate soldier's door, I did not believe Barstow's attitude unjust or over-heedful; I would do the same thing again, were I to walk forth tonight and enter such a cabin in such a season.

Soon, however, we were again mingling in the firelight. Our hostess wore a loose calico dress, either dyed or faded to a brown tone; it hung from her shoulders with such fullness that she would have done well had she tied a sash about her middle. She was a hardy little person with a seamed, knotty face. She wore her long, silver-streaked hair tied at the nape of her neck with a colorless rag, and straggling down her back like a horsetail. But Johnson Tillingbee may even have thought that she was beautiful.

She prayed no longer, nor devoted herself to metaphysical discussion, but went with zeal to various storage barrels at the end of the room where we had stood; and soon sweet potatoes were baking. She drew a slab of hog-meat from a tub where it lay soaking, and filled an iron pan with thick slices. There was corn-hominy, too; the sight of this provender caused the little fountains under our tongues to play and tantalize us.

Naomi remembered the packet of tea, so dearly bought. She gave it over to Entreaty with the admonition that she use plenty of water in the process.

"Tea!" said the old woman, unbelievingly. "It's rich fare. I never thought to look upon the day there'd be tea in this house."

"Treaty," cried her husband, "I don't take kindly to mention of my poverty."

"We'll all have some," Naomi said. "We'll have all we want. But let me help with the cooking."

The old Confederate denied her. "Do squat down on a stool, as I bid you! I don't conduct no tavern, but Treaty will feed you well enough," and then he fetched a banjo from the chimney corner and tapped its greasy drum sadly with the stump of his hand. "I would make a ballett for you Yanks, but I reckon my ballett-singing days are done. I can't pluck the strings with this snag now left to me."

Wind went through the bare tops of swamp oaks bending around the cabin. I felt ready to close my eyes to the unreality of this firelight—the crazy circumstance in which we again found ourselves seated before a rebel's blaze, ready to be fed with his food (while he who heretofore was a single, dangerous stone in the howling gray gravel that rolled toward us across the contested valleys of Virginia, now sat crying his wound aloud, and praying that the day were back when he could have sung to us). But gray uniforms were a common part of Naomi Kincaid's life, as blue had been of ours. She seized upon the banjo. One string was broken; she swore that she could draw music of a sort from the others.

"Sing," she directed Johnson Tillingbee. "I'll find the chords." Barstow and I sat up from the rough floor, astonished to see her bent before the old man, with the instrument ready in her hands. And our noses sucked in the strong odors of steaming tea leaves and browning pork, which choked already in the low-ceiled cabin.

Treaty began immediately, while she knelt in the skirt of the flames: *Not all the blood of beasts on Jewish altars slain....* Her husband spoilt her hymn by declaring, "Treaty, the Lord won't mind a mite if we sing play-party songs."

"Secular songs," muttered Treaty, putting a lid over the pork pan.

But the veteran would not be dissuaded. His song, a jargon which God knows I had never heard before, for all my years of singing, came forth in a voice peculiarly nasal, quite unrelated to the calmness and depth of his tone when speaking.

"I'd sell my distaff, sell my reel,
Likewise sell my spinning wheel,
To buy my love a sword and shield—
Com-mel-o-la-lo-boo-shy-doo-rah!
Sho, fly! sho, fly! sho, fly! Roo! . . ."

He sang not much more than the chorus and a single verse, before Naomi was overcome with laughter and could no longer find the chords for him.

"I know that one," cried Barstow excitedly. "There's neighbors of ours used to sing that, out in the Iowa country!"

And Treaty Tillingbee reminded us by direct quotation from the Ninth Psalm, that the wicked should be turned into hell, and all the nations that forget God.

"We ain't forgetting Him," the old man asserted. "I never forget God for one hour. He brung me back to you safe from Pennsylvania, didn't He?"

His wife declared, "He brung you shy one hand, and how we're to get wood for next winter I don't rightly know."

"I did have a nigger man," Johnson Tillingbee explained, "but he run loose, and I conclude he's contraband of the Yankees afore this."

Naomi brought peace by saying, "If God wants soothing, we'll soothe Him." She lifted a clear voice, *On Jordan's stormy banks I stand, and cast a wishful eye to Canaan's fair and happy land* . . . there was power in her singing, and sweetness too; the banjo, warped by smoke and fire and abuse, played her false more times than one.

Yet she sang on, with the old Confederate pounding his bare foot against the puncheon floor and nodding violently when she boasted that no poisonous breath could reach that healthful shore. Treaty took up the burden of the melody, though I was surprised to find that she did not know all the words and made a kind of repetitious doggerel out of such phrases as lingered in her queer little mind.

Barstow bent forward, the ax-helve fallen from his fingers. His eyes never left Naomi Kincaid's face. I felt again the swift, unreasonable hatred which had assailed me before, and tried to dispel it by recounting the debts standing against me in Prentiss Barstow's ledger. Odors of supper suffocated me: the hot, aromatic fragrance of tea, which I had not smelled for so many months, did prankish things with my memory and my emotions. I realized that I was seeing Barstow through a blur of tears.

I knew the song as well as I knew the name of Westfield, and the dimensions of the white church, with dead and buried Presbyterians round about. In our home hymn book it was called "Avon." My uncle was accustomed to roar it on Thursday nights, with the melodeon gasping its asthma in the very ears of the angels.

Now I began to sing, and Prentiss Barstow came in boldly on the final phrase: *Tho' Jordan's waves around me roll, fearless I'd launch away!*

Tillingbee's wife wiped her scorched hands on her gown. "The side-meat's ready to be et. I believe the hulled-corn would be relished by you, though the potatoes won't be ready for a spell. 'I will sing unto the Lord, because he has dealt bountifully with me.' "

They set forth the fare on such plates as they had, mostly tin, upon a cross-legged table which Johnson Tillingbee said he had finished building the day when he first went soldiering. We crowded around, on our stools. When I saw Naomi across the board, in my turn I brought to mind a quotation out of the Psalms—perhaps one that even Treaty Tillingbee did not have lying ready.

Firelight painted us brilliantly and richly, though the logs were shrinking fast; I looked at Naomi to say, " 'The king's daughter is all glorious within: her clothing is of wrought gold.' "

But she only laughed, and Barstow lifted his head from his plate to scowl, and ask me if I too was touched mightily with religion.

"Yank," counselled Mrs. Tillingbee, "you'll do well to leave worship for them than can manage it better than you." She brought the last pan, still flaked on the outside with livid soot, and set it on the timbers of the table. Then she took her place, crowding next to her husband (who was eating as if he had not owned a meal for a week, though doubtless his evening food still filled him), and with a spoon she sampled the contents of the pan—some dark mass, steaming wrathfully.

Barstow asked, "What's that stuff, ma'am?" I wondered as well, for it looked like a very black cabbage.

In reply, she removed the portion from her mouth to her plate with more dispatch than elegance. "I don't know why distant ladies set such store by it. Any kind of greens is better—or garden yarbs."

"Greens?" asked Naomi, sniffing.

Treaty shook her head. She said, "Maybe the folks in far-off lands can relish it, but it's not a pleasurable food to me. I reckon you Yanks have mighty unfortunate taste in kitchen-yarbs! Now catch me a mess of wild lettuce before the white juice is in it, and stew it in a pot with a ham knuckle, and—"

We heard no more, for Naomi arose with a scream and plunged her two-tined fork into the kettle. She brought up a mound of the contents—the smell was there, and the steam, and it was something we had scented before.

"One hundred and twenty-seven dollars, Confederate!" whispered Naomi. "A pound of green tea . . ." Barstow and I lay back to roar, while the Tillingbees looked at us as if we had gone mad, as indeed we had.

7

THEY told us to lie down and sleep, afterward, and they were ready to offer up their bed to us whom at one time Johnson Tillingbee would have slain with his dutiful musket. We would have none of such doings, naturally enough, so we stretched before the fireplace that still resounded with the minute poppings of red-charred logs. The dog guarded us, and yawned of it. Once more all voices speaking or singing were gone silent, and I could not sleep, but watched Naomi's hair and Barstow's boots near my face.

We had not found the path to Lame Mercer's; perhaps we should never set foot upon it, but we had found a friend in gray clothes. He loomed solid and unmistakable on the edge of our disordered lives, and his figure was the more benevolent by contrast with the thorny wastelands studding his valley.

It was easy to reason that he had not questioned us further, nor had his wife, because their minds were simple; and yet that knowledge in no way satisfied me. I might deliberate just as sanely that I had no business in killing the men I had killed, or in being shot at by those who, a hundred times, had fired their charges at me. . . .

I wondered what would come of it all, in future years when this cabin had rotted into the red clay soil of Virginia— when these bones of men and women now wrapped in the tissues of the living, would contribute as food to the plants that grew in that valley—flowers to be plucked or trampled by hands or feet as yet unimagined. I wondered whether the same childishness which made men in mass to be enemies, and men singly to be valued as friends, would persist when the years lay like thick sod above us all.

Certainly I swore that the North should triumph, for up there we had food and men and many new boys growing into men. In these parts the food was scattered like the winter store of squirrels; and what men there were had vanished along lonely roads, taking the boys with them. We had the manufactories and the great ramparts of ore, the equipment for smelting metal into guns and their food. No matter, said I, if a dozen Joe Hookers are dazed or drunk at a dozen Chancellorsvilles, or if a hundred McClellans cause us to wear out our rifles with sandpaper: I knew that the hoard of rifles and cartridges, and the men for managing them, was by no means scraped to the bottom.

The world would go on, whether we lived or died of it. The downfall, the wastage of these straggling Southern towns and quiet country places was bound to come, unless our Northern statesmen grew wearier than the armies had grown. And when that happened there would be no more shaved-headed vagabonds wandering intricate paths, crying out to know if a man might shelter them.

There would be other wrongs and other misfortunes and inconveniences: of a sudden these fancied future ills multiplied like mice in my brain, and over-ran me with their disastrous little feet until I had to turn away from considering them. Once, when a boy, I had stood on our doorstep and looked at Orion and his minions, trying to settle myself in a voiceless emptiness which must have preceded their creation. I had done this until I cried, and my mother sent me to bed, with an eclectic liver pill for good measure. Now I was equally overcome by contemplation, not of what had gone before, but of what might come afterward; and I whipped my spirit back into its inglorious body before it should be undermined by the little ants of the future.

Here was my sworn enemy and Barstow's, lying by his wife's side, with his mighty snore filling the room. A thousand other enemies waited between us and our lines; when we met them we dared not expect the charity of Psalms and hominy. *My life,* said I, nearly aloud, *my life and my breath and passion, and the others' as well. We shall cling desperately to whatever small futures we have.* My whispering made Barstow shift his feet, and cough, and made Naomi turn her head until her eyes looked at me and smiled and closed again.

Long before dawn crawled the woods, Johnson Tillingbee had incited us to our journey. "I conclude nobody is pressing you close," he said, "but they do say Mr. Vestry has National feelings; and folks call Lame Mercer a black Yankee scalawag, and maybe they'll hang him some day for it. So be off, e'er you get et up by the Home Guards! They come by here frequent in the day."

He told us of a certain pine woods surrounding an old family burying-ground, on high land some two miles to the north. There it would be well for us to spend the day; we must be off the road before other travelers were abroad.

"I can't make you out, reb!" Prentiss Barstow burst forth. "It's not understandable, how you treat us this way with food and all, and don't ask more questions than you do!"

"I done told you," replied the old man, simply, "that I ain't fitten for more soldiering," and he waved his blunted wrist before our eyes.

Entreaty Tillingbee gave us the three baked sweet potatoes which had not been eaten. She said that many a time the Lord turned His anger away, and didn't stir up all his wrath; so Barstow put into her hand thirty dollars, Confederate, from our common treasury.

We left this cabin we had not expected to come upon, following a path as the veteran directed us, and carrying a pine knot until we found the road. Past the first thickets we saw the dead tree which marked another path, undoubtedly the correct route to Lame Mercer's, but there was no need to travel it now. A fine rain, cold and silky on our faces, gathered around us before we reached the ridge— before we saw the wooden headboards of the burying-ground leaning all directions in the first clamminess of dawn—before we crouched under our blankets among the mouldy cones, and took our turns at watching for those who might come to kill us.

8

THAT day we ate the last rancid bread from our packs, spreading it with a film of jelly which still remained in the glass. And now, of our original stores, we had left only half a jar of bacon-fat and the uncooked rice, beans and cornmeal, besides some salt and barley-coffee. But Entreaty Tillingbee's sweet potatoes were a blessing.

Soaked by the persistent unkindness of an all-day rain (far crueler to wanderers than the most damaging thunder shower, for it chills the body by degrees and saps all fortitude) we turned to our applejack and drank it down. As a consequence, we grew reckless, as soon as the rain stopped. Although it lacked an hour of twilight, we set out into the north, pretending we did not care whom we met. Luck rode beside us, and the only other voyager abroad was a toothless, middle-aged woman who sat astride a mule.

We came upon her at a rise of ground, and could not have avoided the meeting had we wished to. Despite the fact that the road seemed little used in these stark, weather-beaten miles, she was not interested in observing us closely. We said, "Howdy," and Barstow, garbed in Union blue, stood still for a moment with the ax tight-gripped in his hands. He had turned the edge of the blade that day, working patiently with his whetstone; and though he complained that only a circular grindstone would do the trick properly, the ax was a more dangerous weapon than when first he snatched it up at the Carpenters'.

Whatever color they might be, this woman saw uniforms only as an evil to be ignored. She responded wearily to our greeting, and rode straight ahead, not looking back as we watched her out of sight.

There were houses, too, but not many of them, and soon the damp night had swaddled us. It was dusk when we came to the Main Louisa Road, as shown on the map we had taken from Mr. Carpenter's book. In less than a mile our own road branched once more to the north; with Barstow pushing at my buttocks, I shinnied up a sign-post to make sure this was the route we wanted. A faded sign, barely to be read in the gloom, announced that Tolersville lay in this direction. We went on, sullen because the warmth of the brandy had left us. Our wet shoes rubbed our heels, and the night refused to offer us comfort.

Now was the hour for fault-finding and recrimination, if ever. Cold and wet, semi-starvation and exhaustion can bring out the evil in a human heart more deftly than any reagent known to apothecaries. Only the habit of walking our wilderness path, prevented the outburst which was bound to come. I have seen the same thing happen in the cavalry—where growing antagonism between man and man or officer and officer, rises with bared fangs, to be kept from biting by the necessity of the very ride which has raised it into danger.

The drama of pursuit was lacking. Now we regretted that we had not reached Lame Mercer's instead of the Tillingbee cabin, for probably the negro would have given us counsel about reaching another Conservative Person in the leagues beyond. We forgot that we had ever eaten; the homely flames of the Confederate veteran's hearth refused to warm even our memories; back among the cedars on either side of the road we heard the multiple drip, drip of icy rain-drops which had gathered among the rusty foliage during that day, and would come down throughout the night on whatever unhappy creatures passed beneath.

Naomi Kincaid, inspiration of our chief distrust, was the person who enabled us to set it aside and find an end to our miserable, mud-trudging night. Half an hour past the Tolersville sign-post, she stopped and told us that she had become possessed of an extraordinary idea.

"The country hereabouts is growing wilder and wilder," she said. "That's easy to see. No dogs have barked at us, all evening. We haven't once heard a cow or a human voice. I think it would be perfectly safe for us to build a fire."

Barstow and I scorned the idea. "That's well enough," jeered Barstow, "if you want some more Home Guards down on us," and I inquired sarcastically whether she wished to go back to Goochland Court House and build the fire there.

"You're fools," she said coldly; "both of you are. I wonder that I should share my common sense with you." Then, coming closer in the darkness, she gripped each of us by a shoulder. She patted me with her hand as she talked, and I think she did the same with Bar. "We'll gain nothing by going on all night this way, boys. Except pneumonia—or some kind of fever. We ought to reach the railroad in another hour or two. I remember that much from the map: Tolersville is on the Virginia Central, between Louisa Court and Frederick's Hall. They're well up in Louisa conuty. Spotsylvania is just beyond, and it's a howling wilderness."

"You weren't an engineer for Bob Lee, by any chance?" I wanted to know.

She said, in her level voice, "I used to hear a lot of conversation from Colonel Mokranowski and other officers." She made me feel shame, when she said it, and Barstow became more polite. We listened while she explained her plan.

Beyond the railroad line the farms grew fewer; consequently the intervening timber-tracts would be broader, and would offer more security to fugitives in their depths. Naomi believed that, once penetrating a thick wood, we would be safe in warming ourselves at a fire, if indeed we could manage to kindle one.

There was a rashness in this proposal which acted as a stimulant to us. It was intuition which neither of us could command, but from which we stood to benefit. Furthermore, knowing that Home Guards were abroad in this land, we might not run so readily into an ambuscade. Naomi told us that she did not flatter the Home Guards' devotion to duty by believing that they chose to prowl the wet forests on a night like this, with no special object in view.

It seemed not long afterward, though doubtless it was all of forty-five minutes, when we came to a break in the forest: the clay road rose slightly before us, and we found ourselves standing in a corridor cutting through the pines. I stumbled over a tie, and half fell upon a metal rail.

There I sat, clenching the thing with both hands, realizing that we had reached a definite height in our climb from the enemies' land. This was the road on which trains carried their grain and powder to the gray armies south of the Rapidan. The longer I fondled the iron rail, the more I realized that I was a Federal soldier, and not merely a prisoner to be ordered about by my keepers like any starved steer. I wished that we had the hands, the strength and the levers to sunder this staunch roadbed, and tear the metal from its anchorage. But enough of my patriotic ambition: Kilpatrick's men had done the job a week before at Frederick's Hall, and they were past masters of the art.

Once we had crossed the railroad, the forests squeezed us again. We turned along the border of trees on our right, hunting for an opening. We had three false hopes. Indeed we followed one of them, concluding that journey five minutes later in a marsh. Barstow got a bad bruise on his forehead when he walked into a tree on the way out; but the fourth time we were successful, and plowed for half an hour along a narrow path overgrown and treacherous, but a path for all that.

No more could I scorn the promise given me repeatedly in the Sunday School library of my youth. We had demonstrated to the Lord that we chose to help ourselves; and when at last we grew tired of hunting a glade where we could find wood and space for the asking, where we could lie unperceived in the sacred heart of the forest and hold safely to our miserable independence, we groped in the coverts and found a rotten bole of oak where a limb had been torn out long before.

In this miniature cave the punk was dry as tinder. We wrenched out a handful, which Barstow lighted with his second match. The tiny flame reassured us with glimpses of other twigs near at hand—the frizzled toothpicks that adorn only those trees in the deepest recesses of woodland, and which comfort the heart of him who needs fire more than any other gift of nature.

Feeding our blaze with care, we brought it to a healthy peak inside of five minutes. It shed enough light to tell us that we stood at the edge of the very shelter we had sought; we moved our sturdy fire, and built ourselves a kennel around it ... the intangible structure that houses each lonely camp-fire and makes it into a hearthside, when man sits down beside it. The wet trees were around us, but there was an opening through which our flames piled aloft, pointed as the heads of spears.

The path we had traveled was barred, time and again, by broken boughs and rustic abatis which the wind had made. No doubt the Pamunkeys had run there, hunting their game or their glory, centuries before. But man had passed it by during these modern years of war, and had left its exploration to us. With the wisdom of the wolves we copied, we could smell our way through entanglements where other men would have lacerated themselves, and sworn that no path ever lay in that direction.

I remember how our laughter went ringing through the soaked underbrush, at each little log we found, dry enough to burn. Naomi and Barstow worked to make a rack on which our blankets could be warmed and dried in some degree, while I took the largest pan from my pack, and went in search of water.

I was a long time finding it, too. In such woods the springs drip forth only along hidden ravines, and into those I dared not wander. But at length I floundered through a quagmire, and felt my way over the hummocks until I went down on my knees in a pool that was deep enough to satisfy. I stayed there, uncomfortable but motionless, until I supposed that the water had settled enough for me to dip up a pan full of it. Then I fought my way back, passing fairly beyond our blaze before I saw it stabbing at me through the trees.

When I came in, ready to brag about my accomplishment, I might as well have had a staggering blow across the mouth. Naomi had divested herself of her clothing. It hung on the poles close by the fire; and she sat wrapped in one blanket and the Quarles's coverlet, with her toes toasting in the heat.

The thought of her making such intimate comfort, alone in the woods with Barstow while I went searching for water in our mutual cause, was more than I could stomach. Barstow felt the glare that I turned on him. He grinned proudly, though if I had not been eaten up with jealousy, I might have known that his pride was only that of one who had been trusted and permitted to share a confidence.

"She took a notion, Clark," he told me, when together we were dragging up a big log. "She said she wasn't going to set around and catch the pleurisy. She just told me to turn my back." And then, when I did not answer, he whispered,

"She's a wise woman, Clark. I reckon we ought to have sense enough to do the same."

"Strip yourself, if you want to," I managed to snarl. "It's no concern of mine!" But despite his speech, he was loath to venture it by himself.

Forest muck stood in the water I had brought, but it was heavy and went to the bottom; by carefully spooning the purified contents into another pan, we acquired a pot of tolerably clean water. Into this we poured a quantity of our beans, wondering how they would taste boiled up without any previous soaking, but ready to eat them dry if all else failed. With salt and the last of our bacon-fat added, we felt that they would be a substance we could contemplate with reasonable satisfaction; hours later we ate them to the last rubbery crumb.

So we had food cooking, in this kitchen carved from the wilderness. Not all the water was needed for our beans, we could soon see; and having wiped mud from the first pan, we salvaged a few cupfuls of the liquid, and put it close to the fire to make barley-coffee. The fragrance (if this strange odor could be so poetically termed) assailed us in another five minutes ... we drank the stuff, taking delight in the way our cups scorched us as we tried to sip the contents. The drink was badly made, its dregs swirled as dark as the original muck, but we drew inspiration from the roasted grain itself. It raised our spirits with every breath, but poisoned us in a peculiar tonic way.

It was written that we two soldiers would be active rivals to the last ditch. We were fiendishly eager for the physical meeting, bound to result sooner or later; we were willing to flay ourselves of every gentle impulse, in order that one or the other could claim the supremacy to which he felt himself entitled. As primitive as when we left the Island, but never so weak and childishly hysterical—in this fashion, Prentiss Barstow and I eyed one another across the blaze.

We heard the woman talking. I know that neither of us attached any importance to whatever comments she made about Mr. Vestry or our journeyings of the night ... *I am the strongest,* Barstow's steady stare seemed to tell me. *Remember what we said in the tobacco house, and don't forget that you couldn't fool me then, no matter how hard you tried. ... Try to take her,* my eyes must have been telling him. For God knows, that was in my mind.

And she was bound to be aware that we were two beasts in a herd of three, and would go against each other with hoofs and teeth like any wild horses in the barren lands of Mexico. When at last (seeing how cozy she looked, wrapped in her blanket) we told her to bury her face so that we might prepare our own clothes for drying, she must have received the coarse assurance that we were going back into a spiritual nativeness, skinned of manners as well as of the cloth which hung around us. I saw Barstow's body, thin and red in the firelight, and of course he saw mine. He must have been remembering, as was I, the time when we undressed in the farmhouse kitchen, before our maleness came out of its starved prison.

Naomi began to speak, once we had joined her—blanket-wrapped near the fire, with our ugly pantaloons dangling nearby. She found a way of bringing up herself as the subject, as if by this time eager to have us know her life.

How she began her quiet revelation, I cannot remember. She must have done it wisely, or we would have growled that it made no possible difference in our relationship. It was as if (still set on being as brave as she knew how) she trembled in contemplation of a time when mere womanly courage would not suffice, and she would need to rely on a masculine charity which had played her false before.

The mention of home does strange things to the man who is without one, or who cannot regain the home that is rightfully his. The mention of a mother and a father conjures up the mothers and fathers of those who listen, else people would never snivel into their handkerchiefs at a theater where mawkish sentimentality is wedded to brutal incident before their very eyes. And yet, if I attribute a motive to Naomi Kincaid's story, I build her into the calculating, hard-reasoning person she never was.

Rather than that, perhaps she felt a love for both of us, there in the twist of the flames; and it caused her to offer confidences that were the literal truth beyond any doubt—and yet which we would have hooted out of court, when first we met her.

9

Naomi could remember her mother. Not alive: caged by glass, surrounded with peonies. There was an echo of fright in this memory which should have had nothing but sorrowful peace in it (since she said that her mother had been sickly for years, and doubtless was better off without the nuisance of a husband who only fretted her, and seldom managed to provide). Naomi herself suffered at the sight of peonies and the very slight odor they carried, until she was grown. She did not remember the hearse, the melancholy intoning of the minister, or any other grimness in the shopworn pomp of death, doubly grim in the case of poverty.

She went out of that room, she said, as fast as her legs could carry her. She climbed a cherry tree near the house, and got her frock and hands sticky with the amber cherrygum. Later her grandmother came to fetch her, and probably would have spanked her at any other time. But the house and yard were filled with neighbors, so she put Naomi to bed instead, and that was all Naomi could remember about it.

There was a wooden well, a place of danger where she watched her grandmother put butter and Dutch cheese into a bucket, and lower the bucket deep in the well, and draw it up again when needed.... There was a cat named Hector. He had sore eyes, and one day disappeared, and Naomi's grandmother would answer no question about him.

Her father's visits were infrequent; they were attended by hysteria which left her undisciplined for days following. The house towered cold and gloomy as any haunted mansion (whereas she thought, looking back, that there could not have been more than four or five rooms). The grand-mother passed her days in the restricted misery of illness, short-commons and disappointment; the air of that horrid little house chilled Naomi's infancy instead of blowing softly on its flame. So she used to play that she was her own grand-mother, walking a similar life from stove to bedroom and back again, and those were the rare occasions when the grand-mother would smile at her.

When Naomi's father came, it was often enough in the night. Sometimes she awakened to hear him. It was like the coming of Santa Claus, or the rallying of a hundred other folk from fairy tales: the creaking of wheels, the dark tram-pling of hoofs, the banging of barn doors—if her father came driving his own horse, as he did sometimes. She was never allowed to get up and greet him; once she remembered lying, tactful and silent, pretending sleep when he came into the slant-ceiled bedroom with a candle in his hand. There was another night, too, when she did not hear him arriving, but awakened to find him lying beside her (fully dressed, on top of the bedclothes) and so weary that he slept until morn-ing with his boots on.

Once he stayed for a long time and gave music lessons about the village, and tried to organize a singing school at the church. The people who did not approve of singing schools of any kind, and more especially disapproved of those held in churches, soon saw to it that nothing came of this venture. On one occasion, early in the project, the benches were all filled of a Wednesday night, and Naomi herself was placed upon a table to sing a song. It was a song about a teakettle (the steamy hum of melodies coming out of its nose when it boiled on the hearth) but she could not remember the tune after she was grown.

Her father's name was Asa Kincaid. He had been a teacher at a young ladies' seminary—a very poor one attended by

Naomi's mother. He did not reside at the school, but came in each day to instruct the young ladies in music, French, sketching and other graceful arts, of which he had much understanding if little skill, and for which his fee was low enough to suit even the tight-fisted widow who conducted the school.

His elopement with Naomi's mother in the second year of her course, must have shaken the seminary to its creaky foundations. They returned to Mrs. Kincaid's native village a few months later, when the bride's father died; after that they made their home in Harrisburg, Pennsylvania, until the baby was born. The grandmother, Mrs. Pomeroy, opened her home to her erring daughter only in the emergency of childbirth.

Asa Kincaid had the roving foot, people said. Frequently he left situations which would have provided him a decent living, for no reason except peevishness at his clients. Naomi was perhaps six years of age when he turned up at her grandmother's, driving a cubical canvas-covered cart in which he had an apparatus for making Daguerreotypes. Where or how he had acquired it, no one knew; probably through misused credit. He received immediate commissions there in the village of Castle Hill, but his craftsmanship left much to be desired; people did not like the pictures he made of them. And one day when he was gone to the country on foot, soliciting more orders, a man with a badge and papers came to Naomi's grandmother, harnessed the spavined horse to the cart, and led it away down the road.

Naomi never knew just why she was taken from her grandmother's house, but suspected it was because the old woman grew tired of Asa Kincaid's voluble promises, and refused at last to succor him with food and lodging, or permit him access to his child. He came one day in the rain, driving a single buggy with a leaky top and a horse which was older

than the other, if not so lame. In half an hour he had Naomi
bundled into the buggy with him, though her throat was
sore that day, and she had an old crocheted shawl pinned
around her shoulders. He put her little canvas box of clothing and toys on the buggy floor for her to rest her feet upon,
and drove off through the mud towards Carlisle. Naomi
doubted that her grandmother suffered pangs of bereave-
ment. The old woman was ailing badly, and no match for a
spoiled child of seven or eight.

The man Kincaid had corn-colored hair that grew like
thick moss, low around his ears, low on his neck, and tufted
in horns above his forehead. Though he was long past his
fortieth birthday, there was not a streak of silver in his hair
at that time. There were intricate lines around his bright,
watery, blue eyes; he wore square spectacles with steel bows,
and sometimes he grew chin whiskers and sometimes mutton-
chops after the English fashion. His clothes were shabby, the
black cloth turning to green on each of his lumpy shoulders.
But he had a waistcoat of white linen with bright brass buttons, and he wore that (with a high collar and Scotch-plaid
stock) whenever he went forth to solicit orders for some com-
modity, or the right to give lessons.

They lived in boarding-house after boarding-house
throughout eastern and southern Pennsylvania, Maryland,
northern Delaware, and even eastward into the state of New
Jersey. (I pricked up my ears at this, and hoped they had
come to Westfield, and perhaps had bought medicines or
horehound in my father's store; but Naomi was sure their
wanderings had never taken them north of Princeton.) Sometimes the child was left for a week or ten days in the care
of a woman who might or might not have the virtues of a
mother, and sometimes she accompanied her father night and
day, for weeks on end, and slept in the buggy.

When the horse got chronic farcy, and died of it, Asa

Kincaid found himself a situation as a clerk in a hotel at Wilmington. He worked there some weeks while Naomi lived with him in a small room off the third floor hall, and ate in the hotel dining room, and made friends with commercial travelers on the hotel piazza. Asa Kincaid gambled—the first time that his daughter knew of his doing it—and he won a hundred and forty-odd dollars. Strangely enough, he had sufficient wisdom to buy a horse the next day, which he did for sixty-five dollars; and he lost the balance of his winnings two nights later at euchre. There was a fourteen dollar debt, besides, which he had been unable to pay. Naomi laughed as she told us of their flight: clipping through the autumn moonlight, with a wicker box of food from the hotel pantry weighting heavy as sin on Naomi's lap.

They reached Baltimore and remained there nearly four years. Kincaid was retained as instructor in a boys' academy, and doubtless gave a creditable account of himself, since Naomi said the school was a good one, and would never have retained Asa Kincaid if he gave way to follies. The headmaster was a scientist who had studied abroad, and his great passion was for the collecting and identification of insects. This hobby was well to the liking of a man like Naomi's father; he could gratify his roving foot on Wednesday and Saturday afternoons (and on the Sabbath, if he proceeded with caution). The headmaster—one named Gerlich—paid him seventy-five cents and necessary expenses each time he went into the fields or forest land outside Baltimore, to collect insects. He had a butterfly net and a great tin box, and bottles which he said were poison, and Naomi was afraid to touch them.

Those were pleasant times, she said. They would drive well beyond the city, unharness the horse and tether him where the grass grew comfortably; and when Naomi's legs grew tired from chasing about, she could climb into the buggy and sleep.

It was the poison in one of those small bottles (prussic acid, she thought) which terminated Asa Kincaid's connection with Baltimore and the academy. Professor Gerlich got some of the stuff upon his hands, and ate a pear, and died. He had been Kincaid's mainstay at the institution; the new headmaster quarreled with the protégé of his predecessor. Professor Gerlich's wife gave over to Asa Kincaid the tin box, the butterfly net and sundry other articles used by hunters for insects, together with many specimens from the professor's collection. Kincaid bought a hair trunk and had it covered with layers of oilcloth, and fastened on bars behind the buggy. He filled it with this inherited impedimenta; in April he drove down into Virginia by way of Washington City, and Naomi went with him.

They lived in Alexandria, Fredericksburg, Richmond, and even journeyed as far as the Old North State. They came back to Richmond when Naomi was fifteen or sixteen—she was never sure about her age.

Age as such, and especially the age of a child, counts for little with a man who can neither recognize nor cope with the responsibilities of existence. Sometimes Asa Kincaid told Naomi that she was eight and sometimes that she was nine. When she was thirteen she might indeed have been fourteen, and her father was not certain (though certain of each at different times) whether the year of his marriage was 1842 or 1843. And so, when Barstow and I came to know her, she might have been twenty and she might have been twenty-one, and she cried that it was senseless for her to worry about it.

But by the time they came again to Richmond, Asa Kincaid was established in the profession which he would follow until his death. It dated from his association with the entomologist Gerlich, and was also suggested by his inclination toward peddling, and the puttering with matters artistic.

He caught butterflies and moths and similar creatures, especially those of great beauty; and having killed them, he took their wings and trimmed them with the tiniest, sharpest scissors, and built the fairy flakes into mosaics which were satisfying to the eye. These mosaics (or designs made from the whole wings of the more vivid butterflies) he prepared under glass, or on tortoise-shell protected by shellac. He made pin-trays and the lids of powder-boxes for ladies, and great oval trays on which wine glasses could be set out, paraded amid a flowery wealth of colors too fantastic to name. He constructed shades for candles and lamps, and all manner of bric-a-brac—each piece ornamented with scraps of turquoise and ebony and magenta and sea-green, which he had stolen from the creatures who were born with them. On silk, on parchment paper, on fine-grained wood perhaps, or resting in the silvery whiteness of milkweed blossoms, he planned his intricate beauties. He sold them readily.

The girl was grown enough to aid him, long since. She said that we would marvel at how she could trap the hastiest, fluttering blue moth in the bag of her net. The quick turn of the wrist, the lightning twist of lacy folds; that was how it was done. You snapped your wrist in a back-hand turn that baffled the eye, and brought up your net with its captive locked by the slender weight of gossamer against the metal ring. . . . Though there were plenty of people, even so, who declared it wicked to ensnare such little handmaidens of the Creator, as they called them; and they ordered Naomi away when she offered her wares. Strangely enough, those were the people who never hesitated to ride on fox-hunts.

And more than these arts, the round-shouldered mountebank taught his daughter. He counseled her in philosophies he had never been able to follow, and put before her the dog-eared books he was forever buying in stalls near the state capitol—the accumulated, fine-printed wisdom of centuries which he had never put to profit, but which might prove the happiness of a shrewd woman. He chanted Greek hymns when he and Naomi were abroad in the fields; and while he pinned specimens and arranged them in rows for drying, he intoned the Latin of Virgil and Horace. She learned also, she said, of poets never preached in seminaries; and she heard about a man named Confucius as well as one named Christ.

They had rooms with a kitchen and tiny parlor, in a respectable house around the corner from Grace street. And though in time she came to know good families at the church, Naomi's social position was a matter of endless puzzling and argument amongst the Richmond folks. Obviously Asa Kincaid was a gentleman, for his manners could be as grand as those of any gentleman in his neighborhood, and no one but a gentleman could tell you about Odysseus. But obviously, too, he was a peddler, an artisan—and not only those, but also a disheveled lunatic who chased over the meadows of Manchester with a net in his hand, and was apt to frighten the field-servants. All in all, Richmond excused him for a Yankee with amusing eccentricities; though many women looked askance at Naomi as soon as she put her hair up.

Asa Kincaid had no political commitment worth mentioning, but he resented it when men went out of their way to threaten him, during the early months of 1861. Old Mrs. Trewant, who kept the house where they lived, grew haughty and more polite than usual, though she was as kindly as ever towards Naomi.

Kincaid journeyed forth in May to deliver a huge decorated serving-tray to a woman who had bargained for it: the woman's brother was at home, and remarks were passed, and the woman's brother said that if it were not for Kincaid's age and frailty, he would take a walking-stick to him. At which Naomi's father cursed the man out, and the rest of Richmond with him, and left the tray shattered all over the drawing room instead of bringing home the fifteen dollars which had been promised him. When Naomi (now a Secessionist, for reason of influence by her contemporaries) pleaded with him to apologize, he stalked out muttering; and he neglected to take his old mackintosh, although the wind was coming up with rain in it. Asa Kincaid went to bed immediately on his return, that night, and pneumonia claimed him a few days later.

There were two families in the town who invited the girl to make her home with them, at least temporarily; when she chose between them, she made her first great mistake. Her father was less than a month in his grave when the husband of the woman who had befriended her so kindly, showed clearly (at one o'clock in the morning, and in her bedroom) that it was destruction for her to remain even through the next day. She went back to Mrs. Trewant's and the unsold trays and candle-shades and powder-boxes which were stored there. But scandal was yelping behind her. Twice men said things to her when she went about offering the trinkets for sale; and there was a dangerous hour when she risked gypsying out alone for the collecting of more butterflies and chose a woodland in which a certain newly-fledged lieutenant was riding.

She told all this in the hot light of our fire; from this point on, neither Barstow nor I could meet her gaze. We watched the fire instead, and I think both of us felt uncomfortable to know that we were men, although muttering mainly our resentment toward the women who had talked about her . . .

Richmond was intent on war that summer; even in 1861, money problems became acute. No one cared for the rose and cobalt of butterfly-wings, when the accumulation of needles or belladonna or condiments was far more important to every household. Naomi cried at home, she said, as any girl might. But there were parties all over town, and an especially festive train of them after First Manassas. Invitations came to her to attend those balls which the young ladies of proper families might not attend, and finally she went, and finally she met Colonel Mokranowski.

And she told us no more (at this time) but I built it up from there on—on to the uncertain conclusion. And I saw her driving out in a good rig which the colonel had provided, a small sunshade clasped in her hand; and I heard the mutterings and annoyance of brother officers who were compelled to wink at open scandal which dared not cost them the services of an experienced European soldier who had been awarded a medal after Palermo—by the king of Italy, no less; and I saw her going to walk, and saw the women drawing their skirts away from her when they met on the narrow sidewalks; and I heard the restless importuning of other men, and the silence with which she faced them down; and I imagined how desperately she grasped even the stale portion of love offered by one who already had a wife and two sons in Poland. No doubt Mrs. Trewant wept bitterly at such tragedy. But I was ready to wager that Naomi Kincaid never shed a tear where man or woman could know about it.

That the Colonel treated Naomi with kindness, or at least such kindness as the character of a European military man could permit, I had little doubt. In most ways her fortune became no worse than that of a million women who, through the ages, have sat up open-eyed in their beds at night and looked on the husbands slumbering beside them, and who have thought, "Oh, why did it have to be you?" But mainly those same wives have carried out their duties of wifehood (or mistress-hood, as the case might be) with the resolve of the sharpshooter who is ordered to an uncomfortable post where the falling case-shot will find him in time. And I think that Naomi Kincaid carried out her share of the bargain, made or implied, as stanchly as possible, until the last sharp extremity.

It could not have been all misery: there must have been laughter and there must have been midnight suppers on the delicacies which a provident and selfish officer could secure, even in Richmond. I know there was music, because she mentioned it; and Colonel Mokranowski had a fine baritone voice and could sing in German or even in Italian. Under his bed he kept a great accordion with silver mountings.

He told Naomi of Vienna, and the wanderings which he had been compelled to pursue about Europe. When a very young man he had fought in a Polish revolution, and much of his life was spent in exile. Whatever simplicity, whatever hourly comfort Naomi could make out of her relationship, she must have made; that was her nature. And it seems doubly strange (after so long a time, when she had endured the emptiness and social blacklisting that came down upon her while her Colonel was away with the armies) that it could have been her hand which cut him down, and opened up his adventurous body as cruelly as our Yankee bullets had done.

She would never say that she hated him, nor that he tormented her beyond endurance. Certainly there was some chasm between them: a black and howling breadth which he repeatedly ordered her to cross, and from which she shrank, pleading, until he lost his temper and tried to drag her through it. That would seem the reason why at last she turned in violence against the man who had sheltered her, who had never been a rapt worshipper at her feet, but who had regarded her as an inviting diversion in the meager, hard-working life he led.

Long I have considered the enigma, in those Louisa county woods and later; and even now I am not certain about the wrong, actual or supposed, which drove Naomi Kincaid to her desperation. But I have felt that Mokranowski demanded from her that last complete capitulation of body and self, which is hated by the law and scorned by many of us who might have desired it in secret.

10

THE night dripped on, but we were not fit for sleep—not with the mettlesome suspicion which still played like lightning between Barstow and me. Now the strong thought lived in my mind: "She is cut away from the Colonel, the first man who had her and who was close to being her husband. She is cut away from Richmond. Her life will need to be put together again."

Naomi Kincaid had never intended to sprinkle salt on our sores. But in final analysis, her autobiography (orally recounted at so parlous a time) had provoked us to new savagery. I think she recognized as much, when we made no move to prepare for sleep, but only watched the rough logs becoming blistered in the fire—puffing out with the irregular fudge-squares of burning, and tumbling apart when we laid fresher, heavier fuel atop them.

This was the first campfire of size which we men had watched since before we were captured; it brightened with the nostalgic allure which such fires will ever have for the soldier who has spent many nights beside them. We were not romantic poets, and we did not see hide nor hair of the Sixth Wisconsin Volunteers or the First New Jersey Cavalry, parading amidst the coals. But we saw the lives we had lived, and the strength which had been ours in another year; we were hypnotized into believing that the vigor of the past—its dreams and appetites and fervency—was fabricated within us once more.

I came out of my musing to hear Naomi reading from the works of Lord Byron. She held a tiny volume with marbled covers, containing four poems: "The Giaour," "Bride of Abydos," "The Corsair," and "Lara." It was the same book she had been reading at the Carpenters'. Now I remembered how, at the moment of our flight from the house, she had run into the north room and had come back, thrusting something into her pocket as she hurried.

It was the first time I saw her with her prize, though later we learned that she had read some of it aloud to Mrs. Quarles during the hours of captivity at Goochland Court House. Apparently Mrs. Quarles was hard-put to cope with names like Maugrabee and Carasman and Bey Aglou. I was, too, in this reading, as I had never yearned toward Lord Byron when he traversed the citron-scented avenues of the Ottomans. God knows what Barstow thought of it, since he said that poetry offered no passion to him, and since he had never had opportunity to read much besides Rollo books and the Bible. I think he enjoyed the scenes of warfare, for there is a compelling ring to any metal that Byron smites upon the heads of his listeners. But I must say that I did not hear half of the first canto of "The Bride of Abydos," being perplexed with my own doubts and eagernesses, and not caring for any heroine named Zuleika.

I was startled to life somewhere in Canto Two on the line "My breast is offer'd—take thy fill," and I shuddered a bit at the next stanza:

> *"My slave, Zuleika!—nay, I'm thine:*
> *But, gentle love, this transport calm,*
> *Thy lot shall yet be link'd with mine;*
> *I swear it by our Prophet's shrine,*
> *And be that thought thy sorrow's balm.*
> *So may the Koran verse display'd*
> *Upon its steel direct my blade,*
> *In danger's hour to guard us both,*
> *As I preserve that awful oath!"*

At this point Barstow yelled roughly that he had had enough, and Naomi closed the book.

"You didn't seem to want to sleep," she said.

"If I did want to sleep, I couldn't—not when you're reading all them poems. They'd plague anybody to death—keep him awake all night."

I said, "Somebody ought to be on guard."

"Well, all right, Clark. You go on picket duty, if you're so set on it!"

Naomi told us firmly, "First watch. I'll keep the time." And she took her clothes, and went into the damp shadows to put them on. When she was dressed and back by the fire, I gave her my revolver, cautioning her that the spring was stout, and she would have to pull hard to cock it.

Already Barstow was motionless; whether he slept, I could not say, as his face was turned from the fire. I lay down near him, and was awakened only when Naomi called on Barstow to take the second turn. As soon as she had lain down, he got into his clothes. I did not stir in my waking. Apparently both of the others believed that I still slept.

And perhaps I did sleep: for now ensued an experience which had every quality of fever's delirium (when the patient is dangled into an unresisting void, and comes out periodically to view the world, but finds it charged with alarm and peopled by chattering termagants ready to pounce upon him if he fails to hold their stare). The fire sizzled and exploded, brittle logs broke beneath the heaviness of others. . . . Several times Barstow came to tend the blaze. Once he went off for more wood, and I heard him swearing under his breath when he laid on a rotten stump, and found it too saturated to burn.

As a fireman he was no more successful than I as a sleeper. But not for one moment did he think that I observed him. With the blaze going lower and less vigorous, minute by minute, the ring of light shrank around us two who lay near its hub, and our guard was left in outer darkness.

A long time elapsed, I say. It must have been close to the hour for my going on watch, and still Barstow did not rouse me. At length I heard acorns crunching beneath boots; and raising my heavy eyelids a bit, I saw Prentiss Barstow advancing rigidly toward me. The waning firelight was like sunburn on his face; it turned his jacket and ragged trousers to purple, and glistened on his stubbled beard. He resolved himself into a menace—an intimate menace—and by that reason, more terrible to contemplate.

Because the ax was in his hand, instead of the revolver appurtenant to his rôle of picket. He held his left hand clenched on the helve, immediately below the blade; his right hand grasped the handle farther down, and splinters of light danced along the steel which he had sharpened that very day.

Still, in the first moment, I did not realize that he thought of killing me where I lay. I had supposed that he stalked a forest foe on the opposite side of the blaze—a snake or a noxious lizard, perhaps, or some such scaly threat creeping at us from the nearby marshes.

But when the light found his eyes and held them, they were set only upon me, and Barstow moved with the stolid persistence of the sleep-walker. . . . Then I was sitting up, with the blanket fallen across my knees.

Barstow stopped in his tracks. For a long while we surveyed each other. He made no sound, but I could see the muscles stiffening and relaxing along his bony jaws.

"Bar," I asked, "what were you thinking of?"

The ax fell from his left hand and remained hanging, blade down, still gripped in his right. "Well," he muttered, "I reckon you know."

I cried, half aloud, "Why don't you do it now?"

"No," he said, shaking his head. "Not now."

I stood up. The wrapping fell from me, and I faced him naked, and the wind felt cold on my chest.

"We can't travel together, Bar, with things like this."

"Well," he said, "maybe we can, at that."

Naomi stirred; we watched her. But she seemed asleep, and I began to put on my clothes. Barstow retreated to a fallen tree, where he had been sitting during the long interval that preceded his approach.

"It's time for you to stand watch," he told me when, fully dressed, I came toward him. "Here's the revolver," and he offered it, butt end first.

"What's to prevent me from killing you, when you lie down again?" I asked.

"I don't know, Clark." He gave a laugh. "God, maybe!"

"God didn't keep you from it, just now. I woke up."

He said, "Maybe God woke you up."

Then we were silent for a considerable time. Beyond some untold, unplumbed distance, I heard a dog barking, telling us that we were not alone in the wilderness, but that other life still breathed across the borders of our lonely existence.

I asked Barstow what had come over him, to make him creep upon me in that fashion; and he said, haltingly, that he could not explain it. He had been watching me for a spell, he said, and thought I was asleep. Then he was driven forward, as if some one else were handling his body; and he had no plan for concealing me after he had struck me to death, nor for explaining to Naomi.

"Do you think you'll try it another time?" I heard myself asking.

He put up his hand and clenched my wrist, squeezing it until it ached. "Clark," he whispered, "I did save your life, more than once. You got to admit that."

"Yes. . . . I know what's happened before this, and I know how we talked in that tobacco shed. But I can't understand it. I've been wanting to fight you all along, but—"

He said, "You never sat, watching me sleep in front of you—not since all this came about."

I pointed out that the fire was low; so the two of us went abroad, Barstow ahead, hunting for more fuel. We made a great crashing in the underbrush and when we came out, dragging the top of a thin pine that had been broken off by the wind, we found Naomi sitting up. We dragged our tree across the clearing, the brown needles squeaking and whistling over the leaves, and we dropped the heavier end with a smash that sent the sparks high.

Flames curled around the trunk; branch by branch the drier twigs sputtered as fire licked them. Now there was plenty of light in the glade; and I fared forth after more wood, while Barstow lay down and wrapped himself in the blanket still warm with the heat of my own body.

By this gesture, it would seem, he laid himself at my mercy. It was his part in a rite calculated to make us forget our enmity—at least when one of us should lie helpless in sleep, and the other should be awake and able to do him harm.

I charged it against Naomi's poem, when I sat down to keep my vigil. The line, "Upon its steel direct my blade," haunted me whenever my eye found the ax. I was confident that those words had implanted murder in Barstow's brain; I recalled that it was only two lines thereafter when he ordered Naomi to stop reading. Thus she had offered him the notion of a wrong never contemplated before, through the very act whereby she hoped to wean us both from our perversity.

If he had broken down and wept, when I rose and accused him—if he had given vent to visible anguish and throes of conscience—our ensuing days had been easier to live. But he did no more than seize my arm, and squeeze it until it was bruised and swollen.

Oh, I had discovered him in unestimated weakness. We could never be the dependent companions we had been a week earlier, no matter whether he snatched me from destruction or whether I acted as his personal saviour. The matter was not settled, nor would be until some violence from within or without, melted our jealousies together and slew them for all time.

Naomi Kincaid's innocence seemed that of the veriest virgin, so far as the hatred between Barstow and me was concerned. She sat up for a while, after I had rebuilt the fire. She said nothing, but appeared to count the webs of flame fluttering from each tentacle of pine.

Not until afterward, did I know that she too had awakened at the time I sat up; that she had heard everything occurring between us, and had wondered in agony if it might not be better for her to take herself into obscurity where the mad Barstow had intended to send me. Only our youth saved us, that night. We could still digest the bitterest poisons and arise unharmed, to face final perils waiting between us and the Rapidan river.

BOOK III

The Symbol and the Menace

1

IN THE hours before dawn, a heavy frost came down on Virginia, as if God were bent on emphasizing the spell He had laid on our hearts during the night. The frost found us lying so close to the fire that we were in danger of being burned, and indeed Naomi's knit coverlet was charred on the hem. When dawn rose up, the gloom dissolved into a white fog, and if one had strayed twenty yards from our camp he could not have found the way back.

We had eaten the last of our cooked beans during the night, so now we chewed a few dry ones; we tried to eat some rice and cornmeal, but could not manage. Thus we were regaining the state of ordinary mankind, when palates and souls shrank in revulsion from what we would have held as highly satisfactory a scant week before. Barley coffee was out of the question, too; and when at last we floundered away through the forest, we were ravenous, and hoped that we might capture a bird or two.

Where the birds had gone I do not know, but the thickets did not twitch with their presence. On one occasion we heard a large animal scrambling from our path, and Barstow said it was a deer. Naomi spoke her fear of wildcats, but I believed it to be a hog such as run wild throughout the year in the southern woods, and are killed only when they have grown fat on acorns.

We were pursuing an erratic course in a wet, gray world where no sunshine revealed the direction. We called upon Barstow to bring a woodsman's knowledge to bear upon our situation, and he had two suggestions: first, that we hit upon a stream and follow it throughout each devious winding, for it might bring us eventually to the North Anna river; and second, that since there were three of us, we could patiently follow a direct line by moving at spaced intervals— the one in the rear marking a bee-line through the middle man to the person ahead, and thus continuing the process, though it was bound to be slow.

Since we were not yet positive that we had crossed into the watershed of the North Anna, and since following the ravines would cut our speed by half, we decided to try the second plan. It was wearisome work. The devil himself seemed to have constructed the thorniest fortifications across our route, and again and again we were compelled to make concessions as to distance and direction. I think now that we might have done fully as well if we had set off blindly, without any regard for tricks of path-finding.

In measuring our road in this manner, we necessarily called back and forth; our caution was leaving us, when simultaneously we heard some person chopping with an ax, not far ahead.

We huddled in the fog, wondering about it.

"If it's a white man," Barstow whispered, "he's apt to give us to the Home Guards."

"Not unless we offer him the chance," I said, examining my revolver. "But there may be more than one man."

We both appealed to Naomi—not with spoken questions, but with the silence which showed her, and us as well, that we had found her advice to be valuable.

"We cannot afford to lose the chance of food," she said. "We might wander for days in these woods, if the fog doesn't let up. Let's go on cautiously, and see who's there."

So we crept through tangled oaks and hickories, worming our way toward the chopping—standing motionless when it abated, and moving only when the clicking ax sounded afresh. The fog lay like rain over the trees, and turned to moisture along the boughs; it dripped constantly to cover our approach.

We crossed a clearing where yellow chips were scattered; and coming up behind the stumps of beech trees, we were amazed to see the ax-man not twenty feet beyond. The pattering moisture and very heaviness of the fog itself, had served to muffle his chopping; we had thought him far ahead of us still.

One of us must have made a sound: the man turned. We lay flat while he tried to see through the mist—mistaking the direction, and searching on our right so carefully that he would have seen us if he had turned completely around. Then he fell to work again. He was trimming boughs from a cedar which he had cut down.

Barstow hissed at me, and made war-like motions. I reasoned that where there was a man, there must be something to eat, and surely our wood-chopper was not an active member of any armed force, or he would not have been about his solitary occupation in this remote place. So I put my revolver over the stump, and sang out to the man that I had a bead on him. He yelped; he dropped his ax and stood with upraised arms, not turning as we came.

"Stavey Allen," he cried, "I reckoned you'd get me sooner or later, but I never expected you today!" Then, when we stood beside him, he fell silent, knitting his heavy brows and opening and closing his lips as if he struggled to speak more amazement than he had uttered before.

"Who are you?" I asked.

Still he regarded us in perplexity and wonder. He was a fine figure of a man (but too fat around the midriff) and he had shoulders like a horse. I judged that he was no older than I. He had a coarse brown beard; he was dressed in homespun and the tags of a gray shirt, his feet were bare, and though the morning was close to freezing, the sweat sat in jewels along his arms and in the hollow of his throat.

"Speak up," commanded Barstow.

The man gulped, and shook his head blindly. "I thought certain it was Stavey Allen," he said. "He's a drafter, and he's seeking me."

"We don't know Stavey Allen," said Naomi. "We're Yankees," and I was amazed to hear her say it.

"Do the Yankees have women-folks fighting in the war?" the fellow asked in bewilderment, while still I held my revolver before him. Barstow picked up the ax, comparing it with the one he carried, and then tossed it away as an implement greatly inferior to his own.

I ordered, "Speak lively, and tell us who you are, and where you live!"

He then tried to lower his hands, but I made him put them up again. He said that his name was Deaton Jones and that he lived in a cabin which he had newly built, with his wife and an uncle. Formerly, his home had been twenty miles distant. He had been ordered into the army, and when he ran away—either before or after enlistment, for he didn't say which—the man Stavey Allen undertook to hunt him down. He had come to live in these woods solely to avoid conscription or whatever penalty the authorities planned to inflict.

"I don't want to fight in no war," he said. "I'm scairt to death of shooting-irons, because a shotgun went off close beside me, when I was a baby."

This seemed a lame enough excuse, to us who had fought on the Union side; though Naomi pitied the big fellow for his cowardice, and smiled at him.

We ordered him to lead us to the cabin, which was about fifty rods distant. In spite of my injunction that he be silent, he began to roar his wife's name, "Lina! Lina!"

when we were still some distance away. The cabin door was swinging open as we approached, but the wife did not peep out.

"I feared as much," he sighed. "She's gone to her mammy's place, and there ain't nobody home but Uncle Deaton."

We followed him into the house. Uncle Deaton was nowhere in sight; the cabin appeared to have but a single room and a loft. Outside, there was a solid lean-to built on one end, and I had noticed that its door was shut and fastened with a rusty chain.

When we demanded food, Deaton Jones brought willingly what he had: a pan of side-meat left from a previous meal, and covered with the cold brown grease of its frying; several dry pones of bread; a few raw turnips. "That's all we've got, till Thursday," he said. "My wife's pap is to bring us some pork then, and I reckon our meal's about out, too."

Since we were eating up the last of the Jones's provisions, and very speedily at that, I muttered to Barstow that we should leave them some money. He growled that he didn't wish to pay any skulkers for food, and rebel skulkers at that; but Naomi prevailed upon him, saying that after all, the Confederate shinplasters would be no use to us once we were north of the Rapidan. But Barstow would leave only a ten-dollar note, even so, and I think the food was worth more than that.

All the time we fed ourselves, the young man sat with his bare heels under him, squatting against the wall of the miserable little cabin, and eyeing the revolver which I held across my knee. Evidently he was very happy that we had not turned out to be Stavey Allen and a posse, for he repeated several times that he was dead set against going into the army.

When we had eaten our fill, there was left a large slab of cornbread and some tepid spring-water in a stone jug.

"Do you-all want that pone?" the young man asked.

"We'll take it along," Barstow said.

Naomi cried decisively, "We will not! What about that poor woman, his wife? He must have eaten before he went out chopping, but perhaps she hasn't."

"Oh, for God's sake," I cried, "she can get plenty more at her mother's farm."

"Can she?" Naomi wanted to know of Deaton Jones.

He said, slowly, "I reckon her kin will provide for us, but I was just recollecting about Uncle Deaton. I ain't given him his food this morning, and maybe Lina never did."

We chorused, "Where is Uncle Deaton?" for we had begun to think he was some kind of household god, intangible but still prevailing in the place.

"Come along," said the man, "and I'll let you take a peek at him. He's mighty quiet today."

Taking up the cornbread and the jug of water, he went out of the door. We all followed, with me still carrying the cocked revolver in my hand. Round the corner of the cabin we went, and there in the end of the lean-to (opposite that side occupied by the door) was a window or shutter made of a piece of plank, and operating in a crude sliding frame.

Deaton Jones pulled out a peg which held the board steady, squeezed the shutter inside, and peered through a rectangular opening. He said, "That's Uncle Deaton in there," and then stood back, while we crowded around the hole, entirely forgetting in our curiosity to cover Jones with the weapon.

For a moment we could see very little of the dark interior, although light came in at numerous cracks. And then we made out a human figure, sitting on the floor with his back against the cabin walls. He was clad in rags as scrofulous as those we had worn away from Belle Island; the very sight of him made Barstow and me imagine that once more we were beside the James.

Uncle Deaton had a variety of small objects on the ground before him: pine cones, straws, bits of bark and little sticks. His thin hands moved rapidly, sorting them into piles, taking away a straw here and a pine cone there, and never seeming satisfied with the division. He talked in a harsh whisper, wholly oblivious of our watching faces at the little window.

Now and then he shook his head, seeming dissatisfied, and once in a manner of rage, he struck several of the scraps furiously aside.

"Not for my mess," he mourned. "I reckon we've had all the worms we want. I don't call worms in no way nourishing. Out you go, worms! We'll offer them to Conway.... Mess Number Nine, I'll divvy up with you. Schmidt's a Dutchman and he don't want none, but I'll give him a cone." Then he began to cough; and shaking his head, he went on all fours into the darker corner of the lean-to, hunting the objects which he had scattered a moment before.

He had a few other things in there with him, such as an old comforter spread across corn-husks for a bed, a bundle of rags tied more or less into the semblance of a doll, and what appeared to be a wooden gun very crudely whittled out.

Now Naomi whirled from the window, flinging her hands over her eyes.

Deaton Jones stepped up to the place she had vacated, and thrust his big arm through the opening. "Uncle Deaton!" he called several times, but he had to call again and again before the creature inside would notice him. He offered the jug and the piece of cornbread, which Uncle Deaton took without a word. Then the poor lunatic retreated to his comforter on the husks. He did not eat the corn pone, but hid it carefully under the covers.

We stepped aside, Barstow and I, while the nephew drew the wooden plank across the opening, and fastened it.

"What, in the name of—?" I asked.

"Well," said Deaton Jones, "that's Uncle Deaton I was telling you about."

Bar grunted, "What's the matter with him?"

"He's lacking in the head," replied Jones.

"Was he always that way?"

"No," said the young man. "He used to be a mighty smart figure, but he got brain fever when he was with the Yankees. They put him in a place name of Fort Delaware, and he didn't get near enough to eat."

Barstow howled, "We don't treat rebs that way. That's a God damn lie! We feed them enough and to spare!" He knotted his fist, and I thought he was going to strike Deaton Jones in the face.

But the young man said, earnestly, "Well now, maybe that's so. If you've been off to the war, you know a sight more than I do. Uncle Deaton came back to live along of us; and then he got brain fever again, worse and worse; and finally we had to shut him up in the shed, so he wouldn't come against no one."

The fog had lifted slightly. We took our leave of the place; Naomi was still very pale, paler than usual because of what she had seen in the lean-to. We pressed Jones for information about the route, and were amazed when he told us that we were not much over a mile from Tolersville.

"Not New Tolersville. Old Tolersville: that's clear off from where the trains go. You must have been going around in the brush, over along Contrary Creek."

He then said that the road which we wished to travel (since we told him frankly that we were journeying toward the Union lines) followed along a ridge running north between the valleys of Christopher Creek and Contrary

Creek. There were several little brooks which flowed together from the forest where we had spent the night, and their confluence became the creek called Contrary. But on west— and he pointed it out—if we could safely pass the few houses that constituted Old Tolersville, and cross the road and a farther tributary of Contrary Creek, we would come upon another wide belt of forest.

"There's a road that people can travel, some miles to the north," Jones concluded. "About a mile past that, there's another log road which no wagons can get over any more. Maybe you'd be safest taking that one. But they'll both bring you out nigh Ware's Crossroad, and then you want to look sharp. The North Anna lays close beyond."

We warned him about telling others of our presence in the neighborhood, but he only laughed. "I scarcely see a face from week to week, except Lina and Uncle Deaton. I reckon the Tolersville folks know I'm in these parts, but my wife's kin won't never turn me over to the drafters."

Before we were out of the clearing, he turned back toward the scene of his wood-chopping. The last sound we heard, came from the lean-to—a muffled outpouring as if the crazed veteran inside were lifting his voice in a song.

Naomi felt only the acid of pity and revulsion, which beset her so that she could scarcely speak for hours; and Barstow was angry at what he considered a political falsehood told against the Federals. But I found some grim strength in contemplating the fact that all the sins of a war are not visited by one side upon the other. Mankind as a whole, irrespective of army, is responsible for their instigation.

This is a knowledge not fit to be contained in any polite philosophy; but it made me forget our private disaster and the hatred which had tried to destroy us during the night— the antagonism of flesh, which would stalk our party until we came to the conclusion of adventure. Thus the woes of the world serve a horrid purpose, in driving out the secret jealousies or mournfulness of one's own heart ... but still the fog's dampness wrapped us, through most of the day.

Not since the time of our first meeting with Naomi, had we traveled for long by daylight, but we made a good thing of it now. It was easy to avoid the straggling remains of Old Tolersville, and we crossed to the west side of our road, unperceived by any one but the rabbits. The creek ran beyond, as Deaton Jones had described, and we walked into the shrouded, interlacing forests that would shelter us throughout the day.

By afternoon we were torn and scratched in a hundred places, and my shoes began to give me much trouble, with one sole loose and having to be tied every now and then. Despite the fact that we had eaten soon after dawn, we were starved before we came to Ware's Crossroad, miles to the north. There we lay, in gravest danger among the trees, with the fog lighter as the wind came up, and our eyes turned towards a ramshackle store where people went in and out.

In front of the store were tied five horses, and with the glass which we had carried all this way and now used for the first time, we saw that three of the animals wore Union army saddles. But God knows the solitary gray-clad man who watched them was never sworn to the Union cause. Inside that store or tavern, there would be four other men— Confederate officers, we had no doubt. So at length we fell back in starved retreat among the friendly cedars, and drove ourselves toward the North Anna, crossing some stubble-fields, but seeing no houses.

I do not think we were much over a mile due north of Ware's Crossroad, and it was late afternoon, when Naomi cried out, "Oh, look at that!" and we turned our faces, following the direction of her out-thrust hand. A light wind had come to dispel the bands of haze—grandchildren of those heavy fogs covering the country at dawn. Shred by shred, mists dissolved and were blown clear; framed as if in a picture, pure cobalt in the northwest, we had our first glimpse of the Blue Ridge.

Naomi had never seen it before, for when her father took her south he went by way of Fredericksburg. To Barstow and me, the cloudy, unreal mountains were a ghostly reminder of what had happened to us since last we saw them. But there we sat, all three, having struggled through spongy clay to a little weed-covered eminence; and without speaking to one another, we watched until wind and failing sunshine disappointed us by bringing back the haze again.

The Blue Ridge was gone from our sight, but not from our memory. Still we stared at a dull horizon where, for a brief period, the vision had shown itself to us. Why we made so much of that momentary landscape, I could not understand at the time. We did not expect to travel there. The Ridge extended far west of the army lines we sought, and was as remote from the hopeful course of our lives as it might have been from the lives of the old Virginia colonists who gazed at it two centuries before, and dreamed vaguely of strange, threatening pastures which were said to lie beyond.

I think that the quick color and shape of mountains against the northwest sky was, in important degree, an inspiration. It spelled masterful attainment, the fulfillment of the cryptic dreams which a person throughout his entire life finds unrealized in any moderate happiness of wealth or love or friends. Mere mountains are a peculiar reward for a leader to establish on horizons, beyond the toilers he would encourage. But we owed a debt to whatever leader ran before us, that day.

Still, there was the night to come—the intrigue, the

striving for benefits which could not be shared equally between us. The steel was sharp on Barstow's ax-blade, and my eyes burned when they looked at him.

In the dusk of that evening we waded the North Anna, below a mill, below a bridge where wagons were rumbling. And now my shoes were wholly worn out.

2

Two hours after dark we captured a negro, in the road slightly north of the North Anna bridge. Our starvation had become a rapacity that fairly screamed inside. One way or another, we were supplied with food during the week just past—more food for that single week than Barstow and I got our hands on, during any month on the Island. Ours was the heedless petulance of the angry living, not of the half-dead. We would eat, or know the reason why; we hid behind some thorn trees along the high-road, waiting like wolves for whatever victim might appear.

The negro came from the direction of the grist mill, which could be heard grinding seriously away in its valley—stopping not for one instant while this part of the Confederacy, at least, stood in need of its solicitude. We heard our man some time before we saw him, and in the gloom he seemed to be carrying a weapon; indeed, with more courage about him, he could have used it as such, for it was a clevis-pin belonging to a wagon.

Barstow and I rushed out of the thorn trees and fell upon him so quickly that he did not have time to resist.

"Marss Pateroler," he cried, when he could recover from the surprise of having a revolver against his back, "I got my paper! I got my paper in writing, from Marss Carey Mc-Keever."

We told him to hush, and prodded him up the road, with Naomi following on and bringing our bundles, two of which Barstow now took from her. We wished to put more distance between ourselves and the mill before we questioned our captive as to his Loyalist sympathies, and presented ourselves to him (we hoped that it would be safe to do so) as escaped Federal prisoners. Thickets were close on either side, and since the man had no lantern, we could not tell much about him other than his race; and that we could tell from his manner of speech.

Some hundreds of yards ahead, at a place which seemed for the moment safe and where the sound of the mill was beyond earshot, we halted our prisoner and told him that neither of us was the Mr. Pateroler whose name he had cried out, and that we did not care what sort of paper he had.

"I reckon I know who you are," said the man, fearfully. "I done thought you was paterolers, but now I guess you robbers!" He said, after further questioning, that his name was Wilse, but that most people called him Yellow Boy on account of his color; that he was twenty years old, and that he belonged to Mr. Carey McKeever who lived nearby. He wailed in conclusion, "Please don't take me away. Marss Carey McKeever he won't think I got caught by nigger-snatchers; he think I done run away, and he whip my old woman."

In all this talk of slavery and running away and whipping, Barstow could remain silent no longer, but told the negro that we were escaped prisoners trying to regain the National lines; he added harshly, "And how does that set with you, anyway?"

The boy shrank away from my revolver; I put it against him again. "Marss," he whispered, "that sets mighty well with Yellow Boy! Yes, marss, I loves the Yankees. I loves Marss Lincoln and all kinds of Yankees."

"Are you one of the Right Sort of People?" asked Naomi, out of the darkness in front of him.

But he seemed unable to understand her meaning, and certainly did not recognize her as a woman, though he kept reiterating his faith in Yankees and his willingness to do anything he could to help us. We demanded food at once. He said that if we followed him quietly to his cabin behind Mr. McKeever's big house, he would give us some mush and chicken gravy which he had there.

We commanded, "Lead on, then," but warned that we would shoot if he turned treacherous.

Now he was our guide as well as our captive, and he took us to his cabin by a very round-about way. He might have eluded us in the gloom but for Barstow, who gripped one of the negro's galluses throughout the journey. Before we turned into a path at the left of the road, we saw a light over to the right, and swung toward it. The man cried out, "No, marss. No, Marss Yankee! That's the Knuckles place, and they got a bad dog. You just follow Yellow Boy, and I get you some gravy."

The path crossed a stony field; and then, having passed through a spur of timberland, we reached the McKeever property—at least Yellow Boy said that this was it. We circled between corn cribs and sheds, keeping a tight rein on the negro meanwhile. Two dogs came up to smell around us, but were cajoled into silence by the fervent whispering of Yellow Boy. The man was in a dreadful panic; we could smell his body, wringing wet with perspiration.

At length he halted near the door of a cabin, unlighted save by a low fire. "Marss Yankee," he whispered to Barstow, "now you got to let go. My old woman's inside, and she don't love Marss Lincoln like I loves him. Then I bring you out some mighty fine victuals."

Barstow, however, would not release his hold upon the gallus-strap until we had toured completely round the cabin, and had seen that it possessed but one door. "All right," said Barstow, at last. "You can go in alone, but we ain't taking a chance with you. We'll be watching that door."

"We'll pay for the food, Yellow Boy," added Naomi, but he was gone into his kennel like a shot.

The night grew colder. We shivered as we crouched behind an old sledge, near another outbuilding. There were lights in the big house, a scant hundred yards away, but no sound of voices came forth. All we heard was the perpetual rustling of corn husks, wind-blown across the barren ground, and a squeaking of rats in the shed nearest us.

The rising fire in the cabin showed deep red and then paler, as its flames went up; we had little doubt, now, that the slave would feed us as he had promised. Barstow muttered about the untrustworthiness of darkies. For my part, I did not like this one as well as the others we had met—for instance, Ernest at Mr. Vestry's. Also, he reminded me of Fatridge—not in color or physique, God knows—but in the mouthy fervor of his patriotic utterances, which seemed too glib to be true.

Ten minutes had gone by, when the negro appeared at his cabin door and hissed at us. We came forward. I had put my revolver back in the holster, but left the flap unfastened. "My old woman asleep," whispered Yellow Boy. "You Yankees just sit down quiet on the stoop, and don't make no talk." He put a good-sized pan of mush on the step beside us, though there were but two spoons in it, and those were all that Yellow Boy said he could find. He did bring out a broken-handled knife, which he said one of us might use, but I scorned it. "You two go ahead," I directed Naomi and Barstow. "I'll wait to have a turn with one of the spoons." This remark was prompted by no sacrifice on my part, but because I wanted to get my full share of the chicken gravy, and did not see how I could manage it with the knife.

The gravy came out, too, in a steaming skillet borne by a Yellow Boy who walked on tiptoe and spoke in whispers, but seemed to chatter with fear at every breath he drew. "Good victuals, yes, sir," he muttered. "I reckon old Marss Lincoln never have any better chicken gravy in his life!"

"I think it stinks," said Barstow coarsely, but eating just the same.

Naomi told me, "Ollie, you've forgotten. We've got spoons, plenty of them." She put down her spoon and bent toward the packs.

But at this moment I was thinking not so much of spoons as I was of shoes, for I had seen by the firelight that Yellow Boy was not barefoot.

"I'll buy your shoes," I told him.

He hovered in the doorway, rubbing his round head with both hands. "Marss, I can't spare these shoes. Marse Carey McKeever whip me, if I let these shoes off my feet."

But I had heard enough of the Southerners and their ways with darkies, to doubt whether Mr. Carey McKeever (from a view of his farm in the darkness, I classed him as only a third-rate planter) would have provided shoes for a field servant. It seemed to me that Yellow Boy had acquired his shoes from another source, and that it would be no cruelty to force him into selling them, since with money in hand he could get another pair. All three of us, no doubt, were bolder and more brutal each day we lived, and so I felt little compunction about dealing in a high-handed fashion with this youth, even though he was feeding us at the door of his cabin.

I patted my holster, and ordered him to remove the shoes. He did so at once. Tearing off the sodden things which were so heavy on my own feet, I tried the ones given me. I would need more than one pair of woolen socks, before these shoes might prove wholly satisfactory. They were coarse and heavy, but better by far than the worn-out relics I possessed.

Meanwhile, Naomi opened the wrong pack and could find no spoon in it; I urged her to get on with her eating, and said that I would join in with the knife, as we must not linger in such a dangerous situation over-long. But Barstow turned, and spat into the yard with disgust.

"Clark," he said, "I can't stomach this chicken gravy. It fairly spoils the mush."

Behind him, the slave began a chattering whisper: "Marss Yankee, everybody likes that chicken gravy! Everybody—"

And then, and not until then, a thought struck me which should have come before. I stood up, facing Yellow Boy. He retreated into the cabin, and I saw the saliva drip from his mouth. "Marss," he cried, "them's good victuals!" His voice was raised to a pitch which would have awakened a dozen sleeping wives, let alone one.

I was after him, inside the cabin door; my first glance showed me a single bed, and no one in it. Yellow Boy retreated, babbling pleas and apologies, but a rude table close to the fireplace held more attraction for me than he did. It was cluttered with dishes and pans: I saw a side of bacon which Yellow Boy had not mentioned to us. And more than that—a paper sack with rounded corners, and printing on its side. I snatched it up; I was aware of a chemic odor before ever I read its legend, by the light of the fire: *Walsh's Meal. The One And Original Specific For Use In Exterminating All Manner Of Rats, Rodents, Weasels—*

I screeched, "For God's sake, don't eat any more of that!" In another second, Yellow Boy was out of the door and across the stoop. He leapt to the yard like a monkey, but stumbled over one of our bundles, and went staggering through the gloom, trying to regain his balance even as he ran.

I cried, "You son of a bitch, come back here!" and he

split the night with unearthly pow-wow: "Marss Carey! Marss Carey! Marss Carey!"

I had my revolver out; I could not see any too well, with the firelight and the flames and the memory of that poison sack, all glaring before my eyes. I began to shoot, guided more by the direction of the man's yells than by my none too steady gaze. I emptied the revolver, which held six rounds, and it must have been at the fifth or sixth report when Yellow Boy screamed as if I had shot his heart fairly out of his chest, which indeed I hoped I had.

There were no more yells for Marss Carey. Barstow and Naomi had the packs; we blundered through the litter of the black farmyard—that amazing, indescribable mass of abandoned cartwheels and chicken coops and broken tubs which seems to persist on every farm served by negroes, and some that are not.

Doors were opening, at the big house. The dogs were vociferous. We heard one voice crying, "Yellow Boy, what in damnation is the matter with you?" and another more dangerous voice saying, "Hold Pedro, Bobsey! I'll get the shotgun." Then we found a rail fence and were over it, wallowing through brush-grown land that bordered this side of the barnyard.

In flights of the past, in our lame reconnoitering across two counties, we had been hurt by vines and jagged twigs, but at no other time had we pressed ourselves into lacerating blackness as heedlessly as now. We made no attempt to find a path or woodland road; several times we were far separated, one from the other; we fought our way together again, bruised and scratched by the trees. I had one of my trouser legs torn off at the knee.

The outcry of dogs fell farther into the background, and why the men at the house did not shoot at random into the woods where we had gone, we could not then understand.

Later we decided that for a certainty I had killed Yellow Boy, or at least had wounded him so badly that he was unable to explain the shooting. Perhaps the McKeevers believed he was the victim of a brawl with another slave from a nearby plantation. His was the untrustworthy, mealy-mouthed demeanor of a fellow who might well embroil himself in a domestic entanglement of the sort settled with razor or pitchfork, if not with the revolver no black man was allowed to own.

Time and distance dissolved behind. Once we sprawled through a watercourse; we were drenched to the shoulders as we fought to the opposite hill crest, and on through the dry trumpet-vines. We fled until our breath gave out, and I knew that Prentiss Barstow was running a hard race against time. As I scampered, I tried to remember whether Naomi had eaten any of the mush after Yellow Boy brought out the chicken gravy. No matter how baneful the poison, I thought that Barstow might survive it, since I had seen him recover from other virulence on the Island.

When at last we fell into a ravine, shredded and bleeding from the relentless thickets, we could not speak for a long time, but could only gulp in miserable exhaustion.

"Barstow," I asked, finally, "how do you feel?"

"I don't know. What was it, Clark?"

"Poison," gasped the woman. "You said, 'For God's sake—'"

I said, "Rat poison."

"What made you think—?"

"I don't know. He kept saying how good it was! How do you feel, Bar?"

Naomi cried, "Oh my God, Ollie! He was the one who ate so much of it. Was it just in the gravy?"

"I don't know."

Barstow was groaning—whether from the tainted food or whether from his fresh abrasions, I could not yet tell.

"I don't think it was in the mush," I declared. "Neither one of you complained about the taste of that. Just the gravy. Did you eat any of that, Naom?"

She believed that she had not, although in the haste of horrid revelation, she could not be sure; and she thought it unlikely that Yellow Boy would have added rat poison to the cornmeal mush, which was already cooked up, cold and solidified, when the slave brought it out.

Now we made out the sound of a hidden stream trickling in the darkness somewhere on our right, and I crawled forward to find it. We were in a bowl of the hillside, and the little brook made an even deeper chasm about fifty feet beyond. I investigated this, and found that Barstow could creep down easily. I had cudgeled my memory to decide what antidote my father would suggest, were he there (since he was an apothecary, among other things, and accustomed to treating people in similar emergencies). As we possessed no drugs, such speculation was worthless. Even in broad daylight, and knowing what leaves (granting that any could be found in so unseasonable a time) might bring a favorable reaction, I am not sure that I could have persuaded Barstow to try them.

Fortunately, I recollected that copious draughts of water would serve to bring about a regurgitation, and thus empty any stomach, although perhaps already the chemicals had begun their work in Barstow's body. Too, the water should have been lukewarm to be wholly efficacious, but it was cold water or nothing.

Barstow said now that his stomach felt unbearably swollen, but all he wanted to do was lie there and hold it. "Leave me alone, Clark," he kept insisting, "I've come through worse things than this," and again he would give himself over to rolling and tossing, and beating the ground with his hands.

It was darker in that valley than at the bottom of any well in the world. Still, as if the night were smudged into visionary dawn, I was confident that I could see Bar's face— the swollen terror of his eyes, the half-open and anguished mouth with its dribbling froth at the corners.

"Come," I said, "you've got to drink. You can't wait any longer."

"God damn you, Clark," he sobbed, "let me alone! I can't move."

Naomi struggled to make him sit up. "Bar, mind what he tells you. You've got to drink some water!"

"The last thing I want," he screamed. "I've got all the water in the world inside me. I'm dripping with it."

"Ollie!" she whispered to me. There was inescapable command in the one word she said.

So I took Barstow by the shoulders, fastening my hands in his armpits, and began to drag him slowly toward the steady rippling.

It seems strange that I did not hold this hasty calamity to be an act of Providence, determined and brought about for the purpose of settling our recurrent antagonism; surely Prentiss Barstow might die, and the stain of his death not be upon me. Strangely, on the other hand, I did not recall the unflagging zeal by which Barstow had brought about my escape from Richmond ... those miles traversed on another Wednesday night, a long generation earlier, when he pried me from the vat of the dying.

I was possessed only of rage against Yellow Boy, a hatred for his treachery, and a desire to keep him from attaining his purpose. Yellow Boy, to my mind, was a witch doctor ten grandfathers removed from the witch doctors of the Congo, but born to the toe-bone necklace, the leopard's skin and antelope horns of savages who mixed more terrible poisons than Walsh's Meal. He was a destructive force, challenging me to exert my own fortitude and charity, and I was not going to let Barstow die if I could help it.

Bar was heavier than I, and stronger; he fought against the plan we had in mind. He kicked with his feet: Naomi exclaimed, and I knew that he had kicked her. I kept dragging him, and tussling with him. Foot by foot I got him toward the little gully where the water sang. I could not reason aloud. I could only condemn God and appeal to Him, in the same breath; and I yelled to Naomi to get the large tin cup or a pan from one of our bundles.

She found a cup, though not the large one. Dipping it full from the stream, I sat on Barstow's chest and tried to force his jaws apart. Naomi helped me: we fought with him, bereft of every sense except the power of feeling with our bodies, as a fever-stricken patient wrestles foes in the abysmal darkness of his disease. The first cup was spilled, and another as well, but I was choking Barstow until his mouth spread open and I heard him gag at the flood of water pouring into it.

"Swallow," I told him, "or I'll choke you to death." And that was senseless enough, since he would die at any rate, if he did not swallow. But we were stronger than he in will, and in the force of our arms; we drowned him with water, which seemed to boil like venom inside his body.

"No, no," he gargled, time and again. But we would not stop pouring it down. At last I felt his stomach muscles tightening and contracting rapidly, in unprecedented spasm; he rolled over on his side, his knees went to his chin, and we stood back wondering if even this violent reaction would do any good whatsoever, since so long a time had elapsed.

The body is possessed of subtle villainies, and one of the gravest is when it spews forth its vomit. We stood at the bottom of the wilderness, there in this narrow ravine, and I thought of sounds I had heard every hour, on Belle Island, and yet which never before seemed so terrible to me.

Gradually, the paroxysms lessened. When Barstow sobbed out at last (and spoke a distinguishable word or two) we heard clearly as any passage of animal, the rattle that Death made, going away through the underbrush. Still, the anguish came back to him every few minutes; once again we poured the stream into him, until he lay helpless in a ghastly sweat, but living in spite of torment.

When I felt his pulse, it pounded stronger than I should have thought. I heard Naomi whispering, "Cover him up, Ollie. He'll get pneumonia if he lies like this...." Working away in the darkness, and scattering some of the small objects in our packs until they were lost irretrievably, we got a blanket between Barstow's body and the damp ground; we brought up the folds on either side, and laid them across him, and then put the comforter over the top.

He muttered that he was too hot. But the woman believed a siege of perspiring, thus protected from chill, would work him more benefit than harm. We hovered beside him, wondering why the McKeevers did not come ranging into the forest after us, and thinking that perhaps they had come, in the wrong direction. No birds whispered in the raw night, but on a hill above there were evergreens, and the branches mourned continuously as if the dream of an ocean wandered through them.

Here was opportunity such as I had fancied when we lay at the Vestry farm, with Barstow *hors de combat* and the woman beside me. I attempted to rage at myself, when I could muster only the hope that we might yet emerge from this woodland trap where we lay chained by sickness and starvation and the fear of worse things. My anger was as difficult to summon as my passion.... Once I heard myself mumbling a swear-word, until Naomi's hand came through the blackness and touched mine, and her voice wanted to know what was the matter.

"We're here," I said, "like this, with no food in sight, and you ask what's the matter!"

She said, "You've been worse starved before, haven't you?"

"But I wasn't so hungry. I don't think I've ever been so hungry."

The hand stayed with mine. "You'll find something, in the daylight. We all will. . . . You ought to feel proud of yourself."

I told her, "Well, I'll never feel proud of myself until I have one thing," and guessing rightly at what I meant, she slid her hand away, and even shifted her body from near mine. But it was the hollowest boast of ambition I had ever uttered; she should have laughed at me, instead of punishing me with silence.

We were glad to hear Barstow snoring, however painfully. The woman was trying to snuggle into a position of some comfort, so that she too might sleep. I bestirred myself, hunting about for the remaining blanket and finding it still wrapped around a clutter of utensils, and tangled annoyingly by cords. The knitted coverlet I could not find until, exploring toward Naomi, I discovered that she had wrapped it around herself before I detected her in the process.

"What is it, Ollie?"

"Nothing." My jaws began to tremble. "It's cold," I whispered.

"Yes," she said. "We must draw close together."

3

THUS again we found ourselves in as beggarly a condition as when we slept in a pig-sty, far south in Goochland county, with Naomi huddled close between Barstow and me, and sharing our coverings. After his misery, Barstow had an odor about him that was unpleasant (reminding me of Bubby Voss, and Belle Island) and I wondered that in this plight I could take umbrage at it. The coldness tried to hunt us out, and succeeded: the little creek crawled with a thin, wintry trickle; pines cried their woes in a rising wind.

The woman slept before I did, and for an hour I listened to her breathing, the muttering that Barstow made in semi-delirium, and the whimsey of the upland breeze. At last I slept as did the others; with morning I witnessed a dank grayness round about, and saw the disordered pile we made there.

More than that, I heard voices. Naomi heard them on the same instant, and rose to her knees with a smothered exclamation of terror.

"Ollie," she whispered. "They're going to find us."

I, too, thought it must be the McKeevers scouring the underbrush with their dogs, although I heard no barking. The sounds came from beyond the ravine, and I was morally certain that we had not crossed any such gully in our wanderings; therefore, it was amazing to learn that the plantation people searched for us in that direction.

I remembered that my revolver was empty, and set to work to reload it, dropping the caps from numbed fingers and picking them up only to lose them a second time, until it seemed that Fate was distracting me from the work of defense.

Naomi awakened Barstow, who sat up weakly. It seemed that the poison had turned his face into a blackened smear. But it was only the blood of numerous scratches, dried in an unholy mask amidst his beard-stubble; and when Naomi shrank from me, I knew that I must look as bad or worse. I could feel cuts on one cheek, stiff and inflamed, and blood was dried in my eyelashes. The woman had escaped with one bruise on her chin and a nick in her ear, although her arms and hands had suffered like ours.

Above us, the indefinite murmur prevailed through the dull dawn; it came no nearer, it moved no farther away. We could recognize now the trampling of feet through the mud, an occasional metallic clatter—blended to symphonic majesty, as if a tide of invaders moved in endless current above the clouds concealing those woods. How the Mc-Keevers had assembled so many men for the search, we could not imagine; perhaps they had aroused the entire countryside.

Barstow muttered that he felt improved, but he could scarcely get to his feet unaided; and he looked like a bugaboo emerged from a worse hell than the Island, if such a place were conceivable.

With this conversation of hosts beyond the ravine, advancing no closer and threatening us no more seriously than when first perceived, we plucked up hope and began to count on avoiding recapture. We gathered such of our belongings as we could find easily, though as I have said, they were tossed about in the leaves. But we made sure of the blankets, and some other things; we set out timidly down the chasm, encouraged as the daylight increased, despite the curdled mists.

The sound of marching humanity was now on our left,

high above the hill's crest, and no one of us could fathom
it. At length, when I heard a man's voice sing out clearly,
"...*reckon it was coffee!*" my curiosity got the better of my
alarm. Deaf to Naomi's imploring, I ascended the left side
of the deep-split valley; at the crest there was a growth of
young pines intermixed with jack-oaks, and here I dropped
flat on the ground, stricken by what I saw. There was a
road beyond these saplings, and along this road paced a
column of rebel infantry.

Even as I lay there with my nose bent against the soil, I
took pride in what we had accomplished, proven thus beyond
any doubt: we had emerged close upon the theater of war,
and possibly we were now not more than a long day's march
from the opposing lines themselves. From the time which it
took these troops to pass (reckoned from when we first
heard them until the last straggler limped through the mud)
I judged this to be at least a brigade. I saw little of them—
desiring mightily to catch a glimpse now and then, but struck
so hard with fear that each time I tried it I would drop to
the ground again. As for Barstow and Naomi, they stood in
the ravine all this time; they could see my limbs hanging
over the hillside above, and they knew I watched some sight
more arresting than we had imagined.

But I observed enough to know that these soldiers were
mainly recruits, no doubt moving on Orange Court House
to reinforce the army there. The officers may have been
veterans, but prevailing through such squads as I saw were
the pale faces of young boys, the scraggly beards of old age,
and the taut, overwrought visages of the unfit, who go to
war only in an emergency more grim than the invalidism
overwhelming them.

Uncomfortable amid the chilly pines, I waited until there
were no more men to come—only the narrow road, voiceless
and gloomy in its empty windings, with clay unsettled by the

passing of many feet. Then I ventured into the path where they had walked: fogs sealed either end of the channel, though not such compact fogs as those of the previous morning.

My companions came up when I called them; Barstow made hard work of the ascent, and Naomi carried his ax. We tried to reconcile ourselves to the devious character of the country where we stood. Certainly this road was not the main road north from Tolersville, near which we had crossed the North Anna; for the mists were lighter on our right, and we knew the rebels had marched squarely away from the sunrise. We recalled that Yellow Boy's plantation lay to the left hand, as we went north from the river; hence, we must still be to the west of the main road, for we had crossed no cart path in our run-away of the previous evening.

While discussing our situation (childishly happy to find that no pursuers were at hand—and with Barstow able to grin under his domino of dried blood) we were startled by a movement in the eastern mist.

It was a wagon, drawn by two sorry horses, with tattered canvas hanging limp from the bows. This much we saw, and then we went digging like rabbits into the shelter of the pines. All the while the wheels wrenched toward us, sucking and hissing in the gluey road, I considered what I should do when the vehicle came abreast. We were hungry from twenty-four hours of fasting, and Barstow especially was in a weakened state. We needed food, no matter how great the risk involved. I could not cower in the shrubbery with undisturbed conscience, when I remembered how Barstow had braved his way into another road three days before.

Accordingly, when the wagon came opposite I leapt out at it, surprising myself almost as much as I did Naomi and Barstow and the men in the wagon. There were two of them, both dressed in butternut: a patriarchal driver, and a

guard sleeping beside him—one no older than the boys at
the Carpenter farm.

He sprang out of his trance, trying to blink slumber
from his eyes, and to aim his rusty shotgun. But I threatened
him with the cocked revolver; the driver obeyed my yell by
dropping his reins, while the boy lugubriously passed the
shotgun down to me, stock end first.

By this time Naomi and Barstow were at the roadside,
though Bar was tottering and finally sat on a stump. I put
the shotgun into Bar's hands and, giving the revolver to
Naomi, I got into the wagon from the rear. To my sharp
disappointment, it was not filled with food. There were
several knapsacks and satchels, evidently belonging to
officers; a portable field desk; and a battered trunk labeled
J. F. R.

"There's got to be something to eat in this wagon," I
cried to the Confederates, "or I'll blow somebody's head off."

The boy was sniveling (not so much in fear, I think, as
because he had lost his shotgun). The old man sat gravely
facing the front, hands lifted, as if he had sat thus through
a dozen previous captures or assaults.

"You're the most ornery-looking bushwhackers ever I
see," he said, without turning his head.

Barstow yelled to me that we could shoot one of the
horses.

"No, no!" protested the old man, in alarm. "Don't kill
this team; that won't do you no profit. They're all I got!" I
remembered, as he said it, that contrary to our custom in
the Federal army, most of the rebel horses were the property
of the men who drove or rode them.

"There's a keg of pickled meat, back there," went on the
teamster, still without turning, though the boy swung round
to look at me, wet-faced and doleful.

I found the keg, concealed in a corner next to the military desk. It was more of a tub. I dragged it to the tailboard, and it tumbled off into the mud without splitting open.

"Crackers, too," the teamster said; and so I found a case half full of them. I looked at the field desk and trunk, wondering what secrets might be contained there. But I knew that we dared not linger, if indeed we had thrown out the entire cargo, to explore it at leisure.

In another second, the ambitious notion assailed me that we might seriously consider capturing this wagon, team and all; and disguising ourselves as rebels, journey north in the Tolersville road. It was a scheme wild enough to have done credit to Barstow in his worst delirium of the night before. We would have been exposed to the sight of every narrow-browed Home Guard in the country, and probably the team itself would have been recognized. Too, we should have had to kill the wagoners in cold blood, to insure our success, or at least leave them trussed up to starve in the wilderness; and that sort of viciousness had never overcome us yet.

We had meat and crackers, more than we could ever eat or carry with us. "Pick up those reins, and get along west," I told the old man. I dropped down beside our spoils.

The teamster groped for his reins; once more the wheels began to jolt through the mire. The old horses whinnied at the cessation of this unprecedented rest, which was too short to suit them, and they moved ahead only under the compulsion of leather across their butts. We three fugitives gathered round the box and tub, and threw the latter over on its bottom, so that we might pry off the cover or break it in.

We made a handsome target, even in that dun-colored dawn. Heaven preserve me if I do not search another such wagon more thoroughly, should I have occasion to waylay one in my well-mannered old age. . . . The Secessionists were perhaps a hundred yards away from us when a pistol barked, and a bullet creased the air above Naomi's head.

Barstow fired one barrel of the shotgun (which came near knocking him flat, as the powder charge was heavy). But I think the shot scattered too wide, at that distance, for there was no outcry in the wagon. It continued into the west, disappearing among fogs at a half turn of the road; and though Barstow cried to me several times that I ought to shoot, I owned too few rounds of ammunition to waste in such a retort.

Now we caved in the head of the keg, and seined into the saltpeter for chunks of beef, which we brought out all scummy, but fairer to our noses than the Garden of Eden. We filled our mouths, even while we filled our pockets and packs with the smelly ration. Emptying the wooden box of crackers, we moved into timberland across the road.

Far in the forest's heart, we had our feast. We ate with no fear of poisoning, this time. But Barstow was not yet at his strength, and he lost his meal as soon as he had eaten it. Nevertheless, we had food in plenty for him, once he was able to assimilate it; in spite of his vomiting, he said that he felt braver than before.

We were stained and bedraggled, in more deplorable case than at any time since we left the Island. So we disregarded the rain which came soberly through the trees before mid-morning, and washed ourselves at a clay-lined stream. Naomi indeed bathed herself, going around a bend of the stream to do it and coming back in rejuvenated beauty, though disgruntled at having to put on damp clothes, and soiled ones at that.

Since Barstow could not travel until he had rested and eaten, I ventured to make a fire. It was hard work, and would have been impossible in those woods by night. But at length I found a spot of reasonable dryness, beneath the tangle where an ancient wind had gone through the forest like a plowshare. In a fox-hole depression at the roots of one torn-out tree, I scraped together enough dead bark and twigs to give us a flame. We hugged it lovingly; it grew harder and harder to find wood which would burn, as the rain continued through the hours. Drying our clothes or blankets was out of the question.

Naomi and I at least were fed; we fancied ourselves as becoming whole again. We looked into a valiant day ahead of us (or a night, if it came to that) when once more rested and fed into activity, we should be able to pit our determination against the distance ahead. We talked of it, too, though in monosyllables; and Barstow dozed in a sickle-curve, close to the protecting blaze. Naomi said at last that she thought she could sleep too, for an hour or so; so I was left to the solitude of a sick-hearted fire and a soaked forest.

But I was not discouraged by the constancy of this bad weather, nor by the ominous miles which still stretched between us and the Union lines. My eagerness for life and for the fruits of complete escape was stimulated by the victories of that morning. I wondered, as I sat watching Naomi Kincaid, asleep so close to me, why the urgency of my first desire did not yet exalt itself. Then, the more I stared at her and considered the courage and sympathy which she had brought to our adventures, the more I found myself entering into devotion.

4

THIS was the first time I had felt gentleness and a wish to plan for the future, instead of a desire to betray it. I could not take my eyes from Naomi's hair. I got down on my knees and, close worshipping in the wan light of our hissing fire, I saw the activity of Naomi's life going on beneath the skin of her neck: the tiny pulsation of veins the flutter of breathing, of swallowing.

Reminiscence was bound up in this adoration, newly sprung to existence on so unhappy a night. For I remembered when I had looked at another woman, although a very young one—three years old, in fact—and had seen her sleeping in a bed as clean and comfortable as she deserved; and I had marvelled at the perplexing significance which the Creator makes us attach to those of another sex.

This sleeping child I had worshipped, was my sister. It would follow naturally that I should wish her every happiness and that I should be, in youthful irritation, half frantic at unnamed vicissitudes which were sure to come upon her when she grew up. I wanted to draw a charmed circle around the bed, widening it to include the blue and red toys which she held so dear and which lay in the moonlight where she had thrown them. (Such a circle we boys used to draw around a lucky marble, and we believed that no one could hit the marble or take it from us, if we appealed to the forces of witchery.) But I knew well enough, although perhaps seventeen years old at the time, that it would take a more potent magic than my spit-wet finger, to charm the demons away from my sister's bedside, and from the side of whatever bed she might lie upon in years to come.

Man considers his lust to be iniquitous, no matter how delightful he may find it and no matter how proud he may be of it. He does not mingle it with the gentler loves which he has been taught are the only kind worth having—that is, not until he centers his lust upon some woman, and then awakens from a siege of passion, amazed to learn that he is considering this woman for his wife. So a phenomenon more common to man than I then believed, had befallen me in this most desolate thicket of Spotsylvania.

I stayed there for a long time, on my knees, and fought to keep my hands from examining Naomi's hair. I was wrathful at the ugly years behind Naomi Kincaid, and vowed that I should make unidentified malefactors suffer for them.

And then, when I could lift myself out of the thunder-struck present, I journeyed with the woman into a panoramic future even more arresting than our glimpse of the Blue Ridge mountains. I strode there, the most enthusiastic ex-plorer ever to walk abroad. My pockets were filled with valuables which I could give to Naomi whenever she wanted them, and sometimes even before she asked. Our food and clothing were unimportant, except when they made us the envy of vague unfortunates who could not be we. I saw every object which man or woman regards as treasure, and somehow each one belonged to us.

I endowed this woman, whom permanently I had claimed as my own, with phlox, honeysuckle, sunsets, the silver of music. She could possess the whetted satisfaction of exploits accomplished so well that the world remarked on them; and still she could demand the simpler glories hemmed by lamp-light and nursery. In a moment, I shared with her each charm which had come my way in the past; a door flew open be-fore us to reveal the paths of amusement and tender oddity I had not yet visited, but might now take Naomi along. Out of this door, voices sang to us. . . . I longed to talk with my lip

buried in the cup of the woman's ear, to tell her what had occurred and to hear her say, perhaps, that she had known it
all the time.

Never before had I known love, as true love deserves to
be set apart from ordinary passion, however true that passion may be; and now, as an old man, I do not blame myself for thinking that nothing like this had ever happened
to any one else. To my notion, the very trees studding New
Jersey hillsides those hundreds of miles distant from Spotsylvania county, took on the imposing aspect of trees woven in
a tapestry; and surely the swamps of the Watchung hills were
moistened by deeper springs than man had ever tasted.

I would keep Naomi Kincaid, I vowed, safe from smallpox and consumption and lesser or even more vicious ills
that come to eat at people. I would transcend all science of
the past, and arrange better sciences for the future; and
while making available to her the old arts which the world
had loved, I would devise more intoxicating arts; and would
see that special classics were prepared for her benefit (though
she would share them with the world, being generous at
heart).

The magic circle, the spit-wet finger of childhood, should
forever be described adjacent to her. But it would be drawn
by a finger tanned in suns never penetrating to this earth,
and wet in dews that drained from Sharon. Hail, hunger, the
misery of the bereaved, the damnation of the cold-hearted—
these evils would be warned away. And when, in weakness
following my unearthly vision, I considered the existence of
Prentiss Barstow, I saw him not as a rival who might con-
ceivably offer similar dreams for Naomi's delectation, but
as an out-wanderer to be pitied by the two of us, and to be
the recipient of charities.

God knows how long I dreamed, bending over her and
wondering why such love had not come upon me before, in-

stead of the less respectable, but more provocative, panting after fornication. I thought that God had something to do with it, and perhaps the devil too; and the devil had shown me a satin-lined seraglio (and had promptly snatched it out of my reach), only to have the Lord take holiday from less inviting endeavors, and come down into March woods for the purpose of instructing me.

The smugness of my concept did not occur to me, any more than it ever occurs to a youth who discovers spiritual love, or the reflection of it, for the first time. I pitied Barstow from the bottom of my heart, and I thought of finding him a situation in Westfield, as the work of a frontier farm would be too overwhelming for him after what he had endured. My belief in the enchantment of the flesh was as strong as ever, but now seemed an excusable belief, and not a lechery to be smuggled through the dark. My belief in beauties, material or evanescent, became a private festival which no man who had seen Belle Island should in righteousness have attended.

This charm grew into vice: I saw a forbidden peak where no wanderer has ever walked. Yet upon it, with the billion other dreamers of all time, I imagined myself drinking a triumphant horn of the moon's white brandy. I grinned in tolerance at lesser souls who should not have aspired to that summit—God-created for Oliver Clark—and planed off like a finished gem for him alone, from the moment the first winds blew.

5

Much of our impedimenta was abandoned this day, and we went stripped to the limit, for our last sortie against the forces besetting us. As if destitution and poisoning and rain were not enough, coupled with our ignorance of enemy country, we had now full warning of another danger.

No Home Guards threatened us this time—but full-fledged soldiers, trained in the art of detecting a thicket rustle or a splashing step along a midnight road. With every yard we gained toward the Rapidan, in like degree would resistance be whistled up. In a matter of hours, now, granted that Barstow suffered no relapse and that we hastened with some semblance of our former desperation, we should approach the campaign ground where I had been captured, and where certainly picket fires would smoke on the ridges against a surprise movement and early spring incursion by the Federals.

Mine Run was a stockade in itself—or better than that, a moat where the bones of late November might make a fortification of their own. Nervous suspicion breeds in she-bang or officers' quarters, when the winter is long in passing. Early this day we had seen infantry; once we had crossed into Orange county, there were few roads where we might not all too easily run afoul of gray cavalry.

We had our map, though it was smudged and water-stained. We saw that we must now be crouching in the extreme southwest corner of Spotsylvania county. Antioch Church lay to our north and west, Verdierville beyond that, and the lines of the Old Plank Road and the Orange Turnpike crossed beside them: arteries for the body and soul of the Rebellion.

Still, when we tramped through the wet hazel brush which came growing out of the north before us, we did not skulk in degradation. Perhaps it would have been safer had we done so. But I thought of Yellow Boy, and the meat and crackers we had with us: I had bought revenge and provisions at the point of a Colt's revolver, and still I had eight rounds left with which to assert my savage independence. We had acquired a second weapon, too (although containing now but one charge), and Naomi Kincaid set it over her shoulder as willingly as any private in the ranks; and Prentiss Barstow, once more on his feet, bragged that he could depend upon his ax-blade at close quarters.

In a remote tangle of second growth west of the Orange-Tolersville road, we deposited the Byron book, the bulk of our cooking utensils, and Colonel Mokranowski's field glasses, which we had lugged in sheer foolishness for so many days. There they lie now, for all I know. I have been told that a great share of those who fell in the Wilderness were never taken out of it: odd it would seem if searchers found a saucepan and a rotten blanket, when they could not find the horrid shape that once was a man. Or perhaps, indeed, they were found, and sooner than we could have imagined. Young boys wandering afield from farms that squatted in the clearings, may have picked up the Colonel's field glasses and carried them home, and wondered at the inscription graven on them in a language few Spotsylvanians could decipher.

But we had no regret at leaving any ounce which might retard us in the long swim we were now to make. The woodland was wet as any sea. We carried each his cup, with attendant spoon and knife, tied by cord and jangling from the belt. The blankets and the comforter, stinking as they were, soaked and oily, seeming fashioned from the very clay under our feet—we shucked them off like pea-pods. We could not dry them at any tiny, illicit blaze. The soil itself seemed more suitable for a coverlet.

But Naomi would not part with the knitted shawl which Mrs. Quarles had given her (I suspect because she was a woman, and knew what a task it was to make a knitted shawl, and also because she mourned the boy, Thomas Quarles, who had died at Cedar Mountain). She carried it hanging in a drenched wad over one shoulder, and the shotgun over the other, and she did not enjoy it when I told her that she resembled Robinson Crusoe.

I should like to know our course of that afternoon and evening, and a dozen times I have tried to trace it on maps. I failed, because the pock-marked map of memory permits little accuracy when one attempts an indelible transfer. I have prepared them all—pine forests and hazel-brush and wretched, swampy roads—in the great letter press of the Past, and have screwed the wheel with all my might, but still I could not make my map. I took the water of common sense and moistened my sheet with it, but still I have no certain impression to offer!

And I could go on indefinitely, contriving such figures of speech, but in the end they would all amount to the same thing: *i.e.*, we were traveling probably in a northerly course between the Orange-Tolersville road and the diagonal Orange county line, and probably we traveled about eight or ten miles, from the time we left our fire until we lay in a cedar covert. I think that we went nowhere near any of the crossroad stores or settlements, but instead tunneled stubbornly through the most uninhabited areas. Certain it is that we did not cross the main road again, but only narrow quagmires where wheel-tracks and occasional relics of manure showed that teams had been upon them.

So, since the main road itself bends increasingly toward

the west as it ascends, and since I am ready to take my oath that we covered at least half of a fair day's march, we were in Orange county when we slept.

Again there was no sunset to color our faces or encourage us. The rain was as persistent as the mists that crawled from the long, dead windfalls; the northeast wind walked like a decrepit beast on every ridge, and dragged its tail through the knotted oak trees.

The most amazing change was now evident in Prentiss Barstow, who had been near to dying only twenty hours before. It was as if, in getting rid of the poison that the treacherous slave had fed him, he evacuated himself also of a hundred pettinesses inflaming his inarticulate sullenness. He could eat now, and retain what he ate. He swore that another two days, or three at the most, should see us in Stevensburg.

One of the cavalry boots he wore (split to begin with) had a gap from top rim to the instep, but he tied it tight around his leg with strips of blanket cloth, and he said that if he needed to, he would chop the living boots off the next rebel we met.

My own shoes, taken by compulsion from Yellow Boy five minutes before I shot him, were giving me a good deal of pain. I dared not speak my mind about them—not with Barstow romping in unsteady enthusiasm, and talking of the lines which we should soon regain. I kept my sore toes to myself; finally the mud worked through, and the water, and then with night came a numbness that let me sleep.

We owned beef and crackers, if no blankets. If indeed we could not build ourselves a fire that night, we had the fever of our successes burning inside us. Our camp began with a fumbling, a lifting aside of boughs that tried to spring back, a crawling here and there in the moist shelf of needles beneath the trees. And then, each in his own little nest of cedar refuse, we said "Good night" with a decency we had not managed at any time before.

I can remember the details of our adventures before this night and after it, as well as any elephant in fable remembers him who dropped a morsel of tobacco into his greedy trunk, or remembers the kinder-hearted man who was prodigal with peanuts. But the fogs of the years tangle like cobwebs, in that cedar hedge where we lay until the woods were gray again.

I do remember the trees as being cedars, and not pines. I remember a strange cry which awakened me alone in the night (wildcat or owl, I do not know, but it was not a human being, and its home was in those woods) ; but I cannot recall the positions in which we lay, nor how nearly I came to embracing the woman as she slept, nor whether Barstow moved until his body was between hers and mine. The slate containing the record of our rivalry has been sponged off; perhaps the record of certain leniencies was wiped along with it.

No blankets wrapped us now, but still the night was not too cold to let us sleep. Somehow, I imagine that the warmth of the woman's body was shared without misunderstanding or afterthought, equally by Prentiss Barstow and by me.

We shared her body heat, we warmed ourselves at the crackling fire of her spirit. Before its kindness we hovered with outstretched hands. And yet, if our mutual detestation was neglected for the moment (and firmly I believe that it was), the moment had worn itself out before the haze of a new day was apparent through the woods. Oh, richest wisdom! that the terror of the future shall never be revealed to us who are powerless to avoid it.

6

FRIDAY was our third consecutive day of rain and mist, but now it seemed as if there had been nothing but rain and mist attending us for weeks. I was sobered, but not amazed, when I found that I did not know the day of the week nor of the month; and when I spoke to the others they were not of one mind about it. Naomi said it was Thursday, and Barstow said Sunday, and I was inclined to agree with him. The debate gratified us in a way; it was the sole topic occupying us at breakfast. Eventually, we agreed that we were all mistaken and that, in fact, this was Friday; although Barstow would not believe it to be the eleventh of the month, and stubbornly declared it to be the thirteenth, to the very end.

Small wonder that we failed to catalogue the successive days in their proper order. Evening had merged with dawn too often; and we had got much of our sleep in rainy hours which were high noon for the rest of this world, but midnight for us. One by one, we were possessed of the quivering emotion that retards the traveler who sees his goal nearly in sight, and sometimes circumvents him when he would have succeeded, had he not been so overwrought by his own hysteria.

Fogs lingered in every grove, and hurried to close the roads over which we came; they were in league with us, if viewed from the standpoint of any man who might be pursuing. But they were intangible enemies of ours, as well. Dampness got into our joints and made them red-hot and stiff, by turns. And never once more were we granted a sight of our blue beacon, those mountainous ridges in the west.

These were the mists of spring, but the bitter, flowery smell of earliest spring was not wound up in them. Frogs grumbled at night, but in a weary fashion: as if they prayed against hope for a season mellowed in the sun, that would prove November's misery was not on them before its time. Grass was greener and greener, but every blade of it had the moisture of death; and clay anointed us to our knees.

We tried to draw sustenance from the knowledge that this was not the color of the clay in Goochland county, nor yet in Louisa. In my mind I spread a scale of colored clay, like the charts in books of geology, to mark the Pleistocene or the Jurassic in our gropings out of tarns where it seemed as if we had lain compressed beneath the skeletons of monsters.

The clay of Henrico county near Richmond, and far into Goochland county, was a deep red rust; and machines of war had gone to their death and abandonment there, and rust would permeate the countryside long after the tenth generation had vanished. There was yellow clay atop the long ridges we had followed into the north (each ridge lifted above the sloping land like a backbone, but occupied with successive valleys and convolutions in its own right, among which we had toiled like insects climbing up and down the vertebrae). Brown clay banked the rivers behind us, filling them to ruddiness when the sunlight found their surface. I thought it would have been a wiser symbolism had the blood-red color prevailed into this north, where our blood was so close to being shed.

But no; the plaster through which we dragged ourselves was a kind of corpse-clay, cold and whitish—unhealthy gray in the gloom—and even more spectral when the fog lifted overhead. The iron had gone out of it, and this spiritless path we followed was in a country sapped by disease.

It was more appropriate than I knew at the moment—

far more appropriate than the figure of blood, worn thread-bare by poets who write of war. A certain miserable county where men languish by the thousand, and meet their end in the bullet-spitting tangles as skirmishers become involved, is not so much blood-stained as devitalized: the juice of manhood has been sucked from such country. And so it lies, pale and putty-colored, ready to be embalmed.

We had the glue of Spotsylvania county against our skin, and in it I now see the foreboding of what would happen to Spotsylvania county before midsummer. Stuck close over that was the fresher, oilier paste of Orange county . . . for a hundred years, will-o'-the-wisps will escape from its mouldering soil and flit abroad, suggesting the spirits of men whose last, forlorn chemistry was the creation of phosphorus. There were ten thousand ghosts of the recent past (and a greater number of the horrid, immediate future) who might have trailed us through every wood-lot, and ranted at us along the crossroads, and taunted us beyond endurance by standing in orderly rows around the farmhouses and saying nothing at all.

They did not choose to do so—principally, because we did not permit it. We failed to consider the specters of a national tragedy as more dangerous than the personal disaster we were reckoning so bitterly. Only in the light of advancing years, do we see such things with reason and calm, and know that the race is not shaped in its destiny by whether a Naomi chooses to yield herself within the arms of a Barstow, or whether she turns instead to a Clark.

The clavicles are hidden by moss and slime in various woodland dens, by now, or have been carted away to help build the orderly cemeteries. Also important, in their hollow-eyed grotesquery, are the skulls which then lay among the Orange and Spotsylvania stumps, or would lie there soon. And yet, being like other humans—no more selfish, but at least equally so—we did not stumble over the skulls or feel them rolling about our feet. Instead, we bored our way down overgrown paths, or scrambled in wet weeds of pasture places —driven by no fear of the past, nor of the future, but only by the malignant present that strode with us and would not be put down.

A dozen times we went astray from our rightful path. There was seldom hint of sun behind the mists; we had no compass, and whenever we came upon a road it wound in any direction except the one in which we thought the main highway should conduct itself. Nevertheless, for all our venturing into labyrinths that brought us against dooryards of danger, we managed to follow a course paralleling the shortest route between Tolersville and Verdierville.

We came across no more brigades of infantry. Twice there was unmistakable evidence that troops had moved in the path we followed; and on another occasion we heard a whinnying and rattle, by which we judged that a cavalry patrol was going about its business beyond the smoky screen.

We ate the last of our beef before night came, and had eaten nearly all of our crackers, when we brought up in a mule pen, quivering in our limbs from the increasing violence of our march. When one of the mists had blown away, and before its relatives came back to drip in their impenetrability, we saw houses and sheds and lamp-light, and knew that we were standing on the outskirts of Verdierville.

This would not do, even for people whose legs were ready to buckle. A few minutes later, the slow rumble of a wagon-train descended upon the village, and we took advantage of this sound to circle the settlement, passing close to the southernmost stables. We crossed a main road which must certainly have been the highway leading to Orange Court House; and so we knew that the bisecting road (near which we had stood before) would take us into the friendly north-west, if we had the courage to follow it.

A lonely rooster strolled our way. Barstow caught him up, strangling the tell-tale squawk before it came from his throat. He wrung the creature's neck, and trotted behind us, holding the feathered body out to let the blood drip free.

"If you want raw fowl, you're welcome to it," I said. "We'll never make a fire tonight."

He growled, "Who said we'd have to make a fire?" But when a big brown dog came through the murk, Barstow tossed the chicken into its jaws. Thus he served our cause skillfully, as the dog was too overwhelmed by this sudden gift to salute us with any hullabaloo.

We passed the outlying houses, and I journeyed beyond a fence of crazy planks to hunt for a milestone or a sign post. Such a post I found, but only when I had back-tracked within the confines of Verdierville. While I was peering at the cluster of weathered boards (some carved into the crude semblance of pointing hands, and each indicating a separate compass point) a man stepped out of the twilight, and asked what town I wanted.

Naomi and Barstow were only a few rods up the road. Judging from occasional bursts of laughter at a building in the opposite direction, there were plenty of citizens on hand. God knows—they may have been soldiers, or perhaps this was one of those settlements of guerrillas which I had read about in the Federal press. Military wagons were creaking through the town, though none of them turned in our direction, and it was their rumbling and axle-whine which had kept me from hearing the approach of this stranger.

"Well," I said, when he had repeated his query, "I reckon I want to go over towards the river."

"What river?" he demanded. "You mean the Black Walnut?"

I countered, "That isn't in the same direction as the Rapidan, is it?" to which he replied with an enormous snort.

"You poor fool, you mean to tell me you don't know where is Black Walnut river? Why, those critter-soldiers will take the scalp off your head, if you go sniffing around the Rapidan."

Then his tone changed. He came closer, obsessed with suspicion. I could not make out his features, for it was darker and damper and blacker with each speeding second; I saw only that he had a stringy beard, and perhaps he was a tavern loafer, for his breath smelled that way.

"Rapidan, sure enough," he said, all the while fumbling with one hand in the region of his belt. "But you didn't tell me if you wanted to point to the 'Coon ford or the Somerville ford. This here road spreads apart and—"

With this much said, he managed to catch my sleeve. He held a bowie knife, and he began to shout for help, crying the name "Harris" aloud, and declaring that he would open my gizzard if I turned out to be a spy.

With my free hand, I drew the revolver. Pushing the muzzle against the man's side, I pulled the trigger: there was the muffled click of the hammer snapping down on a rain-wet cap, or perhaps a cap defective in the first place. At any rate, the charge did not explode. So I struck my opponent in the face with the revolver barrel; he loosed his hold, and I went up the road as if the demons were after me (with a big rent in my shirt, but no blood drawn).

Barstow and Naomi had been alarmed at the outburst, but they sang out when I rushed past the weeds where they had taken refuge. So we galloped into the northwest, considering our exhaustion a minor misery of the past.

Twice we paused to listen for pursuit, and heard none. At least we knew that we were on the right road; and probably the stranger who had come up to me when I stood at the sign post, was a person whose word carried little weight in the village. If a man such as he, smelling of liquor and smelling none too good in addition, came into a taproom and announced that his bloody nose was the result of an attempt to capture a spy, I doubt not that his fellow tipplers would have laughed him out of countenance, whether the tavern lay below the Rapidan, or below the Raritan in New Jersey.

We limped forward at least two miles, and finally sought an old hay-rick at the left of the road. From this decrepit haven we saw lights ahead, suggesting another village, although none had shown on our map. Not until long afterward did we learn that those lights must have been the lights of Old Verdierville, two miles removed from the new town of the same name.

Thus the phenomenon of Tolersville was no phenomenon at all, but a chronicle of dissolution and inheritance manifest in Orange county as well, and so throughout the whole of Virginia; and on, it may well be said, through the territory of human experience, wherein the old is abandoned, and the wheel tracks lead to the new; the oats of ancient granaries take root along their rotten doorsteps, and blow pale green in the sun, instead of being eaten by the jaws that are champing in modern mangers.

Did this figure persist throughout the relationship we wanderers bore to each other? Was I the old (I, who had never possessed the citadel to which I aspired, but had only dreamed of owning it), and Barstow the new, to whom Naomi would turn when tired of my importuning? There was every reason for me to wonder about it, this night. Under the ribs of the hay-rick, I heard the stifled breath of an inarticulate man speaking his heart aloud. He spoke with that uncouth honesty which seems obscene and sacred by turns, and yet in the end demands respect, and a silent tongue in the mouth of him who listens.

Perhaps this is one revelation, of all those in our March adventure, which should not be made. I falter in spreading it out, as one has a fear of unfolding the starched, forever-clean pinafore of a child who has died. Yet I have opened my mouth about my own yearnings (no matter how I was plagued by doing it), and may the council of freemasonry that passes on the acts of prisoners who escape together, not condemn me too harshly if I slit the rawhide away from Prentiss Barstow's soul.

He spoke in the echo of thunder and lightning, some hours after we had taken refuge beside the hay-rick. The rick was of a type never constructed on the farms I visited in my boyhood: it was made of undressed poles with the bark still on them, slanting out in two directions from a longitudinal frame, like opposite rows of stiff fingers. In this trough the grassy harvest had been piled (perhaps in the month of Gettysburg) but wind and snow had beaten the remnants into a sodden layer at the bottom. Hay clung near the bases of the poles, like Spanish moss. Cattle and mules had torn their suppers out, until there was little else for them to tear; but they had left the trace of their visits on the ground beneath, and that was the reason I lay exposed in the trough overhead, when the evening storm came down.

Naomi and Bar made nests underneath the contraption; but I was tardy in claiming a home, and so there was no room for me unless I chose to forget that farm animals are, as we, subject to the orders of nature. Voicing my rage and disgust, I clambered up and fell into that soggy fodder still covering the poles.

At first I accounted myself fortunate, and I had breath enough to jeer at the others; but my body, light as it was, began to settle through the layer; soon I had a dozen knots probing my back. I hitched and turned, trying to make myself comfortable, and wondering if after all it might not be wiser to bed myself among the cattle-droppings.

I fell asleep considering it. I slept lightly, and I think for only a short time.... Thunder boomed in my face, like innumerable Parrott guns, and the lightning crackled keenly. I hoped that many rebels might be struck dead by it, but could not muster the courage to move. Rain fell, but we were drenched to begin with; and I believe we felt a scorn for our forgotten selves who would have shunned this violent splashing, and squealed to get away from it.

The shower did not continue for long. It walked away to drench Verdierville and the toilsome country east of it; the retreating Parrott guns rumbled discordant volleys, as I scraped more hay around me and sank to the verge of limbo. Then, fanned from slumber by the lilac motion which still broke loose along the horizon, I heard Barstow declaring himself to Naomi Kincaid. I wondered if I might not be hearing the chant of a goblin left behind by its father, the storm.

No, I swore to myself, *this is no demon bred by the lightning, but the same rapscallion who was once my friend* ... I tried to gloat: I will admit it now. And, sentence by sentence, I weaken in my resolve to put his speech down as he would have said it, quoted completely and marred by the colloquialism of one who never had the encouragement of copy-books and sensible schoolmasters.

He had read the Bible and the Rollo books, as I said before. He brought to his suit the rustic honor of the boy Rollo, and Rollo's willingness to work for any profit in this life. He brought to it the appetites of old Jews, who had reared their dozens of children on prairies unlike the prairies of Iowa, and in tents constructed differently from the tepees of the Sioux. But whether he drew from the Scriptures this dream of conjugality (once we had safely reached the Union lines and once the war was done), or whether he sucked it only from a yeoman inheritance, he spoke with glowing eagerness. He must have voiced every dream of his impoverished youth.

Who was I, to lie spread-eagled on my rick of poles, and hear the declaration which he cried to Naomi? And who am I, now, to publish it in its pathetic triviality (though perhaps people will say that it was no more pathetic and no more trivial than the dazzlement I had dreamed, a day and a half before) and to make believe that the hope of twin futures is more ideal when its roots are in a New Jersey town, than when it springs from the soil of a frontier farm?

He was my comrade once, and my saviour. Something about the hearty nakedness of his utterance made me shiver as the rain had not done. Barstow was proclaiming a plan which I had neglected to voice, and might never have an opportunity to speak. I had spoken to this woman only about my desires—never about the visions I now sought to build around her. I know well enough that desire should live in any home, or one may go abroad to hunt it; but there is more to the melting of two futures than a dalliance, body to body. And that was all I had voiced.

I deserved to hear her tell him that she would go west with him in a wagon, once he should be able to go. She murmured her reply in so quiet a voice that I would not have known she was putting him off as she had put me off, were it not for his expostulation. So I shivered again . . . Naomi had told him that she would not be committed to him, before our journey came to its end.

At last she fell silent, and Barstow as well; and there was nothing I could listen to, except the disconsolate vibration of the thunder rolling itself toward Richmond.

7

WE WERE out of the hay-rick before dawn. We admired the unfamiliar stars studding the arch above us: it was impossible to believe that they had been there all the time. Save for a few army crackers, we had nothing to eat, and the crackers were so soggy that they fell into scraps like cotton cloth. When we came upon an isolated cabin, at sunrise, we went into it with no misgiving except the fear that there would be little food in the place.

An old negro woman was just getting out of bed. She had two half-grown granddaughters, who were up and dressed when we came; and the trio of them caterwauled until we threatened to blow their heads off.

"Soldiers!" the old woman cried, when she got a glimpse of Barstow's jacket. "Lord bless you, marss, I thought you was worse than that!"

Soldiers, it seemed, were frequent visitors to this family, and they hastened to set out what food they had. It was some time before we realized that the old mammy did not recognize us as Unionists, though the girls rolled suspicious eyes at Naomi. At this stage in the conflict, many of the Confederates wore blue jackets or overcoats, for want of gray ones; and with the countryside continually overrun by scouts, it is no wonder that these ignorant folks did not immediately detect our allegiance.

They had a big pot of what they called black-eyed peas, although I had eaten them before (north of the Rappahannock) and thought the vegetable more closely resembled beans. This food having been cooked overnight in a large pot, covered with coals and ashes, was a relief from our ration of gristly beef. The negroes gave us, too, several cups of coffee made from scorched wheat, and we thought it even better than the barley coffee to which we had been treated before.

We sat upon the floor to eat, as there was only one chair in the place, and that had the bottom out of it. When we rose to leave, we discovered that one of the girls had slipped out of the door and was already far down a weedy lane leading toward the highroad.

Barstow was for going after her with the shotgun. But Naomi whispered that we must not let the woman know we were Yankees, if indeed she had not already guessed it.

The old crone shook with high-pitched laughter at Barstow's alarm. "Marss," she said, between squeals, "that poor girl of mine just hie herself over to the Dawson house, where she do field work." She went on babbling about it, saying that in fact they belonged to Mrs. Dawson's father, whose plantation had been burned a year before. Since that time, the woman and her grandchildren had taken quarters in this crazy cottage, and subsisted on whatever bounty the Dawsons saw fit to give them.

The appearance of the shack, with its unmistakable poverty and neglect (such as seldom would have prevailed on a plantation, under the eye of a master) was fit to bear out her statement. Naomi and I asked Barstow to leave some money, which he did, slapping down fifty dollars Confederate with a happy oath, and saying that we would have no place to spend it after this night.

There was reason for us to regret our carelessness. When we were crossing a field, a quarter mile west of the cabin, we heard the sound of riders on the main road. Hidden behind a screen of cornstalks, we saw the negro girl returning. She trotted in the wake of two men, well mounted and carrying guns across their saddles. We stayed to see no more;

we plunged into the nearest growth of jack-oaks, and labored northwest for an hour before we lay down to rest.

Barstow resorted to no recrimination about this event. As was the case with us, his mind buzzed with thought of the liberty lying a few miles ahead. Stevensburg, to be sure, was farther than that, but it marked the main headquarters where the Army of the Potomac lay in winter camp; pickets were said to be stationed all along the north bank of the Rapidan. That was the information we had gleaned at Belle Island from the "fresh fish" who came in, nearly up to the day of our departure.

We crossed the deep gorge of Mountain Run before noon; from there on, our progress was slower. The countryside seemed well supplied with enemies: army wagons, a lone company of infantry marching God knows where or why, and at least twenty uniformed horsemen whom we saw at different times. There was an air of activity and bustle throughout this region, although the main body of rebels rested miles to the west. Ignorant of the changes which had come about north of the line, and had been quickly communicated into rebeldom, we could not imagine why so many patrols were abroad.

But we did not busy ourselves with much speculation concerning them. Our only thought was to avoid their sight, and not be taken by surprise in the road.

Thus, rapidly we approached the culmination of our project. Each hour moved with the ungovernable speed by which events of significance are propelled. I counseled myself to remember forever this tree and that stump and that broken fence-rail, and all the barriers of forest we went through, because by doing so I could savor again the process of our miracle. . . . As surely as I hoped and planned, so surely was I defeated by the emotion which ran with us. Now I can see only a muddled blur of gumwood sprouts, and open fields where the elms stood at ease, and a road slicing into the northwest—the wild northwest, where forever there danced the sparkle of buckle or bit or musket-hammer.

The sun was out, high in the south. But when we lay down to rest in the greatest heat it had yet given us, we could not relax enough to let its balm enter our bodies. We were awake, frantic and tingling, and if my wrists were athrob with fever pulse, I saw a brightness in Barstow's eyes, such as never gleamed in any other sunlight of our venture.

Naomi alone moved in religious silence. Her hands drew aside the tangles of dry creepers through which we men would have gone with a firecracker explosion. Hour after hour, she pleaded with us to be more careful about our conduct; once she hung back at the edge of some yellow pines, and kept us from flinging ourselves down an embankment into the path of two armed troopers who plodded beneath.

Her eyes were dark; her hair wore again the green glow of fox-fire. Perhaps she considered the life she had left behind her, and wondered what she could make of herself in the life ahead. A dozen times that day, Colonel Mokranowski must have ridden across her memory. Still, she was not the sort to let him ride there for long. I had learned that she was braver than I about such specters, and no easy prey for them.

Our march was slow, slower than it had been in fogs of the yesterday that seemed so far departed. We were determined to keep close abreast of the road, that we might not lose our chance at one of the two fords mentioned to me by the man whom I encountered at Verdierville. Far back in leafless underbrush on either side, we might have traveled with greater ease and surely with greater safety; but in our minds the road was a tentacle extending itself beyond the river—a tentacle in which we might be caught and pulled to safer ground.

Late afternoon found us skirting an open mountain

where the timber had been cut off. The road wound aloft
and then down, in a view to be seen from two directions.
We found a watercourse undoubtedly leading toward the
Rapidan, though not so heavily banked with timber as we
might have wished. Here we sprawled among rabbit holes
and over bowlders, with night coming close behind the
mountain.

When we touched the road again, we found a large farmhouse built of logs and stone, beside a little bridge of the
same construction. There was a wagon near the gate, and
sounds of men at work in the barn. We dared go no nearer,
but felt that we should wait for darkness and then make a
dash for the river, which could be no great distance ahead.

Our sunset mixed a variety of nasturtium colors; we lay
like worms among the water-sprouts of hickory, watching it.
It was the last sunset we would ever see together, and perhaps on that account, the Artist did His best for us.

Then, in the thinning light where already a fragment
of moon was changing from gold into white, we saw a rebel
soldier ride down the road from the northwest. The hoofs
of his horse drummed on the little bridge, his stirrup brushed
the reeds where we watched him. His face, as I remember it,
was young and tired and well-bred...

Bringing up beside the wagon at the farmhouse gate, the
soldier dismounted. A girl in a brown dress (boasting its own
shades of rose, in that sunset) came out of the house and
hailed him as "Dicky." It was like some pastoral war in which
blood is never shed—a painting done in thin oils, where gal-
lantry trots without soiling its hoofs in the sink of death.
This was the myth of war which I had held when I left New
Jersey late in 1861; and I considered it strange that the actuality had never confronted me until this moment, flavored
with moonlight and sycamores.

The young soldier went into the house, with the girl

hurrying before him and calling to her mother. If Barstow was touched by the idyllic stain, he forgot it as soon as the dusk grew deeper.

"Clark," he whispered, "maybe he's got something to eat, in his saddle-bags."

"We're too near the river," I said. "It's not worth taking the chance." Though I said it weakly, for after that day of excursioning through the brush, we were ready enough for food.

Barstow whispered, "We can't get his pistol; he took that in the house with him. I saw him. . . . Iron rations! Don't forget that. He must have some iron rations."

I thought as much, too. So I was not led into the making of our disaster, but went in double harness, as it were, and mine were the first fingers to touch the saddle leather. The horse shied and blew softly as we came up to him, but I had not lived with the First New Jersey Cavalry for no purpose at all: I made the kind of chirrup any horse likes to hear, and so this animal let us approach him, one from each side, though standing with his ears pointed.

Naomi waited near the bridge, with the shotgun in her hands. Barstow was armed only with the ax. In the house, candles were lighted; at its rear we heard doors opening and closing constantly, suggesting that supper was being cooked in an outlying kitchen.

Barstow opened the pouch, on his side, and reported finding nothing except a mess of papers and maps. I was still struggling with a refractory buckle, when some one came toward us around a large tree near the gate.

I think it was the Confederate soldier (an officer, doubtless, as his horse furnishings suggested) and his attention had been inspired by the report of some one looking out from the house. All I know is that the front door was not opened. . . .

A voice said sharply, "Mullin, is that you?" and I dropped back behind the horse.

Barstow whispered, "Let's get." Together we went thudding toward the bridge. The man must have caught the flash of Barstow's blue clothes, in the house lights. He blared out, "By God, it's Yanks!" and fired three or four quick shots. None of the bullets hit us. I turned at the bridge and took out my revolver to reply; I could see the figure of a man blocked against the windows of the house, and then it flashed through my mind that there were women inside those windows—yes, and little boys as well, for we had heard them laughing a moment before.

Naomi cried, "Don't shoot, Ollie! You might hit that girl." We ran away up the hill, as hard as we could pelt.

The incline was steep, but not a long one, and at the top we heard simultaneously the alarm of a big bell being rung in the farmhouse yard, and the patter of many hoofs coming toward us from the opposite direction.

At this point, the road had turned toward the north; we tunneled into the underbrush on the west side. The little moon found us, now and then, as we crossed patches of timberland where the trees did not hold its light out, and never before had I observed how brilliant a young moon can be. There was a moment's cessation of the clamorous field-bell or fire-bell, or whatever implement was being beaten so heartily in that farmhouse yard; it was as if the first alarmist relinquished his hammer to other hands; and then the beating began afresh. Soon we heard the rumbling of the bridge, and knew that the Confederate officer had crossed. His galloping approach met and commingled with that of other riders from the north.

Somebody called, "What is it?" and then another man said something about Captain Richardson. Voices rattled, the burden of talk being that no fugitives had come along the road into the north.

All this time, we were retreating. But the ground turned steep, and we found ourselves sliding on a hillside sheer enough for us to tumble down head-first, should we lose our footing.

Barstow said, "They can't follow us here with horses, anyway." We stood, breathing hard, and wondering in which direction we should make our next move.

We heard the shouts and halloos of other soldiers joining in the search. From the sound of their riding, we were forced to the conclusion that the road in which we had stood must, very close at hand, descend this hill along its northern face. It was Naomi who discovered the glint of water below us, and then we wondered why we had not heard the swishing of the Rapidan before.

For there it was (our Rubicon, our Styx and our Jordan), cut along the base of the steepness, flowing at this point almost directly from south to north, with us three fugitives hung up above its face. We caught at grapevines, and put our legs against the tree roots that bulged around us, to keep from sliding.

There must have been a full company of Confederates in that vicinity. All were awakened by the foolish sortie Barstow and I had made; they were clambering out of their inactivity, shouting abroad. We had our backs to our liberty, now, when we hoped to set our faces there.

The next instant, I made out several men creeping down a path that bordered the river a little way upstream. Bar and Naomi saw them clearly, too; they were no imaginary skirmishers moving to envelop our flank and rear. I blazed away; but I had to empty the revolver before I forced them, running, into the upstream region whence they had come. I had recapped the revolver that day, and there was no misfire of any charge. But there were only two paper cartridges left, although I had plenty of caps. Barstow had taken the shotgun from Naomi, and he tried to fire, but it would not go off. We knew that the powder must be damp.

We slipped down the hillside, nearer the talkative Rapidan. Above and beyond, in an increasing half circle, the Confederates wormed their way in our direction.

As passionately as we had welcomed the moon when first we saw it five days before, we hated it now. Sycamores leaned above; their leafless silver-limbed branches did the best they could to shield us from the candid rays. One tree, I remember, must have been damaged by a blight the year before; button-balls dangled stubbornly from its twigs, and I prayed that God might strike this tree into instant foliage, as in a marvel of Bible times. But no matter how hard we prayed, the light found us readily; and if any Confederate were to move between us and the shore, he could see our dark bodies on the hillside.

Squad after squad of cavalry loped on the highest part of the hill; horses trampled along a glen some fifty yards downstream. Likely enough, that was where the road sought the Rapidan ford.

Barstow worked feverishly to reload the shotgun, but I had no great hopes for his powder.

"How many loads you got left, Clark?"

I felt the capped cylinder, to be certain. "Two."

"I reckon we shouldn't take one of your cartridges for priming..."

"It would just cost us an extra charge, that's all."

He whispered, "Well, I'm trying to dry the powder by rubbing it in my hands." Naomi undertook to aid him in this, but I feared their hands were too damp to do much good.

Two men rode along the hill-crest, and dismounted. One yelled, "Are you keeping watch down by the creek, Vance?"

and a distant affirmative answered him. From another direction a man cried, "There's four of us watching the bank, sir."

"Very well," came the officer's voice. "As soon as Bryan comes in on your right, we'll close through the woods. We'll pick them up easy."

Across the white-tipped, rustling water sounded the report of a carbine. As we turned, we saw several more flashes in the willows over there; the echoes battered from tree-wall to tree-wall.

Naomi said, "On the other side. Those are Yankees."

"Yes," we agreed, and stood in silence until the firing had stopped. The rebels replied in only a casual way, and mainly with revolvers, farther downstream.

Somebody called, from the westerly bank, "Hello, Johnny."

"Hello, Yank," sounded the reply. "How you keeping, these days?"

"We're keeping fine." There was laughter. "You better keep out of sight."

A few more shots tore loose; then somebody howled from the opposite shore: "Did you hear we got a new general over here, who's going to whip the didies right off of you?"

A rebel jeered, "Is his name McClellan?" This time the laughter came from the east shore, and the Federal pickets did not retort with so much as a pistol shot.

I had a vision in which the Unionists rode heedlessly across the ford, swimming their horses when necessary, and bringing up against the hillside to sustain us with a ring of fire, and so to spirit us back across the river. But I understood (even as my eyes truly deceived me, and I saw the black forms riding forth) that such a sally would never occur. Probably the patrolling Federals numbered not more than two squads; we knew that a hundred Confederates had brought us to bay.

Barstow tugged at my trouser leg. "We better swim for it, Clark."

"Naomi," I asked, "can you swim?"

"Oh, no," she said. "But I'll wade, as long as I can."

I sobbed, "We'll never make it. Not with that moon."

Barstow began to whisper that we might be able to cross, if the Union vidette would withdraw to a distance upstream or downstream, and would there engage the rebels, volleying across the river, distracting them from their search. "They're coming closer every minute," he concluded.

Without any warning, several men on foot came sliding down the incline above us. After the first crackle of their approach, and after they had dislodged stones which went bounding through the thin underbrush beside us, they took cover. Each stood behind a tree; when we looked against the sky, we imagined shapeless figures distorted by dull patches of moonlight and shade. The officer on the hilltop gave an order. Sticks and stones were crunching under the boots of the men who had advanced upon us.

"I've got it reloaded," muttered Barstow.

"Powder's too wet, Bar."

"Clark, holler to God, if you never have before!" He crept past Naomi and me, and rested the barrel of his shotgun across a bowlder.

The rebels were advancing again. I thought that Barstow would never shoot, and I began to get ready with my revolver, as it was possible that an unexpected blast might send the men scrambling up the incline down which they had come. But when a bush crackled, only thirty feet above, Barstow exclaimed aloud. He pulled one trigger—the wrong one. He pulled the second trigger, even as several men yelped a view-halloo, and the shotgun roared. A heavy body rolled down until it brought up with a thud, against a tree beside us.

A boy screamed, "Joey! They got Joe!" In a moment the bullets were whirring around us, snapping into tree trunks or crooning across the waste of moon-touched water. We slid away, like children on a straw-stack, and brought up among willows and sycamores at the water's edge. The shallow ford gushed and foamed, a few rods downstream.

Across the river, Federals were calling to one another in surprise; well might they wonder why the forests on the eastern slope were spouting with such rancor. Barstow flung one arm around a tree, and leaned over the water. His voice tore itself into shreds: "Don't shoot! We're coming across. We're Yanks. We're coming across!" And promptly, even above the song of the ford, we heard astonished soldiers calling to one another, repeating his message.

The rebels were threatening us from three directions. But most of them were on the downstream side, many more than were fumbling from the steep crest above. An officer ordered, "Keep under cover! Wait till they come out in the light," and it seemed that the staring wafer of moon was as all-perceiving as a midsummer sun.

Naomi snatched at Barstow's hand; she drew him back around the sycamore trunk. "Oh, Bar," she pleaded, "they'll see you, hanging out that way."

Barstow said, "Now we'll never make it! There's too many down below. Naom, you said you'd never—"

"Never what?" she cried.

Barstow jerked his hand away. "Maybe you can get across," he declared. "Mind now, Clark—she said she couldn't swim," and with that last cry he was away, running down the stream-side; and the rifles sounded like a hurricane roar in my ears.

I had believed, all my life, that sacrifice of this sort entailed grave consideration beforehand. Through violent striving, a man prepared himself for the plunge—whether it was fatal only as a figure, or fatal in the uttermost sense of the word. And Barstow, with his sulkiness, I would never have selected as a man to act at such headstrong speed, raking away the last endearing tendrils that bound him to life.

Perhaps we could have given in and been recaptured, there among the sycamores, an inch outside liberty. Though I think, since we shot their man from ambush, as it were, the Confederates would have given us short shrift when they came up the stream and down the hillside with their guns ready. Perhaps Barstow considered this eventuality with a speed his mind had never mustered before. God knows, even a sluggard brain may become a whirling wheel when the wind of eternity whistles against it.

Hours later I might tremble, wondering at the magnanimity that ruled the heart of him who had been my bitterest enemy (until a persecuted intuition told him that the dream of his desire were better left unspoken). The Rapidan splashed to my waist as I leapt over the bank, dragging Naomi with me. I remember to this hour how the pebbly sluiceway that led to the ford itself, caved from the bank downstream.

Barstow was past that point now; and in the dull moonlight I saw him bounding like a colt, squarely toward the colored flashes that twitched among the trees. He still carried his precious ax, and waved it high. He was across the gully that led to the ford, then over the bank and into the water even as we had gone, but under the very chins of the rebel pickets.

He cried out as he went—a wordless challenge, daring every bullet along the contested county line to come and find him. No more of the firing was directed at us. All the musketry of the war, past and future, seemed pointed at our comrade who had run so quickly away from us, and still raged invulnerable, crashing out from the shallows into deeper water far below the crossing. It appeared that he was soaked with the magic of a Merlin, instead of the cold water that sped about him.

"Bar, Bar!" Naomi cried, as I dragged her through the rapids. But the third time she tried to say it, a hidden rock took her feet from under her, and she went down into a deeper current, with my arms struggling to regain their hold. I caught her, too; we went plunging from rock to rock, half swimming, half crawling, and all the while the woman pleaded with me to prevent a tragedy which no man who had not the omniscience of the Lord Himself could ever have prevented.

Bullets still sprayed the water, in that frightful downstream place. As my final view of the eastern shore, I saw the splintering of a dozen guns. But Barstow was gone beyond their attainment. Perhaps the river (appreciating nobility as no other river that ever ran) would bear him all the way to its juncture with the Rappahannock, and there construct a cairn of fecund soil above him—an island dauntless in the floods of successive springs, crowned with willows and vines of the wild morning-glory—monument appropriate for a man who not only laid down his life, but wrapped it in foam and bullets.

Then, before more than two or three of the Secessionists had assembled their wits to fire in our direction, we felt the gravel of the west shore scraping our knees. The half-light loosened its hold, and granted us the sanctuary of black underbrush.

A man came, with his carbine ready, and there was another trooper behind him. "Yanks?" he inquired, hoarsely. "You say you're Yanks?" Then, when I had mumbled some kind of answer, I heard him saying, "Eighteenth Pennsylvania Cavalry. I'll get the sergeant." More men came up to stare at us through the darkness, protected as we were by willow fortresses. I had my arms around Naomi Kincaid.

She was crying. I blew the water out of my nose, and tried to draw in the air of Culpeper county and the atmosphere of freedom with it; but all I could think about was Prentiss Barstow, and how he had died.

Bibliography

Bibliography

Military minutiae included in this book were obtained by the author when pursuing research for *Long Remember* and other work relating to the Civil War. His study of the terrain of Henrico, Goochland, Louisa, Spotsylvania, Orange and Culpeper counties was effected through frequent visits to Virginia, and was aided greatly by Mr. William A. Slade, in charge of reference work at the Library of Congress, and by Miss Clara Egli, Assistant Chief of the Division of Maps, at the same institution.

The author would like to express his thanks to those mentioned above, and also to Mr. Randolph W. Church of the Virginia State Library, at Richmond; to Mr. J. B. Kincer, Chief of the Division of Climate and Crop Weather at the United States Weather Bureau; to Mr. E. F. Sweeney of the same department; and to Mr. Larry F. Page, government meteorologist. Pains have been taken to present the climatic conditions as they must have prevailed, day by day, in this section of Virginia, in March, 1864.

A bibliographical note would be incomplete unless it mentioned Mr. W. H. Shelton's graphic "A Hard Road to Travel Out of Dixie," and the amazingly unprejudiced description of Belle Island by Sergeant T. P. Meyer, included in the *History of the 148th Pennsylvania Volunteers.*

Other books to which the author is indebted in varying degree, are listed alphabetically:

"An Account of the Escape of Six Soldiers From Prison At Danville, Va." William Henry Newlin. Cincinnati. Western Methodist Book Concern. 1889.

"The Capture, the Prison Pen, and the Escape." Willard W. Glazier. Hartford, Conn. H. E. Goodwin. 1868.

"Civil War Prisons." William H. Hesseltine. Columbus, Ohio. Ohio State University Press. 1930.

"My Ecape from Belle Isle." Horace R. Abbott. Detroit. Winn & Hammond. 1889.

"Nineteen Months a Prisoner of War." Gilbert E. Sabre. New York. The American News Company. 1865.

"The Secret Service: the Field, the Dungeon and the Escape." Albert D. Richardson. Hartford, Conn. American Publishing Company. 1865.

"Service with the Sixth Wisconsin Volunteers." Rufus R. Dawes. Marietta, Ohio. E. E. Alderman & Sons. 1890.

"The Soldier's Story of His Captivity At Andersonville, Belle Island and other Rebel Prisons." Warren Lee Goss. Boston. Lee & Shepard. 1867.

MacKinlay Kantor
PULITZER PRIZE-WINNING AUTHOR
OF *ANDERSONVILLE*

VALLEY FORGE is grandly conceived, but the quality is
equal to the concept. The climate of the war, its taste and
smell and the harsh texture of its life, are evoked with
mystery. Neither souped-up nor toned-down under
fashionable pressures, this is an extraordinarily honest
and human book. I am greatly impressed.
—*MARY RENAULT*

Published by SpeakingVolumes

Visit us at www.speakingvolumes.us